THE ACCIDENT

ALSO BY CHRIS PAVONE

The Expats

Uncorrected Proof

THE ACCIDENT

A NOVEL

CHRIS PAVONE

 CROWN PUBLISHERS | NEW YORK

Copyright © 2014 by Christopher Pavone
All rights reserved.
Published in the United States by Crown Publishers, an imprint of the Crown Publishing Group, a division of Random House LLC, a Penguin Random House Company, New York.
www.crownpublishing.com

Crown and the Crown colophon are registered trademarks of Random House LLC.

Library of Congress Cataloging-in-Publication Data
The accident : a novel / Chris Pavone. —First Edition.
pages cm.
1. Accidents—Fiction. 2. Spy stories. I. Title.
PS3616.A9566A63 2013
813'.6—dc23
2013025677

ISBN 978-0-385-34845-4
eISBN 978-0-385-34846-1

Printed in the United States of America
Book design by Gretchen Achilles
Jacket design by
Jacket photography

10 9 8 7 6 5 4 3 2 1

First Edition

FOR MM

THE ACCIDENT

Is it possible to succeed without any act of betrayal?

—JEAN RENOIR

PROLOGUE

He awakens suddenly, in terror. He spins his head around the spare room, searching the darkest shadows in the blue wash of moonlight, sitting bolt upright, head cocked, alert for noises. He reaches his hand across his body, and grabs the gun.

As he becomes less asleep, he realizes what woke him. The gun won't help. He returns the weapon to the end table, next to the ever-present water bottle. He swigs, but his stomach is roiling, and it takes a couple of seconds before he manages to swallow.

He walks to the end of the hall, to the room he uses as an office. Just a desk and a chair in front of a window. The reflection of the moon shimmers in the Zürichsee, a block away from this Victorian pile of bricks and wrought iron, covered in blooming wisteria, its scent spilling through the windows, seeping through the walls.

He jiggles the mouse to wake his computer, types in his password, launches the media player, and opens the live feed of streaming video. The camera is mounted high in a darkened room, focused on a woman who's lying in bed, reading. She takes a drag of a cigarette, and flicks her ash into a big glass ashtray.

He looks away from the invasive image on his screen to a small keypad mounted beneath the desktop. He punches buttons in rapid succession, and with a soft click the drawers unlock.

1

He pulls out the stack of paper, bound by a thick green rubber band. He turns to a page one-third of the way through, and scans the text to identify the scene. He flips forward ten pages, then five. Then back two. He runs his finger down the page, and he finds it, there on page 136, just as his mind's eye pictured it, in his sleep in the middle of the night. One word. One letter.

I.

He thought he'd caught every one.

This current draft of the manuscript is the third; it will also be the final. For the initial draft, he'd written from a first-person perspective, but not his own. Because this book was going to be a memoir, publicly authored by someone else but ghostwritten—or coauthored—by him; they hadn't decided on the exact nature of his credit.

Then circumstances changed. When he picked up the project again, he recast the story from his own point of view, first-person singular—*I did this, I saw that.* This was going to be a more honest book, more transparent.

After he'd finished, and typed THE END on the final page, and re-read the whole thing, he changed his mind. He decided he needed to hide behind omniscience, and anonymity, to create the shadow of doubt about this book's authorship. To give himself some chance of survival. So he'd pored over the entire manuscript, revising everything to third person—*He drove around a long, dangerous bend. He stared in horror.* Deleting passages that no longer made sense, adding sections—adding chapters—that now did.

It was a big editorial job, but hardly a unique situation. This type of thing must happen all the time, in rewrites, revisions, reconsiderations. An author combs through every page, recasting point of view, replacing nouns and verb conjugations. Over and over and over, thousands of times.

But he misses one of these pronouns, or two. Just a little mistake, a couple of typos. Not a matter of life or death.

EPILOGUE

There is no single person in the world who can
verify the entirety of what's in these p ages.
But there is one person who can come close: the
subject himself, Charlie Wolfe. There are other
people who could, if properly motivated, attest
to the individual realities, one incident at a
time, in which they had direct firsthand knowledge.
Perhaps this book will be that motivation to those
witnesses, an impetus to reveal their truths, to
verify this story.

But the author isn't one of those possible
witnesses. Because if what you are reading is a
finished book, printed and bound and distributed
into the world, I am, almost certainly, dead.

THE END.

PART I

MORNING

CHAPTER I

I t's just before dawn when Isabel Reed turns the final sheet of paper. Halfway down the page, her mouth falls open, her heartbeat quickens. Her eyes dart across each typescript line at a rapid-fire pace, accelerating as she moves through the final paragraph, desperate to arrive at a revelation, to confirm her suspicions. She sucks in her breath, and holds that breath, for the last lines.

Isabel stares at the final period, the little black dot of ink . . . staring . . .

She lets out her breath. "My God." Astounded, at the enormity of the story. Disappointed, at the absence of the confirmation she was hoping for. Furious, at what it means. Terrified, at the dangers it presents. And, above all, heartbroken, at the immensity of the betrayal. Betrayals.

She puts the page down on the fat stack of paper that sits on the bedspread, next to a crumpled soft-pack of cigarettes and an overflowing crystal ashtray, a mildly snarky birthday present from a passive-aggressive colleague. She picks up the manuscript with both hands, flips it over, and uses her thumbs to align the pages. Her hands are trembling. She tries to steady herself with a deep breath, and sets the straightened pile of pages in her lap. There are four words centered at the top of the page:

7

Isabel stares across the room, off into the black nothingness of the picture window on the opposite wall, its severe surface barely softened by the half-drawn shades, an aggressive void invading the cocoon of her bedroom. The room is barely lit by a small bullet-shaped reading sconce mounted over the headboard, aiming a concentrated beam of light directly at her. In the window, the light's reflection hovers above her face, like a tiny sun illuminating the top of her head, creating a halo. An angel. Except she's not.

She can feel her body tense and her jaw tighten and her shoulders contract in a spasm of rage. She tries to suppress it, bites her lip, brings herself under the flimsiest tether of control.

Isabel draws aside the bedspread, struggles to a sitting position. It's been hours since she has shifted her body in any appreciable way, and her legs and back are stiff and achy—old, if she had to choose a word for her joints. Her legs dangle over the side of the mattress, her toes searching for the fleece-lined slippers.

Along the wall, long slivers of aluminum shelves—hundreds of horizontal feet—are filled with neat stacks of manuscripts, their authors' names written with thick black Sharpie into the sides of the stacks of pages. Tens of thousands of pages of proposed books of every sort, promising a wide assortment of entertainment and information, produced with a broad range of skill levels.

These days, everyone younger than Isabel seems to read manuscripts and proposals on e-readers; quite a few of those older, too. But she feels uncomfortable, unnatural, sitting there holding a little device in her hands. Isabel is of the generation that's just old enough to be congenitally uncomfortable with new technologies. When she started her first job, she didn't have a computer at her desk. A year later, she did.

Maybe next year she'll start using one of those things, but for now she's still reading on paper, turning pages, making notes with pens, surrounding herself with stacks of paper, like bricks, bunkered against the relentless onslaught of the future. And for *The Accident*, she didn't even have a choice. Because although 99 percent of new projects are now delivered to her office electronically, this submission was not.

She shuffles down the hall, through the darkness. Turns on the kitchen lights, and the coffee machine—switched from AUTO-ON, which is set to start brewing an hour from now, to ON—and the small television. Filling the silent lonely apartment with humming electronic life.

Isabel had been reading frantically, hoping to discover the one assertion that rang untrue, the single mismatched thread that would unravel the whole narrative, growing increasingly discouraged as page 1 at the office in the morning became page two-hundred-something at home in the evening. She fell asleep sometime after eleven, more than halfway through, then woke again at two, unable to quiet her mind, anxious to get back to it. People in the book business are constantly claiming "I couldn't put it down" or "it kept me up all night" or "I read it in one day." This time, all that was true.

So at two a.m. Isabel picked up the manuscript and started reading again, page after page, through the late-late night. Vaguely reminiscent of those days when Tommy was an infant, and she was sleep-deprived, awake in a dormant world. They are very discrete periods, for very specific reasons, when it's a normal part of life to be awake at four a.m.: it's for making babies or caring for them, in the small desperate hours when a blanket of quiet smothers the city, but through the moth-eaten holes there's the occasional lowing of a railroad in New Jersey, the distant Dopplered wail of an ambulance siren. Then the inevitable thump of the newspaper on the doormat, the end of the idea of night, even if it's still dark out.

Nothing she encountered during the 488 pages seemed false. Now she stares at the anchor's face on the television, tuned to Wolfe Worldwide Media . . . That goddamned son of a bitch . . .

Her anger swells, and she loses control—

Isabel cocks her arm and hurls the remote across the kitchen, cracking and splintering against the refrigerator door, clattering loudly to the floor. Then the heightened silence of the aftermath, the subdued thrum of a double-A battery rolling across the tile, the impotent click as it comes to rest against a baseboard.

She feels tears trickling down her cheek, and wipes them away.

The coffee machine hisses and sputters the final drops, big plops falling into the tempered glass. Isabel glances at the contraption's clock, changing from 5:48 to 5:49, in the corner of the neatly organized counter, a study in right angles of brushed stainless steel. Isabel is a passionate proponent of perfect alignment. Fanatical, some might say.

She opens the refrigerator door, with its new scratch from the airborne remote, whose jagged pieces she kicks out of her way. She takes out the quart of skim and pours a splash into her mug. She grabs the plastic handle of the carafe and fills the mug with hot, viscous, bitter, bracing caffeination. She takes a small sip, then a larger one. She tops up the mug, and again wipes away tears.

She walks back down the now-lighted hall, lined with the family photographs she'd unearthed when she was moving out of her matrimonial apartment, into this single-woman space in a new neighborhood, far from the painful memories of her home—of her life—downtown, where she'd been running into too many mothers, often with their children. Women she'd known from the playgrounds and toy stores and mommy-and-me music classes, from the gyms and grocers and coffee shops, from preschool drop-off and the pediatrician's waiting room. All those other little children growing older, getting bigger, Emmas and Stellas in precious little plaids, Ashers and Amoses with mops of messy curls in skinny jeans on scooters; all those self-satisfied downtown bobo parents, unabashedly proud of their progeny's precociousness.

She'd bought herself a one-bedroom in a full-service uptown co-op, the type of apartment that a woman chooses when she becomes reconciled that she's not going to be living with another human being. She had reached that age, that stage, when a lifestyle starts to look permanent: it is what it is, and ever will be, until you die. She was making her loneliness as comfortable as possible. Palliative care.

If she wasn't allergic to cats, there'd probably be a couple of them lurking around, scrutinizing her disdainfully.

Isabel lined this nice new hallway—parquet floors, ornate moldings, electrical outlets where she wants them—with framed photos. There she is, herself, a smiling little toddler being held aloft by her tragically beautiful mother in Central Park, at the playground near the museum, a couple of blocks from the Classic 8 on Park Avenue that her parents couldn't actually afford. And then hand-in-hand with her remarkably unambitious father, starting fourth grade at the small-town public school in the Hudson Valley, after they'd finally abandoned the city for their "country place," the old family estate that they'd been selling off, half-acre parcels at a time, to pay for their life. Then in cap and gown, the high school valedictorian, bound not for Harvard or Yale or even a first-rate state school, but for a second-tier—maybe third?—private college upstate, because it offered a full scholarship, including room and board, and didn't necessitate expensive out-of-state travel. The drive was just a few hours.

Her parents had called her Belle; still do. But once she was old enough to understand what the word meant, she couldn't bear to lay claim to it. She began to insist on Isabel.

Isabel had intended to go to graduate school, to continue studying American literature, eventually to teach at the university level, maybe. But that plan was formed before she'd had an understanding of the realities of personal finance. She took what she thought would be a short-term job at a publishing house—one of her father's school chums was a famous editor—with the irrational expectation that she'd be able to save money to pay for school, in a year, or two. She was buoyed by modest success in an enjoyable workplace during good business years, and one thing led to another. Plus she never saved a dime. By the time she was twenty-five, she no longer thought about grad school. Almost never.

So then there she is, in a little black dress on stage at a book-award ceremony, accepting on behalf of her author who was in South America at the time, chasing a new story. And in a big white dress, aglow, in the middle of the panoramic-lens group shot, the thirty-six-year-old bride with her bridesmaids, at her wedding to a man she'd started dating a mere eight months earlier, short on time, perfectly willing to turn a blind eye to his obvious faults, the personality traits that her friends were too supportive to point out, until the safe remove of hindsight.

That utter bastard.

It still amazes her how quickly youth slipped away, how severely her options narrowed. Just a couple of bad relationship decisions—one guy who as it turned out was never going to commit, another who was a closeted asshole—and the infinite choices of her late twenties turned into the dwindling selection of her mid-thirties, now saying yes to any non-creepy men who asked her out at parties or introduced themselves in bars, sometimes using her middle name if the guy was on the margins of acceptability and she might end up wanting to hide behind the unstalkable shield of an alias; over the years she'd had at least a half-dozen dates with men who thought her name was something else. Half the time, she was glad for the deception.

Another photo, a smaller print, lying in the hospital bed with Tommy in her arms, tiny and red and angry in his striped swaddling blanket and blue cap. Isabel had returned to work after the standard three months, but in that quarter-year something had passed, and she was complacent to allow it. Her husband was suddenly making embarrassing amounts of money, so Isabel hired a housekeeper to go with the nanny. She started leading one of those enviable-looking lives—a four-day workweek, driving the shiny car from the pristine loft to the shingled beach house, a perfect baby and a rich handsome smart funny husband . . .

And then.

She stops at the final photo, spotlit, a small black-and-white in the center of an expanse of stark-white matting. A little boy, laughing on a rocky beach, running out of the gentle surf, wearing water wings. Isabel reaches her hand to her lips, plants a kiss on her fingers, and transfers the kiss to the little boy. As she does every morning.

Isabel continues to the bathroom, unbuttoning her flannel top as she walks, untying the drawstring of the pajama bottoms, which crumple as she releases the knot. She pushes her panties down and steps out of them, leaving a small, tight puddle of cotton on the floor.

The hot shower punishes her tense, tired shoulders. Steam billows in thick bursts, pulled out the bathroom door, spilling into the dressing area, the bedroom. The water fills her ears, drowning out any sounds of the television, of the world. If there's anything else in her apartment making noise, she can't hear it.

What exactly is she going to do with this manuscript? She shakes water out of her hair, licks her top lip, shifts her hands, her feet, her weight, standing under the stream, distracted and disarmed, distressed. It all beats down on her, the shower stream and the manuscript and the boy and the past, and the old guilt plus the new guilt, and the new earth-shattering truths, and fear for her career and maybe, now, fear for her life.

She slips into a soft, thick white bathrobe, towel-dries her hair. She sweeps her hand across the steamed-up glass, and examines her tired eyes, bagged and bloodshot, wrinkled at the corners. The bathroom's high-voltage lighting isn't doing her any favors this morning. She had long ago become accustomed to not sleeping well, for a variety of reasons. But with each passing year, it has become harder and harder to hide the physical evidence of sleeplessness.

From the other room, she can hear the irrelevant prattle of the so-called news, the piddling dramas of box-office grosses, petty marital indiscretions, celebrity substance abuse. Steam recolonizes the mirror, and she watches big thick drops of condensation streak down from the top beveled edge of the glass, cutting narrow paths of clarity through the fog, thin clear lines in which she can glimpse her reflection . . .

Something is different, and a jolt of nervous electricity shoots through her, a flash of an image, Hitchcockian terror. Something in that slim clear streak has changed. The light has shifted, there's now a darkness, a shadow—

But it's nothing, she now sees, just the reflection of the bedroom TV, more footage of yesterday's international news, today. Today she has to consider the news in a whole new light. Now and forevermore.

She gets dressed, a sleek navy skirt suit over a crisp white blouse, low heels. The type of office attire for someone who wants to look good, without particularly caring about being fashionable. She blow-dries, brushes her shoulder-length blonde hair, applies makeup. Sets contacts into her hazel eyes. She assesses herself—tired-looking, inarguably middle-aged—in the full-length mirror, and sighs, disappointed. Three hours of sleep pushes the limit of what makeup can accomplish.

She stares again at the bottom of *The Accident*'s covering page: *Author contact 40004026@worldmail.net.* She types another e-mail—she's already sent two of these, in the past twelve hours. "I finished. How can we talk?" Hits Send. She again receives the frustrating bounce-back message: an unrecognized address.

That doesn't make any sense. Who would go to the trouble of writing such a manuscript and then not be findable? So she'll keep trying, willing herself to believe that it's some technical problem, something that'll eventually get resolved. She stares at her laptop, the gradations of gray of the various windows on the screen, the silver frame of the device itself. The little black circle at the top, the pinhole camera, that she never uses, never even considers.

She could burn the manuscript right now, in the fireplace, using the long fancy fireplace matches that her penny-pinching aunt sent as a housewarming. She could pretend she never read the submission, never received it. Forget about it.

Or she could go to the authorities, explain what happened, let them handle it. Which authorities? Certainly not the CIA. The FBI?

Or she could take this to the news media—the *New York Times*, CNN. Or even Wolfe, for that matter; that could be interesting.

Or she could call the president; she could *try* to call the president. She spends a minute wondering whether it's possible that she, a well-known literary agent at a famous agency, could get the president of the United States on the telephone. No.

Or she could do what she knows she should, and wants to, do: get this published, quickly and quietly to protect herself, waiting for the inevitable ubiquity of the publicity—the public-ness of this book's story, the weight of its accusations—to protect her. She can't be arrested—or killed—in front of the whole world. Can she?

Isabel picks up her phone, and plucks a cigarette from the silver box atop the marble mantel, under her one and only piece of fine art, hanging where everyone positions their nicest framed thing. She walks out to her terrace and lights the cigarette, inhales deeply, expels smoke into the sky. She leans on the parapet and stares out at the dark, sinister-looking greens and blacks of Central Park, across to the skyline of Fifth Avenue, to the azure sky and the fiery orange ball rising in the northeast. It's a spectacular view from up here, on her plant-filled terrace jutting out from her professionally decorated apartment, swathed in calming neutral tones. It certainly looks like a nice life that she has.

She knows that she is the obvious—the inevitable—literary agent for this project. And there's also one very obvious acquiring editor for the manuscript, a close friend who never met a conspiracy theory he didn't like, no matter how ludicrous, no matter what level of lunatic the author. He used to have impressive success with this type of book, even by some of his less rational authors; there's apparently a good-size book-buying audience out there that inhabits a space beyond the margins of sane discourse. He'll be motivated to publish another. Especially this one, about these people.

Isabel tries to fight off the fear that wells up inside her again. She takes a final drag of her cigarette, knocks the glowing ember off the butt, then flicks the relatively harmless fiberglass filter out into the air above Central Park West, where it seems to hover for a split-second, Wile E. Coyote–like, before falling, fluttering out of sight.

She scrolls through her phone's address book, finds the number, and hits Call.

CHAPTER 2

Hayden slips the bookmark into the Icelandic primer. He places the thick volume atop his spiral notebook, a short stack next to a taller stack of reference works, some newish vinyl-covered handbooks, some tattered paperbacks in various states of falling-apartness, held together by duct tape or masking tape, or bound by sturdy rubber bands. These references are increasingly available electronically, but Hayden still prefers to hold a physical book in his hands, to run his eye across the tops of pages, down the columns, searching for a word, an image, a fact. The effort, he thinks, reinforces the learning. He's old enough to recognize that there's a finite universe of information he's going to be able to absorb in the remainder of his life; he wants to learn all of it properly.

He drops to the floor, does fifty push-ups, fifty sit-ups; his late-morning mini-workout. He buttons a French cuff shirt over his undershirt, affixes his enamel cufflinks, knots his heavy paisley tie. Slips into his sport jacket, glances at himself in the mirror. Adjusts his pocket square.

It was during his first posting overseas that he started wearing pocket squares, plain white linen handkerchiefs. He'd wanted to look like a young ambitious conformist American functionary, the type of guy who would proceed immediately from Groton to Harvard to Europe and always carry a white handkerchief, folded neatly and squared-off, in the breast pocket of his suit jacket. He's surprised at how many of those decisions made back then, at a time when adulthood seemed to stretch ahead indefinitely, turned out to be untemporary. Careers and hobbies, spouses or lack thereof, political beliefs and literary preferences, hairstyles and pocket squares.

The sun is streaming through the French doors, casting brilliant white light across the whitewashed floors, the white brick walls, the white upholstery, the occasional piece of unavoidable Danish teak. In the kitchen it's even brighter because of the reflections from the appliances. The brightness is almost blinding.

The elaborately carved front door is covered in hundreds of years' worth of uncountable coats of paint, scraped and chipped and deeply gouged, revealing an undercoat of pale green here, a dark blue there. He removes a matchbook from his pocket, tears out a paper match, inserts it between door and jamb, one match-length above a long gash in the wood.

The street is leafy, sun-dappled, birdsongy. Hayden's bicycle leans amid dozens of others in the jumbled rack on the wide sidewalk, a few blocks from the queen's palace in Amalienborg. He hops on, pedals gently through quiet streets, to the staid brick building on Kronprinsessegade that houses the David Collection, one of the premier resources on the Continent for his new hobby, Islamic art. He spends a half-hour examining the Middle Age artifacts of the Spanish emirate, from a time when Cordoba was the largest city in Western Europe. Cordoba, of all places.

Hayden Gray is, after all, a cultural attaché. He has a large luxurious office three hundred miles due south, in the American Embassy in Pariser Platz, next to the Brandenburg Gate. He still makes his permanent home in Munich, but his new job responsibilities require regular appearances in Berlin, and a legitimate office there. Of course Berlin has always been a fascination for Hayden, indeed for anyone in his line of work. Los Angeles has the film business, and Paris has fashion; Berlin is for espionage. But it's not a particularly attractive city, and the appealing things about it—a vibrant youth culture, a practically developing-world level of inexpensiveness, and the limitless energy of its nightlife—are not compelling assets for him. So he'd rather not live there.

Back on the bicycle, alongside the lush greenery of the King's Garden, across the bridge, and into Nørrebro, the midday street life a mixture of young native artistic types and recent immigrants, alternative bars alongside kebab joints that double as social clubs. He locks the bike just as the rain begins, quick spatters and then within seconds full-on.

Hayden rushes to push the glossy door, climbs a long steep flight of stairs, and enters an apartment, high-ceilinged and large-windowed, but shabby, and nearly empty. The place where he's been sleeping for the past couple of nights is a long-term lease—a quarter-century long, in fact—on the other side of downtown Copenhagen. But this one on Nørrebrogade was hastily arranged a week ago by the woman who's sitting at the window now, a pair of binoculars in her hands.

"Hello," she says, without turning. She can see him in the window's reflection.

"Anything?"

"No. Bore. Dom."

Hayden joins her at the window, looks past the immense streetlight suspended by wires above the boulevard, across to the storefront on the ground level, to the apartment above it.

She gives him the once-over. "Nice tie," she says. "You have anything interesting for me today?"

"*Always*. Let's see . . . Ah, here's a good one: Thomas Jefferson and John Adams died on the same day."

"You mean the same date?"

"I mean they died on the same exact *day*. And that day was July Fourth. In 1826."

She turns to him. "That's not true."

"Oh, but it is."

"Huh. I give that a 9."

"What do I need to get a 10?"

"I'll know it when I hear it." She turns back to the window, resumes her vigil.

He removes his horn-rimmed glasses, uses his Irish linen pocket square to wipe them clean. He holds his glasses up to the light, gazes through the lenses to double-check their clarity. "This is taking a long time," he says. Sympathetically, he hopes.

"This is taking forever."

Hayden knows that she wants to go home, to Paris. Back to her husband, her children, her perfect apartment in St-Germain-des-Prés. She has been traipsing around Europe for a month now, looking for one person. One elusive, clever, dangerous man.

"Tell me why it has to be *me* who's here?"

He watches a beautiful woman in the street pedaling slowly through the rain, one hand on the handlebars while the other holds a large umbrella, covering not only herself but also the big wooden bucket in front that contains three small children wearing raincoats with matching hats.

"I mean," she continues, "it's not as if I speak Danish, or know Copenhagen well. I don't have any special knowledge about whoever that guy is."

In the window across the street, the scraggly man sits at his desk, turned as always in profile. Jens Grundtvig, part-time student, part-time writer, and nearly-full-time stoner, is sometimes typing on his computer, sometimes just moving his mouse around, researching, and sometimes is on the telephone, gathering quotes, checking facts. Grundtvig seems to be putting a fact-checking polish on another man's project, and Hayden's task is to find that other man. After three months, Jens Grundtvig of Copenhagen is Hayden's only substantive lead.

"Because I trust your instincts," Hayden says. "And to paraphrase Proust: you, Dear, are the charming gardener who makes my soul blossom."

She snorts. She knows that this is fractionally true, but predominantly bullshit, and that Hayden is not going to tell her the whole truth. She accepts being in the dark; it's part of their arrangement.

That truth is complicated, as always. And the truth is that this operation is entirely black, absolutely no record of it anywhere. The expenses for the entire team—the woman here in this apartment, the two men stationed at either end of this block, the other two who are off-duty—are funded out of a Swiss account. They're all under-the-counter, off-the-books freelancers.

"You're a hero," Hayden says, patting her shoulder.

"That's what I keep telling my husband," she says. "But he doesn't believe me."

"A hero, Kate, *and* a martyr."

CHAPTER 3

The ringing phone, the sound of dread, of slept-through appointments or horrible news, snatching Jeff Fielder from the tenuous embrace of fitful sleep.

He squints around the small cluttered bedroom for the offending device. Books and papers and magazines are stacked everywhere—on the desk, the bureau, the end tables, even on much of the wide-planked wooden floor. A nearly empty bottle of bourbon sits on the warped, dented floor—did he have any of that last night, when he got home?—next to his ex-wife's second novel, the one she wrote after she left not only Jeff but also her magazine job and New York City for Los Angeles, where TV people had become interested in the magazine story she'd written about their falling-apart marriage, before Jeff was even aware it was falling apart.

He has begun to dip in and out of the book, mostly when he's substantially drunk. Sara is, he has to admit, a pretty good writer. But for obvious reasons he loathes her book.

Jeff reaches for something black and shiny, in the process knocking over a precarious tower of paper that's resting in the seat of a black Windsor chair, only to discover that the thing he has retrieved is an eyeglass case, not a phone.

Another ring tears through his ears, his brain. He catches a glimpse of flickering red light, from there on the floor, yes, that must be the phone, under that bound galley . . .

"Hello?" The two syllables come out as an amphibian croak, from a mouth filled with the dry, puffy cotton of last night's booze.

"Jeffrey?"

At the sound of her voice, he sits up too fast, and his head spins. Despite himself, despite everything, his heart quickens every time he hears Isabel's voice on the telephone. *"Ungh."*

"You okay?"

"Mmmmm," he says, a noncommittal noise. He glances to the dawn-gray window. "Isn't it a little early?"

"Don't whine at me," Isabel says.

Jeff can't tell if the edge in her voice is playful or annoyed. "And don't be pissed at *me*," he says. "Who woke up whom?"

She snickers; he knows it's at his *whom.* There can be a lot of meaning, in a little snigger, between people with a long history.

"Listen," she says, softer, "I'm doing you a favor, Mr. Whom."

"Uh-huh."

"Meet me for breakfast."

"Sure. I'll be there in three, four minutes."

"I'm serious."

"Isabel. It's . . . what time *is* it, anyway?"

"Six-twenty. I've got something for you."

"Okay. But couldn't this wait until, you know, I'm in the office? Or at least *awake*?"

"No."

"Why?"

"Because it's big."

"You mean long? You know I don't—"

"No, you idiot. I mean"—a silent beat—"it's *huge.*"

Over the years, Jeff has heard some of Isabel's pitches that were

23

cynical, and a few that were transparently panicked. But most were earnest, and none was a lie.

"What is it?" He's fully awake now, and his head is no longer spinning. Pounding, yes, but he's not dizzy.

Maybe this is it, the book he's been waiting for. The thing that every editor wakes up for, comes to work for, loses sleep for. The book that changes your career. Your life. As opposed to all the middling, inconsequential manuscripts and proposals that are now sitting on his desk, and in his satchel, and on his bookshelves, and in his e-reader, and even on this goddamned telephone. There are dozens of proposed books in his life, all in various stages of being considered. Or rejected. Or halfheartedly pursued. Or studiously ignored. Or merely waiting, value-neutral, in the queue for his attention, which is always more abundant in the future.

"Just *meet* me."

"Okay, okay. The usual?"

"Yes. At seven-fifteen?"

He guffaws.

"Seven-thirty?" she counters her own opening bid, contrary to what they both know is a fundamental tenet of negotiating. He's tempted to remain silent, to let her dig herself deeper into her own hole, to plumb the depths of her desperation, to find out how many times she will relent before forcing him to counteroffer. But it's just a breakfast hour, and it's Isabel. "Eight."

"Quarter of."

"Done."

Jeff is feeling a little better—or less bad—every second. He rises slowly, picks his way past the paper piles, past the draped and discarded clothes, over the strewn sneakers and shoes. He pushes open the creaky bathroom door, and turns on the hot tap, running the water; it'll take at least two minutes to get hot. The old sink is rust-stained and chipped, with a wildly unprofessional patch at the drain, where it looks like somebody used Wite-Out as compound. And no matter how many times he replaces the washer, a new drip always materializes. Always. It has become part of his routine, buying and replacing washers.

He's an unpaid handyman. The opposite of paid: he himself does the paying, twenty-six hundred dollars a month, to buy and replace the washers in his crappy sink whose water takes forever to get hot.

Jeff lets his razor and washcloth sit in the stream of slowly heating water, and looks at himself in the mirror, disappointed at what he sees. Yesterday ended with late hours at the office, hunched over a manuscript. Then his hard work was permanently interrupted by an off-hours phone call from one of his authors, who claimed he was being driven insane by the copy editor's nitpicking—"pecked to death by minnows"—and demanding satisfaction. Mason actually used the word *satisfaction*, as if the guy wanted to challenge the poor anonymous freelance copy editor to a duel.

"What exactly do you want from me?" Jeff asked.

"Come get drunk," Mason said, matter-of-factly. Mason has a lot of free-floating anger, which is both alleviated and exacerbated by his frequent excessive drinking. "I'm around the corner."

Jeff obeyed, because this is occasionally his job: pint after pint of ale with the occasional gratuitous shot of tequila, punctuated by a revolting plate of nachos and a gruesome order of buffalo wings with their pathetic accompaniment of plastic-cupped blue-cheese dressing and a few sticks of stringy, water-logged celery. Listening to a complaining author, perched there on the adjoining barstool in his studiously overgrown beard—seemingly a contractual obligation, these days, for young novelists—and meticulously curated vintage T-shirt, ranting and raving about all the things that authors rant and rave about. It was brutal.

Today would be a good day to not shave. But today is Tuesday, the weekly editorial meeting, and the executives will be there, so Jeff makes a greater effort to dress professionally on Tuesdays. And, as a rule, he shaves, as he does now, with slightly shaky hands that make him nervous, especially around the Adam's apple.

A few years ago, Jeff himself fell victim to the ineluctable trend, and grew a full beard, bushy as a whole but scraggly in spots. The beard made him look vaguely rabbinical, and if there was one thing Jeff didn't want to go out of his way to look like, it was his second cousin Rabbi Abe Feinberg.

Instead of the unsuccessful beard, Jeff wears his wavy hair longish. His friends from college who earn millions from law firms and investment banks can't have long hair. But Jeff can, so he does.

Groomed, showered, dressed, and ready to go, Jeff takes a wrench to the bathroom sink, and removes the washer, slides it into his pocket. He'll stop at a hardware store today, and buy a new one.

He grabs his sport jacket from the coat closet, amid the golf bag and the skis and poles, a tennis racquet with busted strings, a canvas bag filled with balls and shoes and caps and gloves, the detritus of the recreational athlete.

At the front door he notices an envelope pushed under the door. He looks away from it quickly, pretending that if he doesn't pick it up, doesn't acknowledge it, then it doesn't really matter, or even exist. A late-rent notice. Another ledger line in his broad portfolio of financial failures.

Chinatown is insistently awake, loud and dirty, bright and early. When Sara left him, Jeff couldn't afford to stay in their one-bedroom in Greenwich Village. So he'd moved down here to Mulberry Street. People assume that his address is in trendy Nolita, among the boutiques and bars inhabited by beautiful people. And Jeff doesn't necessarily disabuse anyone of this misconception. But he really lives a few blocks south of the region North of Little Italy with the silly name, in decidedly unfashionable Little Italy proper, which isn't even truly Little Italy anymore, but a tendril of Chinatown that for a few blocks happens to be littered with crappy Italian restaurants.

As it turns out, Chinatown is the only conveniently located part of downtown Manhattan that Jeff can afford to live in, above a grocery store that seems to specialize in various types of dried shrimp, which itself is above a basement-level dumpling factory, on a street choked with erratically wandering tourists and diesel-spewing delivery trucks and dense crowds of Chinese people with their red plastic shopping bags.

Jeff had thought it'd be cool to live in Chinatown. And maybe it would've been, if he were twenty-five years old. But he's not. And at this point in his life he hates this neighborhood, and the circumstances that put him here.

And before long, he probably won't be able to afford even Chinatown. He steps into the brand-new coffee shop on the corner, one of those joints that specifies the growers and regions and acidity levels of their humanely sourced fair-trade beans. He orders a three-dollar macchiato from an alarmingly muscled and extravagantly tattooed woman wearing a wifebeater and a skullcap, operating a machine that bears more than a passing resemblance to a Lamborghini, house music thumping at seven-thirty a.m., a miasma of patchouli. This café is a shot across the bow, signaling impending rent hikes, even for small walk-up apartments with crappy leaky bathrooms.

He considers himself in the full-wall mirror, a forty-something editor wearing the professorial outfit—gray slacks, herringbone jacket, blue shirt, repp tie, horn-rimmed glasses—that's practically standard-issue to people with his type of job, from his type of college. The only nice piece of clothing is the jacket, which is now getting threadbare, purchased at 80 percent discount at a sample sale in a Midtown hotel's ballroom, back when his then-girlfriend Sara was trying to remake him into a more fashionable version of himself. She always had access to sample sales, and plus-one invitations to friends-and-family previews of restaurants, and gratis tickets to film screenings. The stray perks that enable permanently broke young New Yorkers to appear glamorous.

Sara wanted everything. She wanted to be out every night, on every guest list. She wanted to rub shoulders with the rich and famous; she wanted to become one. She'd been deluded by their early relationship, when Jeff was bringing her along to awards ceremonies and book parties, back when people were still throwing book parties as a matter of course. There would be more and more, better and better, and her good-looking successful well-connected husband would help make her Big.

When she realized that he couldn't, or wouldn't, she used him a final time, as fodder for her writing, on her way out the door. That book had already been turned into a goddamned play, for crying out loud. Off-Broadway. There was now a film option. She was carefully orchestrating every aspect of her life for success, and it appeared to be working.

Jeff was astounded at what some people were willing to do, to advance their careers. He was amazed to discover that he'd married one of those people. He'd married the wrong woman. Or she'd married the wrong man. Both.

He steps out of the café. Stands on the sidewalk and takes a glance uptown, then down-, not sure what he's looking for. Then he starts trudging north.

Jeff will take a pill tonight. He has been sleeping badly these last few months, lying in bed, worrying. About everything. Not just at the office, where he has to admit he has been in a multi-year slump. But worried about his whole life. He has never fought for what he loved—in fact, he has never done a good job of even admitting to loving what he's loved. It was Sara who proposed to him; it was Sara who unilaterally decided they were finished.

But soon everything will change. Soon he'll have another great success, like in the old days, and he too will be able to buy a decent place to live, to pay his bills on time, to save for retirement.

Jeff wonders whether *every*one has noticed his midcareer stall: his colleagues, his boss, his college pals, his friends from college, from the beginning of his career, Isabel. Do people sit around, pitying him? He's never really entertained the possibility that he's a loser. Has he been wrong, all these decades? Do losers know it?

These self-doubts are why he made the decision he did, three months ago. The decision to really and truly grow up, to do what needs doing in order to make his way in the world as a successful adult, to be willing to make a genuine sacrifice.

Last night, in the pub with Mason, Jeff was halfway expecting that he'd see that other man. The one who'd accosted him, made the bizarre proposition, in that very same bar.

CHAPTER 4

R*ing.*

Alexis is digging through her purse to find the phone, tossing aside keys and lipstick and a tin of mints and a compact, business cards from young editors and expensive shoe stores and that British woman she met at the party and the MBA-ish guys she met after the party, at the bar, where she has to admit she was flirting like a madwoman, more so as the night wore on, as drink number three turned into numbers four and five, and finally Courtney said, "We really have to get out of here, or you'll end up going home with a stranger and seriously regretting it. Like, seriously."

The caller-ID announces that it's Isabel calling. Her boss. At 6:51 a.m.

"Hello?" she whispers. "Isabel?"

"Hi Alexis. Sorry to wake you."

"Oh, that's all right," she says, slipping out of bed, trying not to disturb Spencer. Before she got into the taxi at 2:00 a.m., she drunk-dialed, standing there in the teeming tenement-filled street on the Lower East Side, teetering on her high heels, watching as a giant black SUV nearly ran down a gaggle of too-drunk-to-pay-attention girls—not terribly dissimilar to herself—and she gasped and dropped her phone midsentence. A degrading denouement. "I was awake."

She tiptoes to the kitchen, shuts the door, takes a seat at the Ikea drop-leaf dining-table/desk/dressing-table/everything-table, an ungodly mess of jewelry and makeup and napkins and pens and a pepper mill, a small leather-bound notebook, and not one but two power strips filled with chargers—Kindle and Nook and Sony e-reader, iPad and iPhone, plus a plain old laptop computer—as well as a cellophane-wrapped brick of ramen that she intended to eat Sunday night but didn't, too busy finishing the manuscript to do anything that resembled cooking beyond tearing open a bag of pretzels to dip in Greek yogurt. And of course the thick stack of paper, for the very unusual submission, delivered very unusually: on paper.

"Everything okay?"

Of the 500 queries, book proposals, and full manuscripts that arrive every year to the attention of Isabel Reed, 490 of them are digital, and at least 9 of the others are garbage. There seems to be a high correlation between paper submissions and unpublishable drivel.

"Yeah," Isabel says, unconvincingly. "Listen: that manuscript you gave me yesterday? Tell me again how it came to us."

This is what she wants to talk about? At dawn? That's not Isabel's style. As a rule, Isabel is an eminently reasonable boss, a valuable mentor, maybe even a genuine friend, not one of those psychopath caricatures. Which there are plenty of, in the competitive corridors of Atlantic Talent Management, and clearly elsewhere in the book business. Alexis has come to recognize that she had been damn lucky to have landed at her particular cubicle.

"Right." She closes her eyes and rubs them, trying to gather lucidity. "Friday. The package was dropped off during the middle of lunch— maybe one o'clock? You were definitely not in the building."

"In an envelope? In a cardboard box?"

"A Jiffy bag."

"Who delivered it?"

"Dunno."

"Well, was it Lucas? Or one of the other mailroom guys?"

"Um, no. It was some guy I don't know."

"As in, you don't know his name? Or you've never seen him before?"

"Never seen him before, I don't think. The truth is I didn't get a good look at him—really, I didn't get *any* look at him—I was on a very, very long call with Steph Bernstein, who was having a massive meltdown about all the negative reader reviews on Goodreads, which have been sort of vicious, on top of that brutal daily *Times* review. Did you ever call her back, by the way? She's pretty anxious to hear the feedback about her new proposal."

"Oh God. I *really* don't want to." That promised to be one of those bad-news conversations with a disappointed client that are the bane of an agent's life.

"So, anyway, I'm pretty sure I didn't know the guy who delivered it. I sort of assumed he was from another department, like commercial or talent or something, or, y'know, accounting. Whatever."

"Was there anything to give any idea who it came from? Or where?"

"Like, um, what?"

"*I* don't know," Isabel says, exasperation rising in her voice. Isabel sounds too frustrated, for this line of questioning, this early in the morning. "Like a *post*mark? A postage meter's stamp? *Anything* written on the package?"

"No, not that I remember. Sorry."

"And there's no other contact info for the author? No note, or letter, or anything?"

"Just that e-mail address, on the cover page. Have you tried that?"

"Yeah. All I get is an error bounce-back."

"Weird."

"Isn't it? So . . . You read it over the weekend? All of it?"

"Yes." It sort of ruined Alexis's weekend. And Courtney gave her so much shit about her weekend geek-out that Alexis caved, agreeing to a Monday-night revelry that runs utterly counter to her work ethic.

Which is how she ended up at a book-launch party, with Courtney and her friends from the Columbia publishing course, huddled together in their chunky eyeglasses and liberal-arts degrees, inhaling pinot grigio and cubes of dried-out Manchego.

Courtney is only two years older than Alexis, but she has her own office—a tiny little windowless cube, with glass walls that face the door to the book-storage room across the corridor, but still: a door. And her own clients, at least some of them. And her own business cards.

Meanwhile Alexis has been entry-level for two years, nothing but incremental cost-of-living pay increases and no additional vacation time. Two years of answering someone else's phone, wearing the headset nine or ten hours a day—wearing that damn headset in the halls, at her desk, in the *bathroom*. Two years of filing someone else's contracts, mailing someone else's bound galleys, reading someone else's submissions. Assisting someone else's life, instead of living her own. And taking someone else's calls, at seven fucking o'clock on a Tuesday morning. Even if that someone is the famous—or once famous—Isabel Reed.

"Isabel?" she asks. "What's this all about? Did you actually read it?"

"Oh, yes. It's incredible."

"*Right?* I had no idea how Wolfe Media got started. And all that business in Europe with the CIA? And that accident? Unbelievable."

"That may be exactly the right word. Do *you* believe it?"

"You don't?"

"It's hard to say. There's so much . . . *negative*, isn't there? Maybe too negative to be credible?"

Alexis wonders if Isabel might be right. Or if Isabel's judgment is clouded. "You know him, don't you?"

"Charlie Wolfe?"

"Yeah."

"No," Isabel says. "Not really. We met a handful of times, long ago." For a few seconds the phone line is filled with nothing but breathing. Then, "Alexis, have you told anybody about the manuscript?"

Alexis is seized with panic. "Like who?"

"Like *anyone*?"

"No, no," she instinctively lies. But there was of course Courtney. And their friend James from ICM. And then—oh God—that British woman, the subsidiary-rights director at McNally & Sons, maybe named Camille, something-or-other . . .

What the hell was she thinking? She was thinking that this is what you're supposed to do, with a hot new property: talk about it. Make people want it, expect it. Try to create an air of inevitability about it.

But she can see now that she'd been too eager. Too early. She'd wanted to feel like a grown-up, like she had grown-up responsibilities, even though she wasn't, and didn't. She wanted her job to catch up to her ambition.

And—fuck!—there was that tweet of hers, @LitGirl, late Sunday night: *Can't stop reading #AccidentByAnonymous! My new favorite author. But who ARE you, Anonymous?*

"Good," Isabel says.

"And the report—did you write it at work?"

"Um, yeah?"

And of course her Facebook status over the weekend, *LOVING this anonymous manuscript that's ruining my weekend.*

"It's not on your laptop? At home?"

This makes Alexis nervous in a new way. Why should Isabel care where the reader's report was written? "No . . ."

"And do you have a copy of the manuscript? At home? Or in the office? Did you make yourself a photocopy?"

Alexis says a knee-jerk "No" while staring at her copy sitting right in front of her. She'd made this set of pages because she was sort of hoping she'd be allowed to run with this project—utter slush, with no referral— herself. But this hope was obviously irrational. Another misjudgment. It's hard to see clearly with ambition clouding your eyes.

"Okay," Isabel says. "Okay, thanks. I guess that's it for now. I'll be in by nine-thirty. See you then."

Alexis's heart sinks. "Not today," meekly. "Remember?"

A long, painful pause. "Oh." Isabel hadn't remembered. "Personal day?"

"Yeah . . . doctor's appointment, errands . . . Is that still okay?"

"Sure, fine." Though it doesn't sound like it. "See you tomorrow."

Alexis takes a deep breath, overwhelmed by all the lies she just told.

She retrieves her handbag from the bedside. Spencer is still snoring, oblivious. She rummages around for the British woman's card—her name is apparently Camilla—and turns it over to the scrawled cell number. Sometimes, Alexis's job seems like an endless series of humiliating calls. She takes a deep, steadying breath, and places yet another one.

CHAPTER 5

The video on the screen is surprisingly sharp, a close-up of a woman who seems to be staring directly at him. He can't see her hands, but he knows they're down there somewhere, typing and clicking and scrolling. All he can see is her face, framed by blonde hair, shorter than it used to be, but still elegant, in an effortless-looking way that he knows requires substantial effort.

Suddenly the image goes black as the woman folds shut her laptop, so he does too. He'd watched her for too long, and now he's running late. He grabs his small duffel and leaves the apartment and tosses the bag onto the passenger seat of the little two-seater Audi. When he'd arrived in Zurich, he'd discovered it was surprisingly challenging to lease a car without a prohibitive level of credit reports and identity checks; if there's one thing that can be said about the Swiss, it's that they're sticklers. So it was simpler and safer to buy the damn thing. And because he couldn't imagine that he'd own this new car for more than a few months, or that he'd ever have a backseat passenger, he chose a sleek fast car with no backseat, just like any other well-off bachelor would.

He guns the engine, and speeds through the tidy streets of lakeside Seefeld, big tall nineteenth-century houses and stout little twentieth-century apartment buildings, well-pruned trees and carefully tended gardens, and the predictable assortment of boutiques and banks and restaurants and bars on a main European drag like Seefeldstrasse, in a neighborhood called the Gold Coast, in a city like Zurich.

This car handles well on the climbing and dipping curves, and he allows himself to have fun with it, driving much faster here in the Alpine foothills than he ever would, back home. He'll probably never drive in America again. Can't imagine he'll ever be there again. By all accounts, he's already dead.

I.

He can't stop obsessing over that missed pronoun. He'd been so careful, so rigorous, about everything. About the Piper crash and the little motorboat and the international flights. He'd been meticulous about passports and money, about hair and eyes and clothing and shoes, about surgeries and recoveries. He'd made logistically complex arrangements in America, in Denmark and Germany and Switzerland, in Mexico. He'd plotted out precise and possibly futile contingency plans that involved France, Italy, Kenya, and Indonesia.

Maybe it was a subliminal slip. Maybe what he really wants is to get caught.

Twenty minutes out of the city, he turns the car between two tall stone pillars, onto a long straight driveway cut through the dense forest. He slows as he approaches a towering wrought-iron gate, stops the car at the security hut.

"*Guten Tag*, Herr Carner." He has been using an alias. "Welcome back," the security guard says, and opens the gate.

He presses his foot down on the accelerator, speeding toward the imposing half-timbered chalet looming at the end of the dark, shadowy drive.

CHAPTER 6

ayden crosses the windswept bridge over the long, shallow lake, Peblinge Sø, back into the bustling downtown district, making his way through the crowded shopping streets to an elegant café at a sharply angled multi-street intersection. Blocking the door are a pair of American tourists—a man his age, with the type of woman you'd expect—consulting a guidebook. Both of them are wearing shorts and polo shirts, white sneakers with athletic socks. Outfits that Hayden simply can't abide.

"*Undskyld mig*," he says, not wanting to give these buffoons the satisfaction of being addressed in their own language.

"Oh, excuse me," the woman says, smiling.

Hayden steps inside, and there she is. The hostess here is the most beautiful human being he's ever seen in his life, a perfect specimen of blonde-haired blue-eyed young loveliness. She's been here every weekday for years; she's the reason Hayden frequents this café whenever he comes to Copenhagen.

This city in general is filled with fantastic-looking people—men and women, old and young, babies and children. The whole city is like a living breathing meta-gallery, an art installation of unfathomable scale. And this hostess, Sweet Jesus, she's heartbreaking.

She smiles warmly, leads him through the dining room. And it's not just that the girl is spectacular *looking*. There's something beyond mere genetics about it, about people here: they look you straight in the eye, and offer a large smile. Not the phony I'm-trying-to-sell-you-something joyless smile that you tend to get everywhere in America, but a genuine invitation to friendliness and openness and happiness. Especially at this time of year, early summer, when you have to make a concerted effort to see a dark sky: the sun rises before anyone in their right mind is awake, and sets well after most people are asleep.

The waiter—like the hostess, surreally good-looking—delivers the coffee to Hayden's corner table, the china Royal Copenhagen, the white tulips in an Alvar Aalto vase, the burnished silver Georg Jensen, the linen crisp and cool and sharply folded, everything arranged just so. No Styrofoam cups here.

His phone vibrates, a call from New York. "Yes," he answers.

"Something you need to hear. I think you'll want to wear an earpiece. You'll be listening to recordings of three separate telephone conversations."

Hayden connects the headphones, puts the tiny speakers into his ears. He watches the hostess at her station near the door, fiddling with a pen, twirling the thing in her fingers. His contentment is quickly washed away as he listens, lips pursed in what he hopes appears to be concentration, but is furor, barely contained. A string of profanities—*fuck damn shit, that fucking fucker*—ricochets around his brain while his face presents nothing more than a thoughtful man, thinking. Hayden doesn't curse out loud, ever. But in his brain he swears like a sailor. An angry drunken broke sailor who just stumbled upon his girlfriend cheating on him. With his best friend.

Fuck.

This isn't the way it was supposed to happen. He should've had at least a day to prepare. He was expecting the delivery to happen via e-mail, which is why he has a tech monitoring the literary agent's e-mail, opening every attachment, as well as the whole surveillance operation here in Copenhagen. Ensuring that whenever it was that the literary agent received the e-mail with the manuscript attached, Hayden would be alerted, and his whole team would spring into action. Because e-mail, he assumed—he was *positive*—was the only delivery method that could possibly make sense in this situation. But apparently he was mistaken.

The recordings end.

"The first conversation is between the agent and someone named Jeffrey Fiel—"

"I know who that is," Hayden interrupts. And that second call, it's between the agent and her assistant?"

"Yes."

"And who is that in the third call, with the assistant?" Hayden is trying to stay calm, but this operation is all of a sudden threatening to come crashing down around him, dragging his career down in the wreckage. "The woman with the London accent?"

"Her name is Camilla Glyndon-Browning. She works at a publishing house called McNally & Sons. Her job title is director of subsidiary rights. I don't know what that means. Do you?"

"Yes."

This is a crap situation. He saw this coming, fifteen years ago. He knew there'd be a price to pay, sooner or later. And here's the bill, finally come due. He's quite certain there will be other installments.

"Anyway," the man in New York continues, not expecting any further clarification from his boss. Hayden doesn't provide unnecessary operational information. "It doesn't sound like the Browning woman knows anything. But the girl, obviously, does. And she seems to be lying about not having a copy of the manuscript."

"Yes," Hayden agrees. Photocopies could be a tremendous problem; every copy will need to be accounted for. He turns his eyes to the window, looks out at the midday busy-ness of Indre By, the heart of old Copenhagen. "Retrieve the assistant's copy of the manuscript asap."

"Affirmative."

"Make no attempt to hide the retrieval. It should be clear to the assistant that someone burgled her apartment, and that only the manuscript was taken. And it should be clear to the agent that photocopies will not be tolerated."

"Understood. Speaking of which: after these conversations, the agent left home, and stopped at a copy shop. I'm sending that video through to you now."

"Okay." Hayden stares out the window, chasing a conundrum in his mind: If the agent received the manuscript, that means the manuscript is finished. But if the manuscript is finished, then why is the researcher still working all day, every day? Surely after completing a book and sending it off, he would take a break . . .

Plus, the agent received a hard copy. But Grundtvig has had a constant tail, and he didn't mail a big package containing a hard copy . . .

This doesn't make sense.

Regardless of the supply-side uncertainties, Hayden now needs to shift his focus to managing the demand side. "Okay," he says again. "I'll be in New York"—he glances his watch—"I'll be there today, late afternoon. I'll confirm."

Back to New York. He was just there a few months ago, for a week, a long series of hopefully persuasive meetings with publishers and editors-in-chief, the people who run the large publishing outfits. He's about to find out how persuasive he actually was.

Hayden ends the call, and opens up the e-mail with the video attachment, a low-quality surveillance camera mounted above the door of a grungy copy shop. He watches the interaction, the transaction, his eyes narrowing as he tries to make sense of this five-minute silent movie, a bit unclear there at the end, but then he figures it out.

CHAPTER 7

sabel climbs out of the subway, gets her bearings. Across the street, a woman is loading groceries into a gleaming SUV with an East Hampton parking permit in the window and a toddler buckled into the backseat, wearing workout gear, Pilate'd and ponytailed and firm upperarmed. Another hyper-fit representative of the urban gentry, driving a moor-conquering truck.

That, Isabel thinks, used to be me. Sort of. One of the flock of women who stream into luxurious gyms immediately after school drop-off, nine a.m. classes in Studio A, followed by bottled water and decaf skim lattes. The Exercising Class.

Isabel walks a long block down Broadway, the early-morning world of Hispanic guys hosing down sidewalks, Twiggy-skinny girls walking minuscule dogs on whisper-thin leashes, scraggly-haired Japanese guys smoking hand-rolled cigarettes. Taxis and Town Cars flying down the street, one after another, shuttling Uptowners to the Financial District.

Her fatigue has created a sort of buzzing behind her temples, a background to the foreground of each of her steps, which she seems to hear not only in her ears but also in her chest, in her stomach, in the vibrations in her elbows as each footfall lands. She can't tell if she's walking slowly or quickly, normally or abnormally.

She freezes on Broadway, aghast, about to step on a cat-sized rat, lying belly-up in the middle of the sidewalk, in a pool of bright red blood; it must have just died. She feels a wave of nausea, with nothing but coffee and cigarette fumes down in her stomach. She shivers, then continues walking down the street, one foot in front of the other.

The red awning beckons, the windows are warmly aglow, like a crackling fire in the gloomy hearth of sooty SoHo. A re-creation of a Parisian brasserie that's so well executed that it has been copied in Paris.

Isabel examines her reflection in one of these large windows. She pulls her hair back over her ear, and straightens her collar, and smoothes the wrinkles out of her tight—too?—skirt. Here in the vague blur of a plate-glass window, she looks okay. It's only up close, well-lit, that the truth reveals itself.

She wends her way through the crowded room, past the *Times* and *Journals* and *Le Mondes* scattered across tables, past tall men in dark suits and beautiful women in dark glasses. She arrives at the banquettes along the east wall, and reaches into her bag, and removes a thick stack of paper.

Thud.

Jeffrey jumps in his seat, looks up from his haphazardly folded newspaper, looks down again at the stack of manuscript that just landed on the tabletop. "Sunshine," he says, smiling, "good day." He tries to stand up, but he's trapped under the lip of the table, so manages only to get into an uncomfortable-looking half-crouch, limbs fluttering.

"Oh sit down."

He sinks back onto the leather bench with a shrug.

Isabel drops her oversize tote, her manuscript bag, now a few pounds lighter, onto the floor. She glances around the restaurant, sees some familiar faces, a few casual acquaintances, and one very young, ambitious, and aggressively cleavaged colleague—rival, more accurately—named Courtney, a faithful soldier in the formidable army of fashionable females, girls with long bouncy layered blown-out hair and meticulously applied makeup, painstakingly accessorized wardrobes that are constantly updated, not just seasonally but monthly or even weekly, operating according to the precept that you should always wear the most expensive, most current item—jacket, handbag, haircut—that you can afford, or that you can pretend to afford.

The irritating girl is meeting with a bright young editor who seems to be everywhere, all of a sudden. The two of them are more than a decade junior to Isabel. People who Isabel thinks of as assistants seem to have "senior" in their job titles, and books on bestseller lists. Meanwhile Isabel's own cohort is receding from the front lines, chucking it all to go make goat cheese in Vermont, or disappearing for a few weeks during the worst of the chemo. Isabel has been startled by the vicissitudes of middle-age.

The editor waves at Isabel, while Courtney raises a perfectly plucked eyebrow, and flips her hair—she's an incessant hair-flipper—but doesn't alter the set of her mouth, the plastered-on toothy smile, one of those Midwestern mouths whose repose is a severe frown, but it's a repose that's rarely allowed to show itself in public, beaten out like left-handedness in a midcentury Catholic school, so the world sees only the forced smile, the dimples, the ingratiating lie of limitless positivity.

"Who's that?" Jeffrey asks.

"You don't know her?"

He shakes his head.

"She's no one." Isabel sure as hell isn't going to be the one to tell him. "Some junior something or other, in my office."

"Looks familiar."

"You mean she looks hot?"

"Well . . ." He tries to fight off a smile, unsuccessfully. "But that's not why I asked."

"Uh-huh," she says, throwing some scorn at him. He blushes, as he always does when any remotely carnal subject arises, usually brought up by Isabel. Under oath and the penalty of death, she'd have to admit that she does this purposefully, as a test, double-checking that Jeffrey still carries his long-lit torch for her, a perpetual crush that serves as her sexual security blanket. There have been moments in her life when she could've returned the sentiment, and not just those two nights, separated by a decade, when they kissed. But there had always been some barrier in the way: her marriage, or his, or other lesser but still important relationships.

Today, though, they're both single. And today, after all she learned last night, she feels an additional tenderness toward him, a gratitude for his constancy, his honesty. Jeffrey has loved her for twenty years, and everyone knows it; there are times when that means the world to her. There are times when she loves him.

Jeffrey is one of those men who seems to get better looking with age— the salt-and-pepper hair, the crinkly eyes, the laugh lines, all make him more appealing every year. This doesn't really happen for women, Isabel thinks.

"I'll be right back with your coffees."

Isabel watches the waitress leave, her youthfully skinny little ass retreating across the room in a pencil-thin black skirt and a prim white apron. Isabel turns to Jeffrey, who has noticed the same thing, but probably with a sentiment that's not bitterness. He has always had a wandering eye, frequently met, a good-looking charming man in an industry predominantly populated by women.

She sees him glance down at the title page to read *The Accident*, by Anonymous. Lower on the page, there's the shadow of disappeared content where Isabel taped over the author's e-mail address and hand-wrote her own contact information, before she handed the stack of paper to the scrawny pallid clerk at the twenty-four-hour copy-shop/postal-center, around the corner from her apartment. There's a lot you can accomplish in New York City, at all hours, in stuffy fluorescent-lit rooms manned by disaffected overeducated underemployed young adults, rooms that almost always have security cameras mounted where they can film the entire room, as much to monitor the clerks as any potential crooks.

"So." Jeffrey taps the stack of paper with the fountain pen he's always carrying around. "What is it?"

She pauses before answering, "The biggest bombshell you'll ever read."

Jeffrey nods, waiting for more, seemingly not getting it. "You're not going to explain?"

"You want a pitch?"

"I guess so."

This is how it's normally done: the agent pitches a project to the editor; the editor reads the material—a proposal, or sample chapters, or a whole manuscript; then the editor either declines to make an offer for publication, or makes an offer; then the agent and editor negotiate.

But apparently that's not exactly how it's going to work this time. Isabel shakes her head.

"*Any*thing?"

"I'll let the content speak for itself. Everything else is hearsay. Bullshit."

He grins at this.

"But I will tell you this, Darling: the project is yours, exclusively." Isabel sports her own little smile, a purposefully disingenuous-looking one. Pretending to be an agent who's pretending to be hard-selling. "For forty-eight hours."

"That's mighty generous of you. May I ask why?"

"Because I love you. Obviously."

"And?"

"Are you suggesting that I *don't* love you?"

"What are you looking for, Sunshine? I assume you have a number in mind. As compensation for the luxury of an exclusive submission."

"You're asking what it's worth?"

"I guess I am."

"Eight figures."

Jeffrey can't help but laugh, then realizes she's serious. "What are you, out of your mind?"

She doesn't answer.

"I've known this was coming, Sunshine, for a long time. But I have to admit, now that it's here, I'm still sort of surprised." He shakes his head. "Which is too bad. Because, you know, I've always hoped that one day we'd settle down, you and I. Exchange artisan-forged rings. Buy a drafty little farmhouse and some foul-smelling, disagreeable livestock."

He's joking, sort of. Actually, she's pretty sure that he's pretending to be joking.

"But not if you're going to be insane."

"I didn't say that's what I'm *asking*. But that is, I'm certain, what it's worth."

"Plus," he continues, "and I'm telling you this as a friend—and you know I love you dearly—you look like crap. If you're going to be showing up in restaurants at eight in the morning, asking for ten-plus million dollars, you're going to have to . . ." He gestures in her general direction. "You're going to have to look less like shit. *Or*, you're going to have to be naked and performing, you know . . . *sexual* acts. Dealer's choice. But you can't be fully clothed *and* looking like shit *and* asking for eight figures."

"You're not looking so hot yourself. Drink too much last night? Again?"

"No, thank you, I believe I drank just the right amount. And you? Did you sleep at all?"

"Not much. Listen, Jeffrey," she plants her elbows on the table, leans in. "This is serious."

"What is?"

"This whole thing is. Not a joke. Don't spread the manuscript around your office. You can tell people what it is, obviously. But don't distribute copies to the whole world; in fact, don't copy it *at all*. Don't tell anyone who absolutely doesn't need to know."

"I don't understand."

"You will," she says. She suddenly feels her energy fading, precipitously. "Listen, I have to go. And you should get started reading." She stands, leans in to kiss his cheek. "Forty-eight hours."

She turns away, takes a step.

"Hey," he says.

She turns back.

"Why me?"

"Because I can trust you. Can't I?"

"Of course."

"But remember, keep it *quiet*."

"Why? I don't under—"

"Because it's *dang*erous, Jeffrey."

"But *why*?"

"Because it's about some incredibly bad things."

"Done by?"

She stares at him. "One of the most powerful, well-known men in the world. Media mogul, is what people call him."

Isabel can see the color drain from Jeffrey's face. Then he cracks a forced smile. "So Oprah does, after all, have bodies buried in the basement?"

"No," she says, "Charlie Wolfe does." Isabel decides to leave him there, excited, curious, motivated.

She makes her way back through the tightly packed tables, pausing to let waiters and waitresses scurry past. The smell of bacon wafts up from a table, and she inhales deeply, savoring something she forbids herself from eating more than once a month.

In the tight space between tables, a man in a gray suit brushes against her, too closely, and she feels uneasy. She thinks for a second that her pocket may have just been picked. She pats herself down with quick sweeps, and realizes that there's nothing in her pockets to pick; in fact, her pockets are still sewn shut, just as manufactured in whatever Southeast Asian sweatshop. She looks inside her black leather handbag, and sees the wallet, the phone, the keys. There's nothing important that could be missing.

Isabel continues on unsteady feet to the front door, to the sidewalk. She lights a cigarette, the smoke flooding her lungs, the nicotine rushing into her bloodstream. She'd tried Wellbutrin and Xanax; she'd used patches and gum. In the end, the only thing that made her quit successfully was being pregnant.

But then, after everything, she couldn't help but start up again. At first it was just a single cigarette per day, or two. Then it became a few, and within months she was back to full-throttle. Over the past couple of years, she's tried to quit a few times, but not seriously. She anticipates—she accepts—failure. Because she doesn't want to quit, not really. She wants instead to try, and fail.

She's the last of her friends who still smokes, which makes her feel like a polio victim in the early 1950s, having just missed the invention of the vaccine. A relic of a different era.

She takes another drag, and glances in the restaurant window, and sees Jeffrey hunkered down above the manuscript.

The generic-looking man in the standard-issue gray suit ambles through the dining room, drops his bag in a chair. "Excuse me," he says, leaning over Jeff's table, "may I borrow your pen for a moment?" The man points at the Sheaffer on the tabletop.

Jeff glances down. "Sure."

"I'll be right back." The man picks up the pen, walks to another table.

Jeff returns his attention to the stack of paper in front of him, to the manuscript that he hopes—that he *knows*—is the thing he's been waiting for. Now that it's here, something this big, he's worried, unconfident. He hasn't had something this important since that Pulitzer winner a decade ago. He's out of practice, afraid of how to handle it, how to present it to his boss, his colleagues. Of how to manage Isabel, and her expectations, and timetable. Afraid of other editors to whom she might submit it, afraid of a bidding war, an auction, a humiliating defeat. Afraid of other, less easily identifiable issues, prickling his psyche. Afraid of the decisions he will face. The decisions he will make.

When the man returns, leaving the pen on the table and saying "Many thanks," Jeff barely glances up, lost in thought. He never thought this manuscript would actually happen.

The unmemorable man retreats, replaced by the sexy waitress in her white shirt and black apron. What is it about women in servile uniforms? "More coffee?"

Jeff looks up at the waitress, past her, to the table where the man should be. But there's no one there. Jeff looks down at his empty cup. "Yes, thank you." This is going to be a long day. He flips to the middle of the manuscript, and starts reading.

Before long Wolfe Worldwide Media was operating
two dozen news websites across Europe, and buying
up stakes in newspapers and television stations.
They had begun the process of launching the
American cable news network, whose awareness-
building publicity blitz entailed giving countless
interviews with other media, reporting on itself,
the media's favorite topic.

　During one of these interviews, Charlie was
asked if there had been any particular event that
triggered his reform, the total transformation
of his lifestyle that began the summer after
his junior year in college. He gave up alcohol
and drugs entirely. He dedicated himself to
studies, and his spare time to volunteer work.
Almost overnight, he evolved from a singularly
irresponsible, selfish, substance-abusing teenager
into an extraordinarily serious, sober, and earnest
young adult.

　"No," he said, with a relaxed, easy smile
spreading across his face, maintaining unflinching
eye contact with the camera. "I just thought it was
time to grow up."

CHAPTER 8

"Come on, come on, come *on.*" Alexis tugs on Spencer's arm. "*Please.*" After she'd hung up with Isabel, she'd thought, what the hell, the damage was already done. No further harm in a good-morning quickie. "Dude," she'd said to Spencer, slipping under the sheets. "Wake up."

But that was more than an hour ago—it wasn't that quick, when all was said and done—and now he won't get up. She studies this man lounging in her bed, the pretentious, obnoxious, but good-looking and undeniably talented writer—a tech blogger now, submitting short stories and working on a screenplay—she'd met a few months ago, at a party in a Bushwick loft to which she was dragged by a hyperactively social, unfailingly upbeat publicist she knew from a publishing house—assistants like Alexis aren't on guest lists; they're the hangers-on, the plus-ones—after they'd had an insanely unaffordable round of drinks at one of those Midtown hotel bars populated mostly by forty-something men wearing a strict uniform of bespoke suits with working buttonholes at the cuffs.

It was quite a different selection of men out in the Brooklyn ex-slum, feral beards and architectural mustaches, tattoos and piercings, plaids and engineer's boots and jeans with clunky key chains dangling from the pockets. Another type of uniform, perhaps even more complex and studiously maintained than the one in Midtown, just not as expensive.

She glances again at her handheld screen, the blurry digital line between personal and professional. Facebook won't be a problem; only a few people liked Alexis's status update, and Isabel isn't especially engaged with Facebook anyway; she's a weekend lurker. But Twitter, that's a whole different story. Almost everyone at ATM is tweeting and retweeting constantly. Isabel isn't one of them, thank God, but still she's going to hear about it. In the kitchen, or the ladies' room, or in a conference room waiting for a meeting to start, someone will turn to Isabel, and making conversation will ask, "So whatever happened to that anonymous submission that Alexis was loving? You sign that up?"

And then Alexis will be fully fucked.

She tugs Spencer's arm, trying to actually drag him out of bed. "*Please.*" He has broken up with Alexis more than once. As it happens, they are at the moment broken-up.

He finally rises, starts pulling on his paint-spattered jeans and concert T-shirt, a New Wave show that took place in the East Village a few years before the guy was born.

First item today will be a long, punishing, atoning workout. It's time for her to start getting ready for this year's marathon; she's a little behind schedule, slower than usual to recognize that winter ended and it was time to start outdoor running again. Then a doctor's appointment, then a wax, a mani-pedi. And finally some unglamorous shopping—running shoes, underwear, toiletries, groceries. Not exactly the *Sex and the City* retail fantasy.

Nor was her weekend, spent immersed in that damn manuscript instead of the beach and binge drinking lifestyle of one of her six allotted weekends in Southampton, a summer rental she's sharing with at least two dozen friends, acquaintances, and strangers; the list of who's entitled to what bed on what weekends looks like the org chart for a Fortune 500 corporation. But while everyone else tanned and partied, Alexis sat on peeling white wicker in the shade on the sagging back porch, turning manuscript pages in her lap, swatting away mosquitoes.

But once again, this will be another author and project she will not get a chance to represent, yanked out from under her, at dawn.

Her gym bag is now packed, except for reading material. She looks at her little leather Luddite notebook, re-reads her scant editorial notes on *The Accident*; there's practically nothing she thinks should be changed about the manuscript. Then she glances at the compulsively maintained Excel spreadsheet in which she keeps track of her reading. She runs her eyes across row #709, whose column A reads ANONYMOUS, column B THE ACCIDENT. She auto-sums the 2:15 and 5:15 and 4:30 and 3:30 and . . . she spent more than fifteen hours reading this photocopy that she denied having, because of the impure motive that led her to make the copy in the first place: the hope that it could be hers, and hers alone.

She wakes up her Kindle and opens a newly imported file, a submission from a friend of one of Isabel's notably unprofitable clients. Alexis reads the first page—not bad. She learned the hard way to always read the opening page before committing any further time to anything; you can learn a lot on first pages about the many different ways that a manuscript can be awful. But this page 1 is not, so this is what she'll read on the elliptical machine. Or something else. She has three dozen submissions loaded onto the device.

She played it wrong with *The Accident*. She was too impatient, too gregarious, too reckless. She needs to buckle down, to get serious, to continue to pay her dues. She's only twenty-five years old. Even if there are other twenty-five-year-olds who've risen above her current station, they're the exception, not the rule. Her own time will come. But that time is not now.

Finally Spencer is dressed. Alexis pulls him out the door before he has a chance to dawdle, ask for coffee, whatever.

They step out onto the Hell's Kitchen sidewalk. A delivery truck rumbles past, drowning out all other sounds. A taxi screeches to a stop. A small army of Hispanic contractors, all wearing tan work boots and jeans, loiters in front of a newly converted manufacturing building, waiting for the strike of 8:59 a.m., when they'll be allowed to access the unit, to begin their noisy messy undocumented day of sanding floors and plastering ceilings and installing sound-dampening double-pane windows to three-million-dollar lofts.

At the corner she stops. "So," she says.

In the ATM office, only three of the assistants are men, and at least one of them is gay, probably two. The third is on every level unacceptable. So Alexis needed to seek out broader dating horizons—perhaps not dating; whatever this is—often in Brooklyn, where most people her age live, unrelenting boosters of their adopted borough, disdainful of Manhattan. But Alexis's vision of herself has always been in Manhattan, walking to work at a literary agency or a publishing house, surrounded by the throbbing, insistent life in the center of the city.

"This is where we part?" Spencer asks.

She nods.

"That was killer." She knows he means the sex. Their conversation last night was nil, and this morning consisted almost entirely of her trying to get him the hell out of her apartment.

She's beginning to suspect that Spencer doesn't actually like her all that much. And she has to admit that the feeling is rather mutual. Maybe she should stop sleeping with him. "I'll give you a call."

"That'd be awesome," he says, without meaning it. For Spencer everything and everyone is awesome and killer, or, when he's feeling retro-ironic, groovy and neat. It drives her bananas. "We'll hang."

"*Mmm*," she says, and turns and walks away, past the Korean deli, where the cute Mexican kid is swabbing the sidewalk with an eye-burning bleach solution. "Morning, Miss," he says.

His familiarity makes her realize—*damn*—that in her haste to get rid of Spencer, to get out of her little hovel, she forgot her wallet. She needs her ID for the gym. There's a new morning-front-desk guy, a prissy officious little twit who she knows will not let her in without the damn card.

Alexis takes a step off the concrete curb and down onto the blacktop pavement, distracted. She takes another step, then another. She hears a car screeching, and she turns to face a black sedan—

The Mexican kid yells, "*Cuidado! Cuidado!*"

But she's frozen, unable to move, staring at the oncoming grille.

"Miss?" The boy is holding her arm, as well as his mop. "Miss? You okay?" She nods.

"The fuck ya thinkin'?" It's the driver of the sedan, his window rolled down, yelling at her. "Ya know what a red light means? *Do. Not. Walk.* The fuck?" He asks, and clearly wants an answer; this is not rhetorical. "The fuck?" He shakes his head in disgust, and pulls away.

She stands, trembling, electrified with fright. She retraces the long half-block back to her building, shakily. Opens the front door to the standard-issue tenement, red brick and dirty limestone, rusty fire escapes, security bars on the windows. She walks down the short, dim hallway. Inserts the key to her apartment door, the worst unit in the building—1F, first-floor front, two steps below grade, facing garbage cans.

Alexis pushes open the door, steps inside, shuts the door behind her. She turns away from her door, into her apartment—

A man is standing on the far side of the room, holding the manuscript. Caught in the act, surprised, yet moving very quickly, while Alexis remains frozen, again.

CHAPTER 9

"Is your car handy?" Hayden opens the closet, takes out a small suitcase, places it on the bed.

"Yes," Kate answers, turning from the window, surprised. She didn't expect to see him again today.

"Good." He opens the top drawer of the bureau, filled with her under-things. He should have known better. Should have opened a lower, non-underwear drawer. "Um . . ." He beckons Kate. "Could you, uh, help me pack?"

"What's going on?"

"We need to wind down this operation."

"By *wind down*, you mean terminate? Immediately?"

"This instant."

She sweeps up bras and panties and socks in her forearms, dumps them into the bag. She seems out of joint.

"Don't worry, Kate. You did *good*." Hayden gathers up a small stack of her jeans and T-shirts, neatly folded. "This development has nothing to do with *you*. But something else has happened."

She doesn't say anything while she gathers another armful, sweat-ers and outerwear, and transfers the pile to the leather and canvas bag, a piece of quietly elegant luggage that Hayden suspects cost at least a thousand euros, tactile evidence that she has a lot of money to spend on luggage, and on vacations, and in fact on whatever the hell she wants. He resents it, a bit; she works for him, after all.

On the other hand, it's true that Hayden too has a couple of swollen bank accounts. One of them is just a bit of family money, the proceeds from the sale of his parents' Back Bay house. The taxes and maintenance were exorbitant on Marlborough Street, and his Boston-based sister wouldn't deign to live in such a grand building, after Goo and Ga—their nicknames, for a half-century—died. Willa called the house a mansion, and it clashed with her career, and the persona that went with it, as a mediator, specializing in gang intervention and conflict resolution, driving around South Boston in a filthy banged-up Hyundai. And of course Hayden didn't have any use for a tall gloomy six-bedroom townhouse in downtown Boston; neither did his other sister Ellen, a well-manicured Greenwich housewife.

So they sold the big brick heap, paid the taxes, and split the proceeds. Which is how Hayden found himself with three-quarters of a million un-earned dollars, parked in electronic records managed by private bankers. He has never felt the urge—and never really had the time—to spend it. So it's still sitting there, more patiently than he thought money could be, awaiting a catastrophic illness, or a late-life-crisis. He'd long anticipated a debilitating midlife crisis, but midlife seems to be coming and going without relevant incident.

The other swollen account is a numbered one in Switzerland that contains roughly twenty-one million euros, or somewhere north of thirty million dollars, depending on exchange-rate fluctuations. This too is a chunk of unearned money, albeit from a completely different type of source.

"Let me get this straight," Hayden said, a year ago, in a different country. "Your husband is the person who stole fifty million euros from Colonel Petrovic?"

Kate smiled, tight-lipped and joyless. Then she shrugged her shoulders, an afterthought add-on to the noncommittal smile.

"And you want immunity for this? For Dexter?"

"And for me."

"For you?"

Kate nodded.

"Did you play any role in the theft?"

She shook her head.

"But you knew about it?"

"No, not . . . not at the time. It happened last winter."

He leaned toward Kate, his elbows on the table in the café atop the Georges Pompidou Center. "Then why do you need immunity?"

"I don't, really. But you never know."

This was bizarre. "And where *is* this money?"

"Well, we have—that is, *Dexter* has—half of it. The other half is, uh, unavailable. At the moment."

Hayden raised his eyebrows.

"Dexter had a co-conspirator. She has the other half. I think."

"You *think*?"

Kate huffed, blowing a slow stream of air out of swollen cheeks. "I just discovered this, Hayden, and it sort of ruined my life. So give me a fucking break."

Hayden looked away from Kate, out over the café on the Beaubourg rooftop, off to the south, the picture-postcard images of Paris—the flying buttresses of Notre Dame, the severe geometry of the Louvre, the machine-age elegance of *La Tour*. This beautiful city, onetime capital of the world, center of high culture and international intrigue. Now a political backwater, an engine driven by food and fashion, by tourism, by the centrifugal pull of the big city in a small country, irrelevant.

Paris is still important to the French, but it's no longer the European center of what matters to Americans. Germany is by far the biggest economy; Spain and Greece the loci of unrest; London the capital.

There are Muslims growing militant in Scandinavia, and gangsters growing restless in Russia; there are the perpetually downtrodden and occasionally revolutionary hordes of Eastern Europe, the religious strife and ethnic tensions of Southern, the strategic oil reserves of Northern.

There are always important developments in Europe to monitor, to influence; there's a never-diminishing assortment of unsavory characters to handle. But there's an increasing reluctance in Langley to prioritize, to authorize, to legitimize the European desk. In the wake of 9/11, all their focus shifted to the Mideast, and to American-targeted terrorism. The subtleties of Europe had been growing increasingly elusive and unmanageably intricate to the crop of Agency bureaucrats raised on MTV, with the attendant attention spans. They thought they understood the blunt dynamics of Middle Eastern conflict, short-form conflict; they had very little patience with the longer arc of the European narratives.

Beginning in the late nineties, Hayden had run some extracurricular operations, a mutually symbiotic relationship with an international businessman; they helped each other create the news that Hayden, as a representative of the CIA, desired. But as that man grew more influential and visible over the subsequent decade, that business by necessity waned, and then disappeared entirely.

Which is why Hayden has been toying with the idea of setting up something new, something different, an off-the-books fund to run a free-lance team that he could use for the types of operations that would no longer get approved by cover-your-ass Washington oversight. Disinformation. Counterintelligence. Character assassination.

Perhaps this was it, right here, falling into his unprepared lap in the soft early-fall gloaming, high above the busy streets of the 3ᵉᵐᵉ *arrondisement*. Not only the operating capital, but also the point person, the most important personnel member. He could make some sort of deal with Kate. He could take her stolen millions in exchange for her husband's immunity. Sort of. And he could give her the job she wants. Again, sort of.

He considered Kate in the falling light, leaning away and breathing evenly, anxious for his answer but trying to hide it. A vulnerable woman, easily manipulated.

"Okay, Kate," he said, reaching across the table. Every once in a while, Hayden felt like both the luckiest and the cleverest man in the world. This was one of those moments, sealed with a handshake. "You have a deal."

"Are you going to tell me what the hell happened?" Kate asks. Hayden nods.

"Thank God."

"Oh, please, feel free to call me Mr. Gray."

"Har-har."

He hands her the final stack of clothing. "It looks like our subject may not be the correct individual."

Kate stares at Hayden, uncomprehending. The freelance techs at the university in Heidelberg have spent months searching for this guy, mining the planet-wide ether for someone who could be fabricating a biography of one of the most powerful men in the world. Finally the German nerds found an IP address that was regularly clicking through to old newspaper articles, to video clips and photos, all consistent with researching Charlie Wolfe. They matched this web-access ID to a telephone number in the same location that had been placing calls to the States regularly. Calls to Wolfe's family and classmates, to colleagues and politicians, to journalists.

That's when Kate descended on Copenhagen. She'd been chasing other leads around the Continent—an apartment in Seville and a farmhouse in the Dordogne, a cottage in the Cotswolds and a villa on Lipari—for the better part of the spring. She hastily rented this apartment across

Nørrebrogade, moved in bare-bones furnishings, and hired the rest of the local team, freelancers. After a couple of days, certain that she'd found the author, she called in Hayden.

"How is that possible?" She zips her bag closed.

Hayden grabs the handle of Kate's bag, hefts it to the floor.

"Grundtvig is a diligent researcher. We've—*I've*—listened to *all* his calls." She's defending her own diligence, her tactics. Defending herself. "And what he's researching is definitely Wolfe."

"Yes he is," Hayden agrees. "And we've seen *every*thing he's done, correct?"

She nods.

"But somehow a few days ago a hard copy of his manuscript—what we have to assume is his *finished* manuscript—was delivered to the expected literary agent in New York, without any of us seeing him *mail* a hard copy. Without us having intercepted an e-mail with a manuscript attached. And most puzzling, without the researcher"—gesturing at the window—"ceasing to *work* on the manuscript."

Hayden can see Kate's gears spinning, trying to figure this out, just as he himself was, an hour earlier.

"What's going on across the street," she says, "isn't what we think is going on."

He picks up a flat-head screwdriver from the kitchen counter. "No, it doesn't look that way."

Hayden has always known that Grundtvig is not the real author. But he was hoping that Grundtvig would have regular—or at least occasional—contact with the real author, and would lead to him. It's almost inconceivable that this hasn't yet happened.

He walks across the room. With a quick shove of his foot, he moves the mattress to an angle. He kneels on the bare wooden planks, and uses the screwdriver to pry up a board. He reaches into the floor cavity and removes two pairs of gloves. He hands one to Kate, then pulls on the other, tugging and twisting the snug leather into place.

"What are we doing?" she asks.

He reaches into the floor again and retrieves two inexpensive 9-millimeters, clean untraceable weapons with the identifying markings filed off. Hayden's general conviction is that very few problems are solved with a gun. The violence just shifts the problem, usually compounding it. But sometimes there's really no choice.

"Our friend"—Hayden motions with one of the guns—"must have some connection to the actual author. We haven't found that connection through his web or phone activity, but I have to imagine we'll find it on his hard drive."

Hayden checks his ammunition clip, and screws on a sound suppressor. Kate does the same with her weapon.

"We're going to *rob* this guy?" she asks.

Hayden laughs, and slips the weapon into the patch pocket of his herringbone sport jacket. "No, Dear. *I'm* going to rob this guy. You're going to wait on the street, in case something happens. When I exit the building, I'll give you the laptop. I'll get on my bicycle. You'll drive." Hayden places a bud in his ear. "To leave Denmark, don't take the ferry to Germany; go over the mainland."

She nods her understanding: avoid chokepoints.

"Take your bag to the car now." He connects the wire to his phone. "Then wait across the street, and watch."

They both look around the apartment, checking for stray items. There's nothing.

The stairs are worn and creaky, the banister wobbly. Hayden takes the stairs slowly, deliberately, aware of his gathering nerves, careful not to slip and fall, pointlessly.

For the entirety of his adult life, Hayden has chosen to be an American abroad, meddling in the affairs of foreign governments. He bears culpability for the decision to live this type of life. If this gets him killed, he will not be a victim; you're not a victim if you bring it on yourself. Hayden believes in self-determination, and self-responsibility.

He will not blame the person who eventually kills him, in a situation like this. But he always hopes it doesn't happen today.

Hayden waits for a few small cars and a large flotilla of bicycles to pass, then walks across the street with a measured pace, trying to keep himself calm, or at least calm-looking. In front of the building next door, a cigarette-smoking Middle Eastern man tosses his butt into the gutter, turns away, and steps through the glass door covered in lace-trimmed curtains.

Hayden pushes open the apartment building's big wooden door, steps into the tiled vestibule, and confronts a modern glass-and-aluminum door, next to a panel of buttons beside name labels, half of them blank. He considers buzzing randomly until someone admits him, then decides against it. This door looks flimsy enough, and a couple of whacks with the pistol ought to disable the lock, or shatter the glass.

But first he tries pulling on the handle, and sure enough the thing simply opens. Oh, Scandinavia. How trusting.

He climbs another set of rickety wooden stairs, turns on the landing, approaches the door. He takes a deep breath, removes the weapon from his pocket, and uses the butt to knock.

Nothing.

He waits five seconds, ten. He bangs again. Then calls out, "FedEx!"

"*Jeg kommer!*" comes the answer. He can hear the scraping of chair legs against the wood floor, then footsteps, then the click as the lock disengages—

Hayden throws his shoulder and all his weight against the door and explodes into the room while grabbing Jens Grundtvig by the shirt and raising the pistol and placing the nozzle directly on the man's forehead.

"*Shhhh.*" Hayden hisses. He kicks the door closed. "You are very close to dying right now."

Grundtvig's eyes are popping out of his head, stumbling backward, losing his balance, but Hayden is holding him up by the shirtfront.

"But I don't want to kill you. What I want is to know what you're doing."

The man opens his mouth, but no sound emerges.

"Excuse me?" Hayden asks.

"Please do not kill me."

They have moved all the way into the room, to the desk. "Sit down," Hayden orders.

The man collapses into his chair, panting.

"Now tell me: what are you *doing* here?"

"Research. I am doing research."

"For whom?"

"I do not know."

"Who is paying you?"

"I do not know his name. Or her name. I do not know. I am paid every week. Kroner are deposited into my account."

"You are researching Charlie Wolfe? His companies?"

"Yes. That is all. Research."

"And what do you do with your information? Do you send it to someone?"

"No I do not. My file is uploaded to a server every Friday night at midnight."

"How is that set up?"

"I do not understand it. But the computer and the arrangement came with the job. The flat too. This is all I know."

Hayden takes a couple of steps away from this man, breathing space, and allows himself to look around this large cluttered room, office and living room and bedroom combined in one, with an untidy kitchenette in the corner—

His earpiece crackles to life. "We have a problem from next door,"

65

Kate says. The storefront to the west is an Arabic-language social club whose members appear to be primarily—perhaps exclusively— recent Turkish immigrants. A few small tables covered in oilcloth, an old television on a high shelf in the corner, a fat lazy cat, teapots and glasses.

"Two men, possibly armed, entering lobby."

Until this moment it had been unclear if the club had any ties to questionable activities. It is still unclear what exactly is going on, but there's obviously some connection to Grundtvig, and it can't be something good.

"I'll bring up a rear position."

Hayden can see in his imagination Kate entering the building, holding her weapon carefully in front of her, creeping through the same door he entered a minute ago . . .

His eyes dart around the room, looking for cover. He can hear the men trudging up the stairs. That's when he notices the video camera that's aimed at the front door.

Grundtvig shifts in his chair. "Get up," Hayden growls quietly.

"Me?" Kate whispers in his ear.

"No, I was talking to him." Hayden grabs Grundtvig by the shoulder, makes the Dane face the door in front of Hayden. A human shield.

The trudging stops. The men are just on the other side of the door.

"Can you attain visual on the door in ten seconds?"

"Yes."

"Starting now."

Hayden counts the seconds in his mind—one, two, three—his weapon aimed at the front door—four, five, six—

The door bursts open. But there's just one man standing in it, aiming a gun at Hayden. Six, seven—

The two men stare at each other for a second—eight—before Hayden understands.

"Kate!" he says—nine, ten—but realizes it's too late.

The man in the door smiles. Then he steps into the apartment, making room in the doorway for Kate, held at gunpoint by the second man, who'd obviously lain in wait. Who'd known that another American would be coming up the stairs.

They'd been set up.

CHAPTER 10

The author shuffles out of the exam room wearing supple leather slippers, wrapped in a cashmere robe, indulgent items he purchased at an efficient, well-edited little men's shop off the Bahnhofstrasse, the highest high street in Switzerland, with the streetcars gliding by and the flapping canton flags above the clean wide sidewalks lined with a comprehensive collection of the most famous luxury brands in the world, a rich assortment of expensive-looking handbags dangling from the arms of expensive-looking women.

He's still occasionally caught off-guard by the staggering prices in Zurich, for taxis and coffee and groceries and socks, his sense of propriety offended at some unreasonable price tag or another. But what does he care, really? As they say, you can't take it with you.

This is one of the things he ended up thinking to himself over and over, as he was telling his same sad story again and again last fall, to hundreds of people over the course of an interminable week, in person and on the phone and even by e-mail. Explaining to all these shocked and sympathetic people that his diagnosis had come out of the blue, after a season of not feeling well, tired, flu-ish, losing weight, constantly sniffling, his systems compromised by something or other.

But as he made sure everyone knew, he was one of those ostentatiously busy super-professionals who can never get around to vacations or automotive tune-ups or doctor's visits, not until crisis hits, which was in the fall, right before Thanksgiving. Then it took just a few days, cycling through specialists and tests, until bam: stage IV.

His mortality rate was supposedly higher than 95 percent, though no doctor or physician's assistant or nurse would admit how much higher, exactly. Forty-four years old, would be lucky to see forty-five. Extremely lucky. It'd be a good idea to get your affairs in order.

He went to New York for the holiday, as planned, as every year, the one weekend of the year when DC truly empties out, a few weeks after Election Day, when 100 percent of the people in the vast political machinery are willing to say "No thanks" to the producers of *Face the Nation* and *Meet the Press*, "I'm going home for the weekend."

He attended the annual Thursday supper at his mother's house in Brooklyn, the whole big hodgepodge of extended family and friends, now mostly people who could only be characterized as old, people who'd once held him as a baby, far-left-wing people who looked at that grown-up baby with the unmistakable disenchantment that accompanies shattered illusions, not just in a person, but in the unremitting disappointments of their historical materialism, embodied by him.

On Friday and Saturday he attended hastily scheduled medical consultations, sitting around in bland waiting rooms, inoffensive nonrepresentational art in aluminum frames, three-month-old magazines, tissue boxes. By Sunday he was nearly delirious from exhaustion, a long weekend of mostly sleepless hotel-suite nights, staring out the enormous picture window at the vast dark of the big park, rooting around in the cluttered little minibar-fridge, taking brief unsatisfying strolls through the hall's humming fluorescence to the hulking, groaning ice machine.

He took a long Sunday walk, and paid a rare visit to his ex-wife. She was the first person he told. Then Amtrak back to Washington, the train pulling into stations and occasionally sitting there, actionless, waiting for the timetable to catch up to the reality, the emergency lights glowing green in the aisle, like a runway, guiding passengers to the bathroom, to the bar car, to the exit, with the whirr of the circulation fans blowing too hard and unevenly, something caught in a duct, the bathroom door sliding open and clicking closed as a drunk disheveled man emptied himself from either end. A young woman was talking low-volume nonstop into her phone, next to a college kid with his chin on his chest and a variety of textbooks strewn around in pretend studiousness, in front of a West Indian couple, the man's mouth filled with gold teeth.

He was surrounded by all these strangers, alone with his regrets. Despite having been raised to disdain money, he'd made a lot of decisions in his life based on its pursuit. He'd started making those decisions way back in college, and had continued throughout the quarter-century since, as if on capitalist autopilot. For a while he told himself that he was merely professionally ambitious, not money-hungry greedy, and it's hard to disentangle success from wealth. Each is a measure of the other, inseparable.

The train traveled in fits and starts down the spine of New Jersey, passengers boarding and disembarking at Newark and Trenton and Philadelphia, at surprisingly slummy Dover and relentlessly bleak Baltimore, at the big parking lot of BWI and finally abundantly gentrified Union Station, Washington DC.

He arrived to the offices just after dinnertime. From down on the street, he could see that the lights were on in Charlie's corner. He headed straight to his own big office, the opposite corner from Charlie's, with his luggage in tow. It was unusual but hardly unheard-of for someone like him to arrive at this hour, at the close of a holiday weekend, distracted by everything that would need to be accomplished tomorrow, starting tonight, everyone wearing khakis and polo shirts and running shoes, eyeglasses instead of contact lenses, the commonplace camaraderie of Sunday colleagues.

He poured himself a glass of Scotch, strong and smoky, practically thick. He started working, automatically, mindlessly refreshing his heavy tumbler, getting uncharacteristically and unintentionally drunk. And increasingly maudlin, staring at his computer screen, at his face reflected back at him, reflecting on all the things he had lost in his life, and would never have the opportunity to regain.

Sometime about nine he looked up to see his boss filling his doorway, a tall square-shouldered silhouette. "What's going on?" Glancing at the bottle, the glass, the red puffy eyes. "You okay?"

"Oh, you know." He fingered his glass, not trying to hide it, or downplay it. Admitting it, emphasizing it. "Thanksgiving."

Charlie Wolfe took a step into the room, backlit, his face unreadable. "Are you drunk?"

"My mother? She hates me. My ex-wife . . . doesn't exactly love me. My kid?" He shrugged, took a swig of booze, fighting back tears, then planted the heavy glass back on the tabletop with a thud, louder than he intended.

His relationship with Charlie had been deteriorating, as long relationships have a tendency to do. During their years building Wolfe Worldwide Media, the author had learned some things about his friend that he didn't much like, in addition to the unappealing things he'd known for decades, not to mention some not entirely pleasant things about himself. And then a few months earlier, after the disaster in Finland, they'd had that atrocious conversation. And the deterioration accelerated, unsurprisingly.

"Charlie, what we've been doing . . . ?" He shook his head.

Even back at the start, the author had always had misgivings about their niche—deprofessionalizing the news-gathering media, and deobjectifying the news itself. It seems so obvious, even banal, now. But back when they started in the nineties, the news was dominated by the nightly broadcast on the three networks, delivered by ten-million-dollar-per-year anchors wearing suit and tie and scrupulously sculpted hair, or by the *New York Times* and the *Wall Street Journal* and *Time* and *Newsweek* and the Associated Press and UPI, ponderously reporting on the impenetrable nuances of ethnic conflict in the Balkans. The news was a vast apparatus of careerists—producers and editors, publishers and reporters—with degrees in broadcasting and journalism, and internships and entry-level jobs and promotions, and associations and awards, and rules and standards. A profession, populated by professionals. Quaint.

Wolfe Worldwide Media's implicit mission was to de-news the news, to legitimize sensationalism. They launched one website at a time, country by country, in Europe, where web development and usage weren't as advanced, and competition for capital and clicks and advertisers not as fierce. They instituted a system of newsgathering by amateurs who had no legal relationship or responsibility to the publishers, with a content bias toward gossip and innuendo, voyeurism and scandal, openly espousing unabashedly partisan rhetoric. Not aiming to deliver the objective so-called news to the entirety of the potential audience, but rather providing a subjective current-affairs-based entertainment to a much more finite audience. An audience that was much more easily identifiable and targetable, with a much clearer set of appropriate advertisers and sponsors.

This was not the news, in the traditional sense of objective fact-based and double-sourced reportage. It was something sort of new, at a moment before camera phones and social media and news aggregators and streaming video, when things could still be new. When people were still as a rule willing to wait a week for a fresh edition to hit the newsstands so they could read about celebrity divorces. Though of course they were very excited to not have to wait a week. To not have to wait at all.

"If this is our legacy, Charlie?" The author looked down again to the warm glowing amber in his heavy etched-glass tumbler, and again considered telling a particular truth for the first time in his life.

But when he looked up, Charlie Wolfe was turning, and walking away, and then was gone. The life-defining decision was made for him, by Charlie, not for the first time. And the truth just hung in the air, unspoken and silent, yet vast.

———

For a few minutes after Charlie left, the author sat motionless in his dim, cavernous office, lit by only the computer's glow and the cone of light from the small desk lamp. Then he stood up, a bit shaky. He crossed to the far side of room, to the wall with the built-in file cabinets, in deep shadow. He was plastered. So it took a few awkward stabs in the drunken dark before he managed to insert the key into the lock of the set of secure drawers.

He could've turned on the overhead lights, but didn't want to.

He pulled open the bottom left drawer, the least accessible, least used. He removed the rubber-banded manila folders from their hanging green hammocks.

They'd had an earnest, reasoned discussion about writing a full-length book, as opposed to giving short interviews for broadcast and periodical and web. Their business was bite-size infotainment, and they knew what could and couldn't be accomplished this way. It's easy to quickly assassinate a character; it takes much longer to build one.

The author opened his weekend bag, and pushed aside his socks and boxers and jeans, his Dopp kit and his laptop, to make room for the files.

Then he staggered down the hall and around the corner, and pressed the unlock button to release the glass double-doors, through the lobby and past security and out onto the dark deserted downtown DC streets, trudging through the cold two miles home to Georgetown, alone with this new secret, layered atop the old secrets, pondering a life that had been defined by secrets.

CHAPTER 11

Bradford McNally examines his CFO's worn, grimy, ill-fitting plaid suit. The frayed collar of his not-particularly-white shirt, and the slouched-down lint-speckled black socks, and the exposed expanse of pale, hairy, flabby calf, and the unshined, scuffed, fashion-reverse shoes. The moist, shiny bald spot in the middle of his head, and the stubbly hollow on his neck where his razor failed to shave, beneath the nearly nonexistent chin.

This guy is repulsive, sprawled in the worn leather club chair, a sheaf of papers in his fat lap, the top page defaced with violent red scrawls. "The bottom line," Seth says, wheezing slightly, filling the air with too much of his unappealing presence, "is ten million."

"*What?*"

"Ten and a half, actually."

"Beyond budget?" Brad knew that the number would be approaching this, but he thought it'd be less. Six, seven million. Something with one fewer digit. "Ten *million* dollars?'

"And a half," Seth corrects. "In excess of all current projections. And the Wolfe buyout offer drops by a quarter-million every week. But you know that."

Now Brad contemplates his money guy not just with disgust, but with something that could accurately be described as violent loathing.

74

Brad doesn't pretend to be any type of financial genius. But even he knows that there are two fundamental ways to solve any type of money problem: one is to get more of it coming in, the other is to have less of it going out. Going out, there's nothing they can do—no salaries to cut, no production costs to shave, no publicity campaigns to be shortchanged—to close a gap this wide. And receivable, they have no books hitting the marketplace with the potential to become the types of blockbusters that could generate revenue of this magnitude.

There's only one way to come up with this type of additional cash: acquire a massively important manuscript right now, publish it quickly, and pray that whatever the book is about, Americans care immensely. They have a half-year. Enough time, barely.

But that scenario is highly unlikely, and Brad needs to face reality. He must sell the company, to the only party that has expressed interest in buying. The predatory conglomerate Wolfe Worldwide Media.

How the hell did he become the person making this type of decision? Has it really been a quarter-century since he was a ski instructor in Utah, leading a wake-and-bake lifestyle? Now he's apparently the father of two children who are on summer break from college. Private college.

Brad tunes back into the present. His CFO has launched into a familiar refrain, an anti-intellectual, anti-artistic attack on their business. Originality and voice and blah-blah don't mean a thing when you're trying to sell books. Prizes and reviews don't pay the rent. Never have, never will. Topicality. Personality. That's what sells books. Always have. Always will.

Brad stares out the window, at the bustling park across the street. There's no doubt that he should've gotten high before work today. He runs his hand through his thick salt-and-pepper hair, meticulously maintained with biweekly visits to his barber, one of a seemingly infinite supply of guys in New York City named Sal who cut hair.

"Mr. McNally?" His secretary Lorraine is standing in the doorway, peering over her confrontational eyeglasses, rectangular frames in lime green and magenta, frames that scream, something unpleasant. "Jeff Fielder is asking for five minutes?"

Brad glances at the CFO.

"That's fine," Seth says, "I gotta piss anyway." He heaves himself out of the chair, nearly toppling backward before regaining his balance.

Jeff and Seth nod as they pass each other; neither is a fan of the other.

"I have something," Fielder says, wielding a sheaf of paper, looking hopeful.

Brad gestures at the chair opposite his desk. All his editors come to this office on a regular basis, clutching a project they want to acquire, some proposal or manuscript that's important or lyrical or un-putdownable. Fielder doesn't come as frequently as he used to, and he's no longer as passionate when he does. He's now tentative, easily talked out of things, which Brad does mostly to see what projects his editors can*not* be talked out of. Those are the ones that he gives them permission to make offers on, to acquire, to publish: the things they won't be talked out of. The books that can be argued for, successfully.

Whatever fate befalls McNally & Sons, Inc., most of the editors will be fine. But probably not Fielder. He's a senior editor in his mid-forties who used to be at the top of the game, with bestsellers and prize-winners and positive postmortem P&Ls. But when his wife left him, it all seemed to come crumbling down around him. It doesn't take long for an editor to cool off. For agents to scratch you off their submission lists. For sales executives to stop believing in your enthusiasm; to stop believing in you.

Which means that now Fielder's career track has a foreseeable end, and it might be right up ahead, at the next round of layoffs, or a buyout, or whatever event makes a publisher take a hard look at his list of editors, and say—probably without much handwringing—"It looks like we'll have to get rid of Fielder."

Someone like Jeff Fielder probably won't recover from something like that. He may never get another job as a book editor, ever again. Brad wonders if Fielder knows what a precarious position he's in; surprisingly, people frequently don't. Brad is more than a little worried that he himself is in the same type of tenuous situation.

"Tell me what you have, Jeff."

The editor takes a deep breath. "It's a book about Charlie Wolfe," he says. "An exposé."

Oh God, Brad thinks, leaning back in his chair. He certainly didn't expect Fielder to be the one. He's shocked. But now upon closer thought, it's obvious.

"I don't yet know what bombshells, exactly," Fielder continues. "But the agent seems to think the revelations are, um, *newsworthy*. And she is—or might be, I'm not sure—looking for an eight-figure advance."

Brad almost falls out of his chair. "You're kidding."

Fielder shakes his head.

"Who's the author?"

"It's anonymous."

"Who do you *think* is the author?"

"No idea," Fielder says, but Brad can see in the guy's face that this is not particularly true. Maybe there's a good reason for the lie. If this book is what Brad suspects it is.

"Who's the agent?"

"Isabel Reed."

Of course.

"And for forty-eight hours," Fielder continues, "I have it exclusively."

"What? Why?"

Brad can see that Jeff is getting nervous with this conversation, the challenges in Brad's questions. Everyone has seen this type of thing time and again, in meetings: you come into the room wanting something, maybe even needing it, and at first everyone is neutral. But then someone turns against you and nay-says, and next thing you know the surrounding personnel fall like dominoes: first one person says it sounds dubious, then another chimes in, and by the third person—this can be thirty seconds into a conversation—they're heaping insults upon injuries, eventually even mocking and ridiculing you for bringing your crappy desire into this room, maybe even turning hostile, resentful for wasting their time and energy, belittling, humiliating, until you retreat like a beaten dog to hide under a car.

"She knows I'm interested in this type of thing." Fielder shrugs. "She knows you're motivated."

The two men stare at each other across the desk.

"Here." Fielder lays a small stack of paper on an already covered surface. Brad doesn't keep a neat desk. "A sample, from the beginning." Fielder stands.

"Okay I'll take a look asap. End of day latest."

"Thanks." Fielder turns, walks away, then turns back. "Brad, I've never been a boy who cries wolf."

"Yes, Jeff, I know."

"But I'm pretty sure about this." He smiles uncomfortably. "So: wolf."

This is one of those moments that defines you as a publisher. Hell, as a *person*. Do you put yourself—your career, maybe your life—on the line, to do what's right? Rather, what you *think* is right? Or do you follow the rules, stay safe, protect yourself and your family? Isn't that a different type of doing what's right?

Brad watches Fielder retreat as Seth returns, and blah-blah-blahs some more before departing with his sheaf of bad news and his medley of bad clothing.

Brad sinks lower in his chair, loses himself in thought. His brief reverie is broken by a rapping on his door, and he looks up to see Camilla being ushered in by his unfailingly grumpy and disdainful secretary, Lorraine, who's sneering at the curvy, hyper-sexual director of subsidiary rights. Lorraine seems to hate almost everyone in this office, with the exception of those who fawn over her, willing to play the hackneyed game of pretending that it's the boss's secretary who really runs the show. Camilla isn't one of those; Camilla doesn't get along all that well with women.

They'd had a thing, Brad and Camilla, a few years ago. Ignited one long boozy week at the Frankfurt International Book Fair, and burning for a couple of hotel-room months in New York, then fizzling before anyone found out, before anyone was hurt. Brad was left with the distinct feeling that he hadn't been the first married man with whom Camilla dallied, and wouldn't be the last. But she had been his one and only extramarital affair, and it wrecked him. He doesn't intend to do it again. Then again, he didn't plan on it the first time.

But God, look at this woman, her curves straining the confines of her suit. "Hullo McNally," she says. "Just a quick check-in before I'm off. Anything?"

It takes Brad a second to register what she's announcing, and asking. Is this what Alzheimer's feels like? But now he remembers: Camilla is leaving for one of her West Coast trips to meet with film producers, and agents, and whoever. Brad has never been entirely clear on the precise utility of these LA trips. Camilla explained it to him once, but he'd been too busy imagining her naked to accurately assess her argument.

"No," he says, instinctively glancing down at his desk, at the photocopied inch of Jeff's manuscript. A hundred pages?

"What's this?" Camilla taps it with a recently manicured red nail, smiles coyly with freshly red-painted lips. "*The Accident*, by Anonymous. Intriguing."

"Nothing," he says. "Something submitted to Fielder. We don't own it yet. I don't know what it is." He shrugs, and gives his affable chuckle, the laugh he started using as a nervous teenager, and never stopped employing, even after he was no longer a teenager, nor especially nervous. He knows that everyone thinks he laughs too much, when things aren't funny. But that's sort of what it is to be affable, isn't it?

Camilla leans forward, affording—insisting upon—a resistance-melting view of her black lace bra. "Are you *lying* to me, Love?"

"Come on." He chuckles again. "Do I ever?"

She straightens, languorously, pushing her chin up, breasts out.

"Listen, McNally, I know my department have not been pulling our weight. And I won't blame you for making me—as we say back home—redundant." She purses her lips. God, those lips. "I'm not claiming it's my *fault*. The business has changed. Musical chairs, and I'm odd chap out. Or will be, soon. So I'd understand."

He makes a noncommittal grumble. It's true that much of the subsidiary-rights business has disappeared entirely, and most of what remains is controlled by literary agencies. Camilla is running out of relevancy.

"But until that happens, please—*please*—give me every chance of surviving." She inclines her head down at *The Accident*.

"I wish I could, Camilla. But honestly, it's just not ours to shop around, to anyone, for any reason. Also, as I said, I don't even know what it *is*."

"Rubbish." She smiles wider. "If you didn't know what it is, it wouldn't be here, on the middle of your desk. It'd be over *there*." She nods at the coffee table piled high with stacks of manuscripts and book proposals and finished books and bound galleys. All the stuff Brad is supposed to read. Or review. Or whatever the hell he's supposed to do with the hundreds of thousands of pages piled on that goddamned table.

"Don't forget," she says, rising, reaching out across the desk to place her palm on his cheek. "I *know* you, Mr. Boss-Man." She withdraws her hand, turns, and walks away, slowly and deliberately.

And then he's alone, for the first time all morning. Alone with this manuscript, and this decision. He turns to the small stack of pages that Jeff left for him, flips to the rear few, and starts reading.

The bar had stopped serving alcohol a half-hour earlier. The deejay changed the soundtrack from fast dancing to slow going-home. The lights came up. People started shuffling to the doors, raucously or dejectedly, to the parking lot, to drive their third-hand Datsuns and their parents' deaccessioned Acuras to the handful of college campuses within striking distance of this dance club on a quiet, rural road along the sparsely populated stretch of lakeshore.

Charlie was on a bench against the wall, making out with a brunette, a girl who he'd acquired sometime in the past fifteen minutes. It always amazed all the fraternity brothers how quickly Charlie could find a girl, at the end of the night. "Swooping in" is what people called it. He'd done it again.

The night hadn't been unusual for an end-of-term blowout, with exams finished, and summer vacation about to start. Eric was headed to a newspaper internship in Cleveland, résumé fodder for an English major and school-newspaper writer. Dave was going to be staying at his mother's house in Brooklyn, working a job at a Midtown advertising agency. Charlie was meeting his family for a few weeks in the South of France, followed by a month in East Hampton, lightly studying for the LSATs when he wasn't sailing or partying.

This was the three friends' last night together of their junior year, a night to celebrate. But

also a bittersweet night. They were about to start
their final summers as undergraduates. Everyone
understood, in a nonspecific way, that this
meant the end of something. The end of carefree
childhood.

At midnight Eric became morose, as he often
did, and soon disappeared without notice, catching
a different ride back to campus, which was not
unusual for him.

Dave sucked down the last of his Coca-Cola,
striving for sobriety and alertness, determined
to not allow Charlie to drive; Charlie was pretty
much never in driving condition by last call. And
Charlie did indeed hand over the car keys without
argument, his arm wrapped around the waist of the
girl, named Lauren.

"One minute," she said. "I need to say goodbye to
my friend."

That other girl, slender and blonde and looking
tightly wound, was leaning on the bar thirty
or forty feet across the room, fending off a
slobbering jock, a big Golden Retriever of a boy
with meaty paws. As Lauren leaned in, giggling,
that blonde turned to stare through the thick
stratus of cigarette smoke, tinted blue by the beer
lights, trying to assess the trustworthiness of the
two cocky-looking boys. But she was too far away to
tell anything.

Lauren returned to Charlie, giddy, ready to
ride back to Ithaca with the tall, handsome, rich
boy. To be taken to that other more selective
institution on that other nicer hill. To a towering

Gothic fraternity house, to a secret basement tap
room with more beer, to a balconied bedroom stocked
with cocaine and condoms . . .

Or that's what Charlie thought the girl wanted.
Because back then, that's what Charlie always
thought all the girls wanted.

CHAPTER 12

The elevator doors open, and Isabel steps out into the basement. She looks left, right. She walks toward the sign for SECURITY, a plain steel door at the end of a cinder-block-walled hall, painted beige, pipes hanging from the ceiling. The bowels of the office building. It couldn't look more different down here than up on 58, in the plushly carpeted, floor-to-ceiling-windowed, glass-and-steel-and-leather offices, the hustling hubbub of a major international agency—all-in-one Literary and Talent, Motion Picture and Television, Commercial and Speaking and the vague, bullshitty Brand Management. Hundreds of people in the New York headquarters, buffered from the public by a towering double-floor reception hall with cantilevered stairs and a wall of windows behind the desk, a million-dollar view of Midtown Manhattan. A billion-dollar view.

The security chief opens the door to the surveillance center. "Hector Sanchez," he says. "Pleased to meet you."

Isabel looks around the cramped, dark room. There are dozens of little screens streaming real-time video of public spaces, monitored by a morbidly obese uniformed guard. "This is Reggie," Hector says. "Please"—beckoning off to the side, a stand-alone monitor on a small metal table—"have a seat."

Hector takes a stool next to Isabel, and they begin to scan through Friday's footage, slowing down and speeding up to examine various men, suspicious looking or merely unfamiliar.

"Can you pause there?" Isabel asks. "That one?"

They watch a portion of tape, then Sanchez shakes his head. "No, that's a lawyer from the firm on fourteen." He seems to know everybody who enters this building.

"How do you recognize all these people?"

"Guess it's my job."

The video continues. Five, ten, fifteen minutes. Isabel looks around, taking in this grim windowless room, the decrepit old monitor she's been staring at, trying to identify a totally unidentifiable man. The more men she looks at, the more convinced she becomes that this is hopeless.

She asks to take a closer look at what turns out to be another lawyer. She didn't even know there was a law firm in the building. There are apparently nine of them.

"Do you have any idea what you're looking for?" Sanchez asks. He doesn't sound frustrated, just curious. "Any identifying characteristics you're looking for?"

"Not that I know of."

"So is there any chance we're going to get anywhere?"

"I highly doubt it."

But then a minute later, Sanchez notices something. He hits rewind. They watch a section of footage from the lobby. The revolving doors spin, and discharge a man, wearing a baseball cap low on his forehead, hiding his eyes. Medium build, Caucasian. But no defining features of his face are visible.

There is no audio to accompany the video. This security room is eerily silent, just the low hum of electronic equipment, the labored breathing of Reggie across the room. Hector clicks the mouse again, and the video switches to the high-rise elevator banks. The man swipes a key card at the turnstiles, enters the elevator waiting area.

Different camera, in the elevator. The man's face still not visible. And again at ATM's main floor. The man moves quickly but calmly from one area to the next, never pausing, never stopping to talk to anyone, never looking around, never making eye contact. An anonymous man. Who seems to know exactly where he's going.

The camera in Isabel's corridor is mounted high in the corner. She sees the man striding toward her office from the far end, toward her assistant's cubicle. Alexis's face is buried in a manuscript. The man barely slows as he slips a Jiffy bag into the in-box and continues down the hall, approaching the camera, nearer, nearer.

"There," Isabel says. "Rewind a sec."

Hector freezes the footage, clicks a mouse, scrolls back. Now the man is directly below the camera. The bill of his cap still obscures his forehead and eyebrows. But at this angle, for a split-second, they can see some of his face. He's a complete stranger.

This stranger is no ordinary messenger, and Friday clearly wasn't his first visit to Isabel's office; he knew where all the cameras were. Which means she'd been surveilled, stalked. Here, upstairs, this man had been on her floor, more than once. And he probably hadn't limited himself to locating security cameras; he probably hadn't confined his snooping to the hallways.

This man had probably sat in Isabel's chair, at her desk. He'd put his hands, and who knows what else, on her computer.

"Is that him?" Sanchez asks. "That's gotta be him. Do you recognize him?"

Isabel looks at Sanchez, stupefied. What had she already explained? She couldn't recognize the guy because she never saw him in the first place.

Sanchez returns the video to the beginning, to the man's entrance to the elevator banks. "Reggie?" Hector asks, over his shoulder. "You see this time stamp?" It's 1:22, in the dead center of lunchtime.

"Yup."

"Can you check the ID scan at the north elevator bank?"

Reggie hits his keyboard, pauses, taps some more. "Sorry. There must be a mistake." Reggie types again, shaking his head. "I don't understand," he says. "The ID he used? It's Isabel Reed's." He turns to Isabel, points a finger at her. "That's you, ain't it?"

CHAPTER 13

This is not at all what Kate expected out of this operation in particular, out of this job in general, out of her life as a whole. She has her lovely little Jake and Ben, and a wonderful husband, and by any measure she leads an enviable expat existence in Paris. She doesn't need to be standing here in a Copenhagen tenement, on the verge of being shot in the head, for something that has nothing to do with her.

There was a long period when Kate was certain that she'd made the right decisions about what to do with her career, how to live her life. That certainty was a great comfort, lulling her to sleep quickly every night, getting her out of bed energized every morning.

Then the husband and children introduced doubt, levels of qualms that waxed and waned over the years. Sometimes she has been deep under the doubt, drowning in it, unable to see daylight up above; sometimes floating on top of it, a gentle backstroke to stay afloat. But it has always been there, always threatening.

Should she have a safe comfortable desk job instead of this dangerous operational fieldwork? Should she be home more? Home all the time? She wasn't terribly satisfied with that life, for the couple of years that she experimented with the stay-at-home-parent lifestyle in Luxembourg and Paris. She was bored, and resentful, and unfulfilled. Not to mention constantly worried that when the kids had finally left the nest, she'd have spent a dozen years without a job, and for all intents and purposes she'd be unemployable. At least, unemployable in any capacity that would appeal to her. She'd be career-less, one of those at-sea middle-aged women grasping at a second act, a docent at a third-rate cultural institution, or teaching English to foreigners.

On the other hand, it was indisputable that no one lies on her death-bed lamenting that she spent too much time with her children, and not enough time working. No one sane, that is. She'd like to think of herself as sane.

Plus of course "working" doesn't often mean—shouldn't mean—getting shot in the head in a Danish apartment by Turkish drug dealers. If that's what these guys are.

She watches one of them take another step into the room, and another. His gun is trained steadily at Hayden's head, above the shoulder of the hostage that Hayden is holding in front of him. She suspects that these Turks don't have any particular interest in keeping Grundtvig alive, so perhaps "hostage" isn't the operative concept for the poor student's function in front of Hayden. The Dutch kid is merely a physical shield, a nice thick mound of bullet-absorbing flesh.

This situation is very, very bad. Exactly the type of scenario that Kate envisages when she's awake in the middle of the night, away from her family, pondering the question, What's the worst that could happen?

This. This is the worst.

And this particular situation is probably not going to improve over time. Every second is working against her. She needs to make something happen, to change the course of this action.

She mouths the number five at Hayden, and he nods infinitesimally, confirming his understanding of the tactic. He begins another count-down in his head.

Four, he mouths, setting the pace.

The first Turk is now just ten feet in front of Hayden, and continuing to move forward.

Three.

Kate inhales deeply, her shoulders rising with the effort, moving the barrel of the gun slightly off her skin, a half-centimeter.

Two.

Hayden blinks on the beat of the final second.

One.

Kate's right hand shoots up across her face, to her left temple, and grabs the barrel of the weapon that's resting on her skin, changing the angle just as an explosion rings in her ear, while at the same time throwing her left elbow backward, sinking deep into the paunch of the Turk behind her.

Bits of the ceiling fall on her head, her shoulders, from the bullet's damage. She spins around, still holding the barrel of the weapon pointed at the ceiling with her right hand. With the heel of her left hand she hammers this guy in the face, an upward thrust, but she misses somewhat and hits his lip, his front teeth gouging her, but she doesn't pause, doesn't give him time to recover, and strikes again, this time to the trachea, and he crumples.

She seizes the weapon, just as she hears the other Turk's gun fire twice, and every muscle in her body tenses, preparing to have been shot, to be about to die here, in what is now clear has been the wrong decision, the absolute wrong way to live her entire life.

CHAPTER 14

amilla stands in the threshold of Jeff Fielder's office. The editorial meeting is still in progress, so this end of the hall—the editorial department—is completely unpopulated. She glances around Fielder's assistant's desk, looking for an appealing pile of manuscript, but doesn't notice anything special other than the boy's leather bag, which can only be accurately described as a handbag. A lamentable fashion trend.

She wants to get the hell out of New York City, for good. After growing up in dismal England, then living in dismal New York, *ça suffit*, as the teachers used to say at boarding school. Enough of these tiny apartments and overpriced grocers, enough of these self-obsessed poufs with their hand luggage and arrogant financiers with their trophy wives, enough of the crap weather.

So she needs to get on this plane to LA, to continue her purported mission of trying to sell rights—UK book rights, domestic magazine rights, Canadian calendars, whatever derivative rubbish she can pitch—to raise emergency cash. She doesn't need Brad to tell her that the situation is dire. She can feel the desperation hanging in the air, a miasma of impending financial apocalypse.

The ruin sure did come upon her quickly, more a Pompeii than a Rome. Just a few years ago she was Ms. Midas, conjuring six-figure paperback deals out of thin air, being consulted on everything, courted, seduced. For a while, she looked totally vindicated in her rejection of the family concern, Dad's string of shoe stores in the north, a Manchester lad made good enough to buy a house in the part of Pimlico that could pass for Chelsea for those who didn't know better, and send his girls to school in Switzerland, and drive a pathetically endless string of new Jaguars.

Boarding school backfired when she met an American cousin of her best friend, on ski holiday in Lech. It was love at first sight, nineteen-year-old style, and by May she was ignoring Mum's entreaties and putting off university and securing a job as a summer au pair for one of those bankery families whose women and children spend their summer in Bridgehampton while Dad comes out at the weekend to get tight and grope the help in the butler's pantry.

By Labor Day, it was clear that the romance with the cousin was ill-fated. But the ghastly summer job led to a receptionist job at a literary agency—attractive young girls with English accents being the sine qua non of receptionist candidates—and Camilla rang home to announce that she wouldn't be returning to England or Switzerland, refusing even a single quid from that belligerent insecure old man, thanks-I'll-make-my-own-way. And she did, for a good long while.

But then that big bully of a beast rose up and ate her profession. First the web devoured book clubs, then magazines, and now its maw is agape, ravenous, ready to swallow the whole bloody publishing business. She had done nothing wrong, other than to not get out sooner. Now it's almost too late.

Camilla takes a step inside Fielder's office, then another, pulling in her wheeled luggage, setting her tote bag atop the suitcase.

It's funny that no one in America has ever questioned her about her university degree. Just as no one looks down upon her for her class, because as far as they know she's upper.

Camilla sees what she's looking for: a tall stack of paper in the middle of the desk, Fielder's antique pen sitting on the top sheet. She takes another step. She cranes her neck forward, takes a step closer, to the edge of the desk, and thumbs through the stack to find the title page: *The Accident*, by Anonymous. The same thing she noticed on Brad's desk.

Coincidentally—or not—this is the very same manuscript that Camilla heard about last night, at the party, from that high-energy assistant at Atlantic Talent Management. The girl had obviously been drunk, talking about something she shouldn't have mentioned. She'd called Camilla first thing this morning—on Camilla's mobile—to disavow last night's conversation. Loose lips, apologies. Should've known better, and so forth.

"Of course, Love," Camilla told the girl. "I won't mention a thing to anyone."

She looks over her shoulder, out the door into the quiet hall, a phone chirping. "Fuck all," she mutters. If there's one thing she has learned in her decade in the book business, it's that this is the only type of book that *always* seems to work: the thing that one day, all of a sudden, *everyone* is talking about. *The Accident* is going to be that thing. Already is.

Camilla sweeps up the manuscript and carries it down the hall, around the corner to the photocopier. A young woman is standing at the machine, collating pages while talking on a cell phone. "Hullo," Camilla says. She doesn't know the girl's name. "I need this."

The girl scowls, but knows better than to engage a fight with a director, so picks up her papers and huffs away. Camilla feeds her stack through the machine, reading stray paragraphs while the copier gobbles in and spits out fifty pages at a time.

Still no one at Jeff's office when she returns after five minutes. Camilla leaves the pile of paper as she found it, and takes a step out Jeff's door, then stops. She returns to the office, the desk, trying to remember what bit of evidence she's forgetting . . . the chair? . . . the mug . . . ? No, it's that old pen of his, which she left sitting near the mouse pad, instead of atop the manuscript. She reaches out to the pen, but is interrupted by her ringing phone, an incoming call from a 310 number. "Hullo, Camilla Glyndon-Browning."

"Hi, this is Jessica calling from Stan Balzer's office, confirming four-thirty this afternoon."

"Looking forward to it."

"I see that there are no agenda items. Would you care to add any?"

Camilla stares at the manuscript. In truth, this LA trip is serving a purpose that's much more important than selling rights: Camilla is looking for a new job. She'll always have a soft spot for Bradford. For a month, she was even in love with him. After a fashion. But she will not go down with his ship. She knows that loyalty is a virtue, and that deception is, well, *not*, but what is she going to do?

She is going to fly to California to find herself a new career. She has always wanted to try the film business, and now is the time. But she can't just *land* in LA. She needs a parachute.

"Yes," Camilla says, "a brilliant property called *The Accident*."

CHAPTER 15

For a split-second that seems to last forever, everything freezes. Sound disappears.

Then Hayden can feel Grundtvig's body relaxing, beginning to pitch forward, shot somewhere in the thorax. Hayden shoves the guy in the back, impelling his collapsing body forward, into the outstretched arm of the Turk, knocking his gun to the side, this armed intruder now paying the price for being an amateur who'd advanced too far, too close, too carelessly. Hayden takes a quick stutter-step with his right leg to achieve the correct distance to swing his left, a strong swift kick that explodes into the hand with the weapon, which goes flying, smacking against the far wall and then clattering on the tile floor, as Hayden hammers the now unarmed, stunned guy once, twice, three times in the jaw and nose, staggering backward, collapsing, and then Hayden kicks him again across the face, knocking him unconscious.

And then everything is silent except the sound of his own panting.

"You okay?" Hayden asks. His pulse is pounding in his head.

"Yes," Kate answers, a muffled sound, as if underwater. "You?"

Hayden nods. He bends over to check Grundtvig for a pulse, finds none.

"Should we kill them?" Kate asks, panting herself from the quick expenditure of energy, from the spike in heart rate, from fight-or-flight epinephrine levels.

Hayden glances from one fallen guy to the other. He doesn't want these guys to die. Those types of deaths would get reported, investigated, and then he'd have to start lying about this—"Nope, wasn't my people, don't know a thing about it"—despite that he's in Copenhagen under a pretty flimsy premise, so the whole thing would look questionable, at best.

As of right now, the scenario is nothing more complex than that some local kid—a habitual drug user, at that—got shot. That's not international, not diplomatic, nothing to do with the CIA. But add a couple of Turkish immigrants with criminal ties, and three bodies at a shootout with no apparent motive, and people will start asking questions. Asking Hayden questions, ones he wouldn't be able to answer.

He shakes his head, then looks around the room. He takes a couple of long strides to the desk and yanks an electrical cord out of a monitor and an outlet, and tosses the two meters of rubber-clad wire to Kate, who makes quick work of tying the hands of one unconscious guy while Hayden yanks another cord and ties the other. There's nothing for them to do about the dead one.

"Now we need a bag," he says, fumbling to disconnect an external drive, then unplugging the power cord of a laptop, disengaging a hard line that connects to a telecom jack.

He can hear Kate rummaging around, then she arrives with a big shopping bag—recycled fibers, bright colors, a planet-saving slogan— just as he collects a stack of CDs, places them in the bottom of the sturdy bag. He looks around the desk, the shelves, for other data-storage media. He grabs a thumb drive and tosses that into the bag.

"Okay," he says, walking quickly to the front door, Kate trailing. It's been maybe ninety seconds since the shots were fired. "Let's go."

He takes the stairs two at a time, adrenaline coursing through his body, tense and quick, into the vestibule. "There's a rear door," he notices and says at the same instant, looking at a fire door in the far corner of the shabby lobby. "You go that way"—handing her the bag—"and get started on the digital as soon as possible. Is there a place you can stop?"

"I'll find one. But why can't I go to the apartment?" The Agency apartment, on the other side of town, is what she means.

"You need to get out of Copenhagen," he says. She looks confused, rightly so. What's the point of a safe house if not this? "Find a place in the countryside, a motel," he continues, not giving her time to question him. "Examine the hardware. Call me when you learn something."

"And where are you going?"

"New York. Now *go*, Kate." He squeezes her shoulder.

She turns and walks out the rear. He takes the front door to the sidewalk, back into another world, one that he hasn't inhabited for what seems like an eternity, but has been only five minutes. If that.

He glances around. No one out here is screaming or running or pointing at him, just another man in jacket and tie, walking across a busy city street, climbing onto a bicycle, pedaling, turning a corner and crossing a bridge, tossing something over the ledge, something that breaks the surface of Peblinge Sø, a small splash and concentric circles of tiny waves as the weapon sinks, then settles into the muck at the bottom of the lake. That gun is not something he wants to bring with him.

And then he hears "I'm in the car" from his earpiece.

He can picture Kate cruising along the urban highway beside the train tracks, the low red brick industrial buildings, the electricity wires, the trash-strewn scrub that lines train tracks everywhere. She'll speed west across Zealand toward the Great Belt Bridge and over to windblown Funen Island and then sparsely populated mainland Denmark, where she'll find a hotel room and unpack the computer and start sifting through Grundtvig's digital trails.

Tomorrow morning, she'll check out of the hotel, and pay in cash. She'll drive into northern Germany, through Hamburg and Bremen, a route parallel to the North Sea coast, eventually across Belgium and finally into France. There aren't any guards at any of these intra-EU borders; there aren't, really, any borders.

Tomorrow night she'll be home with her family, after three weeks on the road and in the Copenhagen apartment that's now no use, never will be again. The total rent was nine thousand euros, paid by an interest-bearing checking account linked to the numbered one in Switzerland. The same account that pays Kate her three thousand per week year-round, plus the salaries and expenses for the other personnel on a week-by-week basis, and of course supplies like the weapons and computers and software, and modest hourly fees to computer engineers in Heidelberg, as well as electricians and telecom consultants, not to mention bicycles and sandwiches and museum tickets . . .

This operation incurs a lot of expenses. On the other hand, as Hayden expected when he opened the account, twenty-plus-million euros in capital also generates a healthy revenue stream, even when invested conservatively.

"I'm on the highway," Kate updates in his ear.

Hayden is still the only person in the world who knows how to access this money. Indeed, he's the only one who really knows it exists. Kate thinks she knows, but what she thinks is that the money is in a secondary account to the Agency's general European operational fund. This is not exactly true.

"Good," Hayden says. "Be safe, Kate."

Back in Amelienborg, Hayden packs almost nothing, just a few items into a small canvas duffel. He leaves most of his clothing in the bureau, and the bulk of his toiletries in the bath; all his books on the coffee table, and his full-size bag in the closet. He removes his necktie, hangs it from a doorknob; he won't be needing a tie. He gathers his Joseph Lyons passport and a wad of cash and a satellite telephone, all slipped into the duffel.

Hayden takes a seat in the unexpectedly comfortable wooden chair near the front door. He removes his right shoe, holds it upside down. Grips the sturdy leather-and-rubber heel, pulls it away from the sole, and twists. The heel swivels open to reveal a tiny airtight compartment, into which he places a small silver key and an equally small thumb drive; a physical parachute and a digital lifejacket, both in miniature.

He quickly scans the living room. He'll be able to collect the rest of his belongings when he returns, hopefully in a few days. And if he never returns, it will certainly not look like that was intentional.

On his way out the door, Hayden snatches up his Icelandic language text, which he tucks into the bottom of his neighbor's rubbish bin, beneath a big moist bag that smells a lot like rotten fish.

CHAPTER 16

Isabel massages the bridge of her nose, with both elbows resting on the desk, and her eyes closed. She takes a deep breath, and exhales. Deep breath, exhale. Trying to beat back the fatigue, the tension, the fear.

If Isabel does this for too long, she'll fall asleep. Which might not be such a bad thing; she's exhausted.

But no, she can't take a nap at her desk. So she opens her eyes to her nearly empty desk, the few items arranged just-so. Isabel can't tolerate anything out of place. It's one of the things that made it difficult to live with her ex-husband—he was an unrepentant slob—after so many years living alone, in complete and compulsive control of her environment.

Isabel's vision is blurred from the pressure of the rubbing, and the world returns to focus in layers, like peeling back the folded tissue paper under the gift wrapping on a professionally packaged present. With a startle she notices that her boss's assistant is standing in the doorway. The poor girl has clearly been there awhile, waiting too patiently, too meek for her job. Angela will be fired, soon. Meg fires her assistants regularly, standard operating procedure.

"Isabel, hi," Angela says softly. "Meg wonders if you have a minute?"

This can't be good; it never is. Isabel stands, smoothes her skirt. She glances at Alexis's empty chair in the cubicle, the desk and cabinets covered in stacks of manuscripts and contracts and reports and things to be filed, the piles that haunt publishing people for their entire careers. Sometimes the only way to escape your pile is to leave, to quit, squirreling away your pile somewhere—a supply closet, a book-storage room—until you're safely out of the building, and have collected your final paycheck, and can leave a by-the-way message for your replacement.

Isabel stops at the adjoining cubicle, Ryan's, who's covering for Alexis today. All the assistants have coverage buddies, like kindergarteners' hall partners, holding hands to make sure no one wanders off in the wrong direction. This ensures that no business is lost, no money is wasted, no call goes unanswered because some twenty-four-year-old is out with a head cold. The assistants answer every single call, 8:00 a.m. to 6:00 p.m., never taking off their headsets. Ryan is answering Isabel's line today. "Going to see Meg," she tells him. He blinks his understanding; he's on a call.

It's too bad Alexis is out today. The young woman has turned out to be one of Isabel's smarter, abler assistants. Over the years Isabel has had a dozen of them, mostly women but also a few men, nearly all from upper-middle-class suburban families, on their second or third jobs after graduating from top-flight colleges with liberal arts degrees, hardworking and broke but not exactly poor, dining on four-dollar-per-plate rice and beans but also accompanying their parents on thousand-dollar-per-night vacations, and never worrying about catastrophic health problems.

Isabel sees bits of herself in every kid she hires, wide-eyed and eager, seduced by the glamorous aspects and not yet disenchanted by the quotidian, the crass, the ugly.

Despite their superficial homogeneity, each of these assistants has been remarkably distinct, with different results. Some have lasted only a few months, and a couple fled after a year to the security of law school, business school. A handful stuck it out in the media, at publishing houses and literary agencies but also at a news website and a branding firm and a Hollywood studio. One is a senior editor at a major publishing house, a regular on Isabel's submission list, capable of making mid-six-figure offers with bestseller bonuses, securely ensconced in an insular industry where you never stop running across your old bosses, or your old assistants.

Alexis will probably be one of them. She has the passion and the work ethic, she has a good critical eye, she recognizes the difference between beautiful writing and a viable book, and perhaps most important she understands the commercial nature of the enterprise: the publishing business is a business, and books are published for an audience to buy from bookstores, who buy units from distributors who order cartons from publishers who acquire titles from literary agencies who sign up careers from authors, money changing hands at every transaction.

Isabel follows Angela down the long gray-carpeted hall, around a corner, and into the boss's large anteroom, where she sheds her young escort amid couches and coffee tables and carefully staged displays of ATM's recent bestsellers. Meg hired one of those stagers who style fancy—but not quite fancy enough—apartments for sale, rearranging the furniture and artwork.

A smug looking Courtney emerges from Meg's gold-painted double-doors, her layered blonde hair bouncing. Isabel's hair used to do that; she used to have it styled for bounce, she used to walk for it too. But she doesn't think she can pull that off, anymore. Or rather, she doesn't think she should. There's something suspect about forty-somethings with bouncing hair, something perhaps pitiable, especially single women. Isabel doesn't need to go out of her way to find new ways to be pitied.

But that's not a consideration for Courtney and her Charlie's Angels coif, her curves, her whole flirty demeanor, cocktail party catnip for socially awkward writers, young men with unfortunate complexions and ill-fitting clothing. Isabel has seen Courtney in action, titillating these men with the playful touch and the exaggerated laugh, the perfectly timed hair-toss and the coy little slap to the chest. They see what this is, these men, they know she's toying with them, seducing them, but still they're helpless to resist; they will all go home and masturbate to the fantasy of Courtney. And when their manuscripts are finished, Courtney and her pendulous breasts and feathered hair will be at the top of their submissions lists.

The two women exchange tight-lipped joyless smiles. Isabel imagines that the younger woman lives in perpetual fear of having her hyper-styled hair mussed, which Isabel has a nearly uncontrollable urge to do. Almost as if mind-reading, Courtney flips that hair, then walks away, bounce-bounce.

Now it's Isabel who's standing in someone's doorway, waiting for a superior to notice, to tear herself away from the device in her lap, to acknowledge her presence. Isabel waits a few seconds, then a half-minute. She clears her throat.

The president of the literary division of American Talent Management holds up one finger, give-me-a-sec, but doesn't immediately look up to see who's waiting. Then she does. "Oh hi Isabel thanks for stopping by come on in have a seat."

Isabel mumbles thanks. She perches on the edge of a chair, not settling in, projecting that she is busy, no time for leisurely chitchat. She glances around the roomy inner sanctum, the walls adorned with ultra-shocking contemporary art, black-and-white nudes and garishly bright abstract paintings and a giant black canvas covered in scrawled obscenities.

Meg is an angry-looking, alarmingly skinny woman with a diligently earned reputation for tossing crazy bombs into meetings, for having absolutely no shame when it comes to the vulgarity of her language and the lack of boundaries to her privacy—Isabel once heard Meg boast in a conference room full of people about the responsiveness of her sexual organs—and for a wardrobe dripping in logos: the six-hundred-dollar eyeglasses and the two-thousand-dollar bag, the thoroughly expected tank watch and the unmistakable red soles of her unmanageably high heels. The same uniform shared by all the women of a certain type in Meg's zip codes in Manhattan and Southampton, a Logo Woman, every brand the luxury cliché, the It: the big *H* and the interlocking *G*s, the checkerboard pebbled leather and the plaid silk lining, the badge on the shiny sleeve of the puffer jacket.

"Sorry just let me finish this e-mail I'll be right with you thanks for your patience." Half the town seems to be making people wait while they communicate with other people, on smart phone or tablet or landline, on anything, sending different communications in different directions, including the simple age-old communication of making someone wait, merely for the sake of making a person wait.

"Isabel, hi," Meg finally says, plastering on a wide smile, placing her device on the desk in front of her. Attention, though certainly not undivided.

"Good morning." Isabel attempts her own smile, but knows that hers too is phony, and phony-looking. She's not trying to hide the phoniness.

"So, Isabel. Who're you lunching with these days?" Perhaps the most insulting question in the book business, coming from your boss. "Or breakfasting?"

"No one in particular."

Meg looks at Isabel, eyebrows raised, trying to intimidate her into saying more. Saying something. But Isabel won't.

"Okayyyy," dragging out the second syllable, an obnoxious forty-five-year-old teenager. "*Any*way . . . How *are* you, Isabel?"

Isabel has heard this question before from Meg. It's not a question, in the traditional sense of the asker wanting an answer. It's a throat-clearing. A prelude to a criticism or an attack. It's not that Meg doesn't care at all. It's just that the caring isn't an important part of her.

"I'm fine. And how are *you*, Meg?"

Meg smiles, knowing that her disingenuousness has just been thrown back at her. "Not bad. Thanks for asking."

"*Mmm.*"

The two women stare at each for a few beats.

"How long have we known one another, Isabel?"

"*Each other*," Isabel whispers, to herself. Mostly to herself.

"Excuse me?"

"Twenty years. Roughly."

Nearly every night of those two decades, Isabel has read. She has read experimental fiction, narrative nonfiction, memoirs, biographies, genre novels. She has read until she's fallen asleep, then she has woken up and read some more. She'd lived paycheck to paycheck, and managed to remain idealistic for far longer than most of her contemporaries.

"What was that first big deal of yours?" Meg asks. "Belinda Coleman?"

"Brenda." It had been Isabel's first million-dollar deal, at auction.

"And I invited you to drinks," Meg continues, ignoring Isabel's correction of her error. As a rule, Meg surges right past her own mistakes without slowing down. It's other people's errors that stop her cold. "The Four Seasons, wasn't it? I said that we could offer you a job tomorrow." Meg shakes her head, after all these years still impressed by her own impressiveness. "Do you regret it? Coming to Atlantic?"

Meg never, ever refers to the agency as ATM. Legend has it that back in the mid-eighties, when automated teller machines were being installed everywhere, one of the young agents pleaded with the owner-founder-president that he simply *had* to change the name, or the agency would become a laughingstock. The president's answer was a definitive no. "If it turns out like you say, everyone will just call us Atlantic!" Two decades and millions of cash machines later, there are only a handful of people who ever refer to the agency as Atlantic.

"No," Isabel says, "I don't regret it." She'd been tired of being poor, tired of being obscure, tired of being idealistic. So she moved out of the mom-and-pop shop in the grungy downtown open-plan loft, into the multinational corporation in the fancy Midtown skyscraper. She took the fancy salary and the fancy expense account. She brought Brenda Coleman along with her to ATM.

Within a year Isabel found herself barely reading anymore, selling most of her projects based on one-page pitches backed by jargon-heavy marketing budgets, signing up new clients after smoothly orchestrated beauty-pageant meetings, connecting already rich celebrities with the international corporations that could make them richer. She herself earned a large salary and hefty year-end bonuses.

"Then what happened, Isabel?" Meg looks, and sounds, earnest.

It's not a very complicated answer. First she got married, then pregnant. Her husband started making a lot of money, and they became another Manhattan couple lifted by the rising tide of irrational M&As and unsustainable real-estate appreciation. Then she was a new mother, well on her way to becoming one of those women with a casual but lucrative career, dabbling at a job with erratic hours and too much vacation, with questionable commitment and dwindling ambition, a drive that was increasingly keeping her from the things—the people—she increasingly wanted.

She was becoming a woman who was resented by nearly all other women, because her life was so very perfect. Until it wasn't. Perfection is always impermanent.

And after, when she managed to come back to work, she made a purposeful decision to adjust her priorities. To give much more attention to a much smaller client list, holding their hands, being all things to all of them. To try to be a good mother to every one of her writers, to make up for the moment when she had been a bad mother to her flesh-and-blood child.

But Isabel's new strategy didn't fit in with the ethos of ATM, which was to sign as many clients and make as many deals as possible before the so-called brands became mature. The deadwood could then fall away, replaced by younger, hotter talent with their best years ahead of them, not behind. "Forecasted client attrition," this was called.

There had been a long period when everyone respected Isabel, at first for her hard work, and then for her taste, and then for her profitability. Then there was the period when everyone pitied her; when she pitied herself. A period that has continued to this day.

Isabel knows she still carries the disconcerting scent of grief about her, the twinge of tragedy. Very few people know exactly what happened—Isabel doesn't talk about the horrifying particulars, never did—but the general idea was more than sufficiently heartrending.

Enough already. She wants, needs, to gain back the respect. She hopes that starting her own shop will do that. But she shouldn't simply march out the door. That would be failure, or at least look like failure. She needs to leave ATM triumphantly, with a big new client.

"You know exactly what happened to me, Meg."

"I don't mean what happened to *you*. I mean to your *career*."

"They're different?"

"Listen," Meg shifts the angle of her head, jutting her jaw out, projecting a new level of confrontation into the conversation. "You know, the end of the financial year always sneaks up . . . What with summer holidays, you blink and next thing you know, it's September, and we're tallying the numbers."

When Meg had been elevated to the president's position a couple of years ago, they'd had a laugh, agreeing that it would probably become awkward, someday, for one old friend to be the boss of the other. But in such a small business, everyone finds themselves working for friends.

"So I just wanted you to be, um, a*ware*, that . . . that your year-to-date numbers haven't been . . ." They never imagined it'd be this awful, this soon. "Unless things change pretty dramatically in the next month or two . . ."

Isabel folds her arms across her chest. It has recently become clear to Isabel that she never really liked Meg.

"You know, Isabel, you'll always have your *job*, right? I mean, as long as *I* have anything to say about it?"

This, Isabel suddenly realizes, is not true. Isabel has never had this type of conversation before, but she recognizes it: advance warning of being fired. A soft pre-dismissal.

"But I don't think you should count on a bonus, this year. In fact, Isabel, I'm afraid we're going to have to consider scaling back."

"Scaling back?"

Meg responds with a thin-lipped smile, then leans away from her employee, from this conversation, this confrontation.

Isabel stands. "Is that all, Meg?"

"Sign up anything new recently?"

"Not really."

"No. You sure?"

Isabel shrugs. She doesn't want to overtly lie, but she's certainly not going to tell the truth. What she wants is to get the hell out of this room. Out of this building. She'd sort of been expecting this, for a while now. She knows she hasn't been pulling her weight. There are outfits in the book business where well-respected middle-aged professionals can coast by for years, even decades, with sub-par production. Not many outfits, but more than zero. ATM, however, has never been one of them. Here, you're only as good as your last year. Isabel's last year wasn't good, and the current one is not going to be better.

"Nothing to Jeff Fielder, this morning?"

Of course: it was that Courtney, who was at the brasserie this morning, who reported to Meg, just before Isabel came into this room. That devious little bimbo of a fink.

"Nope."

Meg knows Isabel is lying, and she knows why.

"Is there anything else, Meg?"

The Accident is her ticket out of here. And today is, apparently, the day she'll be leaving.

"Don't fuck with me, Isabel." Meg glowers. "You'll be sorry."

Isabel's heart is racing as she pops the thumb drive into her computer. She starts copying important files—her contacts, some recent contracts, a couple of manuscripts, all from a folder titled Most Important Docs that she created for this exact purpose.

Her hard copy of *The Accident* is already in her bag. She picks up the small silver frame with the picture of the little boy, and slips it into the bag, along with the slender digital storage device. She glances around quickly, then shrugs in her brain, and walks out of her office, forever.

She hurries down the hall. From around the corner, she can hear Meg, probably on her cell phone, laugh loudly—an ugly burst of nasal noise—and then say, "Of course, St. Barths is just *not* worth the hassle if you're flying commercial."

Isabel glances left and then right, frozen, wondering where to flee, but she runs out of time—

"Isabel." Putting her finger over the mic of her phone. "Where you going?"

"Lunch."

"At eleven-thirty?"

"It's an early lunch. Excuse me." Isabel brushes past her boss. Ex-boss. Ten steps away, she can hear Meg say, "Call Security."

Then Isabel is rushing down the stairs, hurrying through reception. Pushing, pushing, *pushing* the elevator call button. Just as the doors are closing, another elevator arrives, and two security guards hurry to the ATM doors.

Halfway down to the ground floor, Isabel reconsiders her destination, and presses *B*.

She steps into the eerie cinder-block basement. She walks past the security office, turns into a long corridor. She passes a maintenance man, pulling a dolly through a door. He eyes her warily. "Can I help you, Ma'am?"

"No thanks!" Trying to sound cheerful. Probably sounding panicked, or insane. She turns another corner. Now she can hear men talking behind her—"Where'd she go?"—"That way"—their voices bouncing off the hard, cold surfaces.

Hurried footsteps are now behind her, closing in.

She breaks into a run.

A red exit sign beckons at the end of the hall. She pushes through this fire door, out to a loading dock, an empty bay, a blast of hot air and a whiff of diesel. Down a few concrete steps with a broken banister that snags the sleeve of her suit jacket, jerking her to the side, ripping the fabric loudly.

"*Shit!*" She extracts her sleeve from the cut-off pole, and herself from the stairs, hustling across the shallow driveway. And then she's on the sidewalk, a busy Midtown midday street, just another face in the crowd. She falls into step behind a trio of gray-besuited men, joining the stream of westward-walking pedestrians in the outside lane of the sidewalk, facing off against the east-bounders on the inside lane. Those are the enemy, walking east against her; these are her allies, walking west with her. It is anonymous, it is arbitrary. Just like any teams, any conflict. You were born there, I was born here; you believe in that god, I in this. You want to kill me, and I don't want to die.

Isabel doesn't know where to go; she hasn't thought this out. She wades through the thickening humanity of impending lunchtime on a sunny summer weekday, walking among hundreds—thousands, tens of thousands—of people.

She doesn't know what to do.

She is unemployed for the first time since—when?—high school? Yes. It's been more than a quarter-century since she was last totally jobless.

She is possibly, *probably*, in physical danger. She double-checks the security of her bag with the manuscript. Does someone else in New York—in the world?—have a more dangerous thing dangling from her shoulder? Only perhaps a person with a tactical nuclear weapon, a neat little one-megaton device in a hardened suitcase, standing in bustling King's Cross Station, or sitting in the lobby of the Pera Palace Hotel in Istanbul, or perched on a hard bench on a subway that's stalled between stations underneath Tokyo.

Or maybe loitering right here in the crush of Times Square, in the middle of New York City, the people and cars swirling above the rumbling of the subway and beneath the neon lights and television studios and skyscrapers and Jumbotrons.

She doesn't know whom to turn to, if anyone. Can she trust Jeffrey?

Isabel takes out her phone, stares at the screen, preposterously tiny here amid these others, these electronic screens the size of billboards, of buses, broadcasting diluted approximations of genuine news.

She begins to type an email with her thumbs, a short note, just three words. Another inquisitive to the anonymous author. She isn't absolutely positive, but she's pretty sure who the recipient is. Even though she'd been under the impression that this person was dead.

CHAPTER 17

After a series of hastily arranged succession meetings over the course of a few hectic, exhausting days, the author left the office for good, amid tears and hugs and the firm but reasonable handshakes of people who shake a lot of hands, professionally.

He retreated to his Georgetown house, to the upstairs bedroom he used as his home office, on the web and on the phone, sending e-mails, phoning doctors, collecting information, making the arrangements he'd been advised to make.

He and his ex-wife had never gotten around to writing wills until she was pregnant, and even then continued to put it off until the last minute. So it wasn't until she was at thirty-six weeks that they'd sat in that generic East Midtown conference room, cherry-tabled and windowless, discussing with the T&E lawyer every conceivable combination of deaths and incapacitations and their implications for the fiduciary and physical custody of their as-yet-unborn and -unnamed child. Preparing for every version of horror, except the one that actually occurred.

Now he called that same lawyer in New York, and had her change some particulars. He took the revised paperwork to a local office with a notary and his self-important little stamp.

There were a lot of arrangements to make. There were surgical options to consider, doctors to consult. There were the densely woven secrets he and Charlie Wolfe had been sharing for two decades, and the portion that he'd been keeping to himself. There was also the new possibility that Charlie actually wanted him dead. Would maybe even take steps to cause his death. So there was his security to consider.

When he was finished, he made efforts to conceal the work he'd been doing. He shredded documents. He destroyed files. He cleared the history from his web browser. But even though for a long time he'd been the day-to-day chief of what was something of a tech company, everyone knew that he was not particularly adept, technologically. He wasn't the type of guy who'd be savvy about his digital footprint.

As he takes a turn onto a minor road high above Zurich, his mobile dings, an incoming e-mail, another message received to an account with extraordinarily convoluted ownership, and no practical way of tracing it. He won't answer. The sender will get another of those auto-response bounce-back messages. Keeping her off-guard, making her think she can't find him. A little unavailability is always good to help control the conversation. It'll be driving her nuts.

He glances at the little screen: *Is it you?*

When all his arrangements—financial, logistical, psychological—had been finalized, he drove out to the airfield in the Maryland suburbs. He climbed into the small Piper that he'd bought secondhand as soon as he'd received his pilot's license, back when he'd first started earning unmistakably disposable income, already looking forward to a time when those amounts of money would be indefensible, unspendable. It came on quickly, the hubris that accompanies wealth.

With that first big check he'd gotten a sudden urge to learn to fly, either because of or despite JFK Jr.'s memorable disappearance into the Long Island Sound, one of the flight paths the author started taking regularly. His wife refused categorically to get into any aircraft piloted by him, ever. But there were plenty of other people in Manhattan who were willing to keep him company on tours up the Hudson Valley, over the Catskill Mountains, out to the Vineyard.

The flight from the DC suburbs to the countryside of the Eastern Shore was short and quiet, the landing uneventful, the taxi out to the Delaware beach house exorbitant. He spent a few days in seclusion. He stood on the cold bleak December beach for hours, gazing at the Atlantic. Being seen by the neighbors: the old couple down the shore who took out their big standard poodle at dusk; the platinum-blonde boob-jobbed realtor who power-walked, fists pumping, clutching dainty little dumb-bells. Pink dumbbells.

At the general store, in front of the dairy case in the rear corner, he broke down sobbing. This was witnessed by a handful of people, one of them the local gossip, who he was certain would be more than willing to share her theories with the police, in the coming days.

He wrote a rambling emotional letter addressed to "Everyone," and a separate, very short note to his ex-wife, apologizing "for everything." He left both on his dining table, under a conch shell.

He registered an early-morning sightseeing flight, and set off past the southern reaches of Delaware, following the Maryland coastline past Assateague and Chincoteague, out over the uninhabited barrier islands and marshes that separate the Eastern Shore of Virginia from the Atlantic Ocean, vast stretches of coastal wilderness, uninhabited and unmonitored.

It was a beautiful morning for flying.

Somewhere in that thick stretch of wetlands, the Piper went down. There was nothing in the voice-recorder that suggested any problem with weather, or turbulence, or pilot distress, or the aircraft; there was nothing in the forensic examination that indicated any mechanical malfunction. As far as anyone could surmise, the crash must have been intentional.

The plane broke apart on impact, a total wreck. The body, of course, was never recovered.

Dave rubbernecked around to try to catch a glimpse
of the street sign he'd just passed. He didn't know
where he was going. The old silver convertible was
Charlie's car, a toy given to a spoiled child by
an indulgent mother. Dave didn't have a car of his
own, and hadn't done much driving in Ithaca, and
none of it in this area up the lakeshore.

In the backseat, both the girl and Charlie had
their heads lolled back, perhaps passed out. Or
maybe they were asleep. Or just staring up at the
sky, letting the wind wash across their hot faces
on a muggy May night.

Then Charlie stirred, jolted alert by a quick
turn around a long bend. Dave looked in the
rearview, saw that Charlie was leaning over the
girl, with a hand on one of her breasts. She didn't
appear to be awake.

"Not cool," Dave said, softly.

Charlie looked up, caught Dave's eye in the
mirror. Put his finger up to his lips, *shhh*. He
turned his attention back to the girl, beginning
to undo buttons, then his hand was inside her bra.
Her neck was leaning on the leather headrest, head
angled in a passed-out pose, mouth agape, chest
rising and falling with quick shallow drunken
breaths.

"Charlie," Dave said, trying to project warning
into his voice.

But Charlie ignored it. He started fiddling with
the clasp of her bra, a front-loader.

"Charlie," Dave said, more insistently.

That's when she came to, startled. She jerked her head upright, and she saw what was going on. She took a second to digest the situation, and she realized it was not good. She had no clue where she was, in the backseat of some car with her breasts hanging out and some drunken lecherous guy leaning over her. She looked to the side and saw an unfamiliar landscape, no streetlights or buildings. For all she knew she was in the middle of nowhere, with two men she didn't know.

"Stop," she said. "Stop the car." She was panicked.

"It's okay," Dave said, trying to sound reassuring.

"Stop this fucking car, right now," she said, pushing herself back into her bra and fumbling with the clasp. But she was nervous and kept losing her grip and couldn't get the thing closed.

"Okay," Dave said. But they were going around another long curve, not a good place to stop, too dangerous in the middle of the night. So he kept driving, slowing, until finally the curve ended. He pulled the car to a scrubby shoulder, just a bit of weedy grass along the side of the road.

"I want to get out," she said.

"Okay," Dave said, "take it easy." He shifted into Park but left the motor running. He got out and released the seat forward so she could climb out. Charlie was splayed out back there, not saying a word.

The girl stumbled around the car, onto the grass.

With her back turned to the boys, she closed the buttons of her blouse. She started walking away. "Where are we?"

"Edge of town," Dave answered. "Not sure. Honestly I'm a little lost."

She was still stumbling away, crying. Dave started to follow her, a nonthreatening distance behind, on foot. The weedy grass of the shoulder gave way to dirt. "Look," he said, "I'm sorry about Charlie. But let's get back in the car, and we'll get you home. We're . . . I don't know where exactly, but it can't be far . . ."

She was crying.

Then Dave and the girl both heard the car's gears shift. They turned and saw that Charlie was now at the wheel, inching the car forward.

"Here's Charlie!" he yelled. Dave turned back to the car, took a few steps toward it, then broke into a run, a sprint. As he got closer he could see a scary look on Charlie's face.

Dave ran straight at the grille of the creeping old Jaguar. If Charlie insisted on continuing to drive, he was going to have to run over his friend. Dave put his hands on the hood, and started back-peddling as the car crawled forward in first gear.

"Charlie," he said, "come on, man."

Dave glanced over his shoulder, saw that the girl was now running. She was about to disappear around the next bend in the road. He couldn't let her vanish like that, in the middle of nowhere, in the middle of the night.

"Charlie, come on," I said, "stop the car."

CHAPTER 18

*R*ing.

Isabel pushes through the dense Times Square throngs, the foreign tourists and the domestic ones, the flip-flops and the fanny packs, the tween girls in their scandalously short skirts and the lanky acne'd boys in lacrosse jerseys, bored and awed at once, holding aloft shopping bags from American Girl and Abercrombie & Fitch, posing for smart-phone lenses with obscene gestures, grotesque grimaces, age-inappropriate flirty pouts. Immortalizing their childhoods, regrettably.

Ring.

She makes her way past the human mess of the converging avenues, into a reasonably calm side street in the Theater District, the famous-name marquees announcing the presence of visiting royalty from Hollywood, or resident Broadway lifers, plus "special guest appearances" and "8 Tony Nominations!" and raves from the *Village Voice*.

Ring.

Her call is rerouted to Alexis's voice-mail box, again.

Strange. Maybe the girl is resentful about that early-morning call, on her day off, to discuss methods of manuscript delivery; Isabel wouldn't blame her. Or maybe she set the device to mute so she could lie in bed peacefully, sleeping off whatever she did last night, perhaps with whomever she did it, not so peacefully, extending last night into today. Or maybe she's at the doctor's, legs aloft, staring at a rip in the wallpaper to distract herself from the doctor's cold instruments and fingers. Maybe, perhaps, whatever: Alexis not answering. But they really need to talk.

Isabel doesn't leave a message. She picks up her pace, and crosses Eighth Avenue, now definitely out of the Midtown business district and west of the Theater District and properly into residential Hell's Kitchen, which according to real-estate agents is now supposed to be called Clinton. Trying to rebrand a whole neighborhood. But there's apparently backlash, a re-rebranding back to the gritty old name and its mean-streets connotations, nostalgia for something that's only a few years outdated, and not even gone. People who've lived here for four years consider themselves old pioneers, the avant-garde, yammering proprietarily about "back in the day."

Isabel consults her phone for the address. She's never been to Alexis's apartment, doesn't know what type of building it will be, but her suspicion is one of those soulless contemporary high-rises, with a doorman and a health club and concierge service and a lobby filled with black-leather Mies van der Rohe knockoffs. Buildings with logos. Branded buildings, in rebranded neighborhoods, orchestrated by branding consultants. She walks by one of these new developments now, stares up at a banner that proclaims "limited edition residences." As if there's any other type. She hates those goddamned buildings, and the spoiled entitled people who live in them.

Isabel herself had never been especially political, but she was embarrassed—she was humiliated—when the seemingly apolitical man she'd married started veering sharply to the right. Luckily, he wasn't the only one in town. As bank accounts ballooned in the nineties and aughts, a lot of New Yorkers leaned away from their youthful ideals, their philosophical intentions. Personal politics raced to catch up with the practicalities, rationalizations to catch up with greed.

She stops in front of the number for Alexis's building, but this can't be right. Isabel looks again at the building, then back at her phone, then up again. At the sloppily painted steel security door with the ripped lock-smith stickers, at the rusty fire escape, at the security-gated windows with the Reggaeton spilling out, at the scrawls and the soot and the screwed-on signs prohibiting loitering and drug use and solicitation. At this mini-slum.

Isabel peers at the aluminum panel of the intercom: MAURIER, 1F. Sure enough. Isabel knows from 1F: the very worst apartment, bottom floor front, down at street level, windows facing the garbage cans, the big industrial plastic rat traps, the baggies filled with scooped-up dog shit that people toss in the general direction of the bins, often missing.

Poor girl, in her poor crappy apartment. This is the opposite of what Isabel was expecting, and she feels embarrassed at her own ungenerous assumptions, chastened.

She presses the wide horizontal button. No answer.

She waits a half-minute, and presses again.

Isabel was hoping to recruit Alexis now. To take the girl along in Isabel's flight from ATM, to help open up the new agency, in exchange for sincere promises of equity, independence, fast-track advancement. Isabel doesn't want to do this completely alone; she can't. There will be a lot of work, a lot of hustle, a lot of calls. It will all start today.

She buzzes a third time, waits a few seconds, but finally gives up, starts to walk away.

Then something occurs to her. Isabel turns back to the building, opens the gate to the dry moat, walks past the garbage cans, to the thick iron security bars at what she presumes is the 1F window. She opens her phone, hits redial. She holds the phone down at her stomach, pressing the earpiece against her body so she can't hear the digital ringing through the device, straining to listen for ringing in the physical world.

Ring.

From inside the apartment, through the half-open window, past the fluttering drapes.

Ring.

120

Isabel leans forward, holding the black iron bars, and looks inside. The glow of a newly ignited electronic screen catches her eye. The girl's phone is lying on the floor.

Ring.

Then something else catches her eye.

Isabel is having trouble breathing. She grips the bars tightly, the rusty flaking iron scratching her fingers and palms, struggling to hold herself upright on wobbly knees.

She turns away from the horror on the other side of the parted curtains, stares at the building's walls, at the vulgar graffiti, the mottled discolored stone. Her mind reels with the implications of this situation for herself. She tries to grasp, firmly, the reality of what's going on, but her thoughts keep sliding away from her, slipping toward irrationality.

She needs to calm down, to think.

In an instant it's now clear to her that the manuscript is, without a doubt, true. It's an accurate account of Charlie Wolfe's life and career, and the shocking activities of Wolfe Worldwide Media, written by someone in a unique position to know. If this information is published, if it's brought to light in any way, it will bring down Charlie Wolfe, and initiate a tremendous scandal implicating multiple American presidents and CIA directors, and create a crisis of confidence in one of the most visible media companies in the world. A shitstorm. No question about it.

So there are a lot of powerful people who would want to suppress it, if they were aware of its existence. The author would of course understand this. So he would write a book like this secretly, and possibly anonymously. He would hide somewhere as he wrote, and he'd probably stay hidden until it was published, and hope that the publicity kept him alive. Or maybe he'd stay hidden forever.

And of course it would make sense—it would be practically inevitable—that he'd entrust his manuscript to Isabel.

But what if he wasn't able to keep his project a total secret? What if someone—Charlie Wolfe, or the CIA director, or maybe even the president of the United States—found the author? Knew what he was doing? Discovered that he'd sent this manuscript to Isabel?

What would they do?

Isabel turns her head back to the window, looks inside again, at the girl lying in a pool of her own blood, a gaping hole in the middle of her forehead.

This is what they would do.

PART II

AFTERNOON

CHAPTER 19

She should call the police. Isabel feels it in her bones that she should, while at the same time that she shouldn't, terrified . . .

She needs to be deliberate. To articulate to herself: *why* precisely call the police? It won't help Alexis. There's no way the girl is alive, with that hole in the middle of her head, lying in that pool of blood. No phone call is going to save her.

Isabel stands on the sidewalk in front of the dingy building, and fumbles out a cigarette with trembling hands, manages to ignite the lighter after five tries, takes a long desperate drag of nicotine. She's flooded with nausea. A convulsion begins deep in the pit of her stomach, works its way quickly up through her alimentary canal. She drops the cigarette to the pavement, and closes her eyes, trying to will the queasiness into submission.

She feels her phone begin to vibrate an instant before the audible ring. It's her office's main number, probably Meg, almost certainly calling to fire her, explicitly and vociferously. She hits Ignore.

If she dialed 911 right now, the police would want to know who she was, and she'd be questioned, maybe even detained. Could Isabel herself become a suspect in Alexis's murder? Of course she could. Then she'd have to explain everything: the manuscript, the subject, the probable author. And as implausible as her story sounded, the police would have to consider her explanation. Then what? Then they'd call someone in Washington. And then . . . ?

And then she'd be ushered into the back of a tinted-window SUV, and that would be the last anyone ever saw or heard of Isabel Reed. Because if they were willing to kill Alexis Maurier, they wouldn't feel constrained to stop there.

No, Isabel won't be safe in any police station, or in police custody. She needs to stay away from the police. But someone ought to find Alexis's body. Someone should call the girl's parents, tell her friends. She can't just lie there, *rotting*, in her sad little apartment, ground floor with all the mice and the rats, *feeding* on her flesh—

There's a pay phone on the corner. Do you need a coin to dial 911 from a public phone? It's been . . . how long? . . . it's been never. Isabel has never dialed 911, from any phone. She picks up the gray handset, then remembers the ubiquitous presence of security cameras, of surveillance cameras, of little globes integrated into ATMs, of traffic-safety cameras in sturdy boxes affixed to streetlamps, of good-old generic scare-tactic federal-government cameras . . . There are more than thirty million security cameras in America, aiming everywhere, recording everyone, all the time, producing hundreds of millions of hours of footage, every single day.

Isabel puts on sunglasses, trying to hide from whoever might eventually triangulate this audio with some visual, recorded from who knows what device, where. But it will happen.

It occurs to her that it may not be solely cameras that are watching her. From the privacy of her dark lenses, she scans the street life, taking mental snapshots. A man is standing across the street, leaning against a lamppost, talking on his cell phone. Across the avenue, two youngish guys are sitting in the front of a crummy-looking white Toyota sedan, both wearing sunglasses. A woman is standing in the gutter, as if to hail a cab, though plenty of unoccupied taxis seem to be passing her by, and her hand isn't raised.

Isabel turns to the keypad, punches in the three buttons. "Someone has been shot." She gives Alexis's address, then replaces the handset without identifying herself.

She looks around again, standing in the semi-seclusion of the cut-off-at-the-knees phone booth, watching through the scratched cloudy Plexiglas, waiting for the stoplight to change on the avenue, for the heavy stream of downtown traffic to resume. The light turns green, and the cars pull away, one after the other, half of them occupied taxis, until she sees the telltale lit-up sign, then she takes a couple of long strides to the curb and off it, her arm shooting up, hailing the taxi.

She pulls the door shut. "Penn Station please."

"You got it chief."

She scrolls through the address book on her phone, chooses a contact, hits Call.

"Isabel! What a surprise!"

"Hi Dean. You in town? At your normal spot?"

"I am."

"May I come talk to you, for a few minutes?"

"Oh for fuck's sake, Isabel. Are they asking for their money back? Because I thought—"

"No. This is not about you, at all. Can you see me?"

A pause. "Of course. Always."

She hangs up as the car is pulling to the curb. She tosses a ten into the front seat and ejects herself into another dense crowd, swarming in and out of the hideous train station that's burrowed under the unfortunate monstrosity of Madison Square Garden. Into the wide Amtrak room, through a busy corridor to the subway. She swipes her MetroCard, dashes up the stairs to the platform as an uptown express is pulling in. She hops onto the sparsely populated car, in the one situation when she'd prefer it to be packed to the gills, sardines, body odor and bad breath, the stench of McDonald's, tinny treble leaking out of headphones, bicycles and strollers and backpacks and skateboards, too many people with too much stuff in too small a space.

But today it's just herself and a dozen others. An overweight Italian-looking guy wearing sweats and sneakers and a Mets T-shirt, gold necklaces and bracelets, reading the sports section of the *Daily News*, gives Isabel the up-and-down, and nods appreciatively, as if the sommelier just presented him with a taste of nice Barolo. Everyone else ignores her, and one another.

Isabel doesn't ride the subway a lot, but it's often enough that she carries a fare card. For a few years she'd sworn off subways and buses entirely, making a statement of it, if to no one other than herself. That was back when she started at ATM, when she finally got her first taste of living beyond paycheck-to-paycheck, with enough extra income to dispose of it with a weekly cleaning lady, and proper vacations in real hotels without agonizing over the cost of every poolside drink, and erasing her price-sensitivity on toiletries and groceries. Enough to take taxis instead of the dark, smelly, crowded subway. She had risen above the subway.

It took a few years to change her mind about public transportation, among other similar choices. She stopped trying to appear to have more money than she did, and started aiming for the opposite.

The subway pulls into Times Square, the doors open. Isabel steps onto the platform, then hops back into the car. Then as the doors are closing, she jumps out again.

She hurries up the stairs and across the mezzanine and down the stairs again to the downtown platform, a local arriving on the outside track. She boards this train, takes a seat on the hard gray plastic. She feels the vibration thrumming her thighs, the regular rhythm, *thump-thump, thump-thump, thump-thump.*

Despite the adrenaline, she feels exhausted, spent. She could go to sleep right here, like tens of thousands of people do every day. Simply close her eyes for a second, let her neck relax, head lolling to one side or the other or straight down, chin on chest, dribbling drool here on the Seventh Avenue IRT . . .

But she stands, and exits to another platform under another neighborhood, then the Greenwich Village sidewalk, striding to the curb, her arm aloft again, beckoning another taxi to a screeching halt, another destination, another ten-dollar bill tossed across another bulletproof divide.

She looks through the Chevy windows, left and right, front and back. No, she thinks: there's no way anyone could've followed her.

Isabel discharges herself onto a cobblestoned street in the Meatpacking District, another bustling rebranded neighborhood. This area hasn't changed its name, but it has almost entirely relinquished its raison d'être, as well as the rough trade in transvestite prostitutes that accompanied the stinking bloody eponymous business.

A man holds open the discreetly labeled door to a private club, and she enters the cool dark lobby. A stunning girl at reception directs Isabel to the roof, and after the elevator she reemerges into the bright sunlight, a bar and couches and coffee tables, a decorative restaurant under giant canvas umbrellas, a small blue swimming pool occupied by a half-dozen model types. Isabel scans nearly the full 360 degrees before she spies the person she's looking for, sprawled on a chaise in the far corner of poolside.

She makes her way around the perimeter of chairs, sunglasses and towels and bikinis and biceps, magazines and newspapers, books and tablets, cigarettes and wineglasses and tall beady bottles of sparkling water. What are all these people doing here, in the middle of a workday? This isn't LA or Miami; people are supposed to *work* in New York City.

On the small table next to Dean is a frosty bucket, with the telltale silver foil of a Champagne bottle peeking out from the ice water, and a used ashtray with a packet of cigarettes and a silver lighter, and a phone, and a couple of half-full flutes, one with a lipstick smudge. There's a lithe woman half his age in the next chair, just a few square inches of Lycra removed from naked.

"Isabel, hello." Dean stands, proffering a cheek kiss, leaning close to let his hair-tufted chest brush against her. Dean goes to great pains to paint himself as an action hero sort of character, tattooed and scarred and ropy-muscled, unfiltered cigarettes and excessive quantities of liquor and cocaine, a shameless womanizer. "Great to see you. This"—gesturing at his companion—"is Betsy."

"My name's Brecka," the girl says with a scowl. She doesn't hold out her hand, or move from her prone position.

"*Really*?" Dean asks. "*Breck*a? That's a *name*?"

The girl exhales a plume of smoke in his general direction.

"Are you absolutely sure?"

She stares at him.

"Oops. Apologies." Dean mugs at Isabel, shrugs. "Just the same, Brecka, give us a minute, will you? Isn't that friend of yours Laura over there at the bar?"

"*Her* name"—the girl stands—"is Laur*el*."

"Yeah, well." Dean pats the girl's rear, shooing her away while copping a feel. Multitasking.

Isabel takes Brecka's place on the chaise, but leaves her feet on the floor. She feels ludicrous up here in her business attire, amid all these bathing suits. Like walking into the lobby of a five-star hotel wearing sweats, but the opposite.

Dean removes his sunglasses, revealing a black eye.

"Jesus," Isabel says, her heart falling into the pit of her stomach. Is Dean involved too? "What happened to you?"

"Oh this?" He points at his swollen blue-black flesh. "It's nothing."

"Come on."

"You know about my anti-Hummer, er, cru*sade?*"

Dean has a tendency, when plastered, to walk around the city leaving windshield notes, *Hummers are for douchebags*, a word that he thinks is the all-time greatest linguistic innovation.

"Well, one of the douchebags caught me in the act. He was with his uh, posse, a whole douchemobile worth. I didn't stand a chance. But I don't regret it one fucking bit." He picks up the wine bottle. "So. It's a rare pleasure for my esteemed literary agent to hunt me down in the middle of a workday." He holds the bottle by its neck, tilts it toward Isabel. "Or, rather, *week*day."

"No thanks." She too removes her sunglasses, in the shade of the umbrella, and places them on the table.

"Especially," he continues, "considering that I'm now—what is it?— *ten* months late with my manuscript delivery?"

"Two years."

"*Mmm.*" He takes a deep drag of his cigarette. "As I think we both know, I'm going to finish that book . . . Let's see, *right*: the day after never. And yet here I am, whiling away another day with sparkling wine and unfiltered cigarettes and underage women." He taps one out of the pack, lights it.

"How do you earn a living, Dean?"

"*Earn*? A *living*? You know damn well that I don't do any such thing."

Dean is one of those fearless journalists who specializes in dangerous places, batting around Bosnia and the Sudan, Afghanistan and Iraq. Through the unpredictable alchemy of the book-publishing process—an inexact mix of sales-force enthusiasm and word-of-mouth industry buzz, of long-lead magazine coverage and full-length newspaper reviews and weekly-magazine squibs—Dean's most recent book, about an obscure corner of the Afghanistan war, achieved the much pursued status as being *the* nonfiction book of the year: international editions in thirty languages, and audio books and e-books and paperbacks, and a fast-track film from a major studio with first-name recognized leads, and then movie-tie-in editions . . . Royalties are flowing in from dozens of accounts on six continents. And in the meantime a prominent magazine has hired Dean as a contributing editor, providing him with a business card and a monthly stipend in exchange for a commitment to supplying five thousand words per year, which as a rule he does in one fell swoop after returning from some war-torn hellhole, a cocaine-fueled stream-of-consciousness dump of experiential prose, unconventionally punctuated and ridden with misspellings and grammatical errors. But there are editors to fix that; it's what editors are for. The rules of stylistic consistency are beneath Dean. Hobgoblins of small minds.

He takes a deep drag of his Player's Plain. It was the most available cigarette in Pakistan when Dean lived there in the 1990s, and he never gave it up, despite increasing challenges to procurement. "So: to what do I owe this very *special* pleasure?"

"Dean, you were nosing around DC when David Miller killed himself, right?"

One of the benefits of working in the publishing world is that Isabel knows—or can easily access—at least one expert in practically any subject. Geopolitics, pediatric medicine, Spanish cooking, whatever. The leading lights in every field write books about their areas of expertise; even the leading experts in the field of writing books write books about writing books. And all experts have literary agents.

Dean, an expert in the duplicities of politics, exhales a cloud of smoke, but doesn't say anything.

"Were there any rumors?" she asks. "Rumors wouldn't have reached me, you know."

Dean stares at her, clearly debating whether to engage in this subject, and to what extent. "Yeah," he says, resigned. "Of course there were rumors."

"Rumors that he was murdered?"

"Ah, yeah. Inevitable, the rumors. Important man, suddenly no longer alive."

"And?"

He shakes his head dismissively. "There was nothing to it."

"Were there suspects? A motive?"

"No, not really. And honestly the murder possibility wasn't the most compelling, ah, *alternative* explanation for his disappearance."

"Which was?"

"Which was that Miller's death"—Dean turns his head more directly toward Isabel, strains his neck in her direction—"was a *hoax.*"

This is what Isabel had been expecting to hear; this is the idea that she'd been unable to suppress since she began reading the manuscript yesterday.

She takes one of Dean's cigarettes, lights it. She coughs, the unfiltered too untamed for her lungs.

"Was there any evidence?"

"A few days after his disappearance into the Atlantic, someone who looked a lot like Miller arrived in Brussels on a flight that originated in the Bahamas. Different name on his passport, of course. A passport that turned out to be stolen from someone who lives in DC and works in the Administration."

"And then?"

"Unfortunately—or is it really *un*fortunate? Who's to say?—the trail ended there, in the Brussels airport. But Brussels is a gateway to anywhere. By connecting flight, by train, by car. It's a very convenient place to arrive, if what you're planning is to end up somewhere else."

Isabel takes another drag, much less harsh than the first. That seems to be how it is with things that are bad for you.

"Are you certain you don't want any Champagne? You look like you could use something."

"Did anyone look into this, Dean? Did *you*?"

He nods. "Found nothing, nowhere."

"What about alternative cancer-treatment centers?"

"Oh, Isabel, is it really as bad as all that?" Dean looks down at his cigarette. "It's true that I can't *quite* seem to shake this cough—"

"I'm not talking about you."

"I know what you're talking about. Of *course* I investigated the medical angle. Miller definitely consulted with a variety of doctors, as well as with a number of his colleagues. He contacted cancer-treatment centers in different parts of the world. I wasn't able to get any hard information about recommendations or possible treatments or anything specific; medical professionals tend to take patient confidentiality rather seriously, everywhere. But yeah, I investigated this angle thoroughly. And I found nothing.

"As you know, Mr. Miller was—*is*?—rich. And smart. A rich and smart man can easily buy himself a new identity, in a well-protected hiding spot. And he can stay safely hidden for a very, very long time."

He leans toward Isabel. "Especially if he's scared."

CHAPTER 20

The author walks into one of the large front-facing rooms of the sturdy old *Schloss*. This would've been a bedroom, back when the building was a residence. All these rooms retain their eighteenth-century character, person-size fireplaces and Persian rugs, heavy wooden furniture and ornately framed oil paintings on the walls. It's the back of the building that's twenty-first-century, brushed steel and gleaming veneers, bright flat shadowless lighting systems and a mesmerizing array of cutting-edge medical technology.

He settles into a creaky leather armchair facing the big mahogany desk, and catches a glimpse of himself in a gilt-edged mirror, nearly unrecognizable, an entirely different person here in Zurich than he'd been in Washington.

When he'd arrived in Europe in the early winter he'd had no belongings, no luggage. Lost by the airline, is what he claimed to the thoroughly uninterested clerk at the grubby hotel near the Bruxelles-Midi station.

For a few days he walked the damp cold streets of the big Belgian city, buying a whole new wardrobe a few items at a time, paying cash for skinny suits and slim-fitting shirts to replace those formless sack suits of DC, American clothing designed to hide the pear shape of the typical American man. He bought snug shoes, the types of footwear you really don't find on men's feet in the USA. He was trying to look like someone who belonged in Europe, who lived here, maybe even was from here. Not an American on the run.

But his first order of business had been to trudge through the narrow medieval streets around the spectacular Grand-Place—gift shops and chocolatiers, unruly school trips and the inevitable Japanese tour groups—looking for a busy barbershop that cycles through men at a production-line pace, quick clips and close shaves, *snip-snip buzz-buzz*. He found the right sort of busy anonymous shop in a covered arcade near the Bourse, and had his dark curls shorn down to a tight crew cut. He'd also stopped shaving a few days before his fateful Piper flight, and after a week this purposeful neglect had blossomed into a short beard.

He visited an Internet café that also sent and received snail mail from all over the globe, and picked up a package that he'd mailed to himself from a similar outfit in DC.

He bought thin angular eyeglasses and acquired tinted contacts to hide the bright blue of his eyes, the first thing anyone ever noticed about him, the most important detail to disguise. But he didn't start wearing these contacts until he'd rented a car and driven out of Belgium and across northern Germany to Berlin, where a new identity—Stuart Carner—was waiting for him courtesy of a Russian forger and twenty thousand euros cash, a disappointingly thin stack of banknotes, forty pieces of purple paper.

He didn't care for the name Stuart, but it was better than Stu; there'd been a jackass Stu in college who had permanently tainted the name.

Herr Stuart Carner was his second new identity. The first had been the passport of a Treasury wonk who was the author's virtual doppelganger; for the past few years, people were constantly remarking that the resemblance between the two men was uncanny. And everyone who knew this glorified accountant also knew that the guy never, *ever* left DC, much less America, except for a famously disastrous trip to Cancún a few years earlier. He was unlikely to miss his passport.

It hadn't been much trouble to find someone willing to break into the guy's apartment; the hard part had been convincing the burglar not to steal anything besides the passport.

So then in Berlin those striking blue eyes became black, cloaked in mourning. He'd also lost fifteen pounds over the preceding few months. Now with the short hair and the dark eyes and the glasses, the skinny suits and pointy shoes, he was nearly unrecognizable, to the naked eye. But he'd still be plenty identifiable, with facial-recognition software, not to mention his fingerprints.

With his new appearance and fictitious identity and his two new suitcases filled with his new wardrobe, he boarded an Air Berlin flight, the stewardesses wearing kinky red leather gloves with black palms, bound for the large Zurich airport and a reservation in a business hotel near the Paradeplatz, a convenient base to explore, to find a place to live, to drive out to this converted old estate up in the hills, this unobtrusive medical complex, which was the primary reason to come to the quiet tidy little city in the first place.

He hears someone enter the room behind him, and a hand squeezes his shoulder as the doctor comes into peripheral view. The tall German settles behind the desk, opens the file, turns a page, turns to the front again.

"So, Herr Carner, how are you feeling?"

"In general I feel good."

"Exercising?"

"Yes." He'd taken up running, for the first time in his life. His apartment is a block from the lakeside's park and its pleasant path along the quai, packed with people on a sunny warm day like today, but deserted in the usual drizzle of Europe in winter and spring.

"I run now, almost every day." Working his way up to respectable distances. And finally able to feel reasonably comfortable wearing headphones while running out in public, overcoming a paranoia that dated back to junior high, when the Walkman was first invented, and his grandparents had given him one for his thirteenth birthday, but two weeks later he was mugged while wearing it, unable to hear the thugs coming up behind him, and they took the Sony as well as the folded-up dollar in his pocket, on his way to Gino's to buy a pizza-soda-ice lunch special for fifty cents, plus a pack of baseball cards from the candy store whose primary business was dime, nickel, and trey bags of low-quality marijuana. Brooklyn in the early eighties.

"And your, ah, appetite?"

"I'm eating fine."

"I am referring to another appetite." The good doctor always seems inappropriately interested in his patient's sex life, despite its apparent irrelevance to the medical issues at hand.

"Oh. That comes and goes. It exists."

The doctor nods approvingly.

It was on one of his first jogs that he'd met Vanessa, both of them stretching their hamstrings on an unseasonably warm March morning. At that point he'd been in Switzerland for three months, carefully sequestered in his friendless little bubble of a life, a paranoid hermit. He was having stirrings, feeling the weight of loneliness, and perhaps getting sloppy because of it. They had a brief conversation, then ran their separate ways. At the time, he was still wearing some bandages.

When the last of the wrappings finally came off he'd started going out, by himself. He bought a few Saturday nights' worth of opera tickets, even though he'd never enjoyed all that Italian screaming. But the opera house was just up the street, and he suspected it was an okay thing to do alone. Put on a suit and tie, stand on the balcony during intermission, struggle to stay awake for Act III.

The cinema too, on the far side of the opera's *Platz*, with assigned seating, and an inexplicable intermission in the middle of the film, everyone strolling out to the lobby for a Coke and a pee. He'd buy cookies from the Sicilian guys' lavish selection at their giant table there in the middle of all the tram stops, and nibble from his pocket.

In late April, when the weather turned, he started going to cafés, once in a while. Mostly the terrace of the Terrasse, a few minutes from home, always packed with bankers and consultants in suits and heels, ties and scarves. But he was still self-conscious, scarred, and scared of talking to women.

Then downstairs at the Widder one night, he ran into that jogger from the quai again. He bought a bottle of Champagne for her table of English-speaking women. He himself took only a couple of sips, but the three women drank with reckless abandon. He would, he realized, gladly sleep with any of the three; he ordered a second bottle. At midnight one of the women left, then he couldn't quite figure out how to move things along—it was late, and he was tired—with either of the remaining two, other than to propose the thing that he suddenly couldn't stop thinking about, not for ten seconds at a stretch, a new obsession.

Unable to resist, he somehow mustered the courage to ask, "Could I interest you ladies in joining me in bed?"

Their jaws dropped in unison. Then the redheaded Irishwoman, with a husband who was out of the country, asked, "*Both* of us?"

After squealing and blushing and grabbing each other's arms, the women retreated to the loo to discuss in private. They returned coyly silent, making him suffer a long wait for an answer. Then Vanessa, the South African, drained her glass, leaned toward and him, and said, "All right then. Let's have a go."

Fifteen minutes later the three of them were naked, in bed. His first and probably last ménage-à-trois.

After that he began to ease back into something of a social life, saying hello to strangers, making small talk at cafés. He could now claim to have a few friends, albeit in the limited way that friendships can exist when one person is lying about absolutely everything, right down to his name.

It's easy to be pseudonymous when you're an expat, and nobody knows you. It's effortless to be anonymous. But it's not fun.

Now, despite the barriers of his wholesale dishonesties, he has something to do, with someone else, once in a while. This isn't a full life he's leading, by any stretch of the imagination. But neither is it the opposite.

And until a few days ago he was working every day, frantic, as authors can become, to finish a manuscript, to progress to the next stage. He had always been one of those people who doesn't forget much, even when he wasn't paying particularly close attention while the information was incoming. So over the years he'd managed to absorb a solid understanding of the book business. He knows enough to be able to imagine the entire process for another author, a normal author, in a normal situation. Sitting there at home, all his hopes and dreams pinned on the manuscript, while the submissions are made to acquisition editors at a dozen publishing houses, waiting for responses—enthusiasm, skepticism, offers, rejections, maybe an auction, frenetic bidding, items in gossip columns and industry magazines.

Then the editing, the dust jacket design, the publicity campaign, the launch party. The newspaper reviews and the morning-show appearances and the bookstore events and the radio interviews, the rapid climb up the bestseller lists . . .

That's how it could work, for someone with his type of story to tell, but without his reason for telling it.

"You are recovering quite well, Herr Carner," the doctor smiles. "Quite well. The incisions are almost completely disappeared, and everything is normal. I will see you again in two weeks. But there is nothing you should worry about."

CHAPTER 21

"I think he may have sent me a manuscript," Isabel says. "An exposé of Charlie Wolfe's career."

Dean raises his eyebrows. "Damaging?"

"More than you can imagine. There's something horrible—unforgivable—in his youth. And then some startling revelations about his business. Startling, and illegal."

"Is the manuscript in your bag, right now?"

"Yes."

"Will you give me a copy?"

"I can't," she says. "I'm sorry."

He shrugs, understanding. But he had to ask. "Is it *true*?"

"I don't know, for certain. But yes, I think so."

"Why do you think that?"

Isabel looks around the rooftop deck, for potential eavesdroppers. She leans in close to Dean, smells the smoke and the wine on his breath. "Because someone," she whispers, "just murdered my assistant."

"Oh fuck." Dean squares his jaw and narrows his eyes to small severe slits. "Are you sure?"

"Positive."

"Are they here, now? Have you been followed?"

"I took, um, evasive maneuvers. Listen, Dean, I don't know what to do. Any suggestions?"

He lights another cigarette, his brow furrowed. "You're not safe with the police, or any part of the government."

"I agree."

"The American government, that is." He exhales. "What would you think about presenting yourself to a foreign embassy? I have some trust-worthy connections. I could escort you."

"What could they do?"

"Keep you safe."

"*Could* they? For how long? A week? A year?" She stares at her client, her old friend. Wondering how much she can trust even him. "I need to get out of town."

"Yeah, that's probably a good idea. Where would you go?"

"Not sure. Maghe a client's beach house, out east."

Dean nods, stubs out his cigarette studiously, staring into the ashtray. "Southampton?"

Isabel swallows, disappointed in this question. Why does Dean care what town she's going to? Mere curiosity?

"No," she says, without supplying an alternative. "But don't be sur-prised if I eventually take you up on that embassy offer."

She steps off the curb, onto the cobblestones, taking care to keep her heels out of the deep crevasses between the blocks. She picks her way slowly across the street, and is relieved to alight on the opposite curb. Such a small accomplishment, crossing the street.

Her phone rings again. The office, again. Rather, the ex-office. She ignores it, again.

She keeps walking inland, toward the meat of Manhattan, away from the river. Lost in thought, weighing her options, plotting her course of ac-tion. She steps into a small triangular park with a fountain in the middle, office workers with lunch in their laps, sandwiches and wraps, smoothies and soups, sitting on green benches in dappled sunlight, everyone wearing sunglasses—

Crap. She left her sunglasses next to Dean's ice bucket. She stops. Should she go back and collect them? Waste of time? But what is she on her way to do? Anything?

She turns around, and walks through the wrought iron gates, out onto the sidewalk of Eighth Avenue. Just in time to see a white Toyota across the avenue, pulling away from the curb. The same beat-up sedan from Hell's Kitchen, with the same two guys in front, wearing sunglasses, rigidly not looking in her direction.

She makes it a block, maybe two, and staggers into a coffee shop, a studiously shabby room filled with mismatched overstuffed furniture and scruffy denim-clad men, working on Macs. She holds out money to pay for coffee, and notices that her hand is trembling. She puts the bills on the counter, covered with her clenched fist.

How can this be? How could anyone have followed her? In a *car*? When she'd ridden on two different underground trains, going in two different directions?

Isabel carries her coffee to the rear corner, a good vantage on the room, on the front door. She collapses into a wing chair, drops her handbag onto the floor beside her. It seems like forever since she sat in that other restaurant, way back at breakfast with Jeffrey, and dropped the heavy manuscript bag to the floor. The restaurant where that man brushed against her, making her nervous, when she was on her way out.

She looks down at the floor, at the crumpled black-leather pile of her bag containing her mobile phone, and she thinks she understands.

Dave walked around to the rear of the car slowly, tentatively, not looking forward to what he would discover back there. The girl's legs were emerging from under the trunk, jutting out at unnatural angles.

Charlie followed a moment behind, his eyes averted. Then he mustered his courage, took a deep breath, and leaned down to get a look. Her skull had split open, spilling its contents all over the dark wet pavement. That's when Charlie threw up, quick and violent and uncontrolled, onto the blacktop, again and again, loudly and painfully, doubled-over, clutching his wrenching gut.

It was drizzling and would end up raining all through the night. Charlie's vomit would be swept away by the downpour, borne into the drainage swale at the side of the road, along with the girl's blood and brains. All visible traces of the event would be washed away.

There was still plenty of retrievable evidence. Not just on a microscopic level, but footprints, crushed branches, fabric fibers, and tire treads for anyone who know where to look. But no one knew.

CHAPTER 22

Jeff is devouring the pages, one after the other, his eyes racing down the lines, turning a new page every thirty seconds, his fingers always on the corner of a piece of paper, ready to turn. Twenty years after graduation, his most practical take-away skill from his Ivy League B.A. seems to be this: the ability to digest reading material very quickly. For an editor whose main job is to grasp the general idea of thousands of pages every week, this means the difference between occasionally getting a full night's sleep, and never.

Jeff fiddles with his Sheaffer as he reads, spinning the silver cylinder in his fingers, clockwise, counterclockwise, flipping it around, upside-down. His phone starts beeping at him, an alarm, time to go.

He can't let the manuscript lie on his desk, unattended, when he leaves the building; he shouldn't have left it to go the editorial meeting an hour ago. Or for that matter to the toilet. So now he shoves the thick stack of paper into his leather satchel, and heads out for today's agent lunch.

Jeff eats with a rotating cast of hundreds of literary agents, three or four days per week, forty-five weeks out of the year, year after year after year. The four most beautiful words in his life are "your lunch date canceled." But there's a complicated calculus to cancellation, a combination of factors including your date's relative power plus possible pending business plus past projects and past lunch cancellations, then minus grudges and resentments and sometimes the weather and, of course, plain old dislike.

Today's date Dan is insufferable, but the guy outranks Jeff on anyone's measure of importance in the publishing firmament. So on this clear bright day, Jeff can't cancel.

Jeff hustles through the halls, over the well-worn and tattered carpets, past the mismatched furniture, the ailing photocopy machines and printers that are wedged into spaces that are too awkward for desks, past the never-quite-clean-smelling kitchen—today it's the perpetual aroma of microwave popcorn, mingling with someone's ill-advised leftover curry—and through reception, and lunges into the closing elevator, which he realizes with a sinking heart is not as empty as he'd thought.

"Hi," Ashleigh says to him, softly, uncomfortably.

"Oh, hi."

Ashleigh is an extravagantly talented junior-ish designer—not a kid, and definitely not a real grown-up, but something in between—who seems able to nail everything on the first try. Not just the dust jackets for hardbacks or the covers for paperbacks, but also promotional bookmarks and one-sheets and web banner ads and all the other detritus that's constantly thrown at designers by marketing, publicity, and sales, an endless array of tactics trying to differentiate one new book from the hundreds of thousands of others published every year.

Jeff had a one-night-stand with Ashleigh a few months ago. It was one of those maudlin going-away nights, a farewell party for an ancient sales rep who'd been on the road during the Nixon Administration. After three or four or five rounds, a half-dozen of the unmarrieds—though not all of these people single, precisely—moved from the quiet up-market going-away pub to a loud down-market getting-drunk one. There were greasy burgers, and ultimately an offer to share a taxi, and then backseat groping, and superfluous vodka-rocks in her tiny apartment . . .

The elevator doors open, releasing them both from the special hell of sharing an elevator with an ill-advised sexual partner, into the cramped, unattended lobby, then the bright sunshine.

"Well," Ashleigh says, "that sure was fun. Bye."

Jeff can't think of anything clever to say before the girl walks away. He stares after her for a few seconds, feeling sorry, though he's not sure about what, exactly.

Then he too starts walking through Union Square's riot of exuberant youth—the summer-school students from NYU and the New School and Parsons, the high-school kids cutting classes, the young underemployed adults and disheveled grad-school matriculants, the street artists and musicians and dancers and chess players, banging on their clocks and checking out the girls who walk by, and dog owners at the dog run, checking out one another. In the playground, bordered by a parking lot of imported strollers, the benches are occupied by groups of well-off-looking white parents alternating with clusters of nannies arranged by their lands of origin—South America, Tibet, the Caribbean—watching their charges with widely varying levels of vigilance. To the east, a decidedly shiftier element dominates, drug dealers and users, crazies shouting profanities, wild-eyed shirtless men tossing garbage into the grass. Skateboarders perform recklessly along the southern steps, where beat cops maintain a lax distance, not incentivized to intervene in any mere misdemeanors. They're here for the felonies.

Jeff walks away from the park, into tree-lined Greenwich Village, trudging through the quiet streets at a steady pace, losing himself in *The Accident*. He can't help but plot out ways to improve the manuscript, crafting the editorial letter in his mind: passages that should be shortened, or deleted entirely; redundancies to be tightened; vocabulary choices that are used repeatedly, ill-advisedly; staccato sentences that ought be lengthened, and unwieldy run-ons that should be subdivided into more manageable lengths. There are elements of the end of the story, he expects, that might be teased earlier, maybe cutting in a different timeline to the otherwise straight chronology. In many books, there are things that should be said at the beginning, about the end. And vice versa.

Can this book actually be true? Completely true? And should its veracity—or lack of—influence his behavior? If some of it is true, how much? And if it's a decent amount that's true—if any of the important events did indeed happen—then does it matter if some of it is untrue, or exaggerated? What's the core essence of the story . . . ?

And is Isabel serious about ten-plus million dollars? In that case—in any case—will Bradford be willing—will Brad be eager—to acquire it? Every month the rumors get more insistent, the chatter gets louder, about a sellout to one of the multinationals. It has become practically deafening, and some speculation even made it into *Publishers Weekly*. Will Brad want to gamble big money while his company is being yanked from under him? Will he want to gamble big money *because* his company is being yanked? Being bought by Wolfe Worldwide Media, of all the goddamned outfits in the world?

And will this manuscript bring an end to the recent unsuccessful interlude in Jeff's career? The part where he has sat in ed-board meetings, not paying any attention, nor being paid any attention?

Jeff has an ex-wife on the other side of the continent. He has arthritis in both knees, and wiry gray hairs growing out of his ears, and a prostate that's beginning to worry him. But he still manages to think of his life as something that's just getting underway; he's still willing to believe that he's on the upslope.

And, of course, can he really pursue this manuscript? Or will he have to destroy it?

"Again and again, I find myself telling these guys"—all Dan's clients are apparently guys—"that if anyone else can write the book, *you* shouldn't. The first step is to ask: what's the one book in the world you're best qualified to write?"

The guy has been pontificating for thirty minutes now, his leg jiggling under the table; he's one of those inveterate leg-jigglers. Jeff wants to fasten the damn thing in place with a nail gun.

"What's the single story that can be told by only one person in the world—*you*?"

At this, Jeff looks up from his food, stares into the distance. Who's the one possible most likely author in the world for *The Accident*? Every legitimate news outlet in America—as well as plenty of nonlegit ones—have poked and prodded through Charlie Wolfe's past, interviewing ex-girlfriends and schoolmates and law-school classmates, colleagues and rivals, friends and foes. The author of *The Accident* would have called the same sources who'd been called before, by people from the *New York Times* and the *Wall Street Journal* and the *Washington Post*, from CNN and ABC and FOX, from *Salon* and the *Huffington Post* . . . Sooner or later, all these sources would've stopped confirming credentials. So if someone called who wasn't who he was pretending to be, these sources wouldn't even notice, much less do anything about it.

And whoever wrote *The Accident* would've had access that none of the other journalists ever had. He would've unearthed some game-changing secrets, and for some reason would've held on to those secrets until now . . . Why? *Who?*

Jeff feels his phone vibrating in his pocket. He hates answering in the middle of meals, or meetings, but because of the manuscript he's afraid to miss calls—from Isabel, or from Brad, or from who knows. Plus he could really use a break from this blowhard.

"Oh go ahead," Dan says, eagerly retrieving his own device from the clip on his belt. "I should check e-mail."

Jeff excuses himself, stands, looks at the phone as he walks away from the table. "Hey," he says. It was Isabel's name on the small screen. "I'm at lun—"

"I need to see you."

"Everything okay?"

"When will you be finished?"

"Um, I don't know. Twenty minutes?"

"Then you're going back to the office?"

"Yes. Isabel, is everything okay?"

"No . . . listen . . . I'll meet you at your office in a half-hour. Okay?"

Jeff has a premonition of a tidal wave sneaking up behind him, a hundred-foot-high wall of water moving at fifty miles per hour.

On Bleecker Street Jeff notices Naomi Berger leaning against a lamppost, seemingly staring off into nothingness in the dappled light under a towering London planetree. They exchange quick cheek kisses, but they don't hug; they're business acquaintances, not friends.

"I hope you're not waiting for Borders to come by," Jeff says, "make you an offer for the store. You know they went out of business, right?"

She laughs, in that way that people laugh when something isn't funny. "Having a book party tonight," she says. "Waiting for the wine guy to return. He got chased around the corner by a traffic cop." She waves her arm in the direction of a meter maid who's sauntering up the shady street, window-shopping amid striped awnings and plate-glass windows and young women walking in and out of boutiques, carrying sturdy shopping bags with braided-rope handles. "They're donating the wine, and I don't want their delivery guy to get a parking ticket to boot. That would make me just too damned unappealing, don't you think?"

Jeff has sympathy for Naomi, and her bookshop, one of the better respected independents in town, among a dwindling population. It must be difficult for her to remain solvent, and it's a crucial business for the publishing community, for Jeff's livelihood. Neighborhood bookstores aren't merely places for customers to purchase products from retailers; they're where readers discover authors, where kids discover reading. Discoverability is what keeps the book business alive.

"Nothing could make you unappealing, Naomi Berger. Everyone loves you."

He thinks he sees her blush under all those freckles. She turns her eyes down to the sidewalk, but doesn't say anything. Sometime about a decade ago, Naomi had popped up in front of Jeff at a party, late at night, all smiles and laughs and even a wink. After a flirty five-minute conversation, it was clear to Jeff that this woman was angling for intimacy. He quickly pecked her on the cheek and ran away. He knew that Naomi was close friends with Isabel.

"Well, nice to see you," he says. "Have a good party."

Jeff continues up the street, around a corner, and walks five steps past the hardware store before he remembers the washer in his pocket that needs replacing. Perhaps if he behaves as if his normal life is ongoing, then maybe it will be. He pauses on the sidewalk for a second, but decides it's more important—much more important—to solve his career problem, to deal with this manuscript, than to solve his plumbing problem. He needs to return to the office. So he keeps walking for another few steps before he admits that now that it's on his mind, he should just stop for a minute and buy this goddamned little thing.

He turns around, retraces his steps while fingering the corroded ring of metal in his pocket. A vaguely familiar man is approaching, but doesn't make eye contact, and continues past on the sidewalk, staring straight ahead.

Jeff feels his stomach fall away, his body flooding with panic.

He walks into the small cluttered shop, his brain clamoring at this development, and absentmindedly spends forty cents on two washers.

He takes out his phone, dials the number. When the man answers, Jeff asks, without preamble, "Are you having me followed?"

There's a lot of static on the line, but no voice. Jeff thinks the call may have been dropped, so he takes the device from his ear, looks at the screen, then hears "No" from the little speaker. "Why do you ask?"

"I'm pretty sure I just saw a man on the sidewalk who was in a restaurant with me this morning."

The man doesn't respond. "I know exactly where you are, without following you."

Jeff looks up at the streetscape, the humongous brownstone Italianate houses, the smaller red brick Federal ones, the awninged doormanned apartment buildings. "This guy is not one of yours?"

Even through the thick static, Jeff can hear the man sigh. "I'm afraid not."

"What should I do?"

"Be *careful*."

He stops into a café, orders a coffee, struggling to distribute the weight of the bag that's tugging his shoulder, heavy from the manuscript plus the unwieldy bound galleys that Dan foisted upon him, advance reader's editions of books that Jeff absolutely does not intend to read. Fuck it, he thinks. He takes the paper-bound galleys out of his bag and deposits them on the café's counter, now communal reading material along with various sections of more than one newspaper, and a few magazines, and the ubiquitous flyers for a guitar teacher.

He negotiates his café exit at the same time as the entrance of a woman pushing a stroller, a whimpering infant strapped inside. This woman is clearly at the very end of her rope, tear tracks down her cheeks, haggard and disheveled, wearing sweatpants and a T-shirt splattered with spit-up, the odor of baby powder trying to mask something funkier. Jeff holds the door for her, and she manages to project thank-you into the raise of her eyebrows. But no small act of kindness is going to make a dent in this woman's despair, not today.

Jeff takes a sip through the sip-top, scalds his tongue.

He glances up and down the street, looking again for that familiar man, or anyone else who might be following him. He walks the width of the sidewalk, and steps to the curb, down into the gutter, to cross the street.

In the middle of the street, his bag strap slips off his shoulder, and yanks his arm downward, sloshing hot coffee out of the cup onto the back of his hand. He mutters *"Fuck"* and looks down at his hand, then up again at a growling sound coming from his left, a car tearing up the street, accelerating as it approaches.

CHAPTER 23

Camilla starts reading while the car is pulling away from the curb. She reads through the stop-and-go traffic of the surface streets, then through the clogged Holland Tunnel, which usually seems too long— can the Hudson River really be this wide? But today she doesn't notice. She reads as the Town Car hums over the gritty black ironworks of the Pulaski Skyway, skimming over the New Jersey swamps, skirting the ominous idea of downtown Newark.

She is still engrossed as the car comes to a stop. The driver leans back to hand her the paperwork. "Miss?"

Camilla looks up. "Oh! So sorry." She takes the little clipboard, signs the voucher. She tucks the manuscript into her tote and climbs out onto the well-policed curb in front of the terminal. She looks around at the passengers in ticketing: the run-of-the-mill business travelers, the college students, the tourists—a normal assortment—who are complemented by passengers bound for both Tel Aviv and Mumbai, with clusters of Hassidim and Hindi in dueling observant-religious garb, strewn around the vast hall. It looks as if the extras for two different period movies have both been called to the same soundstage, milling around, trying to figure out who's responsible for the mix-up.

She arrives at the gate an hour before departure. Peers into her tote at the three-ring binder filled with supporting material for McNally's next-spring list. Camilla is always living six to twelve months in the future, in the space occupied by next Christmas, next New-Year-New-You promotion, next Mother's Day promotion, next summer-beach-read roundup. After a decade of living in next year, and the following year, Camilla has lost the ability to keep reliable track of when exactly it is, right now.

None of the books on next spring's list, in that binder, will be worth anything to anyone in Hollywood. So they're not worth anything to her. Instead she pulls out the anonymous manuscript again.

This is the part of her job that she loves, the part that she'll miss: sitting in an airport or a bar or at her desk, one of the first readers of a not-yet-published manuscript, just a bunch of loose letter-size pages in her hands, which less than a year later will be typeset and printed and trimmed and bound, shipped in sturdy little manageable-size cartons around the country—around the world—and shelved in thousands of stores, in bookstores and big-box mega-marts and gift shops, on new-title tables and in window displays, on bestseller lists in dozens of languages.

And it all begins here, one person at a time reading something that can't be put down. In the past year, Camilla began reading hundreds of manuscripts; she looked at hundreds of page 1's. For at least half of those manuscripts, though, she never got to page 2.

When her boarding group is called, Camilla is on page 109. As the plane pulls away from the gate, her eyes are racing down page 138. At liftoff she's on 146, and she holds her breath and feels a shiver run down her spine, and she knows that this is it.

This is how it happens: you spend your life reading, reading, and reading more, waiting, waiting, and waiting for something to be incredible. Each manuscript you start could be it, but thousands upon thousands aren't. And then one day, always hoped-for but never expected, there it is.

When he finally stopped throwing up, Charlie plopped
down onto the tarmac. He sat there in the drizzle,
shaking his head in disbelief. "Fuck." He wiped his
chin with the back of his hand, cleaning away his
vomit. "What happened, exactly?"

Dave turned away from the car and looked at his
friend. "Don't you remember?"

"Not entirely."

"What? What *do* you remember?"

Charlie shook his head.

"Do you remember being back at the bar?"

"Yes."

"What, exactly?"

"I remember a lot, up until I went to the
bathroom . . . Then I couldn't find you guys. I
went upstairs and there you were, and some girl was
talking to me but I was too drunk . . . So I left
her, I went to sit down . . ."

Charlie put his head in his hands. "And I
remember driving . . ." He started sobbing. "And
then everything went black . . . And then I killed
her."

Neither boy said anything for a minute. Then Dave
said, "Yes. It looks like you did."

Charlie wiped tears away from both cheeks,
snuffled. He stood. He glanced around, then back at
Dave. "We have to get out of here."

Charlie walked to the front of the car, examined
the grille, squatted down and looked at the
undercarriage. He turned to the side of the road,

looked at the heavy brush and trees. "We can . . .
Let's get her . . . let's hide her."

"What?"

"We have to get out of here, Dave. But first we
have to get her out of sight. In there." Charlie
put his hand on Dave's shoulder. "We have to get
her body into the brush."

"Why?"

"Goddamnit, Dave, we don't have *time* to debate
this. Just help me."

"What are you talking about?"

Charlie looked Dave in the eye, searching. "You
know what we have to do."

"We're going to hide the body and run away?"

"We don't have a choice. I'm not going to jail
for this."

Dave opened his mouth slightly, but then shut his
lips, clamped his jaw. He nodded.

Charlie knelt and grabbed the girl's ankles.
Dave clutched the wrists. Together they dragged her
body, with her rear end scraping across the tarmac
and then the weedy grass at the edge of the road.

Upon closer examination the first layer of brush
wasn't that heavy, certainly not dense enough
to hide a body. They'd have to go into the dark
underbrush, where it looked like after a few feet
the land might drop off. Perhaps there was a ravine
or something back there, the reason that the road
curved, following the path of water. Maybe there
was even a gorge, deep and untraveled.

"We have to go farther," Charlie said. He pushed
his way through the thicket, which after a few feet

opened up into a moss-floored clearing, and then a few steps later there was indeed a steep drop. It was too dark to see the bottom.

"Okay," Charlie said. They both took a final sidestep to the edge. "On three."

The two boys looked at each other, a quick painful glance.

Charlie counted one, and they swung her outward. Two, and they swung her back. Three, swinging her out over the empty space, letting go, and then the lifeless body was flying through the air, and then they heaerd the sound of branches cracking and crunching, thuds and crushing and sliding, dirt and pebbles tumbling.

And then it was silent in the still night. But the sickening sounds were reverberating in their memories.

CHAPTER 24

"Two problems," the man says, without any pleasantries. "First is that the young woman—the assistant—had to be, ah . . ."

Hayden covers his eyes with the hand that isn't holding the satellite phone. He's strapped into a bench on a military transport that took off from northeastern Germany, a quick helicopter ride from Copenhagen across the Baltic to the airfield near the Polish border. This will be a long flight to New York, with no doubt a long night on the other end.

"What happened?"

"She returned home unexpectedly while the item was being recovered."

"*Unexpectedly.*" Hayden never kidded himself that there'd be no collateral damage, no civilians harmed. But he wasn't expecting it this early, so far removed from the primary players. This doesn't bode well. "What does that *mean*?"

Silence.

"Does that mean there was no *lookout*?" He presses his fingers into his brow, trying to massage away the pain of this bad news. "No *backup*?"

"Yes sir. That's what it means."

"I see. And the item?"

"Retrieved. Will be waiting for you upon arrival."

Whew. At least there was that. "Okay. You said there were two problems."

"That subsidiary rights director at the publishing house? Camilla Glyndon-Browning? She's on a commercial flight to LAX. As far as we can tell, her first order of business is to meet with a film producer named Stan Balzer. The agenda of this meeting?"

"*No.*"

"I'm sorry, yes. We were able to intercept her confirmation phone call, through sheer luck: she happened to be within range of the editor's transmitter."

"So the editor *gave* Glyndon-Browning a copy?" That wouldn't make sense.

"Actually, it seems like she might've stolen it."

"Oh for the love of God." Do people in publishing houses really steal things from each other?

"What do you want to do about this situation, sir?"

Hayden allows his head to fall back, stretching his neck muscles. "Do we know what Glyndon-Browning is *do*ing, after she deplanes? I mean in terms of transport? Hotel?"

"Yes. We've located her rental-car reservation, and she's booked into a small hotel in Beverly Hills."

"And do we know what she looks like? What she's wearing? Et cetera?"

"Affirmative."

"Do we have someone on the ground in LA? To take care of this?"

"We have Cooper."

Cooper; that's too bad. The guy is dumb as a rock. Hayden's mind runs rapidly through the alternatives. Or, rather, through the possible excuses to reject the only viable alternative. But he comes up blank. "That meeting can't happen," he concludes. "And that copy of the item must be retrieved. And destroyed. The woman too."

"Yes sir." A pause. "Lethal finding?"

This is not how it's supposed to go, not at all. But the situation could spiral out of control, quickly. There's no telling what other producers the woman may have lined up to pitch. One day, two days, and there would be nothing left Hayden could do to contain the manuscript. It would be out there, there would be a book deal or a film deal or both, the deal or deals would be reported same-day on some industry online gossip mill, and then picked up overnight and run in a New York tabloid in the morning, and by midday the online *Times* and AP would have run it, by afternoon it'd be on CNN and CNBC, and the major networks at the 6:30 broadcasts, all within twenty-four to thirty-six hours of this moment, this decision, right now, if he doesn't give the instruction for some dimwitted goon to murder a poor civilian.

"Yes," Hayden says. He has no choice. "Lethal finding confirmed."

"Nothing."

"Nothing?" Hayden puts down his book, a new paperback in German, about a well-known nineteenth-century art dealer. He shifts the sat-phone to his other hand, his better ear. Not much of him is falling apart—he's in remarkably good shape, better than he expected to be by this point in his life—but his hearing in his right ear isn't as strong as it once was.

"Well," Kate says, "not *zero* information. There's plenty of material on Grundtvig's hard drive about Charlie Wolfe and his company and associates and whatnot. But there's nothing here that gives any lead on what we're looking for. No record of his bank account, nor connections to anyone who could be our subject. At least none that I've been able to find so far. And I'm pretty sure I've unearthed everything recent."

Hayden sighs.

"I'm not entirely finished, though," she says, holding out the glimmer of hope. Kate isn't an irrationally optimistic person, but she does try to be supportive. Of Hayden, of herself. She doesn't admit that something is a complete failure until it is a fully completed and indisputable failure.

"You someplace safe?" he asks.

"Safe. Quiet. Completely bereft of anything that could resemble charm."

He can see it, the plasterboard walls and creaky plywood floors under musty orange wall-to-wall, a lumpy mattress, a tiny shower stall with a plastic folding door. There's an awful lot of beauty in Europe, but there's also no shortage of ugly.

Hayden is sure that Kate is wondering why she can't be comfortably ensconced in the elegant apartment in downtown Copenhagen, instead of in some fleabag rest-area motel. But she understands that she's not allowed to ask.

Which is good. Hayden doesn't particularly want to lie to Kate more than is absolutely necessary.

"The tallest people in the world, Kate, are the Dutch. Average adult height is six-one—that's men *and* women, combined average. And second are the Danish, at six-even."

"Oh, come on," she says. "People in Northern Europe are tall? You're slipping, Hayden. I give that a three."

"No one would *blame* you, Kate, for feeling particularly short in Denmark. Perhaps inadequate?"

She laughs. "I'll call you if I find anything," she says, and ends the connection.

When he rehired Kate last year, he never provided her with any specifics about what exact office she was working for, nor how she fit into the organizational structure of the Central Intelligence Agency's European operations. She seemed to accept that she didn't need to fill out any new paperwork, nor undergo any psychological exams or medical screening or physical training. After all, she'd been a CIA employee for nearly two decades before she resigned, and spent a couple of years as a stay-at-home expat mother. It made sense to her that she could be rehired simply, without a lot of fuss and bother, by a man in Hayden's position.

She has no reason to think that it isn't the CIA she's working for. But it isn't. Langley doesn't know a damn thing about Kate, or her team, or this mission. They never have, and Hayden hopes that they never will.

CHAPTER 25

He parks under a towering tree on the steep hill, and walks over to the pedestrian-only street called Oberstrasse, a sidewalk really, interspersed with stairs and switchbacks, with a street sign and a proper name, and a funicular running alongside. He opens the gate to the terraced garden, and attempts a half-smile at the belligerent-looking hausfrau who always seems to be lurking in the garden or the front hall, staring disapprovingly, nodding reluctantly. He takes the tiny lift up to the third floor of the tall house, terraces and turrets, dormer windows under gabled eaves.

There's only one door up here, already ajar, awaiting the new client on the hour. The two men shake hands in the waiting room, then settle into the office.

"So." The therapist pushes up his lips, pressing his cheekbones up under his eyes. But the result is more a squint than a smile; Dr. Studer isn't very good at smiling. It doesn't seem to be an area of particular expertise here in Zurich. "Tell me, Herr Carner: what is new?"

The author shifts in his chair. Even after a few months of this, he's still uncomfortable with the practice of psychotherapy. He has never been a believer. Plus he can't help but think that it's futile, considering all the truths he cannot tell. But he grew up in New York City in the 1970s, when for certain types of people psychiatry seemed to be as required as inoculations and preventive dentistry. So when he found himself with time on his hands, and emotional issues to tackle, and no price-sensitivity, he found Dr. Studer here. It has been of very marginal benefit.

"Last week I completed that big project," the author says. "After a long time working nonstop. It's now off my chest, off my desk. In someone else's hands."

"And how does this make you feel?"

"At first I felt great. Elated. I felt . . . *accomplished*. But then that happiness, it ebbed away quickly, over the weekend. The project that been my mission was suddenly no longer the thing that defined my daily routine, my reason to exist in the world. And now I have none."

"So you are having difficulties finding focus? For your life?"

"I'm having difficulties *justifying* my life. I'm . . . not proud, I guess would be an understated way of saying it, of certain things I've done."

Studer nods.

"I've engaged in major, ah, *mis*representations, about some important events."

The author struggles with his own vagueness. He knows he hasn't been a particularly forthcoming patient, probably an unsatisfying two hours per week in the life of this inscrutable psychiatrist. Even though he felt compelled to try this process, he was sort of hoping that he could just show up to an office and have someone else do the actual work, someone with advanced degrees and board-certified specialties, someone who could diagnose what was wrong and prescribe how to fix it. Perhaps with a pill and some, whatever, stretching exercises.

"There was this thing that happened, back in college—at university. That was the first major instance."

"Of?"

"Of, um . . ." There's an idea just beyond the tip of his consciousness . . . "Of, I guess, *redefining* reality. Of taking an event, and just sort of turning it into something else. Something advantageous, instead of dis-."

He suspects that the doctor has no idea what this means, but neither

165

of them particularly cares. They're not here for the doctor to learn things; the point is the patient's enlightenment.

"I came to the realization that all events, all facts, were to some extent negotiable. And throughout my life, this concept, this ever-present opportunity, took increasing control of my consciousness, and my career. I've spent the past two decades negotiating reality. Manipulating other people's perceptions of it."

Studer looks like a lecture student who has lost the thread of the professor's argument, but is hoping that the topic will expire without anyone asking him any questions.

"I've led a dishonest life. An *amoral* life. And sadly there aren't very many people who care, on a personal level. I'm childless and divorced, and have pretty much no relationship with my ex-wife. My father died a long time ago. And Mom, she sort of washed her hands of me. I still see her once a year, but we don't really talk.

"I don't think there's anything I can do, on a personal level, to improve anything with anyone, and I accept that. But on an impersonal level, I'm finding my legacy . . . um . . . unpalatable."

Studer nods vigorously. "And you would like to *set the record straight*, as they say." He seems relieved to be returning the conversation to a more practical level.

"Yes, I do."

"And may I ask, Herr Carner: Why? Why do you want to set the record straight?"

"Because I want to do the right thing. For once."

"*Is* it the right thing? Will it *help* anyone?"

The author doesn't respond.

"Or will it serve only to assuage—is this the correct word?"

"It is."

"To *assuage* your conscience?"

He has wondered exactly the same thing, many times. Every day. But he already made the decision, irrevocable.

They drove wordlessly through the quiet streets
near the lake, then into downtown. Charlie was
becoming more sober by the second. The bright red
color was draining from his cheeks, and instead he
was looking increasingly ashen.

   They pulled to a stop at a red traffic light.
The car was facing in the direction of their
university, up at the top of the hill. But Charlie
was gazing off to the side.

   "My father is over there," he said. "In that
hotel."

   The two boys stared at the unremarkable structure
a few blocks away.

   "He'll know what to do," Charlie said.

   "Um . . . Are you sure?"

   "I am. I think."

   So Dave pulled the vintage Jaguar around a corner
and into a mostly empty parking lot. They walked
as calmly as they could through the lobby, to the
elevator. Charlie pushed the button for the top
floor. He looked down at his feet and noticed a
blood spatter on the top of one of his boat shoes.
He knelt down to wipe it up, but he realized he
had nothing to wipe with. He paused, thinking,
then rubbed the splotch with his thumb until it
looked like just another commonplace splotch on an
unremarkable shoe.

CHAPTER 26

"Jesus!"

Isabel pushes the door open. "Get in," she says.

"What the—?"

"Get. In."

Jeffrey stands there, dumbstruck, not moving, his coffee toppled at his feet, his bag strap tugging at the crook of his arm.

"Goddamnit Jeffrey! Get the *fuck* in this car! *Right now!*"

He finally obeys, folding himself into the taxi, panic all over his face.

Isabel turns her attention back to the driver, who's staring at her in the rearview. "It's okay," she tries to reassure him. "We're just . . . you know."

The driver doesn't respond.

"Herald Square, please."

"What's going on?" Jeffrey demands. "Where are we going? Did you say Herald Square?"

Isabel yanks a notepad out of her purse. "What do you think of the manuscript?" she asks, but doesn't pay attention to Jeffrey's answer as she scribbles, and thrusts the pad at him:

This a.m. at b'fast did a stranger interact w/ you? Touch you?

He reads, nods, writes: *Borrowed my pen.*

Is pen w/ you?

He reaches into his breast pocket, holds up the Sheaffer for her to see.

"So are you going to want to publish the thing?" she asks aloud, continuing to scribble. "Or not?"

They're listening.

Jeffrey looks shaken. "I'm definitely intrigued," he says. "but . . ."

She writes again: *My asst Alexis just murdered.*

"I know," she says, staring at Jeffrey as he reads her note, mouth falling open into an O, brow deeply furrowed. "There are an awful lot of buts."

The traffic leading into Herald Square is a mass-merge of taxis and trucks and angry impatient drivers of jumbo SUVs with Jersey plates, leaning on their horns pointlessly.

Isabel takes her compact out of her handbag. She holds up the mirror, surveys the reflection out the back windshield. The white Toyota, which was a few cars back when they were down in the Village, became entangled in traffic in north Chelsea, and is now nearly a block back and a few lanes over.

"Driver, this is good," Isabel says, placing another ten-dollar bill in the pass-through. She pushes out the door, and turns to check on Jeffrey, and the Toyota. She thinks she can see the passenger watching her, buzz-cut and sunglassed, across the stalled rows of glinting steel, the air shimmering with exhaust.

They leave the loud bright sunny avenue onto a shady side street, the sidewalk crowded with late-lunchtime jovial groups spilling out of the restaurants in another of the city's micro-neighborhoods, Koreatown.

Isabel looks back over her shoulder, and sees the Toyota's passenger wending his way through the stop-and-go of Sixth Avenue, pursuing.

"Come on," she urges Jeffrey, "let's go." She picks up her pace, sidesteps a group of tourists gawking up. They hustle down the street, a half-block ahead of their lone pursuer. The car will still be stuck in traffic.

At Fifth Avenue she grabs Jeffrey's wrist, yanks him around the corner, another sun-splashed wide avenue with broad sidewalks, with buses and taxis, trucks and motorcycles, whiffs of diesel mingling with the aromas of honey-roasted peanuts and hot dogs soaking in their salty steel baths under striped umbrellas. Fifth Avenue is thick with crowds of visitors from all over the globe, cameras and guidebooks, pamphlets and maps, milling and staring up and snapping photos of the most famous building in America.

"Here," she says, ushering Jeffrey through the doors and into the lobby and to the counter. She hands over her credit card and collects the tickets.

Isabel had been here before, not terribly long ago, with Tommy. The little boy used to regularly ask, "Mommy, when can we go to the top of the world?" She didn't know exactly what he meant, what he was asking to be allowed to do. But she figured this experience was as close as possible to that elusive ideal.

On that prior visit, she learned that if there was one worthwhile extra expense in this already extravagant city, it was paying a premium for the express ticket that grants cutting-the-line privileges; there are a lot of lines here, and they're all long. So now she and Jeffrey enter the special queue for the cutting-the-liners.

Isabel nods at the x-ray machine and the metal-detector, glances around at the large police presence in the Art Deco lobby. "We're getting ourselves some privacy, and some safety. I'm sure that the guy following us is armed."

"There's a guy following us?"

"And unless he's willing to ditch his weapon, he's not going to be able to keep up with us. Plus I'm sure he didn't preorder tickets."

Jeffrey is spinning his head around, looking for the pursuer.

"Plus we're about to find out if he's an actual law-enforcement officer, in which case he'll flash his badge."

That man is standing at the lobby's front doors, trying to figure out how to proceed. He puts a cell phone to his ear, starts talking. Isabel feels like she should wink at him, or nod. But this is not a game, not at all. So she turns away, before she's tempted to make eye contact.

Then she turns back quickly, an instant flash of recognition, something about the way the guy is standing, and she realizes: this is the delivery messenger, the person who brought the manuscript to her office. Is he now pursuing her?

She joins Jeffrey for the feet-shuffling march to the elevator, tries to breathe normally during the long ascent, then steps out into a highly unscenic floor and then up again and out into the bright sunshine, again, this time on the 102nd floor of the Empire State Building.

They stand there perched at the top of the world, a quarter-mile into the sky, with the city spread beneath, the rivers and harbor and ocean, the buildings and highways and bridges, the endless sprawls of Queens and Jersey.

Isabel explains her plan cursorily, in this panicked and rushed state, scrawling on a notepad in the middle of all these people, all this sunshine and wind. She can see that Jeffrey doesn't completely understand her, and doesn't know if he should—if he can—commit to this course of action.

You have a better idea? she writes. She shoves the pad at him.

He turns his eyes away from the expansive view, and glances down. He shakes his head. The wind whips into the notepad, fluttering the pages.

Isabel holds up her hand, bends her fingers, beckoning something. Jeffrey nods. He reaches into his pocket, removes his pen, places it on the ledge.

"Ready?" she asks.

He doesn't look okay, nor ready. But he says, "Sure. Let's go."

They turn away from his antique Sheaffer, bound to be discovered within seconds by some stranger, pocketed, toted along to somewhere else. They make their way quickly through the thick shifting crowds and down the elevator and out into the street. Isabel doesn't see the white Toyota, but she doesn't spend a lot of time looking. It doesn't really matter.

They hustle around one corner and then another, picking their way through the midafternoon crowds of this low-rent version of Midtown,

171

stale air being pushed through the revolving doors from the low-ceilinged claustrophobic lobbies of nondescript buildings occupied by vocational schools and shady accountants and cut-rate matrimonial attorneys, with barbers providing ten-dollar haircuts and delis selling five-dollar lunches.

They descend into the damp chill of the subway tunnels, the burst of wind that precedes the screaming arrival of the uptown local, then after few stops exit directly into the basement of Bloomingdale's. They fight through the aggressive and nauseating gauntlet of Fragrance, and into the nakedly crass ogling at Jewelry. Isabel looks around at the women leaning on the counters, engrossed in their assessments of gold and silver, watches and necklaces.

An overweight woman is examining a trio of bracelets sitting on a black velvet pad. A large forest-green bag dangles from the woman's chunky shoulder, the bag's maw wide open. Isabel pauses at the counter. She reaches into her handbag and removes her mobile phone, a familiar plastic presence in her palm.

"They're beautiful," Isabel says to the woman, who smiles at her quickly, nonplussed, then turns away. Isabel slides her phone gently into the woman's green bag, and slinks away.

They arrive at the relative irrelevance of Men's Accessories, and exit through revolving doors back into daylight. Across a street and around a corner and through the cavernous lobby of a recently constructed tower, glass and steel and marble and soaring negative space, an architecture that practically smells of the relentless optimism of 2005, the cockiness that there would never be anything other than reliably and rapidly escalating real-estate values, ever again.

Out the far side and around a corner and suddenly out of Midtown, on a completely residential block, nineteenth-century brownstone townhouses and linden trees and small fluffy dogs at the ends of expensive leather leashes.

Isabel climbs a wide staircase to an etched-glass doorway flanked by ornately carved potted topiary. She rings the doorbell, and barely a second passes before the door is opened by an explosively smiling young man, all white teeth and an aggressive flip of blond, holding an iPad.

"Isabel Reed?!" he exclaims, and leans in for a cheek kiss, sort of, with skin not quite grazing, lips barely pursing, and no part of him actually touching any part of Isabel. "She's expecting you?!" Glancing down at his touch screen, panicked.

"She's not. I'm sorry. But it's, um, urgent."

"Absolutely! Give me two shakes?!"

The guy turns and takes a couple of steps away and covers his mouth to speak, indecipherable, into his headset. Isabel notices that his suit pants are cuffed high above the ankle, and he's not wearing any socks under his wingtips. "Isabel?" He turns back. "It's no problem! She's down in the office?!"

They walk through the marble-floored foyer, between identical console tables with matching arrangements of densely packed purple tulips, hundreds of them, passing the wide arched door to a hyper-decorated sitting room, wallpaper and throw blankets and a half-dozen area rugs, settees and ottomans and highly glossed occasional tables.

The assistant turns a carved brass knob and opens a painted paneled door, and the three of them descend to the garden level, glossy white tile floors overlaid by matte white rugs, white furniture with glass and steel, white flowers in white vases, a half-dozen cubicles on either side of a long white-walled corridor. An iOffice. And taking up the full width of the rear of the house, the main suite is another study in various gloss levels of white, and opens through a massive wall of casement windows to the garden, teak furniture and stone statuary and rows and layers and heights of greens.

It's a serene garden back there, behind this perfect house presided over by this shockingly attractive woman who's now embracing Isabel, more air kisses, smiles, an upper-arm rub, "*So* good to see you."

"Judy Thompson, this is Jeffrey Fielder."

The doyenne reaches out her braceleted hand for a handshake, a smile, a nod. Judy turns to Isabel. "He's cute. Is he yours?"

Isabel glances at Jeffrey, who's suddenly staring at his feet, blushing.

"I guess." Isabel herself can't help but smile. "Sort of. Now and then."

"Please," Judy says, "have a seat."

The personal assistant plus a couple of other minions retreat wordlessly down the corridor.

Isabel takes a white leather chair, soft armrests, perfectly shaped back.

"Patrick tells me it's something urgent, Isabel. How can I help?"

Isabel takes a deep breath. "I know this is strange, Judy, but: could I borrow the beach house, for a night, or two?"

Judy has offered this house before; Isabel is pretty sure she's welcome to it, circumstances permitting. "Of course, Isabel. Of *course*."

Isabel has sometimes found it difficult with her clients to clearly demarcate the line between professional and personal. But it only ever seems to be a problem with the ultra-successful, filthy rich clients, whose fame and fortune don't come from their books; rather the books follow as a consequence of their other successes. Isabel has quite a few of these clients, Judy here first and foremost among them. Some agents—and some editors too—conflate the relationship with these types of celebrities, and begin to imagine that they too belong in the same summer-house communities, tasting-menu restaurants, and airplane cabins as their multimillionaire clientele. Isabel is conscientious about not making this pretense. But she really needs Judy's resources, now. And not for rubbing shoulders.

"And I know this is, um, unusual, but what about a car?"

Judy snorts a laugh, a surprisingly indelicate noise coming from this famously proper woman. "Please, don't be shy. Is there anything else I can offer?"

"Now that you mention it," Isabel says, "I wouldn't mind any cash you happen to have."

Judy laughs again, but Isabel doesn't.

"Are you serious?"

Isabel nods.

"What's going on?"

"Listen, Judy, I'm scared," Isabel says. "I have a dangerous manuscript, and I'm worried that people are following me. That they want to *kill* me."

Judy's eyebrows raise. "What's the book about?"

"I'd rather not say. For your safety."

Judy knows Charlie, of course. Judy Thompson herself is a version of Charlie Wolfe, a different type of media mogul, with an eponymous magazine and a television show and consumer product lines and prepared foods, plus a decade's worth of book deals on five continents. She hasn't written a single word of any of her dozen books, possibly not even the acknowledgments. But she has deposited a lot of large checks.

"Fair enough," Judy says. "You're afraid to go the police?"

"For all I know, it's the police who're following me. Some form of police, anyway."

"What about going on television? I could help with that, you know."

"Thanks, but I don't have any actual proof of anything. All I have is a manuscript by an anonymous author, and—"

"Anonymous? That's unfortunate."

"And a murdered assistant."

"*What?*"

Isabel struggles to take a deep breath, without crying. She doesn't want to break down now, tries to prevent it, but doesn't really succeed, and the tears spring out of the corners of her eyes, start streaming down her cheeks. "Someone shot Alexis, in her apartment. This morning."

"Oh my Lord. Who?"

Isabel shakes her head, swallows her tears. "And Judy, it's okay if you don't want to be involved . . . I know this is a lot to ask."

Judy gives her a what-are-you-kidding look. "So who's this?" Judy gestures toward Jeffrey, who's standing at the window, staring at into the backyard, silent and unmoving.

"Jeffrey is an editor, and a good friend. I submitted the manuscript to him, this morning. Before I knew that people were going to start *dying*. So I have to assume that Jeffrey also is in danger."

"Did you give a copy to anyone else?"

"I didn't. Jeffrey, did you?"

"Not really," he says, still facing the window.

"What does that mean?"

"I gave Brad a small chunk." Jeffrey turns away from the window, worry etched across his forehead. "Should we warn him?"

"Oh. God, I don't know," Isabel says. "What would we—what would *you*—say?"

"The truth, I guess."

That makes sense, but Isabel doesn't say anything. Instead she leans over Judy's desk and scribbles on a scratch pad, then tears off the sheet. She hands the paper to Judy, who reads it quickly—it's just a couple of lines—and nods.

"Then what?" Judy asks. "Do you have a plan?"

"I don't know. I don't *know*. I just want to . . . I want to go hide."

"Hide? And wait for what?"

Isabel shrugs, then lies: "I'm not sure."

CHAPTER 27

"Hello?"

"Hi Bradford. I don't know how to say this in a way that won't make you panic—"

"Jeffrey, what's—?"

"In fact, actually, you *should* panic."

Brad stares at the LED screen of his complicated landline, displaying the ten digits of a mobile number. "Jeffrey, what's going on?"

"That anonymous manuscript? It was submitted to me by Isabel Reed. You know her?"

"Sure, I know Isabel."

"What about her assistant, Alexis?"

"What about her?"

"Do you know Alexis?"

"No."

"Well, she was murdered this morning, in her apartment."

Brad's heart skips a beat. He forces himself to ask, "You think that has something to do with the manuscript?"

"I do. Isabel does."

"What? Why?"

"Because it can't be coincidence that the morning after the girl finishes reading this bombshell, someone shoots her in the head. In her own apartment."

Brad leans back in his chair, closes his eyes. Is this really happening? "Jeffrey, where are you?"

"Um . . . I'd rather not say."

"Why?"

"Because my phone might be bugged. Or yours, for that matter."

"Bugged? By?"

"Who knows. Listen, Brad, I'm calling to tell you that you might be in danger. I certainly think I am. Be very careful."

Brad stares out at the picture-perfect urban renewal of Union Square. When he was growing up in the 1970s, this park was just another derelict space in a city filled with an assortment of unsavory places. The graffiti'd subway was untenable after dark. Times Square was a pornographic, prostitute-filled cesspool. Most of the major squares—Bryant Park, Tompkins Square Park, Union Square—were Needle Parks, populated by toothless junkies and gold-toothed dealers, broken glass and glassine bags, discarded needles and crumpled packets of Cheetos, menacing teenagers mugging you at knifepoint, taking your wallet, your jacket, your sneakers. "Yo, lemme check out that bike . . ."

Then Brad left for college, followed by a few years bumming around. When he returned to New York, things had changed. Reagan's eighties had deregulated and broadened the paths to extreme wealth while also widening the many routes to abject poverty. There were more rich people in Manhattan, and they were richer than ever, interspersed with new armies of hopelessly poor—homeless, panhandlers, car-window washers. The rich needed new places to live, an expanded geography of luxury. So new residential areas were carved from old industrial ones—SoHo, Tribeca—and gentrification spread like wildfire. An entirely new neighborhood was even constructed in what used to be the Hudson River, built upon landfill excavated to build the World Trade Center.

And Union Square, right here across the street, was cleaned up, anchored by the city's newest largest bookstore on one end and a mega-music store on the other, a farmer's market that seemed to grow every week, a multiplex. Seemingly every retail space alongside the park was replaced; the park itself was replanted and relandscaped, reimagined. The junkies were evicted, mostly, and the square repopulated. To cap it all off, Whole Foods showed up.

McNally & Sons was again in the center of Downtown, just as it had been when it was founded in the 1920s. It had been a long trip to come full circle.

And then a few months ago the agent from the National Security Agency called for the founder's grandson, and asked Sheila for an appointment, but refused to say what it was about. Brad had been curious and a little worried, plus not entirely sure he had the right to refuse. Was it possible that he was employing a suspected terrorist? His mind raced down the hallways, poking in and out of the offices, peering over the dividing wall of every cubicle, trying to remember each face of the hundred people who worked for him.

He thought of one: that junior accountant, Middle Eastern. Brad couldn't remember the guy's name, nor where he was from; probably never knew the latter. He had a vague sense of Lebanon or Syria, but it could just as easily have been Israel, Turkey, Iraq; what the hell did he know from Middle Easterns? Or the guy could've been from Queens, or Atlanta. Brad felt deeply ashamed.

The agent entered politely, giving Brad something of a bow that felt insincere. "I'm Joseph Lyons," he said, shaking hands. The man was older—early sixties, probably—than Brad has expected, which for some reason had been a young thug. And this Lyons was wearing a paisley pocket square, of all damn things.

"Thank you for taking the time, Mr. McNally."

Brad didn't equate pocket squares with badges and guns.

"So, Mr. McNally, I'll get right to it."

"Yes. Please."

"It has come to our attention that some type of biography is being written of the CEO of Wolfe Worldwide Media."

Both men were sitting in wing chairs on either end of the coffee table. Neither had chosen the sofa, whose welcoming embrace projected a certain weakness.

"This manuscript, Mr. McNally, is being written by a freelance journalist who's in hiding in Europe. The project is being directed by a rival media empire, who are paying the journalist what we believe is a million dollars to create this book."

Brad shifted in his seat.

"We suspect that in nearly *all* respects the eventual manuscript will be true. Meticulously researched and factually unassailable, a *thoroughly credible book.*"

Brad now understood that whatever this conversation was about, it was not his employees, nor any existing problem in his private life or his business. No one was working in this office who needed to be watched or fired. Nothing had crossed Brad's desk that needed to be turned over to the feds. This conversation was about something that had yet to enter his world; this conversation was its entrance.

Brad relaxed his shoulders, and released his death-grip on his pen. He glanced down to see that his knuckles were white.

"But there will also be fabrications. We don't have any idea what those fictions will *be*, but we suspect they'll be designed for maximum impact." The agent leaned forward. "The manuscript, Mr. McNally, will be a *hoax.*"

"Why?" Brad was feeling less uncomfortable, enough to start participating in this conversation, albeit monosyllabically.

"The goal is to scandalize Charlie Wolfe, and in fact the whole international enterprise of Wolfe Media, to stage a hostile takeover."

"What? How?"

"By instigating a stock crisis. Wolfe shares are being shorted now, as we speak, building a portfolio that can be cashed out after the crisis hits, for immense profit. Which in turn can be used to take over a company in a calamitous predicament."

"Uh-huh." Brad leaned back in his chair, crossed his legs, and tried to maintain eye contact with Lyons. "What does this have to with the National Security Agency?"

"That's classified. But as I'm sure you're aware, Mr. McNally, our collective safety requires everyday people, *civilians*, to occasionally play a role in law enforcement. Maybe even people in the publishing business."

Brad realized what was going on.

"This is one of those if-you-see-something-say-something situations."

"Are you asking me? Or telling me?" Brad asked. Then he quickly looked away, avoiding the man's stare. Brad still had the occasional urge to Stick It to the Man. And if there ever was such a thing as the Man, it was this agent sitting here, asking him to do something that smelled a lot like snitching at best, stifling freedom of speech in any case, and at worst suppressing information that was in the public's interest.

Lyons was smiling, the small, condescending grin of someone who knows he will win, and that it will not even be close. "I guess, Mr. Mc-Nally, this is more of a demand than a request."

"I see."

Brad had asked the in-house lawyer to wait in the conference room next door, in case of any unforeseen circumstances. Foreseen circumstances, actually. Foreseen and undesirable.

Brad looked Lyons in the eye, trying to stare hard into a hardened face. "And how did you learn all this?"

"The *specific* details of intelligence-gathering operations are, of course, confidential. But I can reveal that we intercepted telephone calls between the journalist and the, uh, *commissioning* enterprise."

"Intercepted phone calls? You're talking about the domestic wiretapping program?"

"That's right." That small smug smile, again. "Although we refer to it as the homeland surveillance program."

"*Mm-hmm.*" Brad was slowly becoming outraged. And cocky. "And so why is this journalist supposedly abroad?"

"To elude our surveillance. And our law enforcement."

"I see. So what is it you want, exactly?"

"*I* do not *want* anything. But what the NSA *requires*, as a matter of national security, is for you to alert us—*me*—if such a manuscript arrives here, to your company."

"Is that right?"

"That is correct."

"And how will I know? If a given manuscript meets these criteria?"

"That would be pretty easy, I should think."

"Ten editors work here. Each receives twenty submissions in a week, of full manuscripts and book proposals."

"This will not arrive as a proposal."

"How do you know?"

"Because I do."

The two men stared at each other, then Brad broke the standoff. "As I was saying, two hundred prospective books arrive here every week. That's, um . . . that's ten thousand per year."

Lyons nodded.

"And you're asking me to find one? One out of ten thousand?"

"I'm sure, Mr. McNally, that it will not be nearly as difficult as you're pretending."

After fretting about it for a few hours, months ago, Brad decided that he didn't need to make any decision, at the time. This preposterous predicament was purely hypothetical. He didn't even bother to consult the in-house lawyer, who was a contracts and intellectual-property specialist, and not exactly an expert in this type of situation. Nor did he call the outside counsel; Brad didn't need to waste the guy's exorbitant billable hours on a long fruitless abstract conversation about the First Amendment.

He had more concrete and actionable issues on his desk, every single day. Until today, when that manuscript became no longer abstract. So Brad places the call, the one he was hoping not to make, but somehow knew he'd need to.

"Bradford McNally?" The voice on the other end of the line is a slow, rich Southern drawl, and you can practically hear the belly protruding through the phone. "So nice of you to call."

"Trey Freeley. So nice of you to *take* my call."

The lawyer chuckles. Both men know that Freeley is more than happy to field a brief call and charge a hundred dollars for it.

"Listen, Trey, one of my editors has a submission that might be tricky, legally."

"*Mm-hmmmmm.*" Freeley's drawl seems most pronounced when what's coming out of his mouth aren't actual words; he moans and grumbles with a thick accent. "What seems to be the problem?" As if he's a physician.

"Well, the project is an unauthorized biography of Charlie Wolfe. It includes some pretty explosive revelations. Or, rather, *allegations*, I guess is more accurate."

"I see." Long pause. "And who wrote this?"

"It's anonymous."

Freeley is silent for another beat. "Who's the literary agent?"

"It's a woman named Isabel Reed."

Freeley doesn't respond.

"She's at Atlantic Talent Management," Brad continues. "You know her?"

"Yes." The lawyer sounds suspicious, or angry, or something not quite right. Freeley is not a monosyllabic type of guy. "If you don't mind me askin', McNally, which one of your editors received this?"

Brad is too mired in his own worries to wonder why the hell the lawyer would ask. "Jeff Fielder got the submission."

"*Mmmm.*" Brad can hear the heavy man's labored breathing on the other end of the line. "Listen, McNally, we should talk in person. I can come up to New York later."

Brad's first, brief instinct is to worry about the cost of such a trip, but then he realizes that if the lawyer is willing to hop on Acela at a moment's notice, the billable hours are the least of his problems.

"Could we grab a drink?"

———

Brad stands at the unfamiliar machine, a relatively new expenditure that he doesn't remember approving. He stares at the little gray screen, considering his options, wondering whether he needs to actively choose anything here, or if he can forge ahead unthinking. He tries it, simply puts the stack of paper into the feeder tray, hits the giant green button, the one screaming "Push me!" The thing starts operating as it should, duplicating pages. Thank God. He can avoid the humiliation of asking someone to show him how to use the photocopier.

He walks away from the cluster of grand rooms that formed the original offices of McNally Publishing at its founding, beefore any Sons were involved. Nearly a century later, and Brad knows he'll have to sell the company to whoever will be crazy enough to buy. His father also knows it, sitting on his veranda on the Vineyard, trying to enjoy the twilight of his life. Though neither has explicitly admitted it to the other, each knows that the other knows.

But if he's going to have to sell this venerable firm, first he's going to try to do some good in this world, using the position he still has, however temporarily.

He walks down the hall and around a corner, then steps down into what he still thinks of as the new wing, even though it's now twenty years old. The lease on the expansion was acquired in the early nineties, when a string of bestsellers created a flush period. The farthest reaches of the new wing is known as Lost Corridor, a long warren of cubbyholes and makeshift workspaces and supply closets and restrooms and the fireproofed vaulted rooms that are jammed with FireKing file cabinets that hold artwork, contracts, and other irreplaceable pieces of paper or film.

The Lost Corridor is where Chester Dumont and his people toil: the copy editors, proofreaders, fact-checkers, indexers, and production editors who collectively read and revise the tens of millions of words per year that are turned into the McNally & Sons' 150 books. At the very end of the corridor, past a large pool of freelance stations, is Chester's office. Every square foot of wall space is lined with floor-to-ceiling steel storage, twelve-inch-deep sagging shelves packed with stacks of in-process books, as well as a comprehensive collection of reference materials. Off to the side of his desk is a podium-style stand for *Merriam-Webster's Unabridged Dictionary*; beneath are the 1961 Third Edition and the 1934 Second. Chester is leaning over this massive volume, peering at the gossamer-thin paper through half-moon glasses that sit low on his substantial nose, when he hears a polite rap on his open door.

"One moment, please," he says reflexively, without looking up, finishing his tiny task of research. Then, satisfied with his new understanding of the *rhombicosidodecahedron*, he turns to the door, and sees Bradford. Chester is pretty sure that the publisher has never before visited his office. And Chester has been with McNally & Sons for thirty years.

"Mr. McNally," he says, "what a surprise." Chester's habit, which he realizes everybody thinks is pretentious, is to use formality. "To what do I owe the pleasure?"

The publisher is standing in the doorway, seemingly unsure of whether to enter. As always, Bradford is wearing a suit, this one a chalk-striped charcoal affair that looks like flannel, and a shirt in what's called French blue with English-style club collar, and an embroidered navy-and-purple necktie knotted in a well-executed half-Windsor. Alan Flusser's *Style and the Man*, Chester knows, is the most thorough reference on men's attire.

"Hi, Chester," his boss's boss says. "May I come in?"

"Of course." Chester walks around his gunmetal-gray desk. "Have a seat?"

The publisher makes his way through the stacks of reference books and manuscripts that litter the floor. He sits in the soft leather Brno chair, designed by Mies van der Rohe in 1929–30, a pair of the few surviving relics of the 1952 overhaul of the office furniture. The chunky illustrated book *1000 Chairs* sits just over Chester's right shoulder.

"Look, Chester, I need a little fact-checking." He taps the small stack of paper.

"Very well, Mr. McNally. I'll have one of the freelancers take care of this soonest." He knows that Doris is about to finish proofing an astoundingly ahead-of-schedule novel. That work can be put aside for the day. Hell, that work can be put aside for four months. Chester starts leafing through the pages.

"I'm sorry, Chester, but I need you to do this yourself. And I need it done today."

Chester glances at the man who signs his paycheck—eighty-two thousand dollars a year. Thank God he never moved out of his rent-controlled Turtle Bay hovel.

"What is this?"

"Part of a submission."

"And what is it you'd like me to check?"

"Anything that can be verified." The publisher rises. "By the end of the day, please."

Chester takes a long slow intake of breath, and starts plotting out a reorganization of the rest of his day, now that this giant crater has been blown into the middle of it.

"Oh, and Chester? This is strictly embargoed. Not a single word, to anyone."

CHAPTER 28

The pavement changes at exit 66, the relatively new black surface giving way to the old gray, rougher, louder, a stronger vibration in the steering wheel of the brand-new Mercedes that they'd collected from the garage around the corner from Judy's house. While they were waiting at the bottom of the ramp, Jeff noticed the rate list: $675 per month for a car, plus an extra $200 for anything oversize or "exotic," plus parking tax of 18.75 percent. AKA $800 a month. For a parking spot.

"You know how to drive, right?" Isabel asked.

"Yeah."

The shiny silver car came screeching around a corner, a wiry guy opening the driver's door while the vehicle was still moving, stepping out smoothly, taking Isabel's five-dollar-tip with a quick "Thank you Miss," scurrying back into the bowels to collect someone else's hundred-thousand-dollar car, for minimum wage.

"You drive," she said. "I need some sleep."

Jeff sank into the soft leather, adjusted the mirrors and his seat, glanced around the dash. Then he pulled out tentatively into the thick snarl of a weekday traffic jam. A hundred yards ahead, a disheveled wild-haired man was standing in the center of an intersection, attempting to direct traffic with no authority whatsoever other than his will to be in

187

charge of some little piece of the world, to preside over something, any-thing, however irrelevant.

Jeff stole a glance at Isabel, collapsed in her seat, staring out the side window, apparently lost in thought. He wondered what her plan really was. He knew that she wasn't telling him the whole truth.

In a sudden burst of multi-vehicle movement, the car was sprung free of the jam, and Jeff accelerated through the intersection, then cruised across a comparatively empty street—"Take the next right, Jeffrey" and "Turn up there"—and then they were ascending a ramp onto the Fifty-Ninth Street Bridge, climbing into the blue sky, on a single narrow lane that seemed to be cantilevered out over the river. This was the scariest roadway he'd ever driven, and it was already the scariest day of his life.

"I really think we need to go to the police," he said. He felt he needed to object, again, to their course of action.

"No."

"Why?" He knew what her answer would be. And he didn't even want the police. But he needed to go through the motions of the argument. "I'm terrified, Isabel."

"*Mmm.*" A sound of agreement, but not of commitment. "Jeffrey?" she asked, lowering the window. A warm wind flooded into the car. "May I have your phone?"

Jeff doesn't drive frequently—he has never in his life owned a car—so he was wildly uncomfortable at the wheel of this luxury car borrowed from a famous woman on this insanely narrow and shockingly exposed roadway high above the East River. So he reached into his pocket and handed the device to Isabel without looking at the phone, or her, keeping his eyes glued ahead. Which is why he didn't exactly see the thing fly out the window; he was just vaguely aware of her arm motion.

"Did you just throw my phone out the window?"

"I did."

"*Why?*"

"Because cell phones are homing devices. Even when they're not bugged."

His stomach was in freefall, yanked down as if attached to an anvil, like the sinking SIM card on its way to the bottom of the East River, with its irretrievable, irreplaceable data.

"You could've just removed the battery," he said sullenly.

"Sorry." She turned from the window, now closed again, to face Jeff. "It was just a phone, right?"

Ninety minutes later, Jeff looks over at the passenger seat, at his companion, sleeping. Her hair has cascaded over the right side of her face, and her mouth is open, her jaw hanging a bit crooked. Her breathing is deep, her chest rising and falling with a slow, even rhythm.

He nudges her upper arm. "Isabel"—quietly—"we're here."

She doesn't budge, doesn't stir, doesn't alter the rhythm of her breathing.

He looks back at the road, sees the exit looming. Little by little over the past hour, the traffic had thinned over the length of the Long Island Expressway, from the urban blight in Queens—the housing complexes and cut-rate motels, the crumbling community centers and seedy shopping plazas—to the dense suburbanity of Nassau County, then the thinning throughout Suffolk, till the unpopulated stretch of the Pine Barrens, the turnoffs to the Hamptons, and finally the sign that Isabel had mentioned, before she fell asleep: EXPRESSWAY ENDS 4 MILES.

"Hey, Isabel," he says, less quietly. "We just passed the sign."

"*Mmm.*" She moves her mouth and shifts her weight, but doesn't open her eyes.

He rests his hand on her upper arm, soft and warm under the smooth blouse. He squeezes. "Isabel, wake up."

She opens her eyes, blinks. "What?" Confused.

"We just passed the expressway-ends sign. A minute ago."

She rubs her eyes, licks her lips. This is a vision he wants to imprint on memory: the sight of the woman he loves, waking up.

"At the bottom of the ramp, turn left," she says. "There's a gas station. Stop there."

Jeff pulls the car into the station, but stops short of the pumps.

"What's the problem?" she asks.

He looks over at her. "What do you want me to do?"

"Now? Fill up the tank."

Jeff looks at the dashboard. "But we don't need gas."

Isabel unbuckles her seatbelt. "Sure we do," she says. "We just don't need a *lot* of it." She hands him a credit card, one of Judy's that she was willing to lend—give—to her suddenly erratic literary agent. "I'm going to the restroom."

Jeff stands at the pump, barely remembering how this works. He inserts the nozzle, squeezes its trigger, stares at the reflection of himself in the rear window. His satchel is there behind the glass, in the backseat. But Isabel has taken her handbag to the bathroom.

CHAPTER 29

H ayden deplanes with his small duffel over his shoulder, puts on his sunglasses to shield against the bright glare of the summer-solstice sun reflected from the vast expanse of light-gray asphalt, the long row of hangers.

A black SUV speeds through a gate in the chain-link fence that separates the airfield from the rest of the military base, and comes to a halt in front of him. The driver's window lowers, and a young man turns to him, at first unfamiliar because of the wrap-around sunglasses, but then Hayden recognizes him. "Hello Tyler," he says. Hayden had just met this guy a few months ago; he's from the musclehead school. Not so much an agent as an enforcer, which is probably what's needed here.

"Hello Mr. Gray."

Hayden sees another youngish operative in the passenger seat.

"Who are you?"

"My name's Colby, sir."

"That your first name or last?"

"Colby Manfield, sir."

Staffing here in the homeland was a delicate challenge. Hayden needed to secure a lot of bodies for all this surveillance, both electronic and physical, with techs and a mobile command unit in New York City, and teams of floaters on standby to keep track of other personnel tendrils—such as the publisher, or the lawyer in DC, and that poor girl this morning—who might present problems, not to mention possible players in other locations, such as Los Angeles, where that inconvenient sub-rights director is creating Lord knows what mischief. It was a lot of people Hayden needed on this operation, in a territory that's not his own, on a mission that's not exactly legal. Not remotely legal.

In the end, the most efficacious thing had been for Hayden to sub out to private contractors for his stateside needs. After 9/11, the personnel landscape had changed dramatically, with paramilitary organizations proliferating, merging with one another, going out of business, renaming themselves, redefining their scopes of operations, obfuscating their ownership and mandates and recordkeeping. There are plenty of crew-cut guys looking for work in America, guys who pride themselves on their discretion, on the sacrosanct honor of sworn secrecy, on an unwavering conviction that the right to security outweighs the right to privacy, at least where other people are concerned. Or if not on any of these principles, on the much more straightforward consideration of cash.

A boom era for mercenaries.

And here's the result, sitting in the front of the big black truck, into whose back Hayden hoists himself. He wonders what type of satisfactory explanation he'll need to produce for these thugs. But he knows it doesn't really matter, and he doesn't need to tell them much. These guys will do simply what they're told—that's who they are, that's what they're for. And afterward Hayden will probably kill them.

"Tell me what's happening," he says.

The driver accelerates while the man in the passenger seat turns to look at his boss. "The agent and the editor have borrowed a car from Judy Thompson."

"Who's she?"

"A television personality, and book author, and who knows what else. They went to see Thompson at her East Side house. Reed admitted she was terrified and wanted someplace to hide; said that someone had murdered her assistant. So she asked for Thompson's beach house, and her car, as well as cash and a credit card. They just used this plastic to buy gas along the route from New York City to that destination, which is in Amagansett. The Hamptons."

Hayden looks at his watch, trying to orient himself to the change of time, change of continent. He's on a military base in New Jersey, which is a very different place from where he woke up this morning. "How far of a drive for us?"

"Too long. Three and a half hours. Maybe four. So we're not driving." The guy points ahead, at a helicopter in the distance. "There's a base in Westhampton. Close enough."

"Good. What else?"

"There's that woman on her way to Los Angeles, the subsidiary rights director."

"We have a team in position?"

"Yes, waiting near the rental-car facility."

"And dare I ask?"

"The plan is for a carjacking gone awry, on the stretch between the facility and the freeway. Two cars, one coming from either direction."

Hayden envisages the screeching tires, the ski masks, the *tat-tat-tat* of the 9-millimeters, the blood splattered across the front seat and the dashboard and the windows.

He hates this. It's one thing to kill a lone girl in New York City, by mistake. It's another to start shooting up Los Angeles, on purpose. Opening fire on civilians in the United States of America. Hunting down innocent Americans to mete out their undeserved comeuppance to his unexpected corruption. What a fucking disaster.

"Do you have the item?" he asks the front seat.

"Yes sir." The passenger-seat goon reaches down, retrieves a canvas bag, passes it over the back of the seat.

Hayden pulls the stack of paper from the bag. *The Accident.* He wonders what the title refers to; no accident had ever been a subject of any conversations he'd had about this manuscript.

His phone rings, a 202 number, Washington. "Hello."

"Good afternoon. This is Trey Freeley."

"Oh hello. How can I help you?"

"Do you remember that matter we discussed? The manuscript."

"Of course."

"It has landed, to exactly the person I expected it would."

No shit. "Yes. Do you have any additional information?"

"A portion—a small portion, I believe—of the manuscript is with the editor's boss. The publisher of the outfit. Do you know who that is?"

"I do."

"He's worried."

"I imagine so."

"I happen to be meeting him for a drink tonight, at the Sailor's in New York. You familiar with that club?"

Hayden's father had been a member of the Sailor's; this is where they'd stayed, the two of them, when they'd visited New York for Hayden's sixteenth birthday. Another era, in a different century. "No, can't say that I am."

"We'll be there at seven o'clock."

Hayden hangs up. The three of them transfer from the SUV to the helicopter. As soon as he's buckled in, Hayden starts to read.

Hayden had met with Buford Freeley III when this operation began, back in December.

"You can call me Trey," the lawyer said in an aggressively Southern accent, holding out his big hand, taking a firm grip of Hayden's. Too firm, something to prove. "Everyone does. We been tryin' to shake the name Buford for three generations now, but can't seem to ditch it." He gestured at a chair. "Please."

Hayden took his seat, glanced out the windows at the Washington skyline, such as it was, with the monument to the city's namesake just a few blocks away, puncturing the sky, dividing it. Hayden had taken a good walk around Penn Quarter, the Mall, Capitol Hill. It'd been a long time since he'd wandered the capital. Washington reminded him more of a European city than an American one: the radiating streets and the traffic circles, the parks and squares, the lowness of the buildings relative to the height of the monuments. It's the least skyscrapery big city in the States; would fit right in on the Continent.

He let his eye wander over Freeley's ego wall, framed hand-shakings with dozens of dignitaries, including more than one president of the United States. Law degree from Duke, undergrad from Princeton.

"The farthest north any self-respectin' Southern gentleman would consent to attend college, isn't that right?"

"I wouldn't know, Mr. Freeley. I myself am not a Southerner."

"No, I guess you're not."

"And only marginally a gentleman."

Freeley squinted across his wide, cluttered desk. "So what can I do for you?"

"People tell me you're a man who can be trusted."

Freeley had an easy laugh, a genuine one, a Southern laugh. "As much as any Washington, DC, lawyer. Isn't that right, Mr.—what was it again? Mr. Lyons?"

"That's right."

"*Mm-hmmm.*" He peered over the rim of his glasses, dubious. "And your message said this is about a book project? Mr. *Lyons*?"

"Yes?"

"You gonna stick with that name, now that you've made it into my office? Or you gonna tell me who you really are?"

Hayden was ready for this, but didn't feel the need to show it. Which is what separates the pros from the amateurs: pros don't need to prove how smart they are.

"What did you think?" Freeley shook his head. "I bill at eight hundred dollars an hour. When I do a book deal, I take fifteen percent off the top, and the top for my clients is usually in the seven-figure range. It takes me a day or two to make one a those deals. And that's when I'm havin' a off-day."

Hayden nodded.

"Which is to say, Mr. Lyons, that I make a lotta money. And do you know *how* I make a lotta money?" He kept his eyes on Hayden, but didn't wait for an answer. "I make a lotta money by *not* wasting time takin' meetings that will make me *no* money. Which is to say, Mr. *Lyons*, that I have a staff whose job it is to research the people who want to walk into this office. To find out who they are."

Hayden was amused by all the unnecessary bluster. "And who am I?"

"You are no one. You don't exist. There is no one meaningful named Joseph Lyons in Washington. Or in the United States of America."

"Didn't someone tell you I'd be calling?"

Freeley snorted. "Of course. Someone *always* tells me someone will be callin'. A senator, congressman, lobbyist."

Hayden allowed himself a full, broad smile of bona fide enjoyment. "But this was from the director of Central Intelligence."

"Oh, is he the one person in Washington who don't lie?"

Hayden couldn't help but laugh. This was exactly the type of guy who he wished he could work with. But guys like this don't work for a hundred grand a year, occasionally getting shot at, sometimes in hellholes.

Trey Freeley had launched himself in the capital as a white-shoe associate, who soon became a famously aggressive literary agent, who then translated his success into a law-firm partnership, where he carved out unique niche for himself, representing nearly everyone inside the Beltway with a big book deal to make.

"I could"—Hayden leaned forward—"tell you another, more complicated, and more difficult-to-verify set of lies. But they'd just be more cover. So for the purposes of this billable hour, let's just assume that I'm a prospective client who will turn out to be not worth your trouble." Hayden took an envelope out of his pocket, handed it over to Freeley. "And I expect we will not meet again."

The lawyer opened the envelope, pulled out a piece of paper, a cashier's check.

"I also do homework, Mr. Freeley. And you hourly is *seven* hundred, not eight."

"Touché." Freeley put the check on his desk. "This is not about a book deal?"

Hayden shrugged. "That doesn't matter, does it? Why I'm here is because people say you know more about the book-publishing business than anyone in DC, and you collect the New York gossip without being a part of it."

Freeley couldn't disagree with this assessment. He shrugged.

"I'm here," Hayden said, "for you to explain it to me."

"Explain what?"

"Book publishing."

"What about it?"

"Everything," Hayden said, smiling broadly again. "That is, everything we can cover in"—he glanced at his watch—"the next fifty-four minutes."

Freeley leaned back in his chair, getting comfortable. "That should just about do it," he said. "It ain't a very complicated business."

CHAPTER 30

Across-continental flight provides ample reading time, especially headed west, into the wind. But *The Accident* is on the long side, as submissions go. So even though the plane is inexplicably delayed, and the trade winds fierce, when the seatbelt light extinguishes and the passengers stand and Camilla slips the manuscript back into her MCNALLY & SONS tote, she's still a hundred pages shy of the end.

She shuffles down the aisle, casting the leads in her imagination. She's partial to relatively young actors for *The Accident*, so they'll be appropriate for the college-age scenes, which will take disproportionate time in the adaptation; there's a lot of visual drama in the beginning of the story. And she imagines that it's easier to age younger actors than to reverse-age older ones.

This will be a *brilliant* film.

She should rent a convertible, a nice one, and spend the week zipping around Los Angeles with her sunglasses on, her long red hair whipping in the wind, trying, like everyone here, to attract attention. She finally has something worth the attention.

And to hell with the limits of her expense account. This is the last trip she'll be taking on the McNally tab, and she'll never even have to justify the charges. Gone by the time the credit-card statement arrives.

Waiting curbside for the rental van, Camilla calls and asks for an upgrade. But they're all out of convertibles. The almost unbearably stupid clerk can offer her a variety of SUVs, but that's not what she wants, not at all. "Right," she says, "I'll take the midsize then."

"No worries."

As Camilla listens to this unapologetic dimwit, she worries that maybe California isn't exactly Shangri-La. "On second thought, no thank you." She hangs up, calls another agency, who sure enough has multiple convertible options. If there's one place that's never short on rental cars, it's LAX.

The other shuttle bus deposits her in the lot, across an access road and a quarter-mile from the lot where she's expected.

She doesn't have sufficient time to check into the hotel before her appointment, as planned. She'll just freshen up here, in the rental-lot restroom, a wardrobe swap and a makeup application. Staring at herself in the mirror, painting her lips under the harsh glare of public-bathroom fluorescence, dehydrated from the flight, she catches a foreshadow of her face in twenty years, maybe ten, eyes downturned at the corners, a bit like a cocker spaniel, and cheeks sagging, a spot of waddle. She'll look exactly like her mum. Not being her mum has been one of Camilla's main goals in life. *The* primary goal, in fact. But there's no avoiding one's genes.

She tosses her luggage into the boot, shimmies into the driver's side, adjusts all the things that need adjusting. She turns the ignition, and steals a glance at the car's clock. She's cutting it close.

Camilla shifts into gear and pulls out of the numbered space, past a security check, accelerating down the surface street, driving like an utter maniac in the rich glow of the late-afternoon sun, on this day of hers that will be twenty-seven hours long, the wind in her hair and an invaluable property in her possession, on her way to pitch a friendly producer.

She loves it here. The palm trees and the mountains, the canyons and the beaches, the valet parking and the central-air. Camilla used to be posh, sort of, before she decided to reject it. Twenty years on, she's reconsidering. Posh had its upsides. She could be posh here, where posh can be earned democratically. In England, posh needs to be bestowed genetically to be worn comfortably.

Camilla guns the engine, feels the automatic transmission turn over to the next gear, hitting ninety on the ascent of the on-ramp.

She doesn't notice that she has pulled far ahead of a burgundy sedan that had been speeding to catch her before she reached the freeway.

Camilla enters the vast outer office, walking with the long strides of an Important Person with Places to Be. But she also softens her face into what she hopes is a sweet, sincere smile.

"Hullo Jessica," she says to the assistant. "It's Camilla Glyndon-Browning."

If there's one thing Camilla has learned about Los Angeles, it's to suck up to the assistants. All it really takes is remembering their names.

"Hello Ms. Glyndon-Browning. He'll be right with you. Please have a seat."

"Thank you, Jessica." Another big smile. Remembering their names, plus really big smiles; it's not so hard. She reaches into her tote and takes out the manuscript.

"Jessica, whilst I'm there, could I impose on you to have a photocopy made? Of this?" She puts the manuscript on the desk. "It's for Stan, of course."

Jessica looks down her nose at the stack of paper, then back at Camilla. "Absolutely." The girl punches a button on her vast telephone apparatus. "Need a copy, George, now," she says into her headset. "Ms. Glyndon-Browning, it'll be ready in ten."

"Thank you so very much."

Camilla crosses to a deep, welcoming sofa. She looks around at the promotional posters for blockbusters, Stan's credit on all of them.

The door to the inner sanctum is open, and Camilla can hear the in-progress meeting within. "We can't have a SAG actor doing the driving, if there are other actors on the bus, and the bus is actually moving," some woman says. "We'll need a Teamster. This is not a big issue, but it's a safety concern, when we've got equipment and lighting in the vehicle, and the vehicle is moving."

Camilla straightens her back, crosses her legs, places her hands in her lap, trying to look her best. Then she leans back a few degrees, trying to look like she's not trying. Then she notices the assistant watching her, regarding her coolly, warily. The girl must see a lot of women waltzing through this office, dressed like this. Camilla suddenly feels self-conscious, aware of what she looks like. Aware of what she is. Fleeing England didn't eradicate the rich tapestry of insecurities that comes with being someone like her, with a dad like him. It just redirected them, disguised them. She recognizes her origins every time she pulls on a skirt she knows is too short, a working-class girl from the North. But she can't help herself.

She tunes back into the conversation, and hears another voice, "That's with all their bonuses maxed out at one mil: the book author, the first screenwriter, the second screenwriter. I'm gonna go back to the second screenwriter's rep to renegotiate. It's been two years, and she hasn't contributed *anything*. Not a single word of hers in the entire script."

Camilla loses herself in the reverie of renegotiating a contract that includes million-dollar bonuses. She doesn't notice Stan's meeting disbanding. "Camilla, Babe." His chunky arms are spread expansively, oversize gold cufflinks glinting at the end of a garishly striped shirt. A handful of people spill through the anteroom, clutching papers and folders and phones.

"Stan," she says, standing, smiling. He has lost a little weight in the half-year since she last saw him, but he's still a bear: six-one, maybe six-two, probably 275 pounds, and a massive everything—his hands, his fingers, his forearms, every part of him is oversized. Like a different species, *Homo producerus giganticus*. It's his gigantic head specifically that's alarming, and not just the circumference of the skull, but a gigantitude in all aspects—elephantine ears, bulbous nose, flesh-filled lips, dome-like forehead. It's a scary bloody head.

Stan Balzer takes up more than his fair share of space in the world. He's a big person with a big car, big houses, a big presence, big bank accounts with hundreds—thousands—of times the amount of money that the average person on this planet has. He consumes more of everything—food, liquor, money, women—than he's entitled to, and he boasts about it. For Camilla—for a lot of people, she imagines—he's the unlikely intersection of repugnant and alluring. He's America.

"Always good to see you," Stan continues, "looking so . . . um . . . wonderful." He gives her a full, slow once-over. What Stan is not is a subtle man.

Camilla thinks she sees Jessica roll her eyes, and she can't blame the girl. Her boss is a letch; everyone knows it. And Camilla has to admit that she herself is—to put not too fine a point on it—a tart, dressed the part in a scandalous skirt, a diaphanous low-cut blouse, big hoop earrings, a choker. Absolutely no question this is a slutty look. And she completes the ensemble, as always, with her plastic-frame eyeglasses, a little bit of schoolmarm there. With her English accent, she's at least a compelling enigma. Surrounded by all these silicone breasts and Botoxed lips, that's all she can hope for. A compelling enigma, plus the promise of a relatively cheap date, in a town filled with wildly expensive ones.

"No calls, Jessica," says Stan. "None. I'm gone. Call Tim and tell him wheels-up in ninety."

Camilla stands in the center of the office, her back to the door, to Stan, facing his unoccupied desk. She knows where Stan is going, but she's not. Not yet.

"Babe," from behind her. "Why don't you join me over here?" She can hear him pat the black leather of his Art Deco casting couch. She wonders if he chose leather specifically, as opposed to upholstery, to make it easier to clean off bodily fluids.

She peeks over her shoulder. Stan is wearing the smuggest of his various types of smug smiles, shoulders thrown back confidently. She turns away.

"In a moment, Stan," she says. "But first, perhaps *you* could join *me*, over here?"

"We have business?"

"We do."

"*Rrrmmm*," he grumbles, walking around his desk. He settles into his vast chair, crosses his legs. "Ninety seconds."

"I need thirty." She'd rehearsed, quite a bit, in the car.

Stan chortles, looks off to the window, whose shades are already drawn. "Go."

"When one of the most powerful men in the world was at university, he killed a girl." Camilla got this sentence out slowly, with a measured pace, a poker face. "His father and best friend helped cover it up. And then they went on to found an international string of news websites, which they expanded into cable television, newspapers, magazines, and book publishers—the largest media company in the world. All built with the illegal, covert help of the Central. Intelligence. Agency."

Stan turns away from the window, to Camilla, with his eyebrows raised. "You have an unauthorized biography? Of Charlie Wolfe?"

"Something like."

"And it's true?"

"It is."

"And it's brand-new? Do you own it yet?"

"Sort of."

"Meaning?"

"We'll cross that bridge when we come to it. *If* we come to it."

Stan nods knowingly. "And how's my friend Bradford? He on-board with this?"

She pauses. "He's not involved."

The look on Stan's face can be summed up in one word: *bullshit*. "How can . . . ?"

"It'll be fine."

"Okay." He shrugs. "I'll definitely read it. You left it with Jessica to copy?"

"I did indeed." Camilla stands, smiling coyly. "But you need to promise me something, Stan."

"Mmm."

"Executive producer credit."

He raises his big bushy eyebrows.

"You know you can screw me, Stan. But I won't let you screw me over."

"There was another girl."

Preston Wolfe squinted at this interloper, his son's friend. "What do you mean?"

The three of them had been in the suite for an hour, rehashing the accident and the aftermath in minute detail, drinking coffee from the tiny hotel-room carafe, Cokes from the vending machine down on the floor below. Both Dave and Charlie had taken showers, scrubbing off any traces of their night, and that dead girl.

There had never been any mention of going to the police.

"The girl, Lauren. She was at the club with a friend."

"Did this friend see you?"

Dave nodded.

"Did you talk to her?"

"No."

"Do you think she could recognize you? Identify you?" Preston Wolfe glanced between the two boys. "Either of you?"

Dave shrugged. Mr. Wolfe turned to face his son. "Charlie?"

"I don't know, Dad. I could barely *see*."

Mr. Wolfe turned away from these boys, from this disaster, sitting side by side on the sofa of his suite. For a few minutes, nobody said anything, as Preston Wolfe stared out at the modest sights and lights of downtown Ithaca, late at night.

"Okay," he finally said. "Charlie, you and I

have to leave town." He glanced at his watch.
"At seven a.m. This will be before anyone at the
girl's dormitory knows she's missing. Before any
investigation could possibly start. But it'll be
late enough that we won't arouse the suspicion of
the hotel staff."

Charlie was leaning forward, elbows on knees. He
nodded.

"I'll take care of cleaning up the Jaguar, in New
York. You'll get on your plane to meet your mother
at Cap Ferrat, as planned. You will of course say
nothing about this to her. To anyone."

"What about your meeting?" That was why Preston
Wolfe was in town, to see the university president.

"I'm ill. I have to cancel." He shrugged. "I'll
write a bigger check."

Mr. Wolfe turned his attention to his son's
friend. "Dave, you'll go back to the fraternity
house, and pack your bags. You can catch another
ride home?"

Dave nodded. At the end of the school year,
the stream of students departing for the New York
metropolitan area was constant, a sort of opposite
Great Migration.

"As long as no one knows, it'll be fine." Mr.
Wolfe was nodding, agreeing with himself, with this
hope of his.

"Dad?"

Preston Wolfe turned his focus back to his son.

"We should give Dave something."

Once again Preston Wolfe's eyes narrowed.

"Maybe it should be annual," Charlie added. "An
ongoing, ah . . ."

"Retainer," Mr. Wolfe supplied the word.

Dave was stunned, aghast. "I don't want any *money*."

"Twenty thousand per year," Mr. Wolfe said. "That sound right to you?"

Dave shook his head. "No."

Preston Wolfe was still wearing his silk dressing gown, one hand in the front pocket. He looked like his other hand should be holding a pipe.

"Better make it forty. For, say, twenty years. No: twenty-five years. That's a million dollars."

"What? I don't understand."

"Because that implicates you," Charlie said. He grasped this intuitively. Dave was at the time the more naive of the two.

"Because," Charlie continued, "the money is evidence of wrongdoing. By you."

Charlie pointed at his friend, as if to clarify something. "In the event that you ever consider changing your recollection. About what transpired tonight."

CHAPTER 31

He brushes his teeth and washes his face and returns to his office. He wakens his computer, and opens the video feed to Isabel Reed's apartment. Her bedroom is dark, and empty. The living room too, and the kitchen, and the hall.

He opens the media folder of motion-activated footage. Since he last checked, there have been about ten minutes of motion, in one stretch, time-stamped beginning 3:08 p.m. local time.

The first activated camera, as usual, is the one in the hall, as the front door opens. It's a different man from the usual, this one tall and blond and muscular and wearing latex gloves, moving quickly, not pausing to listen for sounds, not hesitating, not sneaking around corners. This man, like the others, knows there's no one home; he and his colleagues are keeping close tabs on Isabel, and they know where she is at all times. But also like the others, this blond guy doesn't know about the surveillance cameras that are watching him while he's spying on her.

These cameras are the author's. He had them installed partly to monitor the agent, but mostly to keep track of these goons who come and go, to see what they do, to see if they ever walk away with a manuscript, or, worse, with the woman herself. One or another of these guys has been stealing into her apartment every few days for months. Checking on her submissions. Checking on her.

208

Today's goon disappears from the hall's camera and reappears in the bedroom's, glancing around at the dresser, the end tables, the shelving. He stands there facing the wall of shelves, methodically scanning up and down and across the rows of manuscripts, each with an author's name written on the side. After a couple of minutes he reaches up and grabs a stack of paper, and examines the covering page and the first page, but then returns this manuscript to its proper position, and continues scanning until he reaches the end of the wall.

He walks through the rest of the apartment, looking at surfaces, in drawers. Quickly examining every spot where a manuscript could be sitting, or casually hiding. But not finding what he's looking for. Isabel's apartment is clutter-free, no disorganized piles, no unsorted stacks of miscellany, no mess in which a manuscript could hide. Her fastidiousness makes the goons' job easy.

The man leaves. A few seconds later the video file ends; no more motion.

It had been quick work to establish surveillance on Isabel Reed and her apartment, a three-man team who broke into Isabel's apartment while she was on a four-day trip to a West Coast writer's conference. The whole operation was not nearly as expensive as the author had been prepared for.

Over the course of his career, he'd amassed millions of dollars that he'd never gotten around to spending. At the beginning, entry-level television jobs for poverty-level pay, the only way he was able to pay the rent had been with the help of the Wolfe payoffs. It seemed like a fortune back then, when he had nothing. And those checks continued to arrive well past their financial relevance, as a matter of—what?—moral principle, would probably be how Charlie explained it, without acknowledging the irony.

Then the late-nineties startup years were a different type of lean, with the promise of a big payoff on the horizon, and the satisfaction of building something. And when it started to work, it happened quickly: a half-million one year, and a million the next, as the international websites exploded and the VC money came pouring in. His take from the IPO was over ten million, on paper at least, and he started earning a healthy seven-figure salary. Plus bonuses, of course.

As with so many people, the more money he made, the less time—or even inclination—he had to spend it. Sure, he bought a junky little airplane, and a nice new car, and a couple of houses. But by the time he signed the papers last fall to disentangle himself from Wolfe Worldwide Media, he had eight figures squirreled away, quite a bit of it well-hidden.

Now he needed to spend it. On the surveillance cameras for the literary agent's apartment, though not for her office; the headquarters of an international literary agency would've been much more challenging, much riskier, for much less benefit. He knew the agent's habits, and she took everything home with her. Home would suffice for the video.

He spent a hundred thousand on his own disappearance: the gear and the motorboat that he'd needed after the Piper crash, and the airline tickets and train tickets and rental cars and hotels, the clothes and luggage, the new identities. Another six-figure chunk for the Zurich setup—the apartment, the computer, the Audi, the gun.

A half-million on the whole medical aspect, and the discretion that he required to accompany the surgeries and their recordkeeping.

Then there was the quarter-million for the Copenhagen setup, all for nothing more than misdirection. But the Copenhagen ruse was absolutely essential. Because the author knew without a doubt that after his departure from the office, after his death, Charlie Wolfe would go looking for the book material. When he failed to find anything—when Charlie found a distinct and unequivocal absence of everything related to the book—he would suspect the truth: that his erstwhile right-hand man had not committed suicide, but had disappeared with all this material. And there could be only one reason to do that. The autobiography/memoir was the author's idea to begin with; Charlie wouldn't doubt the author's eagerness to turn it into an unauthorized biography. An exposé.

So Charlie would dispatch someone to find the liar, the thief, the traitor. Most likely someone from Langley. Someone high up, someone who had the wherewithal to run a completely black operation, with no oversight whatsoever from any branch of government. Someone who was as motivated as Charlie to make sure that the manuscript was buried, and its author alongside it. There was only one such someone in the world, and the author was terrified of him.

"I don't care how you handle it," Charlie would say to this guy, "and I don't want to know. Just make sure the book doesn't see the light of day."

This guy would know that it wouldn't be enough to simply find the author and intimidate him, or even kill him. Because that wouldn't necessarily prevent the disastrous story from being out there in the world. They'd have to find and eradicate all traces of the manuscript.

This Langley man would go on a manhunt, and he wouldn't stop until he found something. Finding nothing wouldn't dissuade him. He needed to find the *wrong* thing.

So the author had to create something to be found. Something credible. Something unfinished, in-process; something they wouldn't interrupt. Something awaiting a resolution. Something that was getting more and more specific as time went on; a project that looked more and more like something to be investigated.

The author flew to Hamburg and rented a car and drove to Copenhagen, where he met with an American mercenary who led him to an Austrian skinhead who hired a strung-out Danish student named Jens Grundtvig to fact-check a manuscript about Charlie Wolfe. None of the damning bits; just the straight-up biography, thousands of little facts. No particular rush on this, take your time. New material will arrive on a regular basis over the next six months, maybe nine. And here's an apartment you should work in, already equipped and wired. Yes, those are some shady Middle Eastern characters who hang out in the social club downstairs, but what do you expect for rent-free?

Those shady characters were in actuality bodyguards, after a fashion.

That's how it came to be that poor clueless Jens Grundtvig trolled the

Internet for old newspaper and magazine articles, and placed off-hour phone calls to the States, checking with primary sources, double-checking with secondary sources, jotting down dates and places and names.

The Agency guy and his freelance team would of course find Grundt-vig. His phone calls and web history would be flagged and traced, then he'd be watched. The team would wait, and wait, and wait, until Grundt-vig was finished, or until the author made contact, or showed up.

But Grundtvig wouldn't be finished with his fake task before the author was finished with the real one; and the author would certainly never show up again in Copenhagen. So they would still be waiting, and watching, until it was too late.

Too late was yesterday, when the manuscript began to make its appearances in New York, and the black-ops people—a man and a woman—must have realized that they'd been duped. They stormed into Grundtvig's apartment, and aroused the alarm of those militant Turks who congregated downstairs, all of which was according to the author's plan. Not according to his plan, however, was that they both managed to survive. The best-laid plans. Oh well.

Now the Copenhagen chimera is finished, and the secret has begun its inexorable march toward the public, beginning, as all books do, with a hundred thousand words sent from one person to one other person.

And the person to whom this author sent his manuscript is on his computer screen, in this morning's video feed. Reading in bed, and rising, and showering and dressing, and stepping out to the balcony for her cigarette and a couple of phone calls, and planting that kiss on the framed photo of the little boy, as she does every morning.

CHAPTER 32

Brad is partly proud but partly ashamed that so many of his employees are still in the office at 6:30 p.m. He makes his way through editorial and then the big open Mac-filled space for the designers, past the publicists on the phone and the marketing department gathered in a meeting, into the Lost Corridor, Chester's team of language nerds, red Col-Erase pencils and glue-backed query flags and big thick reference tomes.

The copy chief is peering intently at his monitor, deep in concentration.

Brad raps gently on the door frame. "Hi."

"Mr. McNally," Chester says, looking up.

Brad inclines his head toward the pages on the beat-up old desk. "How's the fact-checking coming along?"

"Rather well," Chester says. "I haven't been able to verify everything; a lot of this seems to be original source material. But what I *have* been able to verify has been accurate. And fascinating."

"Thank you, Chester." He holds out his palm. "I'll take those pages back now."

"Oh but I haven't finished." Chester looks panicked.

"That's all right. I don't need . . ." Brad isn't sure what he doesn't need, or does need. "It's all right. I need the pages back."

Chester nods. He's an obedient character. He picks up the pages, straightens them into a neat stack, and reaches across the table, somewhat reluctantly. It's hard to read just part of this book.

"Thanks again, Chester. Remember, not a word."

Brad trudges up Park Avenue South, passing bars and restaurants with giant windows open onto the avenue, spilling out the sounds and bodies of young adulthood, every single person holding a cell phone, calling and e-mailing, texting and sexting, constantly communicating with people other than the ones they're physically with.

This stretch of Park is traffic-choked, one of the last remaining two-way avenues on the island, its stoplights synchronized to neither direction. He doesn't care for Park Avenue South, which is a very different street from the Park Avenue proper on which he lives. But it doesn't occur to him to take a different, less direct route. Part of the New Yorker mentality of accepting the unpleasantness that's always there, as if it's inevitable, despite being avoidable.

It takes him thirty minutes to get to Midtown, a half-hour consumed with debate, with worry, with obsession. Wavering on what to do about this manuscript. What to do with his business.

He arrives to the narrow grimy side street off Grand Central Station, and the Sailor's, an imposing limestone mansion, beautiful Beaux Arts, with a liveried doorman manning the brass-accented revolving doors, the marble-floored lobby, the dense floral arrangement on the polished circular table, the pennants and flags and black-and-white photos, the sweeping staircase to the oak-paneled bar, the leather club chairs and the Persian rugs, the ancient obsequious waiters in bow ties carrying silver trays to deliver short glasses of amber liquids. This is one of the last places in town where most of the drinks are brown.

This is also one of the last places where everyone who's reading is holding printed paper instead of an electronic device. Trey Freeley himself is deep in a corner, sequestered-looking, draped in an unfolded *Wall Street Journal*, held aloft like a protective blanket.

"Trey, good to see you."

Freeley pulls aside his newsprint, puts it down, shakes Brad's hand. A waiter takes Brad's drink order before he even sits down in a chair that matches Freeley's, separated by a small table, a bowl of mixed nuts, a swizzle stick on a cocktail napkin, a mobile telephone turned upside down.

Brad had never been much of a drinker. He doesn't enjoy the impairment, and he especially hates the hangover. A few times a year, at an awards ceremony or a book party or a benefit, he'll mistakenly have a third drink, or even a fourth, and he invariably regrets it. Not just the physical feeling, but the thoughts he had, the decisions he made. On the other hand, he's never regretted what he's done when stoned. And he's been getting high now for forty years.

Trey picks up his phone, opens the back, pops out the battery, and places the two pieces on the same table. "Would you mind?" he asks.

Brad, nonplused, retrieves his phone, and removes the case, and turns the thing over, around, again. "I can't . . ." he shrugs. "I don't see how . . ."

"Waiter?" Freeley beckons the old African American guy, bow-tied and stooped. "Could I ask you to safe-keep this at the maître d's stand?"

The old guy nods obsequiously, holds McNally's phone as if it's the pillow for the crown jewels.

"You never know" is all Freeley offers by way of explanation. "A few months ago, McNally," the lawyer continues, without any further discussion of the phone, "I get a call from the DCI. Tells me that a guy would be callin' me, and that I should take that meetin'. I of course do.

"So this man, he shows up with a phony name but a genuine cashier's check for an hour of my time, wantin' to learn about the book business. So I explain it to him. And then he admits that he's wonderin' about a very specific type-A situation. Interested to know how it would work."

The waiter delivers Brad's beer, and a fresh bowl of nuts.

"It's a hypothetical biography," Freeley continues, "of a media mogul."

Brad blanches. "Who was this guy?"

"Dunno. Couldn't find anythin' on him."

"Which means what?"

"My guess is that he's workin' for the Agency, in some type-a covert capacity. Maybe he's ex-Agency, or somethin' else in the national security apparatus. And I suspect that this guy's job is to prevent this book from bein' published."

Brad fights the urge to panic. "Why do you think that?" As calmly as possible, which isn't that calm.

"Because I know who wrote it, McNally." The lawyer pops a cashew into his mouth.

"Well?"

The big man shifts in his seat, leans toward Brad. "A year ago, Charlie Wolfe started puttin' out feelers, quietly, about running for Senate. Did you catch wind of this?"

Brad shakes his head. This isn't the type of gossip that reaches him; nor would he pay attention if it did.

"As part of his strategy, Wolfe had begun the process of writin' a book, a memoir, with prescriptive elements—you know, the same bullshit everyone writes when they run for office. An excuse to be on the *Today* show and *Face the Nation*, profiles in *Newsweek* and the *Journal*"—waving a hand at the cast-aside newspaper.

"Aren't those books how you make your living, Trey?"

"Well that doesn't mean I like 'em, now does it."

"I guess not."

"Early on, Wolfe himself came to see me about the book, lookin' for advice; I knew his father, who sent him my way. Charlie was writin' with his lieutenant, who was doin' most-a the heavy liftin', and all the actual typin'. I put together a quickie collaboration agreement for them. They worked on this project for a couple-three months, somethin' like that. Then the coauthor? He up and killed himself."

"You're saying this is the submission we received?" Brad can't quite wrap his mind around this. "You're saying that Charlie Wolfe himself is the author?"

"Well, *author* is somethin' of a misnomer in this situation. I'm sayin' that most of the *information* in this book came from Charlie Wolfe. But some of the story—I imagine there are damagin' aspects to it—was filled in by someone else. Perhaps *invented* by someone else."

"Who?"

"The same person who was workin' on the book to begin with. His college friend, his chief strategist, and his coauthor, all rolled into one tidy handsome package."

"That's Dave Miller."

"That's correct."

"But Dave Miller is dead." Brad realizes he's on the edge of his seat, about to pitch forward onto the rug, which is the size of a basketball court. Maybe bigger. He forces himself to lean back in his chair. "He faked his suicide?"

"That's certainly possible."

Brad rolls this around in his brain, staring across the room toward immense windows, tremendous sheets of streakless glass set into gleaming polished brass. "So you're saying that when Miller found out he had terminal cancer, he had some sort of crisis of conscience, or . . . or whatever, and decided he wanted to finish this book project. To get the full Charlie Wolfe story into the world."

Freeley drains the last of his drink, says nothing.

"But he couldn't just sit there in his living room in Washington, typing away on a computer. Because if Wolfe has skeletons in his closet, he'd never let Miller do this. In fact, he'd make extra-sure that this was exactly what Miller *wasn't* doing. Wolfe would do what . . . ? He'd have Miller's phones bugged, computer hacked, house monitored . . ."

The waiter arrives, and replaces Freeley's empty glass with a fresh full one.

"And if there's anyone in the world who would know how Wolfe would react, and what he would do to quash the book, it's Miller. But still Miller wanted to—*needed* to—publish it. So he faked his suicide. He disappeared somewhere with the old research material, and spent a half-year—is that how long ago he supposedly died?—to finish writing the book."

Freeley takes a sip of his amber liquid, plunks his heavy glass down onto the thick coaster on the thin tabletop.

"That's an awful lot of trouble to go to, for a man on his deathbed. Why would he?"

Freeley still doesn't say anything. He wants Brad to figure out the same thing he figured out, in the same way, without any help. Freeley wants the confirmation that this is the inevitable interpretation.

"Because Wolfe did something truly horrible," Brad concludes. "That's the only way this makes sense. There's something in Wolfe's past that'll absolutely ruin him. Ruin other people too. And that's what's in the book."

Brad thinks Freeley nods, or maybe it's just the motion of chewing nuts.

"And of course Wolfe is certainly aware of his own past, and of the danger. So he'd do anything—*any*thing—to prevent this." Now it all makes total sense. "Listen, Trey: somebody strange came to see me too. Possibly the same guy who came to see you."

The lawyer looks up.

"It was a few months ago. And the guy claimed to be NSA, but I had no way of knowing if that was true. Anyway, he told me that if we received a submission like this—a biography of Wolfe, one that contained bombshell revelations—then it'd be a fake. A hoax, being perpetrated for the purpose of orchestrating a hostile corporate takeover."

Freeley chews on this. "And this man, what did he want from you?"

"He was telling me—he was *order*ing me—to contact him if we received this."

"And have you?"

"Not yet. I called you. What are my options, Trey?"

"*Options*?" Freeley rummages around in the nut bowl, digging for something, finds it. "You don't have any options, McNally." He pops another cashew.

"But what about the First Amendment? What about freedom of the press? What about an informed citizenry being the only true repository of the public will?"

Freeley snorts. "This isn't civics class, McNally. And you're not a crusader, or a revolutionary. You're a book publisher, McNally. A *businessman*."

Brad shifts in his chair.

"And maybe," the lawyer continues, "the manuscript *is* a hoax." He leans forward, rests his elbows on his haunches. "Maybe this is another failure of imagination, on our part . . . I mean, a fake biography *would* be sorta genius, wouldn't it?"

"Who's side are you on, Trey?"

"Ha! Side?! I'm not on anyone's *side*. I don't have skin in this game, McNally. And you need to remember that *neither do you*." Freeley leans back in his chair, satisfied with his own certainty.

"Trey?"

"Yeah?"

"Do you have any idea what's *in* the book?"

"No, McNally, and I don't care to. And neither should you."

CHAPTER 33

I sabel walks past the cashier and around the fast-food counter, the stench of nitrates laying siege to her nostrils, hot dogs rotating on their bed of rotating steel rods. The bathroom is incomprehensibly large, room for three or even four times the number of facilities, and reeks of industrial-grade cleaner. She relieves herself, and washes her hands, and splashes water on her face. She smoothes her hair, and stares into the mirror. She wonders, again, if this is going to work. And what's going to happen if it doesn't.

Isabel plucks a few paper towels. Picks her bag off the floor, walks to an uncluttered corner of the restroom. She wipes down the floor with the towels, then carefully upends the contents of her bag onto this cleanish surface. She sorts through everything, all the familiar items, the compact and wallet and lipsticks and business-card case and sunglasses and other whatnots. The rubber-band-bound manuscript. All this stuff is definitely hers; nothing unfamiliar.

She takes the empty bag itself in hand, the crumpled pile of black leather and steel studs and zippers and clasps, with a designer's name-plate riveted to the side. A conspicuously expensive bag, the shackles of a peculiar form of slavery. She loathes the impulse that made her buy it, another lemming at a boutique, casually sliding her credit card onto the gleaming counter as if a sixteen-hundred-dollar handbag were just another daily purchase, a dozen eggs, a bottle of shampoo.

She runs her hand along the surface of the bag, her fingertips rubbing one leather plane, another, another. Along the seams, across the bottom. She doesn't feel anything strange, doesn't see anything abnormal.

And then finally she does, a stud of a different size, in the wrong spot. She folds the leather over itself and brings it closer to her face and glances down at this thing. It isn't a stud at all, but a different type of little metal disk. She pinches it between two fingertips, and pulls, and the small rivet-like shape slides out smoothly. She turns it over, examines the sharp pin that affixed this thing that's not hers to the thing that is.

This is it, the tracking device. This is what had been attached to her bag at the restaurant, way back at breakfast, when that man brushed past her. This is how she was followed, when it was impossible to have been followed.

She puts the device back on the floor. Uses her toe to push the little thing into the gray grout at the corner where the white wall tile meets the taupe vinyl flooring, exactly where something like this would fall if it somehow detached from her bag, and got kicked into a corner inadvertently by someone who never felt the little piece of metal touch her toe.

So now Jeffrey's compromised cell phone is in the East River, and his bugged pen is probably in the pocket of some tourist from the Empire State Building. Isabel's cell is in that overweight woman's green bag, and this little device here is lying in a film of disinfectant on a gas-station restroom floor. They should now be completely free of surveillance. Electronic surveillance, that is.

And with the purchase of the gas using someone else's credit card, it will appear that Isabel is running from the city and trying to hide, but failing. Whoever is tracking her will still think—will still be certain—that her destination is her client Judy's beach house in Amagansett.

Isabel has known for hours that she was being tracked. She made a show of being elusive, in order to make the next elusion successful. Or at least to appear to be successful. It is not a straightforward cat-and-mouse situation.

She walks back through the convenience store, grabs a couple of things without particularly thinking, pays in cash, pretends to notice the security camera and quickly turns away, hiding her face from the lens.

She returns to the gassed-up Mercedes, clutching a Diet Coke and a bag of pretzels, slipping the new pack of cigarettes into her sanitized handbag.

Jeffrey pulls out of the service station, onto a quiet exurban road that suddenly turns into a cluttered commercial stretch. Isabel notices the sign for an outlet mall, and something occurs to her. "Pull in here," she says.

"We're going *shopping*?"

They hustle into a chain store, men's clothing on one side, women's on the other. "Choose new pants and shirt," she says. "Meet me at the register."

When their transaction is finished—cash, again—she leads Jeffrey back out to the endless stretch of glass-fronted storefronts, finds restrooms in a brightly lit hall with vending machines and water fountains. "Go change," she says. "Throw your old clothes in the garbage."

He raises his eyebrows.

"There could be tracking devices on them. Or transmitting. Or whatever. Just do it."

On the road again, speeding alongside vast expanses of sod, the flat green tracts presided over by massive irrigation sprinklers, looking like the landing apparatuses of UFOs. They drive past fields of corn and potatoes, plant nurseries and paddock fencing, the small nylon flags on the greens of golf courses, flapping in the breeze. White-clapboard churches, tall and tight and towering into the bright blue sky. Farmstands boasting local produce, homemade pie, on hand-painted signs.

The road curves and dips and rolls under a leafy canopy, then emerges into the open, with fields and sky on either side. There are now more grapevines than anything, with signs every few miles to TURN HERE for a winery, a tasting room, a vineyard. They catch their first sight of the water, along a rocky-sandy strip of a beach. Then the road leaves the shoreline again, through woods and a hodgepodge of houses, vinyl-sided split-levels and modest little Capes and ill-proportioned contemporaries, then a tightly clustered collection of Victorians in a dense village, then all at once the trees and houses fall away and there's water everywhere, left and right, sailboats and whitecaps and long stretches of pebbly beach.

She glances over and catches Jeffrey eyeing her, and gives him a coy little smile. He looks sheepish and returns his attention to the road, accelerating across the wind-whipped causeway, speeding toward the end of the continent. Isabel tries to lose herself in the scenery, the idea of being here, out of the city, surrounded by blues and greens, water and sand, grass and trees, alongside this man who loves her, this man she might love.

An escape from life, an escape from reality. But not even that: this is just the fantasy of an escape, a fleeting self-delusion. She manages to get a second's relaxation out of it, maybe two, before the reality of this flight crashes to the forefront of her mind, like a desperate junky bursting into a twenty-four-hour convenience store at 2:00 a.m., waving a gun in a shaking hand.

"Turn left up here."

Jeffrey leans forward, over the wheel. "Where?"

"There, that little clearing."

He turns the car onto the gravel, nuzzling the front fender against a weathered chain hanging from chunky wooden posts. Isabel climbs out of the car, unhooks the chain, lets it fall. She waves Jeff through, then replaces the chain and climbs back into the passenger seat. This is their second stop in five minutes; the first was to buy vegetables at a farmstand. Dinner.

Jeffrey drives slowly, bumping over the narrow rutted dirt path

223

through thick vine-choked woods, climbing a slight grade, occasionally a glimpse of open farmland through the trees. After a half-mile they come to a circular drive surrounding a stand of trees, a shingled house bordered by tall grasses.

They get out of the car, walk to the side of the house, where it becomes clear that they're atop a towering bluff, a steep drop of fifty feet—more?—down to a rocky beach, slate-blue water, a sliver of land on the horizon.

"Nice place," Jeffrey says. "What's that land over there?"

"Connecticut."

"Aren't the Hamptons on the Atlantic?"

She can't tell if he's being genuine or facetious. "Did you notice us driving through any towns called Hampton? Westhampton, Southampton, Bridgehampton?" This is one of those things assumed by New Yorkers of a certain type: that everyone is familiar with the geography of the South Fork of Long Island.

"What do I know from the Hamptons? I thought we were taking a shortcut. The back roads. Whatever."

She shakes her head.

"But isn't Judy's house in the Hamptons?"

"It is. But we're not going there: that's where I want people to *think* we're going. I want them to follow us to Judy's house. But we're nowhere near there."

"Why?"

"Why what?"

"Why do you want them—whoever *they* are—to go to Judy's house?"

"Because her place is next door to a movie star's house with head-of-state-level security. If anyone unsavory shows up there, taking unsavory action, there'll be a full-out war."

Isabel rummages around a large terracotta planter filled with lavender, digs out a set of keys on a hardware-store ring. She unlocks the front door, large and heavy and inset with panels of stained glass, a loud creak as it swings open.

She drops her bag in the foyer and walks into the large living room with the view of the water, shimmering in the late-afternoon light. The beadboard walls offer a very different view, of hundreds of black-and-white photos of every size and shape and type, from tiny Polaroids up through poster-size prints. Each and every one of people.

"So whose house *is* this?"

"Naomi's."

"Ah." Jeffrey nods. "I just ran into her this afternoon." Everyone in New York book publishing knows—or knows of—the owner of the independent bookstore in Greenwich Village, in whose front room many a first novelist had their first readings.

Jeffrey examines the wall. "What's with all the photos? This sort of looks like the work of a serial killer. I didn't realize Naomi was nuts."

"These are Naomi's friends. Her life. These are all people who've visited this house over the past decade. This had been her parents' house; the bookstore was theirs too." Isabel scans the wall. "Naomi loves film, of every sort. She used to be a filmmaker." She locates the picture she's looking for, a glossy eight-by-ten at eye height. "Look." She points. "We spent a long weekend here."

She watches Jeffrey lean in to get a better look, Isabel with her son and ex-husband. She looked so much younger back then; so much happier. But it wasn't that long ago.

"It was our last vacation."

CHAPTER 34

Naomi needs to use both hands to carry the giant bottle of donated Italian white, pouring sloppy splashes into flimsy cups. The bookstore hosts some glass-stemware parties, and some plastic-cup parties; this is one of the latter.

The author finished his reading and Q&A a half-hour earlier, but he's still seated at the small table in the back room, inscribing books and chatting with his friends, who like him are in their late twenties, nearly all the men bearded and tattooed, wearing plaid and porkpies and tight blue jeans rolled at the cuff. The women all seem to have glittering little studs in their nostrils, and ironic eyeglasses or haircuts, or both.

Naomi squeezes the author's shoulder as she walks by, a more intimate gesture than their relationship warrants. But her business is cultivating intimacy with authors, as well as with editors and publishers, publicists and sponsors—the jug wine has been donated, as has the cheap cheese—and bloggers and newspapers, and the community board and the principals of the local elementary schools, and anyone else who can help a bookshop maintain its presence as a neighborhood institution, a cultural center, a community resource.

She walks out the French doors and down the few steps into the backyard, which had always been a neglected overgrown haven for rats and pigeons during the decades that her parents owned the shop. They'd started the radical left-wing bookstore back in the early seventies, when such an enterprise constituted a viable retail segment, bizarrely. Over the years Berger's Books transformed into a general bookstore, reflecting the evolution of the Village itself, from a low-rent haven for artists and writers and musicians and intellectuals, then to the epicenter of East Coast gay life, then to an enclave for yuppies who preferred their gentrification with a whiff of bohemian, and most recently the realignment that accompanied an influx of the downright rich and famous, refugees from Beverly Hills and the Upper East Side who pay five million for one-bedroom penthouses. Bleecker Street was once littered with cluttered little shops selling beat-up antiques and used vinyl and secondhand books and novelty condoms. Now it is almost exclusively high-end fashion.

Naomi grew up in this shop, doing her homework sitting on the floor in the history section, stocking shelves as a teenager, starting the newsletter and building the website. But she always had other full-time-ish jobs in the film industry, while at the same time constantly trying to raise the money to produce her own highly experimental—and admittedly not widely understood—short films. Perhaps this didn't look like a satisfying life for a fully grown adult woman. But as she kept telling her parents, it was.

Then they died; a drunk driver during broad daylight on the Long Island Expressway. Suddenly Naomi was the sole proprietor of the shop. She couldn't bear to simply shutter the joint, nor to look for buyers. So she took the helm, temporarily, during one of those occasional windows when the finances of the book business appear to be in relatively good shape. People in Greenwich Village bought a lot of books, and didn't welcome chain stores; Berger's was doing all right. And Naomi quickly grew fond of the whole thing, the employees and the customers and the authors, the kids and their moms who came to the Saturday-morning readings.

It took her a few years to admit that her temporary stewardship had turned permanent. Then she hired a guy to build a simple counter in the rear, and bought a handful of beat-up café tables, and an espresso machine, and a few baskets for baked goods. A place to hang out on a rainy day. And for when it wasn't raining, she reconfigured the backyard, put some secondhand teak furniture out there, plus a few bins of plastic toys, and all-weather outlets for the computer users—the writers and programmers and start-up dreamers—who swarm into every café every midmorning, living their office-less lives in public, absorbing free wi-fi. Not too many of these café people buy books, at least not regularly; but they do pay for coffee and scones. Some days she sells more scones than books.

But now these backyard tables are occupied by the party's smokers, dropping their butts into nearly empty plastic glasses, getting jovially drunk on a Tuesday night.

Her phone rings. She glances at the screen, and sees something odd: it seems to be herself who's calling. "Hello?"

"Hi Naomi, it's Isabel." Her old friend, calling from the landline in Naomi's weekend house. Another of her parents' follies from the seventies—a ramshackle shingled house atop a tall bluff near the end of Long Island. It was the middle of nowhere, back then; bought for a song, and slowly renovated on the cheap. Her parents were pretty astute investors, for a couple of Communists.

"Are you in my house, Isabel?"

"Is that okay?"

"Of *course*. I have only one best friend who's also my literary agent." When Naomi was halfway through writing her memoir, she'd sent it to a very encouraging, extremely astute Isabel, who helped her re-imagine the whole structure, turning it into a much better book than Naomi would've—could've—written on her own. And then Isabel had represented the project, submitted it to a dozen editors, and within a few weeks had collected a half-dozen offers, reaching all the way up to $110,000. Six figures!

But of course the agent's commission was 15 percent off the top. And who knew that the advance was payable in four separate disbursements? And because it wasn't Naomi's sole revenue in any of the four years of payouts, she had to lump the money into her overall income, taxed at her general rate for city, state, federal. So in the end that six-figure payday translated into four checks of roughly $15,000 apiece, spread over four years.

One of the partygoers is telling a very loud story, and Naomi looks around for an unoccupied spot, a quiet zone. She starts to walk inside. "You know you're always—*always*—welcome."

"Thanks," Isabel says. "Sorry I didn't call to ask, or anything. It's been . . . This has been a very strange day."

Naomi unlocks the door to the tiny windowless office, dim and quiet. "Everything okay?"

"Oh . . . God, it's hard to explain. But listen, Naomi, the cameras in the house: they still work, right?"

For her most recent film project, Naomi had secretly wired the entire ground floor of the country house with small hidden cameras, and microphones. "Yeah."

"Good. Would you mind telling me how you turn them on?"

This was unexpected. "Sure."

"Good, thanks. And Naomi?"

"Yeah?"

"That gun? Is it still here?"

"So we're in agreement?" Charlie asked.

Dave nodded.

"This is exciting," Charlie said, smiling broadly. "Are you excited?"

"I am."

Everything was going better than expected. So they had started talking about what was next, with that optimistic arrogance particular to young men like them. And next was the American cable news network, whose investors were already lining up. Charlie was going to have his own show, the main draw, weeknights prime-time.

"We're going to do great things," Charlie said, gazing out the window of Wolfe Worldwide Media's main conference room, perched atop an old building in Silicon Alley, with open views of the Empire State Building, just a half-mile away. "Great things."

"We are."

"You don't sound too convinced."

Dave tapped his pen on the pad for a few beats. "We still haven't discussed it, Charlie."

Charlie shifted in his seat. He took a sip of coffee, replaced his cup to the table.

"I'm talking about the other girl. The one in the dance club."

"I know what you're talking about."

"She may have seen us. She may be able to identify you, or me for that matter. When you're on television all the time . . ." Dave held out his hands, explaining the rest of that unappealing narrative.

"Then she might recognize me," Charlie provided it, confirmation that he understood. "She might come forward, point a finger: *That's him! The last person with my friend before she disappeared! J'accuse!!* Is that what you're afraid of?"

"Yes, that's right. Aren't you?"

Charlie blinked his assent. "So are you merely pointing out an obvious problem? Or do you have a solution?"

"Do you?"

Charlie picked up his coffee again, but didn't raise it to his mouth. "We have to determine whether that's likely to happen, don't we?"

"Duh. How?"

"First we find her. That shouldn't be so hard. Her name was in the newspapers, we know where she went to college, and when. We should be able—"

"Yeah," Dave cut him off, "I got it: we can find her. Then?"

"We figure out if she recognizes me. Which I'm sure she won't. So we'll be in the clear."

Dave smiled, condescendingly. "Yes Charlie," he said, leaning forward, forearms on thighs, hands clasped in front of him, prayer-like, "but what if she does?"

CHAPTER 35

Isabel pads across the whitewashed floor in bare feet. The wood is smooth and cool against her soles, and the breeze smells of the sea, and the knee-high waves lap at the rocky beach, a circular rhythm that sounds like radio static, someone playing with the tuning knob, trying to get a better signal. She can imagine the low indistinct murmur of a ballgame from a transistor radio in another room, and birds chirping their endless conversations, a car with an ailing transmission accelerating on the distant road, the twang-and-splash of a cannonball into a swimming pool from a sagging yellowed diving board, and the ringing peel of a child's laughter.

She can imagine that it's three years ago, and she's still married, and her baby is still alive.

Her eye is drawn to the built-in bookcases that flank the fireplace, filled with nature books and photography books, with milky white seashells and old green soda bottles, the conventional ephemera of a beach house, plus the electronic equipment hidden in the corners, the discreet circular lenses, the reasons she's here.

The weight of her situation settles onto her shoulders, her soul, her entire being. She can't remember what it was like to feel safe. It seems like weeks since she finished this manuscript, since this whole thing started, but it's . . . is it possible? . . . can it be true that she finished reading the manuscript *this* morning?

Isabel puts her hand on the refrigerator's handle, but she doesn't pull. Instead she leans against the door. She starts to cry, at first just a few catches of her breath and a couple of tears, but it quickly escalates, and soon her shoulders are heaving, her whole body is convulsing, crumpled there against the cool metallic plane of the refrigerator.

The crying stops of its own accord, its urgency dissipated. She takes a deep quavering breath, then another more controlled one. She wipes her cheeks with her right forefinger; her left hand is still holding the handle.

She opens the door to the freezer compartment, and can't help but glance down to the bin on the bottom shelf, the big Ziploc that she tucked beneath the box of ice pops, just its zip-closed top fold visible. Then she pulls out the ice-cube tray, and dumps all the cubes into a glass pitcher ringed with multicolor stripes. As she fills the pitcher with tap water, she can see her reflection in the window above the sink. She's a mess. She wipes her eyes again with the knuckles, then uses a dish towel to do a more thorough job.

Isabel returns to the veranda, where Jeffrey is putting his empty pasta bowl down on the wicker ottoman. He looks over the railing, to where the sun has sunk below the horizon of the water, setting the sky on fire, sending color bolts through the waves.

"Thank you," he says, taking the glassware from her. He fills a glass with water, hands it to her. Then he fills another, for himself. "That was delicious."

A single-person meal, pasta with vegetables alongside a salad, a few dollars' worth of fresh ingredients and ten minutes of cooking time. It's the type of meal she prepares a lot of, these days.

Isabel sets her empty bowl into Jeffrey's, but hers is tilted because of his fork; hers is balanced precariously, while his is steady. She stares at this small edifice, the small unstable structure, perhaps analogous to their lives.

Jeffrey turns back to the sunset, and she follows his gaze. For a moment, the two of them stare silently at the colorful remains of yesterday. Then he turns to her and smiles. She has always felt secure in the warm embrace of his smile.

"I know this must be hard for you," he says. "Being here."

She feels tears welling up again, and struggles to suppress them, to not fall apart here and now and possibly permanently. She's been trying to hold it together for a very long time.

There was nothing worse than Tommy's memorial service. Nothing more heartbreaking, gut-wrenching, tear-inducing. Unspeakably sad, but people still had to speak. The hall was standing-room-only, at least three hundred people wearing black, holding handkerchiefs, sniffling, leaning against one another, hugging, wiping their noses, rubbing knuckles into their eye sockets, running fingers through their hair, staring up at the ornately gilt ceiling, at ten-thirty on a Monday morning. What a way to start the week.

Her mother-in-law was the first speaker. The aging hippie had never looked more formal, in her black shift and tights. Grandmothers know better, she said. They know that everything will pass: every tantrum, every toilet-training mishap, every manipulative strategy for avoiding bedtime, every cold and flu, every stomach virus and scraped knee and busted lip, every vicious meltdown with projectile vomit and bitter, stinging accusation. It will pass, grandmothers know, and the memories of the little annoying things will transform into some of the wonderful things, the lovely things, the things we should have appreciated while we could. And so the unfairness of this, it's unthinkable . . . Then Karla fell apart.

She was followed by a family friend. Then Isabel's parents. The final speaker was Isabel's husband, who spoke for barely a minute, with Isabel slumped against him. But it was too much, not just for him and Isabel but for everyone in the voluminous room, for all the people crushed by the loss of a boy who had was about to start his second year of preschool, who had a best friend named Danny and a favorite teddy named Baba-Beebee and a favorite color orange and a second favorite color green and a favorite television show and movie and song, who had just that Tuesday morning had a tantrum at the toilet—"Pee-pee, come back! Please come back, pee-pee"—because Isabel had mistakenly flushed the toilet before letting Tommy do it himself.

There wasn't a dry eye in the house.

Then three hundred black-clad mourners streamed out of the building onto the gray, wet street, dabbing their eyes and holding hands. Some lit cigarettes, and others flung their arms in the air to hail taxis, and dozens or scores or hundreds reached into their pockets and handbags and opened cell phones, and switched off silent modes, and examined screens and pressed devices against ears, staring off into the low dark sky, heads hanging at angles, listening to messages, concentrating on the details of their lives from which they'd been absent for seventy-five minutes, to the rescheduled appointments and updates and questions, and their eyes were still inflamed when they eased back into their normal lives, untragic lives from which their perfect little child had not been taken, unshattered lives, lives that still made sense, lives with reasons to move forward, to go to work and then to go home, to wake up the next day and do it again.

But not Isabel. Everyone could see that her life no longer made sense. All those new friends she'd made in the playground and the preschool, all those women who spent their lives managing the trappings of their wealth, tending to their co-op lofts in Tribeca and their beach houses in Water Mill and their slope-side condos in Vail, scheduling their nannies and babysitters and tutors and piano instructors and French teachers, their tailors and cleaners and manicurists and colorists and stylists, their personal trainers and Pilates sessions and yoga classes, their doormen and garage attendants, their summer and Christmas vacations, their midwinter breaks and spring breaks, their cars and boats, their French upholstery and granite countertops and reclaimed wood floors, their this and their that, but for Isabel it just didn't fucking matter what Farrow & Ball shade of gray anyone was painting any goddamned foyer.

Suddenly there was no reason to go to work, or to go home, or to wake up tomorrow.

Because she couldn't stop thinking this: we don't lose our babies. That's not part of the deal of life. That's not *fair*.

And while she retreated into her grief, her husband veered further toward his nihilist tendencies, the amorality that had always been lurking beneath his surface. He was angrier at the world than ever, and he was taking revenge by not caring about it.

Isabel couldn't help but think it was her he was angry at. That he blamed her. Because she certainly did.

They had never been one of those hand-holding couples, never called each Babe, never were the ones running out onto the dance floor. But neither had done anything egregious, neither had said anything horrible. It was just that their marriage, which to begin with hadn't been constructed on the soundest foundation, couldn't support the weight of their tragedy, their grief. And Isabel's guilt.

So the divorce wasn't acrimonious. They split their assets right down the middle, without debate. He bought her out of her share of the downtown loft, and she used that money to buy the uptown apartment, to fill it with soft comfortable furniture in soothing shades of neutrals, with top-end appliances and nickel-plated fixtures. He visited the new place once, for a glass of wine on the terrace, soon after she moved in. He brought a housewarming present, a small lithograph by Helen Frankenthaler, about whom Isabel had written a term paper, two decades earlier.

They still spoke, every few months. Or maybe it had become a couple times per year. There were things Isabel still loved about him, various reminders that could be elicited by that ten-thousand-dollar piece of paper hanging on her living room wall, which is probably why he went out of his way to buy the thing in the first place, a thoughtful present for an ex-wife.

She stands at the kitchen counter, leafing through pages, rushed. She doesn't want Jeffrey to discover her in here, doing this.

Isabel knows it's in the scene about the car accident, so it takes her only a few seconds to find, near the bottom of page 136, the sentence that changed everything:

"Charlie, come on," I said, "stop the car."

She can't believe how naive she was, how trusting. She'd always thought of herself as savvy, wary; a native New Yorker's self-assurance in her immunity to swindles of every sort. But here it was, black-and-white evidence that she'd been deceived on the deepest levels, for an unforgivably long time.

CHAPTER 36

"Hello, Hayden." Charlie Wolfe said. The two men shook hands as if they were old friends, free hands on shoulders, wide smiles. But friends are not what they'd ever been. "Nice to see you again."

For a few years in the 1980s, back when Charlie was still in high school, his father Preston Wolfe had been deputy director of Central Intelligence. The Cold War was in its last throes, and Europe was still a crucial theater for American intelligence. Hayden was becoming an important man there, in an important part of the world, so he and Wolfe *père* had gotten to know each other. They'd maintained a relationship at a low simmer for the next couple of decades, over which Hayden caught the occasional glimpse of young Charlie: a cocky high-school kid at an elitist New York private school, then an irresponsible frat boy at Cornell, then a striking transformation into a studious law-school student at Yale, and finally an ambitious and hardworking and sober young adult, immensely ambitious.

Hayden hadn't been altogether flabbergasted when Wolfe *fils* first presented himself in London in the late nineties, looking for a useful connection. Just mildly surprised. But then it had been absolutely shocking to Hayden that they actually started doing business together. The ensuing fifteen years had been good to both of them, in their own spheres, thanks in no small part to the other.

But then it ended.

"Thanks for meeting me here," Charlie said. Hayden had just flown in from Berlin, a special trip to talk to this one man, in this old park.

They took seats in the more upright style of the hundreds of metal chairs scattered on the pebbled paths surrounding the fountain. The more prone style was for reading, or sunbathing. But it was December, and no one was sunbathing. Indeed only a handful of other people were scattered around the Jardin des Tuileries. A pair of guys in loose-fitting overcoats stood fifty meters away; Charlie's bodyguards. Ninety degrees around the fountain, a bundled-up woman in giant sunglasses sat in one of the reclining chairs, facing the weak southerly sun, a book in her lap, looking somewhat asleep. A quartet of retirees—Italian, or maybe Spanish—were eating sandwiches, laughing, having a grand old time. A hundred meters away, a big young guy leaning against a leafless a tree was obviously the watcher from the American Embassy. Charlie Wolfe had become a man who would be monitored, as a matter of course. And that meant, unfortunately, that so would Hayden.

"So," Hayden said, "I thought we were finished."

In early autumn they'd had dinner in Berlin, and Charlie had brought their long, mutually beneficial relationship to a close. "It's been only a few months, Charlie. Have you changed your mind already? Miss me that much?"

Charlie smiled, accepting the joke, but not enjoying it. "Did you know I was thinking about running for office? Senate?"

Of course Hayden had heard about that, and he'd thought it an absolutely terrible idea. He didn't respond.

"I also started writing a book, which was a little bit of autobiography, plus a lot of my vision for the future of America. I was writing with Dave Miller." We would sit down together, Dave and I, for a half-hour at a time, or an hour, whatever we had, whenever we had it. I'd talk, and he'd type, and ask me questions. We'd work together on the phrasing of important passages. He did some interviewing of my family, and my old classmates, gathering background . . ." Charlie trailed off, obviously coming to a part of the story he didn't want to tell.

"Dave kept the working manuscript in his office, with some handwritten notes of mine, and contact information for sources, and law-school papers, and DVDs of my TV appearances. Et cetera."

Charlie enunciated the Latin slowly and pointedly—*et cet e ra*.

"Then Dave was diagnosed with cancer—awful, really." Charlie shook his head. "And then yet more awful was last week, when I found out about the plane going down."

Hayden felt that they were coming to the crux of things, and he watched Charlie's face carefully. That phrase—"found out about the plane going down"—was a peculiar way to refer to his best friend's suicide.

"It took a couple of days before it occurred to me that I ought to retrieve this book material; there'd been other things on my mind. So Monday evening, I went into Dave's office, and had the file cabinet unlocked, and I looked around quickly. Then I looked around slowly, and carefully. Then I looked around exhaustively. But I didn't find any trace of the material."

"This was all hard-copy? What about the digital files?"

"We didn't keep digital files."

Hayden looked uncomprehendingly at the digital-media mogul.

"Digital is too easily duplicated. Too easily *stolen*. Any digital storage device, no matter how secure, is in the end essentially insecure. What's *not* insecure is a stack of paper that no one knows about. That no one will go looking for. So we typed, and printed, and destroyed the word-processing files. The manuscript exists only in physical form. Somewhere."

"I assume you had his house checked?"

"Nothing there. Not in Georgetown, and not in his place at the beach."

"Is it possible Miller destroyed it?"

"Sure. But why would he?"

Hayden shrugged.

"No manuscript anywhere. And," Charlie said, leaning forward, "no *body*."

Hayden stared off into the distance at the French Renaissance elegance of the Louvre looming above the rigid lines of the park. Behind them was the obelisk at the center of the place de la Concorde, and the Champs Elysées, and the Arc de Triomphe, and the Eiffel Tower, over which the dense clouds were draped in folds of gray.

They were sitting in the middle of everything, a wide-open vista, impossible for anyone to surreptitiously listen to their conversation. Anyone else, that is.

"What's your theory?" he asked.

Charlie stared at Hayden for a few seconds, a purposefully pregnant pause. "I think the suicide was faked, and Dave is hiding out somewhere, finishing the book."

"Oh good grief. Why?"

"I'm not sure."

"Don't give me that crap. What *happened*?"

"Listen, Hayden, it's complicated."

Hayden's first instinct when he'd received Charlie's summons, two days earlier, was that this was going to turn out to be something disastrous. He'd learned over the years that his first instinct about these things was unfailingly correct. "So explain it, Charlie. You're not stupid. Neither am I."

Charlie shifted in his seat, uncomfortable. "Dave was always kind of jealous of me. Envious. Of the money, and, y'know, everything. And something happened back in college . . . that was . . ."

"*What?*"

Charlie leaned away, crossed one leg over the other. "There was an accident. A car accident. I was, um, drunk."

"And?"

"And a girl died."

Hayden chewed on this distasteful nugget. "Miller knows about it?"

"He was in the car."

Oh fuck. "But he has remained quiet? For, what, a quarter-century?"

"We paid him."

"Who's *we*?"

"My father. And me. But I guess it was just my father who was doing the actual, um, *paying*."

"You're telling me that Preston Wolfe was involved in this?"

"My dad was in Ithaca, the night of the accident. After Dave and I, ah, *dis*posed of the girl's body, we went to Dad. It was the middle of the night. We went to him for help."

"For help doing what?"

"Deciding what to do. Deciding how to hide ourselves, and the evidence. Deciding to start paying Dave. Forty thousand per year. Not just to keep him silent, but to be able to prove that he was accepting money from us in return for staying silent. To make him a conspirator. In a crime. To ensure that he'd suffer unappealing consequences if he stopped staying silent."

"This was your father's idea?"

Charlie shook his head.

"You were a devious little bastard, weren't you?"

"He needed the money. Did you know Dave was poor? His parents— his mother—a Communist? An actual *Marxist*?"

Hayden didn't answer.

"And then, y'know, Dave helped me start the business, and everything ... We became sort of intertwined. And his relationship with me—our relationship, our business—made him rich. Richer than he ever thought he could be, or should be: he was always kind of uneasy with the money. His Communist mother was ashamed of him, and I think he was ashamed of himself. He had become everything he'd been raised to not become; to *despise*, in fact."

"He was explicit about this?"

"No. But his self-loathing was pretty clear. And then his personal life certainly didn't help. You know about that?"

Hayden nodded.

245

"Then we launched the cable division in Washington, and moved the HQ down there, and it was hugely successful . . ."

"And then?"

"And then Finland."

Their first joint operation, fifteen years earlier, had been an Italian presidential candidate whose campaign imploded with the revelation that he was sleeping with a nineteen-year-old. Then there was the newly elected Liverpudlian MP who resigned after developing a debilitating cocaine habit, caught in the men's room of a club in Greek Street. And the gun-running Dutch financier who was arrested in Athens, and within hours was murdered in jail.

Ruining ruinable lives, for profit and politics.

"I thought you said that was under control."

"Well, I thought it was. Mostly."

Because Finland was different. Not a great idea from the get-go: an unstable target, a web entrepreneur whose muckraking site was making America look bad, and challenging Wolfe's market share, and breaking a lot of laws, all at once. To Hayden it smelled a lot like a personal Charlie Wolfe grudge, and he should've rejected the idea outright. In years past, he would've rejected it. But his moral compass had slowly been corrupted, eventually reset, and north was now pointing in a direction that wasn't true. Compromise had been too good to Hayden, its results too satisfying.

"But then a few months later he announces he's sick, dying, see ya."

"You think he didn't really have cancer? Doesn't?"

"As far as I could tell, yes, he does. He saw specialists, took tests. He looked like shit, lost weight, color. He was definitely sick*ly*. But doctors and hospitals, y'know, don't exactly part willingly with their patient records. Plus it's not impossible to fabricate test results, or medical reports."

"So if Miller really *does* have cancer, Charlie, is this what he's doing on his deathbed? Exposing your accident, and his role in it?"

"Yup."

"And what if he *doesn't* have cancer?"

"Maybe he's doing the same thing. Just not on a deathbed."

This was a pretty unappealing situation. "Do you have any idea where he is, Charlie?"

"Me, I think he's in Mexico. I had some tech guys go through his stuff. He'd deleted a bunch of files from his computer, erased his browsing history. But he neglected to delete the cookies."

"The cookies."

"Yeah, they're a record of the websites he'd visited, which makes it—"

"I know what cookies are. That's odd, no?"

"What?"

"That Miller trashed some files and wiped the history, but didn't delete the cookies."

"Dave wasn't especially computer-literate. That was never his expertise." Charlie shrugged. "Anyway, there was a lot of web-browsing history involving Mexico. Researching places—San Miguel de Allende, Cuernavaca, Oaxaca—where there's a lot of expat infrastructure."

"Why Mexico?"

"As I told you, his family is Communist."

"And?" Hayden squinted. "Mexico isn't Communist. Never has been."

"I don't know. It's, um, *proletarian*. Whatever." Charlie shrugged. "But anyway, he was looking at flights to Mexico. And buses, which are apparently the way people get around the country. Plus my guys were pretty sure he bought a first-class ticket from Miami to Mexico City."

This sounded too good to be true. Sometimes too good to be true was, still, true. But there was no way that these supposed overlooked cookies were going to be the quick-and-easy solution. And Hayden was getting the sneaking feeling that there was another angle that was almost too bad to be true.

"Charlie, how much does Miller know about our business together?"

Charlie stared intently at the ground before answering, "A lot."

Hayden felt his chest pushing in. He turned away from Charlie, whose face was giving away nothing. He let his gaze wander across the fountain at the woman in sunglasses, still sitting there, face turned to the feeble Parisian winter sun.

"Everything?"

Charlie raised his eyebrows, but still didn't meet Hayden's eye.

There were a great many people in the Agency who would do anything to get ahead. Hayden had never been one of them, and he'd taken great pains to make that clear; he took pride in his paucity of institutional ambition. There were plenty of things that Hayden wanted out of life; he was not a man without ambition. But those things didn't include sitting in any office in Langley, no matter how large. He never wanted to live anywhere near Washington, never wanted to be surrounded by the types of people who descend on the capital to try to make their mark in the world. He never aspired to be rich, or famous.

He wanted to live in Europe, amongst Europeans, in their languages and museums and cafés. He wanted to learn interesting things, to surround himself with interesting people, to sleep with interesting women. He wanted his life to be rich with experiences and exposures, with people and places. He wanted to work in the world of espionage, not politics. He wanted the career he already had.

To facilitate his own particular modest ambitions, other more commonplace ambitions had been thrust upon him. Hayden had never thought of himself as corruptible, yet he had allowed himself to be stealthily corrupted. So now there he was, sitting in the Tuileries, staring at the man responsible.

When Hayden had first struck up his arrangement with Charlie Wolfe, it was clear that every operation was on the correct side of the right-wrong line. No one was getting hurt who was completely innocent, and every outcome was to the strategic benefit of the US. This was Hayden's job, and it was a worthwhile job, and he did it well, and he was rewarded for his success with promotions and autonomy. There was nothing wrong with any of that.

A certain degree of mission creep was, Hayden expected, unavoidable. But he now had to admit that he hadn't been nearly vigilant enough, while on the other hand Charlie had been smoothly adept at obscuring the line between what was good for the United States of America and what was good for Wolfe Worldwide Media. In hindsight it was obvious that that operation in Finland was of far greater benefit to Wolfe. Plus, a little kid died.

"Can he prove any of it, Charlie?"

"Depends on your burden of proof, I guess. He can certainly create a convincing appearance."

Hayden stared down at his wingtips, running through this new scenario.

"You know what needs to be done, yes?" Charlie asked.

Hayden turned to him with a scowl. If there's one thing he didn't need at this moment, it was to be condescended to by this prick.

"You should talk to an attorney in DC named Trey Freeley," Charlie said, pushing himself up, out of the green metal chair. He pulled his overcoat closed around his torso, hugging himself in his tailored wool. It was nearly four in the afternoon, December in Paris; the sun would be setting any minute, and it was cold, getting colder quickly. "Trey knows a lot about the book business, and the people in it." He held out his hand for a shake, and Hayden stood, took the hand.

"Thanks."

Charlie nodded while blinking slowly, as if accepting well-earned gratitude for a deeply meaningful favor he'd done, when in fact the opposite was true. He was masterful. Charlie Wolfe would probably make a great politician, if he could get past the potential crisis that was looming. Maybe other crises, ones that Hayden didn't know about.

On second thought, maybe Charlie Wolfe would be a disaster of a politician.

"I'm sorry about this, Hayden. Truly."

Charlie turned and walked away, followed at a comfortable distance by his clunky muscle, ascending the steps to the giant traffic circle of the place de la Concorde, then out of sight.

Hayden set off in the other direction, around the fountain, toward the Louvre, through the park, quiet and cold, little dogs on their late-afternoon walks, young mothers pushing prams, old men with their hands clasped behind their backs, wearing hats with brims, newspapers tucked under their arms, clouds of cigarette smoke.

Just shy of the museum, Hayden exited the Tuileries, and stopped to wait for the traffic light at the rue de Rivoli. He turned to face the oncoming traffic. Out of the corner of his eye, he saw the sunglassed woman from the fountain, trailing him by thirty meters, trying to cloak herself in the dense crowd.

Hayden waded through the teeming crush, and a block later trotted across the rue St-Honoré, and crossed the busy little *place*. He took a seat at the big bustling café, facing out onto the plaza, under a heat lamp glowing red, projecting its warmth down on his chilled head. He rubbed his hands together, and ordered a *chocolat chaud*. It was fucking freezing, colder then he expected, wearing his trusty old Mackintosh instead of a wool coat. It was supposed to rain today, tomorrow. Every goddamned day for months on end, rain was possible. Hayden had owned this raincoat as long as he'd been dealing with Charlie Wolfe, about a quarter of his lifetime.

He scanned the crowd, as ever looking for familiar faces, overcoats, hats. The endless slog of counter-surveillance. Hundreds of people streaming by, disappearing into the Métro, going this way and that, glancing at one another, and occasionally at him.

Then there she was, that woman again, walking across the plaza, toward the café, at a leisurely pace. Daylight was disappearing, but she still wore her sunglasses, which seemed to play a practical function in pinning the paisley scarf that covered her head, and wrapped around her neck, atop a subtle plaid coat with big brass buttons.

She walked straight up to Hayden's table, and took the seat by his side, also facing out to the plaza.

"*Oui Madame?*" the waiter asked.

"*Un café crème, s'il vous plaît.*" She sounded fluent, and she certainly looked the part, red lipstick and snug leather gloves with a fold of fur lining. She removed the dense boiled-wool blanket from the back of the caned chair, and spread it across her lap.

They sat in silence for a minute, people-watching. Then she removed her sunglasses, folded them, placed them on the table in front of her. She unfurled the scarf. Then she pulled the tiny speaker from her left ear, and coiled its thin wire, and tucked the neat little package into her pocket.

"So," Hayden said, "what do you think?"

The waiter delivered their drinks, and retreated hastily to the warmth of the *salle*.

"*Je crois que ça pourrait devenir difficile. Très difficile.*"

"Ooh. *Nice* tense there, Kate." It was just a couple of years ago that she barely spoke a word of French.

She tried to hide her smile in her coffee cup.

"And *fault*less pronunciation." Hayden too took a warming drink. "I agree. This could become very difficult indeed."

Kate had been back on Hayden's payroll just a few months. Nothing except small jobs, for what they'd taken to calling the Paris Substation. But this job, it was clear, was going to be big.

"Are you ready?"

"I am."

They fell silent again, while Hayden's mind chased a few different routes this could take on the way to a rich variety of disasters.

"Do you know what's in this book?" she asked.

Hayden took another sip of his chocolate, wiped his mouth with a napkin. "No one is a villain in his own autobiography, Kate. We all spend our whole lives thinking we're the heroes. But there are, obviously, villains in the world." He turned to her. "Would you agree?"

She nodded.

"Well, Charlie Wolfe is one of them."

CHAPTER 37

As anticipated, it had indeed been easy for the author to find the potential witness. All it took was a couple of minutes on the web and a
single quick phone call for definitive confirmation.

So he found himself loitering in a service doorway across the street
from the woman's office in the Flatiron District, a dark tight street just
a few blocks from the Wolfe offices, nearly all the buildings down here
constructed well before setback laws, the fifteen-story structures rising straight up from narrow sidewalks, blocking out sky and light and
breathing room, claustrophobic blocks of gray stone filled with small
businesses, tech and web, retail and media.

She didn't emerge till after seven, when he'd been standing out there
for two hours, as daylight slipped away and the temperature dropped
fifteen degrees, huddled in a not-heavy-enough overcoat over his best
suit and shiniest shoes, though not the most comfortable, especially
for standing on pavement for hours on end, nose running, ears tin-
gling, hands shoved deep into pockets, gloveless, not as prepared as he
should've been.

She walked west and he followed, a safe distance behind as well as
across the street, head down. Two blocks, then she turned downtown. He
was prepared to follow her onto the subway, or to hop into a trailing cab,

but he was expecting that she'd be going to a bar. It was Thursday night, and she was unmarried.

It turned out to be a subterranean lounge under a mediocre restaurant whose clientele was almost exclusively young gay men, bright-eyed and buff, flexing and preening and laughing too loud, trying to attract the free-floating, fickle attention that buzzed around a room like this.

Downstairs was different, darker and quieter. He saw her settling into a corner banquette, alone, and he took a seat at the bar, facing her, laying his coat on the adjoining stool. He checked his watch, 7:22, and it occurred to him that she must be meeting someone—this didn't seem like a place to have a drink by yourself, certainly not sitting in a banquette like that—and that date would probably be at 7:30, so he had a few minutes. It would be sort of perfect if they got interrupted by someone else's arrival—it would give him the impetus to press the issue—but not if that interruption was a boyfriend. He could tell from his online stalking that she was unmarried, but not if she was completely single.

He ordered a neat Scotch, and took a nerve-steeling sip. It was of course possible that she would recognize not only Charlie, but himself. Or not even Charlie, only himself. Tonight. Now.

He crossed the low-ceilinged room, his anxiety buzzing in his ears. He stopped a few steps from her table, knee-high and mirror topped, a trio of votives flickering, reflecting, scattering light.

She looked up, a pretty woman in her mid-thirties, more attractive than suggested by her pictures on the web. Both expectant and dubious, a look common to women who regularly get approached by men in bars.

"Hi," he said. His voice sounded like someone else's. "Could I buy you a drink?"

It was his job to approach this woman, to make this contact. And it had been Charlie's end of the bargain to procure the gun that was tucked, heavy as an anvil, in the silk-lined pocket of the author's cashmere overcoat.

CHAPTER 38

Jeff watches Isabel pick up her wineglass. She takes a small sip, and swallows, and licks her top lip, her tongue sliding slowly, leaving a trail of glisten, then disappearing back into her mouth. She glances down at the glass and up to him and off to the side, her eyes dancing, flitting and sparkling and flirty.

She drags on her cigarette, the oxygenized embers glowing, her own private candle, the warm flattering light washing over her face, a brightening and then a darkening. Isabel isn't one of those nervous smokers, tamping down on new packs, obsessively flipping ash, moving the cigarette from finger to finger, playing with it, posing. She simply lets the thing sit there in the crook of her fingers, inactive except when she moves it to her mouth, wraps her lips around it, and sucks.

Jeff has always loved the way Isabel smokes.

The last of the sunset bathes everything in a golden tint, giving her skin an extra-radiant glow, highlighting the amber flecks in her green eyes. He has never seen her look more beautiful, and she has always been absolutely beautiful.

"I'm exhausted," she says, shifting in her seat, stubbing out her cigarette, getting ready to rise.

"Me too." He watches her stand, then he too gets up, puts his hands in his pockets. "Are you . . . ?" He loses track of what it was he was going ask. "It's not even dark out." He glances out at the water, at the last slivers of brilliant color on the horizon, and the vast expanses of dark blues on either side.

Jeff's mind flashes back to that night, a half-year after her son died. As soon as he'd entered the dark low-ceilinged room, and saw her slouched at the bar, he'd known that not only her marriage but also her psyche were collapsing, imminently, and totally. And then of course they drank way too much. Then it was late, or maybe it wasn't so late but it just felt that way, the way an evening can get late-night-feeling when it's only the two of you, and an empty pack of cigarettes has been crumpled and discarded, and there are fives and singles strewn atop a polyurethaned bar, the remnants of a lot of rounds bought with twenties, without bothering to see if you've got exact change.

And then they were hugging. There are many different types of hugs, and this one evolved, so then they were kissing, intensely, messy.

And then she was crying.

And then it passed. It had been effervescent, like the fizz from Champagne, flat before they left the hallway in that Irish pub, flat but still drinkable, drinkable till it was gone, which it was when they left the bar, leaving those singles and fives scattered all over the goddamned place, Lord knows how ridiculous a tip they left.

And then out on the street, she hailed a taxi and jumped inside without saying goodnight, without saying anything, without giving Jeff the chance to take any action other than to watch her go, standing there on a sidewalk in front of a bar, swaying.

And he never knew—still doesn't—whether it had been real in any fashion, or whether it could be completely attributed to all the drink, or whether it was the disintegration of her marriage, or this generalized emotional collapse of hers, under the unbearable burden of her grief. Whether it had anything to do with him whatsoever, or if he was not much more than a bystander.

Jeff was also, at the time, married to somebody else.

They never again discussed it, never mentioned it. So Jeff never knew how Isabel felt about it; or even if she completely remembered it.

What he does know is that he didn't do what he should've: gone after her. He should've pushed his way into the cab with her, or he should've called her first thing the next morning, or for lunch the next day, or the following night, or at some fucking point he should've called her and asked, "Can I see you?" He should've been there to pick up her falling-apart pieces when her husband—who it's now clear was a credulity-defying shithead—couldn't, or wouldn't.

But instead of taking immediate action, Jeff kept thinking that tomorrow he would, tomorrow some opportunity would present itself, or he'll see her next week for sure. These imaginary chances kept floating by, like ice floes that he never hopped on, waiting for a bigger one, a more secure one, he was waiting for an ice floe that was actually a luxury cruise ship that would never arrive to rescue him from his isolation, from the slow disintegration of his own marriage.

And Isabel never called. Not in the way he wanted, hoped. She never rang up and demanded that he join her in some dingy bar at an inappropriate time of day. She never called at midnight to say come over.

But now, now she's standing here in front of him, in the falling light, wearing a Mona Lisa smile that he thinks—hopes—is encouraging. And even if he's wrong, he still has to try, tonight.

"Isabel?"

"*Mmm?*"

Jeff takes one of the two steps that separate them. He has always hated this moment, butterflies in his stomach, throat tight and dry.

He takes the second step, and she doesn't retreat. Their faces are inches apart. He leans in farther, not at all confident that this will be successful. When his lips are just a breath from hers he pauses again, giving her one last chance to back away. But she doesn't, thank God, and so he kisses her, and she kisses him back, and he almost collapses in joy. He can barely enjoy the real experience of the kiss, too distracted by the idea of it.

Jeff has been kissing women for thirty years now, and he's never been entirely sure when it's going to work, with whom, and why, or how. The whole thing has always been a nightmare of indecision and insecurity. Except when it's magic, like now, and he feels her fingers on the back of his neck, pulling him in tighter, pressing herself against him—

But then what's this? She pulls her face away, and takes a step back, pouting. But no, that's just a tease. She's smiling, and turning away slowly, deliberately.

Jeff is frozen, watching her walk with measured steps, as if keeping the silent beat of a slow song.

"Come," she says, not turning back, "with me."

He cannot believe this is happening, and he can't help but verbalize this in his mind, this incredulity that she's actually going to take him to bed now of all times, in the middle of this entirely cocked-up situation, about which he has more questions than answers as every minute passes.

Because while Isabel took her late-afternoon nap, and then prepared their dinner, Jeff sat on the veranda and read the remainder of the manuscript, skimming here and there, propelled forward by the magnitude of the accusations, and nearly overwhelmed by their credibility. He'd been expecting something fantastical, something easily refutable. He'd prepared himself to dismiss this manuscript; it's part of an editor's mindset to be ready to call bullshit. And for this project, he was way beyond ready.

But even though he wanted—needed—to not believe this manuscript, he does. And that's an intractable problem.

On the other hand, he's watching Isabel walk across this living room, her body moving in front of him. He's acutely aware of her nakedness under her clothes, of her bare skin rubbing against the flimsy fabric that separates modesty from im-, of the curve of her hip, of the line of her calf as she climbs the first stairs toward the inevitable beds, of the bend of her knee, of the space between her legs . . .

Jeff knew he needed to make a pass at her, tonight. But all he'd been hoping for was a little kiss.

CHAPTER 39

amilla turns away from the party that sprawls across the gently sloping grounds of the Beverly Hills estate, looking out at the lights that have just begun to twinkle in the dusk of the LA basin. She takes a sip of Champagne, her third glass, which is going to have to be her last. Not just because it's time for her to finally check into the hotel and turn in, but because of the one thing she finds supremely tiresome about Los Angeles: the relentless sobriety. Everybody's always driving everywhere—sitting around in brutal traffic, where it seems to take an hour to get anywhere. In New York, the only destination that takes an hour is the airport. That is, the big international airport, JFK. Going to LaGuardia or Newark usually takes a half-hour. Here, it can take a half-hour just to cross the fucking 405.

And with all this driving, and the attendant police vigilance, you simply can't get pissed.

She doesn't really know anyone here, except the midlevel talent agent who'd invited her. He said hello at one of the bars before promptly disappearing. Which was fine. Preferable, even: she's almost too excited to engage in everyday small talk, too obsessed to not talk about *The Accident*. She might as well be alone.

Next year, she'll be at this party again—it's an annual event, apparently—and she'll know everyone.

258

"Hi." A man is suddenly standing next to her, talking. "I'm Cooper."

He holds out his hand. She looks at his face, then down at his hand. This, she thinks, is a fantastic-looking man.

"I'm Camilla. Cam."

"Interesting name, Camilla Cam. Pleased to meet you."

She turns back to the south, to the lights. "It's a beautiful night."

"Yes it is."

She steals another quick glimpse. He must be an actor, or aspiring. "Are you a client of Janice's?" Rumor has it that the host Janice has earned twenty million dollars from bonuses generated by commissions from a single client, a comedian for the teen and tween demo, specializing in sophomoric sexual gags punctuated by scatological jokes.

Cooper smiles, a big, broad, confident smile. "No, I'm not an actor," he says. "I'm a producer." He moves into her line of vision, with his toothy smile and devastating dimples. "I don't think I've seen you around. What do you do?"

"I dabble."

He raises an eyebrow, asking for more information, but she doesn't provide any. They stare at each other.

"Well then, would you prefer to talk about something else?"

She gives a shrug, takes another sip. "For example?"

He smiles, game for the game. In this town, everyone always seems to be glancing over your shoulder, looking for—hoping for—someone more interesting or famous to appear in their line of vision. But not this Cooper. He has the focus of a politician, or a gigolo.

"Is there anything I can do, or say," he says, eyes locked on hers, "to get you into bed tonight?"

She can see a cocky little smile playing across the corners of his mouth, and she feels her own smile sprouting, uncontrollable really; she can't stop herself from smiling as she considers her possible responses, ranging from outrage or feigned indignation to noncommittal procrastination and playful challenge. Does this line work on other women? Probably.

"Honestly," she says, "I've never been all that keen about *beds.*"

The porcelain feels cool and smooth under her hot palms, and Camilla presses down harder, trying to keep steady, sweat trickling down her forearms, around her wrists, her hands, the sweat now sliding between her skin and the surface of the sink, and the sheen makes one hand slip forward along the plane of the side of the sink, and she loses balance and falls forward. Her stomach gets pressed against the lip of the sink, her rear lifted higher in the air.

"Oh," he moans, deep and guttural.

She presses into him, harder. Her elbows are now resting on the sink, her hands against the tile wall. She can no longer see him in the mirror; can no longer see herself. Her face is just inches above the bronze water spout. Or is that gold? She wouldn't be surprised.

She realizes that this is the second time she's been bent over a bathroom sink at an industry party in Beverly Hills. Has she finally discovered her fetish?

He moans again, a sound like he's just about done, and so is she, almost there, and she squeezes her eyes shut, harder, biting her lip, tensing every muscle, thrusting onto him, and for once she's picturing in her mind the exact man who's actually fucking her, even though she can't see him. And that is what makes her come, and her coming is what makes him come, and so his own goddamned handsomeness is the thing that gives him an orgasm.

"Whew," she says. Standing upright again, pushing down her skirt. Neither of them removed a single article of clothing. "That was *lovely*."

"Agreed," he says.

She finds his eye in the mirror, holds it, but he looks away, down, fumbling to get himself back into his pants. He zips up.

They sneak through the hall. They're not supposed to be in the house; the house is strictly off-limits. In the garage, which is large enough to contain a fleet of ten vehicles, are two trailers for mobile restrooms, complete with crown moldings, area rugs, cut flowers, and attendants.

Out a side door, onto a brick-paved path, then around the corner of the house, back onto the lawn.

"I should leave you here," she says, stopped, standing still.

He looks stricken, injured.

"I've a *long* day tomorrow," she continues, justifying herself to him. To herself. "And I'm on New York time, which means I'll be waking at three a.m."

"Can I call you?" There's something surprisingly desperate about him. It's sort of touching.

She reaches into her bag, fumbles around for the soft calfskin of her business-card holder. She removes a card, writes her mobile number on the back. "I'm here through the weekend," she says, wondering whether this is the last she'll ever see of this man. Probably so.

"You sure I can't come with you?"

"Didn't you already come with me?" She smirks at her own witticism. "I'm quite certain you did. Anyway, I really must get some sleep, now. But it's been a pleasure indeed. A genuine pleasure."

Camilla turns and walks across the lawn, regretting this path immediately as her spiked heels sink into the grass, threatening to stick and eject her foot and send her sprawling. But she knows it would be humiliating to retreat, as ever. So with great concentration and balance and, she hopes, poise, she manages to cross the wide lawn without hideous incident, past the couches that have been arranged on carpets en plein air, past the fountains filled with sparkling wine, past the sushi bar and the caviar bar, past the liquor bar and the wine bar, and finally to the well-groomed lip of the driveway, where she hands a boy her ticket.

"Two minutes, ma'am," he says, and literally sprints away, down the drive, in search of her Mustang rental, parked safely out of sight, so the Rollses and Ferraris and Maybachs can occupy the more visible positions up here, by the house, by the guests.

Camilla is pretty sure it's Demi Moore who walks by, coming while she's going. She watches the elegant woman saunter effortlessly across the grass.

She wonders if her life will become elegant and effortless, once she turns this manuscript into an international blockbuster. If other people will envy her, for a change.

The driveway winds down the mountain, past other massive houses surrounded by meticulous landscaping, and then a US-embassy-in-Africa-style gate that opens to release her out of the private community, into the public world, where anyone is free to drive around.

The street continues to spill down the Beverly hills, twisting, switchbacks appearing out of the dark night with alarming frequency. Camilla realizes she's been riding the brake pedal, and shifts into low gear. The car complains briefly, then slows, and the transmission's noise sounds more normal.

Camilla can hear her phone ringing, muffled within her handbag. This is no time to be searching for a phone; that's how people die. But then again, this could be important; it could be Stan.

She notices another car behind her, the reflection of its headlights momentarily blinding her, until she swings around another switchback. After the curve, her hand rummages through her bag, find the phone, pulls it out.

The road levels out at an intersection, and she allows herself to look away from the windshield, to glance down at the device's screen: it is indeed Stan.

Now the road is curving and dropping again, and the car behind is following nearer, closing in, tailgating. She can't answer the phone at this moment. Plus, if Stan is calling already, that means he's interested. It wouldn't be bad to make him sweat, if only a little.

In her rearview, the other car's high beams are blinding. "Bugger off," she mutters.

She leans toward her door, averting her eyes from the reflection. She's beginning to worry that the turn she took was wrong. And this other car is practically upon her. She's getting nervous.

Her tires skid on the gravel of the shoulder. She shifts out of low gear, and the car lurches forward, then steadies, approaching another hairpin turn.

"Fucker!"

After the turn she accelerates on the straightaway, but then has to ease off again as she takes another curve, the tires kicking up gravel. Her heart races, and she barrels through an intersection, barely slowing through the stop sign, rushing to get out in front of this arsehole. She's not merely anxious anymore; she's terrified.

The road levels but takes a long turn around a rock outcropping. Camilla notices a street off to the right that drops down into dark nothingness. She glances in the rearview but doesn't see the lights; the other car hasn't yet made it around the outcropping. So in a moment of panic or clarity or irrationality or brilliance, she yanks the wheel to the side and bumps over the precipice and bounces down this unlit street, under cover of trees, away from the main road, out of sight.

Camilla brings the car to a screeching, skidding halt and turns off the lights and grips the wheel with both hands. She's panting.

She spins around, looks over her shoulder. She watches that maniac speed around the curve on the main road, the sound of the car receding, then gone. Thank bloody God.

Camilla sits behind the wheel, her chest heaving, catching her breath. She's still high up in the hills, looking down at the LA basin, which just a minute ago was a terrifying view; now it's pretty again. She knows that if she keeps descending, sooner or later she'll end up in the flats. She'll be able to find her way once the terrain is level.

She descends this secondary street, past vine-covered stucco walls, past palm trees and orange trees, painted metal gates at the tops of steep driveways. She finds a major intersection with a familiar name, a street that she knows will take her to the bottom of Beverly Hills. She takes a long, deep breath of relief, and turns onto the thoroughfare.

Camilla moves her right foot off the brake and onto the gas. She brings the convertible up to fifty, then what the hell sixty, the wind flowing through her hair.

She never even glances in the rearview to see the other car that reappears behind her, because now its headlights aren't on.

CHAPTER 40

The two-tone wail of an ambulance siren grows nearer for a few seconds, then farther, then is distant and quiet for a long time, the sound waves bouncing off Lake Zurich, before disappearing entirely. The author takes a drink of water, and recommences staring at the ceiling.

He'd met the potential witness again the following week for a proper date, a desirable table at a popular restaurant, a difficult reservation to procure; she claimed to know the chef from business, though she was vague about the specifics, and it seemed marginally unlikely. Plus she was calling herself Anne, which he knew was not her real name, or at least it hadn't been her name back in college. She didn't seem to be particularly trustworthy. Or maybe she wasn't particularly trusting.

But regardless of the lies this woman was telling, she was definitely entertaining, and undeniably good-looking, and smarter than he'd expected, and funnier. She was a good date. Great. And she clearly didn't recognize him from anywhere.

But he couldn't prevent himself from thinking, every few minutes, that he might end up killing her. It wouldn't be a tragic burst of violence in a passionate moment, nor the reckless disregard for life in a vehicular manslaughter. It would be premeditated, purposeful, cold-blooded killing. First-degree murder.

Every time this horrific thought intruded, he forced himself to smile. She must've thought he was an idiot. Or uncontrollably smitten, helplessly amused at every little thing she said.

When dessert was on the table they both started at the sound of a man's voice, booming beside them. "Well, hello!" Charlie Wolfe was standing there, grinning down. "Funny finding you here."

After introductions, Charlie invited himself to join them for a drink. Three vintage ports, elegant little tulip glasses, a plate of almond cookies, another of meticulously painted chocolates.

The woman was definitely examining Charlie closely, maybe curiously, perhaps suspiciously. It was undeniable that Charlie was charismatic, and always had been. The author felt a pang of jealousy intrude on his underlying anxiety with bouts of occasional horror; it was a messy emotional stew simmering inside him, everything but the kitchen sink.

The three of them had all gone to college in the same town, at roughly the same time; they had a lot of Finger Lakes reminiscing they could do. They all lived in Manhattan and worked in the media, so there was a productive six-degrees-of-separation interrogation. It was one of those not uncommon New York conversations, exclamations of surprise at utterly unsurprising non-coincidences, the intersections of Ivy League classmates and Hamptons neighbors, ex-colleagues and ex-girlfriends.

When the port was gone, even smaller glasses, for grappa.

And when the grappa was gone, a sudden look of recognition crossed the woman's face, then a dark cloud. "I know!" she exclaimed, leaning away from Charlie, staring at him. "I know who you are."

The author awakens again in the middle of the night, panicked again, grabbing his gun, again. And again he realizes that the problem that woke him—the thing he's terrified of, tonight—is once again not something that's solvable with a gun.

He collapses back onto the pillow, in a cold sweat, his mind still flooded with dream detritus mingling with real memory, a recollection that seems impossibly fresh and incredibly old at the same time. It was just a half-year ago. But a half-year was a lifetime ago.

He remembers walking out of the hospital, a cool crisp day, fallen leaves everywhere, a foreboding chill in the wind.

"Charlie," he said, after a ten-minute taxi back to the office, a soft rap on his boss's door. "I'm sick."

He'd been losing weight all autumn, fifteen pounds. He was pale and gaunt, his suits hanging off him like a kid trying on his father's clothes in the secrecy of an empty house, the parents at work, four o'clock on a lonely bored weekday afternoon.

"Sorry to hear it, Dave. Take all the time you need."

"No, Charlie, you don't understand." Dave shut the door behind him, the loud din of the big busy office instantly disappearing into a low background hum. "It's not that I have a cold. Or shingles."

He'd been anticipating this conversation for a long time, practicing in the mirror, trying to not sound rehearsed, to not look disingenuous. There was a lot at stake, and it wasn't easy.

"I'm dying, Charlie."

Charlie raised his eyebrows, a question, but not a lot of emotion. Ever since their conversation about the Finnish debacle, Dave had felt a gulf growing between them, a frostiness. Something not dissimilar to the end of his marriage.

"Stage-four cancer."

"I'm so sorry, Dave. That's . . . terrible."

Charlie stood up, walked around his desk. He opened his arms, and they shared a brief, awkward embrace. "What's your prognosis?"

Dave shook his head, looked down.

"How long?"

Dave shrugged. He was prepared to provide a plethora of details, but as it turned it out he didn't need to. He looked down at his feet, and noticed that his right shoelace was almost entirely untied. But now would've been a bad time to fix it.

"I'm so, *so* sorry."

And then there didn't seem to be anything left to say.

The author took a DC taxi to the jam-packed airport, the chaotic throng and din of the busiest travel day of the year, the airplanes and -port packed to bursting capacity, tens of thousands of people moving among one another in oblivious isolation, from check-in to fast-food to rest-room to gate, where the guys with gazillions of frequent-flyer miles and two-brass-buttoned blazers swaggered up to the counter to demand up-grades or bulkhead seats or whatever preferential treatment they thought they were entitled to by virtue of being guys who spend a lot of time on airplanes.

Then flying over the gray denuded landscape, the factories along the rivers belching white plumes of noxious gas, the New Jersey Turn-pike looking like a modern-day Great Wall, the green-gray marsh of the Meadowlands giving way to the brown-gray buildings of Jersey City and Hoboken and then the vast blue-gray of the Hudson River, skirting over the green-gray Statue of Liberty and flying up the length of the gray-gray island, and he could pinpoint actual buildings where he'd lived, then veer-ing over the East River and looking off to the South Bronx, its slummy blight and the pot-holed truck-laden expressway and the gigantic cubes of warehouses, the bombed-out buildings and vacant lots littered with the torched shells of stolen cars and abandoned vans, dropping precipi-tously over *All in the Family*–style Queens and then the terrifyingly close serpentine spit of the mouth of the Long Island Sound, screeching onto La Guardia's tarmac with a brief and mildly alarming bump.

The Grand Central Parkway was choked with the glowing embers of bumper-to-bumper taillights streaming in both directions, commuters and reverse-commuters and the kids coming home from college with backpacks filled with dirty laundry, the business-attired with overnight bags calling to say I'll be home in twenty, the low gloaming gray and ominous, layers of clouds forming color-neutral folds like a soft-focus black-and-white photograph of an unkempt bed, a light rain falling and the wipers set to the second slowest speed, squeaking, and the directional sounding *click-click, click-click*, the wipers sounding *whish-squeak, whisk-squeak*, these November noises and November shades and textures and layers of grayness, the landscape exuding cold and damp that chilled his spine.

And then stop-and-go through north Queens and the brownstony parts of Brooklyn—Cobble Hill and Boerum Hill, Brooklyn Heights, and Prospect Heights—then deep into the thick meat of the large dense borough—as a standalone city Brooklyn would be the fourth largest in America—to the tree-lined street and the sprawling Victorian filled with people who were usually protected from one another by distance and busy-ness, by technology and excuses, all now stripped away to reveal the strains and feuds and simmering resentments, brought to the surface by chores left untended and dishes unwashed and leaves unraked and shoes unwiped and ringing phones unanswered, by poor behavior at the festively decorated table, by late arrivals and unintended slights and overt insults, by seething sotto voce and withering contempt and searing stares and sarcastic solicitousness, everything laid bare in the weak oblique light of Thanksgiving, every year, as ritual, until everyone finally pulls themselves off the sofas and out of the armchairs, away from the televisions and tannic red wine and mismatched mugs of mulled cider, when they exchange kisses and hugs and open the front door and walk gingerly down the possibly icy stairs, and then in the privacy of their nuclear unit they turn to each other and recap yet another in the seemingly endless series of final Thursdays in November.

But this one, suddenly, was his last.

CHAPTER 41

Hayden started reading on the helicopter from New Jersey to West-hampton. Then he read in another overly large SUV, on the long tedious drive from the airfield out to the beach community. He was still reading when the car pulled to a halt within sight and smell and sound of the ocean, a hundred yards on. And now he sits in the backseat, racing through pages, before coming to a breathless stop at the bottom of page 146.

He climbs out of the truck, and walks down to the beach, and stares out at the sea. He had already known generally what was in this part of the book. But reading the specifics affected him strongly. It's always the specifics that are affecting. The boyhood poetry of the guy who was killed. His wife's picture. His son's casket.

He returns to the truck, but doesn't climb in. "Tyler," he says through the window, "you wait here." He checks his sidearm, and tucks it into his waistband. "Colby, you and me, let's scout the perimeter." He fits the earpiece into his ear, with the microphone dangling at his throat.

Hayden surveys the semi-dark country lane. The blacktop is rough, gravely, sandy, its shoulder falling away gently into scrub on one side, while the other's border is cleanly demarcated with landscaping, with shrubs and small trees, with lawn and flowerbeds, with cultivation, civilization. The two men walk on the tamed side, where the vegetation offers more cover.

There are a couple of streetlamps down here near the beach, bathing the tiny parking light in yellowish light, discouraging backseat sex, underage drinking, brazen pot-smoking, the other petty misdemeanors of summertime indiscretions. A sandy lane marked PRIVATE ROAD, parallel to the shoreline, provides access to the driveways of a handful of beach-front houses in a jumble of styles. There's a massive shingled thing that looks newly built, and a modest white cottage with overgrown gardens, and a Victorian with dark clapboard and porches and a widow's walk, and a stark contemporary structure, glass and concrete and steel, right angles and cantilevered planes. This is the only house with lights on.

Hayden and Colby look incongruous here on the beach, wearing long pants and shoes. But it's dark, and no one can see. Hopefully.

They approach the big modernist box from the sand. The ground floor is half-lit, as is one room on the second floor, casting discrete envelopes of light out to the grounds, ten yards of illumination in a few vectors. A wood-plank path cuts through the low dunes to a gate, which Colby opens, and scampers around the western side of the house to a wide lawn in total darkness. Hayden goes around to the east, ducking between a couple of shrubs near the property line, a long arbor of pines. Good cover.

A curtain flutters upstairs, and Hayden can see that it's a woman. But it's not the woman they're looking for; a brunette, not a blonde. They are, unsurprisingly, at the wrong house.

He leans on a branch, fragrant and sappy, weighing the viability of his other hunch, and how he should investigate it.

But then he hears a car engine on the street, and he hears Tyler say "Fuck" loudly in Hayden's earpiece. "Local police arriving."

Hayden's heart sinks. "You hear that, Colby?"

"*Unh.*"

"What?"

271

"I've got"—he can hear heavy breathing—"no cover here. Running."

Hayden can see the cruiser's lights aimed down the private lane, and now he can hear the engine too.

"Move the vehicle one street to the east, at the beach," Hayden orders into his microphone. "We'll meet there. Go! *Now!*"

"Police!" the shout comes from around the side of the house. "Freeze!"

"Oh fuck." Hayden hears Colby exclaim. "Recommend action?"

"Run." Hayden is moving through the yard of the neighboring house, the big Victorian. "Do not allow yourself to be apprehended." He runs across another planked path. "I repeat, do not—"

That's when Hayden hears the first shot.

Colby's earpiece will be the first clue. Then the fact that the man isn't carrying any identification, or a mobile phone, or a wallet, this will all be highly suspicious. But still, these are only small-town police. What will they think?

"The next road is a half-mile," Tyler says into Hayden's ear, electronically. "Can you make it?"

Hayden stops running, takes a seat in the sand against a dune, removes his shoes. "I'm going to need to ditch the earpiece and mike."

"Why?"

"Because if the police stop me I have to look like someone like me would look, out for a walk on the beach." The possible conversation quickly unspools itself in Hayden's imagination. "Listen," he continues, "I need to be someone's guest. Find me a name, and an address."

"Okay."

Hayden slips off his socks, tucks them into his shoes. He rolls his pants up at the cuff, nearly to the knee. He can hear Tyler's keyboard clicking.

"Jon Sanderson. On Bluff Road."

"That's walking distance?"

"You've come about three-quarters of a mile."

"Got it. Now I'm going silent. If you don't see me in twenty minutes, abandon the truck, and abort."

Hayden tugs the incriminating plastic out of his ear, the wire out of his shirt, and buries the thousands of dollars worth of tech in the sand. He heads down to the water, the Atlantic lapping and foaming, his shoes dangling in his hand. Just another guy taking a solo nighttime walk, sulking about something or other. He slows his pace, feels the hard cool sand under the soles of his feet. He hasn't been on a wide sandy beach in years. Decades, maybe.

Christ, what is he doing with his life? Isn't *this* what he should be doing?

He could retire somewhere near a beach, and go for long lonely walks at night. Get himself a big stupid Labrador, make it fetch sticks out of the surf. Buy a new set of golf clubs—his old woods are made of actual wood—and play every day that ends in *y,* as his grandfather used to say. Hayden had once been a two-handicap; maybe he could again find some satisfaction in swatting a small ball around a big park. Other people seem to.

And maybe he could find himself a more permanent, more satisfying female companion, one who's not married to someone else. As entertaining as it's been, Hayden has now had more than a few lifetimes' worth of other men's wives; as with pocket squares and his career, another short-term temporary choice that turned out to be long-term. Married women tend to be easy, and grateful, and enthusiastic; they also have short shelf lives.

Anke's expiration date is nearing, may be past. He met her a year ago, when she took the adjoining plot of land—a meter wide, fifty meters long—at the communal garden he'd joined years ago out in suburban Wessling, a half-hour on the S-Bahn from his apartment. At first he'd been motivated by the idea of growing his own produce; he was carrying an extra ten kilos, and thought that eating his own green beans and such would help take off the weight. It did.

And then Anke showed up, trying to tackle impossible delicacies like tomatoes and strawberries instead of the hard-to-kill crops—potatoes, cabbages, carrots, cauliflower—in which Hayden and other practical-minded Northern European farmers specialized. They went out for a drink around the corner from his flat. Anke had two, then invited herself up; she's not shy.

Year after year goes by, and Hayden keeps expecting his apparatus to stop functioning, but it never does. And over all these years of sexual activity, more than one man has mistaken Hayden for gay; at least a dozen men have come onto him. Women, on the other hand, always seem to know that he's heterosexual.

But these fleeting fantasies of carefree retirement are now dashed. Because Hayden has gotten trapped, protecting the secrets of the well-bred lowlife. That fucker.

"Excuse me, sir?"

The patrolman hops out of the SUV, hand hovering near his holster.

"Yes." Hayden smiles at the man, squinting at the flashlight. "How can I help you, Officer?"

"What are you doing out here?"

"Excuse me?"

"I said, why are you on the beach?"

"Taking a walk."

"Did you hear those gunshots?"

"No, I don't have a *slingshot*. That's a strange—"

"I said *gun*shots, sir. Did you hear them?"

"Oh, sorry. No. I'm a bit hard of hearing." An apologetic smile, then he widens his eyes. "Were those *gun*shots? I thought firecrackers. Kids."

The policeman stares at him. "May I see some ID, sir?"

Hayden pats his back pocket. "Oh. I don't seem to . . ."

The cop frowns, looks up the beach nervously.

"Where do you live?"

"I live in the city. I'm staying with the Sandersons, up on Bluff Road."

The cop still stares, wondering how thorough he needs to be here, given the attempted burglary a quarter-mile away, and shots fired, and the suspect down, maybe an officer as well . . .

On the other hand, chances are pretty high that a man Hayden's age walking on the Amagansett beach is going to be a heavy hitter of some sort. The type of guy who puffs his chest and says, "Do you know who I am?" and "You're going to be sorry for this" and "I'm going to have you fired, I can promise you that." It must be a daily degradation to provide public services around here.

"I'm sorry, sir, but I'm going to need you to come with me."

Hayden puts out his palms, give-me-a-break. "You're serious? I'm just going for a walk."

"I apologize for the inconven—"

That's when Hayden hammers him in the throat, and snatches the man's weapon out of his holster, and pistol-whips him on the back of the head. The cop crumples face-first into the sand.

"Sorry," Hayden says to the inert body. He pulls the handcuffs around the guy's wrists, and leaves him there on the damp sand. Hayden takes the officer's walkie-talkie, and climbs into the off-road-ready vehicle, puts it into gear, and starts to drive away.

Then he changes his mind, turns back. He hops out onto the sand, and drags the policeman far away from the water. Who knows which way the tide is going? Hayden doesn't want this poor guy to drown here, because of him. There may be innocent people who have to die in this operation, but this cop isn't one of them.

Hayden anticipated part of this debacle, but Christ, this is much worse.

He turns off the headlights, and speeds up the beach. At the next road, he pulls onto the tarmac, feels the firmness under the wheels, hears the hum of rubber on a man-made surface. He pulls to a stop at the black truck that's idling on the shoulder, rolls down the window.

"Get the gear and the manuscript," he says to Tyler. "We'll take this instead."

Tyler doesn't question the provenance of the vehicle, just loads the bags into the back, climbs into the passenger seat, laptop open in his lap, the car moving before he even pulls his door closed.

"This geography is going to be a problem." Tyler is examining a map. "We're toward the end of the island, and there are a very finite number of roads out of here, and ferries at a couple spots, and I imagine road blocks will be up soon, everywhere."

"If they're not already."

"Right. Anyway, what the hell happened?"

"We were set up, that's what."

"You mean she called the cops? Had them on alert?"

"I mean she's not there. The woman in that house is not the woman we're looking for. In fact, the woman in that house is, I'm pretty sure, a movie star."

"What?"

"I saw her through the window, just before the cops arrived."

"Did she see you?"

"No. We must've tripped some motion-sensor alarm."

Hayden had expected that they'd be misled, sent on a wild goose chase. But the security-alarm setup was an unexpected twist. Hayden had already given Isabel Reed a lot of credit, but he now realizes that she deserves even more. Just as the author has turned out to be more cunning than expected, so has his agent. Which is, now that Hayden thinks about it, not surprising.

"This is FUBAR, man," says Tyler, shaking his head.

Hayden can't stand all the jargon these kids use. But this is, indeed, fucked-up beyond all recognition. Hayden stares at the road, the painted lines zooming underneath, the shoulder densely populated by excessively bright reflectors.

"So what's the play, boss? We making a mad dash for it?"

Hayden nods. "But we need a different type of transportation."

———

Three days after meeting with Charlie in Paris, Hayden was in Washington, sitting in Trey Freeley's office with its view of the Capitol, and his prepaid hour of consultation coming to a close.

"I'd guarantee that the agent would be a woman name-a Isabel Reed, at a outfit called Atlantic Talent Management. And Reed is thick as thieves with an editor who sees a conspiracy in absolutely everythin'. A real aficionado."

Freeley leaned back in his chair, a hugely self-satisfied smile spreading across his apple cheeks.

"Plus, everyone—and I mean, *every*one—knows that this editor has been in love with this agent for the better part of forever. You understand what I'm sayin'?"

"You're saying that if this agent were representing a manuscript like my hypothetical, you'd expect her to send it to this particular editor."

"No sir, I wouldn't ex*pect* it." The lawyer shook his head. "I'd guaran*tee* it." Hayden had always thought lawyers weren't supposed to guarantee anything, ever. And here this guy was, throwing out gratuitous guarantees willy-nilly.

"Thank you, Mr. Freeley." Hayden looked at his watch, stood.

"Don't you wanna know why it's gonna be this agent?"

Hayden smiled, and reached his hand across the table for a shake. "Oh, I already know that, Mr. Freeley."

The marina is clean and well-organized, every slip occupied by an expensive-looking boat. Hayden walks down the wide planks, looking for evidence of sloppiness, of a hasty departure, of the type of sailor who'd leave an ignition key under a seat cushion.

The stolen police jeep is now in a heavy copse around back of a dark house with a for-sale sign on the lawn, no car in the driveway. That'll buy them some time, but not forever. They need to get the hell out of here.

Hayden points to a Boston Whaler and Tyler hops in, starts looking around, pawing at fiberglass and canvas. Hayden pauses at a vintage little Glastron with a hundred-horsepower motor, a Coleman cooler sitting aft, a couple of life jackets lying on a vinyl-upholstered seat, all the right signs. He climbs into the boat, and sure enough, there's the key, just sitting in the ignition.

He checks the fuel tanks; three of four are full. He whistles, and Tyler trots over.

Tyler fires the engine, which starts immediately, purrs softly. He turns on the running light, and pushes the throttle. The boat lunges away from the dock, off into the darkness.

Hayden takes a seat in the hull, where a small bulb under the control panel provides illumination. Not much light, but enough. He retrieves the manuscript, and continues reading.

CHAPTER 42

S tan is no dope. He knows what his assistant Jessica must think when women like Camilla show up late in the day, with flimsy agendas and flimsier outfits, and he shuts the door and has her hold the calls, then emerges looking satisfied. And of course the girl is correct.

He also knows that when Jessica asks the boy she refers to as George the Slave to make a copy of something for Stan, George makes two copies: the one for Stan, plus another for Jessica herself. Stan knows this because he gave—bribed—George a thousand dollars—ten crisp hundred-dollar bills—to rat on his assistant. Previously he'd paid similar kids much less money for this type of subterfuge, but he'd noticed that George waits around like an adoring puppy for Jessica to pay any attention to him, which she rarely does, occasionally throwing him a perfunctory "You're a doll" to keep him alert, but usually giving him nothing whatsoever, so he slinks away, head down, the overlong cuffs of his jeans scuffing the floor.

So Stan had upped the ante for this pathetic little lovesick spy. Sometimes it's inconvenient to have a hot assistant. This is a lesson that Stan has needed to learn more than once, and probably not for the last time. He can't help himself.

As he walked out of the office, he saw Jessica with her eyes in her lap, engrossed in something there that she didn't want Stan to see, which was no doubt the contraband copy of Camilla's manuscript.

Stan understands the girl's situation; he'd been in it, when he was her age. Picking up something, anything, at the end of the day—a nice long manuscript, or a succinct treatment, or a formulaic 120-page screenplay—and having absolutely *no* idea what it was: to just start reading blind. Like walking down Forty-Sixth Street in New York, with the throngs streaming through wide-open double doors at seven-fifty p.m., and randomly walking in amid one of the crowds, the lights dimming, taking a seat in the back, watching the velvet curtain rise on . . . ? On what? It could be a big-budget musical filled with intricately choreographed dances, pyrotechnic effects, and zoo animals. A tense drama with an ensemble cast of six. A one-woman monologue about the dissolution of her marriage. It could be anything. Just like the manuscript that Jessica is hiding in her lap, chosen for no reason other than it showed up here, to an office where decisions are made about such things.

Stan knows Jessica's life. He knows that she doesn't date, at least not for pleasure, though every week she probably finds herself sitting poolside or loungeside sipping overly oaked chardonnay with some industry guy. She doesn't go hiking in Griffith Park or surfing in Malibu or skiing at Mammoth. She doesn't go to bars at ten or dance clubs at midnight. She doesn't take vacations to Los Cabos or Hawaii or Paris.

What Jessica does is watch television, always DVR'd to skip all the inane consumer-products ads, though she diligently watches all the previews and trailers, all the ten-second spots for other television shows on sister networks, all the thirty-second mini-films for features. And she goes to the movies, at least two per week, but sometimes as many as three films in a single weekend day, if she has fallen behind.

And Jessica reads. She thinks that Stan doesn't read, because he wants her—he wants everyone—to think that. But Jessica reads everything. Three thousand pages are deposited in Stan's office every week, representing dozens, scores, sometimes hundreds of projects. Highly theoretical projects. No-chance projects. Sure-thing projects, even though there's no such thing, in practicality. But whatever. Jessica reads bits and parts or all of every single one of them.

"Good night Jessica," Stan said. Then he climbed into the back of the chauffeured Range Rover, and started making his evening calls. Halfway to the airport, Juan the driver called Tim the pilot—"Wheels up in fifteen"—who got the engine started, and moved the blocks away from the wheels, and ran through his checks while Stan's SUV was gliding through the unmarked parking lot and low-slung office buildings that surround the Santa Monica Airport. When the security gate swung open, the buggy was waiting to accompany the big black vehicle across the airfield. Juan carried Stan's briefcase up the gangplank, and unpacked the bag onto the mahogany worktable that was already unfolded in front of Stan's leather seat. Juan filled a highball with ice, poured in a can of Red Bull, and set the glass in the cup-holder. He opened Stan's door and stood at attention.

That's when Stan climbed out. Just as he liked it—demanded it—the walk from the car to the gangplank was six steps. The plane started to taxi fifteen seconds after Stan sat down.

"Lou," he says into his phone, staring out the window, "we're taxiing."

"Oh, hi," his wife answers. "Good. I'll tell Irene first course at eight-thirty?"

He responds with something that sounds like "*Ungh*."

Stan decided to take Camilla's manuscript after all. He couldn't remember the last time he'd heard someone so confident and passionate about a project. And after all these years of string-free sex—quickies in his bungalow at the Beverly Hills Hotel, bj's in the back of cars, and one uniquely memorable five minutes in the rest room at Spago—he owes Camilla. Not sure it's an executive-producer credit that he owes, but it's something. So he'll read her project. Not the whole thing, for the love of God—books are always so *long*—but some of it. Enough of it.

As the plane made its turn onto the runway, Stan started page 1. He doesn't mention this often—in fact, ever, he *never* admits this—but he can speed-read. The summer between sophomore and junior year in college, living in his parents' house in Greenwich and commuting into the city for his internship at the law firm, he took a speed-reading class. It was on the fourth floor of a building around the corner from Grand Central Station, three evenings a week, ninety minutes a class. He never told anyone—not his parents, not his friends—how he spent that hour and a half. He'd hatched all sorts of elaborate lies to explain the hole in his schedule, but it turned out that over the entire six-week course, no one ever asked.

By the time the Cessna bumps down in Santa Ynez, Stan is on page 198. He unbuckles his seatbelt absentmindedly, without removing his eyes from the manuscript. He tucks the pages under his arm, ducks under the door, onto the gangplank. With each passing minute, he adds another name to his short lists of directors and male leads, smiling to himself at the prospects. He'll own the whole thing.

Stan takes out his phone, and calls Camilla. One ring, two, three . . . He leaves a quick message—"It's Stan, this manuscript is fan-fucking-tastic, call me."

This, he thinks as he leaves his private jet, and settles into the supple seat of another chauffeured Range Rover, en route to his thousand-acre ranch, is the project that will finally, once and for all, make him rich.

Lou scowls from across the table when Stan's phone rings. He glances down at the screen, an unfamiliar number. Someone he doesn't know has procured his contact information. How the fuck did that happen?

"Stan Balzer," he answers, somewhat belligerently. "Who's this?"

Lou rolls her eyes.

"Good evening. My name is George Dryden, detective with the Beverly Hills Police Department."

"Okay. What can I do for you?"

"Oh Sweet Jesus," his wife says. "Will you please . . . ?" She shoos him away from the table, and he glares at her, but then gets up. He's in the wrong, as usual.

"Mr. Balzer, do you know a woman named Camilla Browning? That is, Camilla *Glyndon*-Browning?"

He briefly, ridiculously, considers denying it. But there's so very much evidence to the contrary. "Yes."

"I'm sorry to say we have some bad news."

Stan waits, but the officer doesn't continue. "Yes?" he asks, leaving the dining room, on his way to his office.

"Mr. Balzer, Ms. Browning died tonight, in a car accident. Glyndon-Browning, that is."

Fuck.

"Mr. Balzer? Are you still there?"

"Um, yeah," he croaks out. "I'm really sorry to hear about Camilla."

"Do you know of anyone who would want to harm her? Or why?"

"No," Stan says. "But didn't you say it was an accident?"

"We still need to investigate. When did you last see Ms. Glyndon? Ah, Browning?"

"A few hours ago," Stan says. "We had a meeting. In my office."

"What was it about?"

Stan furrows his brow. "Our meeting?" Why would a cop care? Is it because the cop suspects Stan of something? "It was about a film project."

There's no answer for a moment, and Stan is about to repeat himself, when the guy asks, "What was the project?"

Oh God. That is absolutely not the business of any cop. No cop would ever ask that question.

Stan had begun to worry that he wouldn't be able to make the picture without altering all the identifying details. In fact, he had the creeping feeling that he wouldn't be able to make it *at all.* It would get quashed by some arm of the government. By lawyers.

But now he realizes that if this manuscript is really true, he's facing problems far more serious than lawyers.

Stan holds on to the banister, steadying himself before descending the four steps to the hall that leads to the east wing. This house was designed to echo the rolling terrain, with every room on a slightly different level, so you're constantly on stairs, up and down three steps, down and up two steps, to get anywhere. The guy who built the house was a famously unhinged character actor who enjoyed a remarkable run of a steady work in the fifties, sixties, and seventies. It was in this last decade of his success that he directed the design of Casa Mariposa, named for one of his many insane obsessions, butterflies. He designed all the landscaping to attract butterflies. It's sometimes like a fucking war zone out there, all those damn things dive-bombing around.

Stan is trying to think, quickly. Quick quick quick: what to do? He takes a deep breath, and continues to the office, to the desk that's built into the wall under the windows that afford a view down the hill and its driveway toward the road in the distance, the road that snakes through the canyon. The road to town, to the airport, to his plane, to wherever he might need to go.

"What did you say your name was?" Stan sputters out. "Dryden? With the Beverly Hills P.D.?" His hand is shaking as he jots down the information. "And your number, please? Someone's at my door. I'm going to have to call you back."

He realizes he's been standing for this whole conversation, his legs increasingly unsteady, now trembling, about to stop functioning. He pulls out his chair, collapses into it, weight pushing down on his chest, through his temples, into his eyeballs.

Whoever murdered Camilla is going to try to murder him, and that person may have just been on the other end of his phone.

Stan ignores the phone number he jotted down. Instead he dials information for the Beverly Hills P.D. Gets connected. A chipper voice answers, "Beverly Hills Police Department. How may I direct your call?" Stan wouldn't expect such a lively, friendly answer from the police, at night.

"Hi," he says, then takes a deep breath. "I'm calling for Detective Dryden." Please please please please. Please be there; please be real.

This situation, he thinks, can be assigned values on a continuum that ranges from pretty bad to extraordinarily horrible. As he hears the clicks from a keyboard, he knows he's about to find out where, exactly.

"I'm sorry, sir," the operator says, sincere apology in her voice. "There's no Detective Dryden with the Beverly Hills Police Department."

"This is Brad McNally."

"Hi Brad. Stan Balzer calling. Do you remember me?"

"Of course. Hi Stan."

"Listen, Brad, I've got bad news for you, about Camilla Glyndon-Browning. A few hours after she left my office, she was in a car crash. She's dead."

Silence.

"I'm sorry, Brad. And I'm sorry too if this sounds uncaring, but I have to ask: do you know anything about the project she was pitching me?"

Brad doesn't respond for a couple of seconds. Then, "What did she pitch you?"

"Something that I'm not sure you own."

"I think I know what you're talking about."

"Have you read it?"

Another pause. "No, not really."

Stan is about to ask for clarification on that, but he doesn't really care. "Listen, Brad." He pauses, trying to make sure that anyone who's listening—and he's absolutely positive that this conversation is being monitored—will hear this part, this lie, loud and clear: "Camilla didn't give me a copy of this manuscript. But if you have one, I strongly suggest you destroy it."

CHAPTER 43

Jeffrey finishes with a gasp and a grimace, his eyes clamped tightly shut, his mouth gaping open, as if he's witnessing something awe-inspiring. Then he exhales slowly, and Isabel feels him shudder a final time inside her, an after-shock.

She rolls off him, catching her breath, her chest rising and falling, staring at the ceiling, the fan spinning slowly round and round.

Well that could've been a lot worse, and these days it often is. In the half-decade between when Isabel started dating her husband and when she started sleeping with other men, her field of choice narrowed dramatically. Men tend to want women who are younger than they are, and Isabel is not exactly young. Plus the book-publishing business is disproportionately gay, especially in the editorial realms that constitute her day-to-day universe, and nearly all the rest of them are married. Or they're inappropriately young, or inconceivably old. So perhaps one in a hundred is single, straight, and in her age bracket, where she has discovered that this population tends to have more issues, more challenges, more performance-enhancing pills and unappealing personal proclivities, than the men she'd had in her twenties and thirties.

Isabel has downward-adjusted her expectations. "That was nice," she says. Because in the overall scheme of things, it was.

Jeffrey doesn't say anything.

She pulls herself out of bed. "Thirsty," she says. Isabel isn't sure that she wants to traipse across this moonlit room naked, but nor does she want to yank a sheet off the bed, and wrap herself in it. That seems too un-intimate. "You want some water?"

"Sure. Thanks." There's a bit of an edge to his voice, something that doesn't sound quite right. She probably shouldn't have used the word *nice*.

She hands him a glass of tap water, and settles into bed beside him, her head on his shoulder.

"You should've gotten me into bed years ago," she says, trying to compensate for *nice*. "Decades ago."

The first time they kissed was nearly twenty years ago, when everyone was so young—one, two years out of college, lowest rungs on the totem pole. On weeknights they'd go to readings in bookshops—some of them even had part-time jobs, nights and weekends, in the same stores—and afterward to loud places with bar-size pool tables, short stacks of quarters placed on the bumpers to indicate who was playing next, Nirvana and Elvis Costello on jukeboxes, pitchers of Pabst Blue Ribbon or Molson Golden, sticky floors and plywood doors.

"Fielder," she said, turning to him there in one of those back rooms, everyone else somewhere else. She used to call people by their last names. "Are you *ever* going to kiss me?"

So they made out, standing up in a bar amid the beer lights and the bar stools, on a rainy Thursday night in April, a long time ago, back when she could simply make out with someone in a bar, and leave it at that.

The next day in the office, they didn't happen to run into each other until late afternoon, and neither had the confidence to seek out the other. Their cubicles were at opposite ends of a full floor in a big building.

"Want to do something later?" he asked. They were in the brightly lit main hall, around the corner from a conference room.

"I can't, not tonight." She was having dinner with her mother, who was in the city for a doctor's appointment, never having given up her Manhattan doctors, never replaced them with physicians in the small town where she actually lived, never admitted that the move upstate was full-time and permanent. Isabel didn't want to explain all this to Jeffrey, so all she said by way of explanation was "Sorry."

He nodded his understanding, but he didn't understand. He misunderstood. He thought he was being rejected, and she never mustered the nerve to disabuse him, so he never asked again.

But now here they are, two decades later, just as she always presumed they'd end up, sooner or later.

"I didn't even get you into bed tonight," he says. "Did I?"

She shifts her body, turns her face up to his, plants a kiss on his lips, ready to start up again, wondering if he is too, or could be. "No." She plants a kiss on his chest. "I guess not."

Then they're both seized by the sound, terrifyingly loud in the dark quiet house: *Ringggggggggg*.

The possibilities run through Isabel's mind—wrong number, an old boyfriend calling for Naomi, a live solicitation, a robo-call . . .

Ring—

Isabel reaches across to the night table, picks up the handset midring, cutting short the shrillness. "Hello?"

"Hi," an unfamiliar voice, male. "Is this Isabel Reed?"

All her muscles tense. "Who's calling?"

"Isabel?"

She doesn't confirm or deny.

"My name is Stan Balzer," he continues. "You know who I am?"

She still doesn't respond.

"I got this number from Naomi Berger, whose number I got from Brad McNally, who thought it was possible that you'd be in Naomi's house. You two are close friends, I gather."

"Uh-huh."

"I've made a big effort to find you."

"Yes. Why?"

"I'm a film pro—"

"I know who you are."

"Okay. This afternoon I met with Camilla Glyndon-Browning, the sub-rights director at McNally & Sons, who was pitching me a project: an anonymous unauthorized biography of Charlie Wolfe. Do you represent this?"

Isabel pulls the sheet up to her breasts, but doesn't say anything.

"Anyway, soon after leaving my office, Camilla was killed."

Isabel gasps, and her free hand instinctually shoots to her mouth, and the sheet slips down, exposing her, once again.

"It was supposedly in a car accident."

Jeffrey is sitting up in bed, watching her, listening. She wonders if he can hear through the earpiece, the man on the other end.

"Then I received a call from someone impersonating a police officer. Someone who knew that Camilla and I had met. Someone who knew how to find me, and where, which I have to tell you is not that easy of a thing to do. Someone who wanted to know what we'd discussed, Camilla and I."

Isabel can hear this man breathing heavily, panting from exertion, or fear, or both.

"So I'm calling to warn you that you're in danger."

She can't help but laugh, a thick meaty guffaw, a markedly unfeminine sound.

"I guess you already know that," he says. "I'm also calling to tell you that Camilla didn't give me a copy of this manuscript, and other than her short pitch, I don't know anything about it. And I don't want to."

He pauses, seemingly waiting for some response. "Okay" is what she gives him.

"I'm not involved, in any way. Understand?"

She doesn't, not really. This is an odd and horrifying phone call, in a day filled with oddness and horror.

And then suddenly she understands what this is about: being over-heard. This movie producer thinks that this conversation is being moni-tored, and he's telling whoever's listening that they have nothing to fear from him. That there's no reason for anyone to hunt down and kill Stan Balzer.

"I think I understand," she says. "The truth is that I'm not really in-volved either." No one is going to believe this, other than maybe Stan Balzer, and probably not even him.

"Good luck," he says, and the line goes dead.

Isabel stares at the plastic handset with its long accordion cord, then replaces it to its cradle, a big chunky thing with a push-button key pad.

"What was that all about?"

She turns to him. "Did you give a copy of the manuscript to your sub-rights director? Camilla?"

"No," Jeffrey says defensively. "I didn't even mention it to her."

"Well, somehow she knows about it. *Knew*."

"What do you mean?"

"She's dead."

"*What*?" He seems to be scanning his memory. "She must've photo-copied the manuscript when I was in a meeting. Oh shit. How was she killed?"

"Car crash."

"Good God. Does anyone else have a copy of the manuscript?"

She almost answers, It depends on your definition of *have*. But what she says is "Not from me. Did *you* give it to anyone besides Brad? Would he have given it to anyone?"

"I doubt it."

Isabel nods.

"So there aren't any other copies in the world?" he asks. "Besides the two that we have with us here?"

Isabel turns to Jeffrey, searches his face, wondering again how much she can trust this man in bed with her. It was her ex-husband who'd always lived by the credo that you should never completely trust anyone, and always be prepared for betrayal; you never know when it's going to happen. Over the years this cynicism rubbed off on Isabel. In hindsight, this pervasive worldview was one of the things she didn't like about being married to him. But like it or not, there it is: she doesn't really trust anyone.

"Not that I know of," she says. "Though I'm assuming the author has a copy."

The idea of the author hangs in the air between them.

"You know who it is, don't you?"

"Well, there's certainly one obvious possibility," she admits.

Jeffrey nods.

"But he's already *dead*."

CHAPTER 44

The morning air is crisp and clean, the wind blowing cool from the snow-capped Alps in the south, blowing across the deep blue lake dotted with sailboats and ducklings and ruffled with whitecaps, making the tree boughs sway, heavy with the season's new green leaves. The gravel-covered dirt path feels springy under the cushy soles of his new high-tech running shoes, and his legs have grown rubbery, in a not-unpleasant way. He leans into his jog, his torso pitched forward, propelling him onward, toward the simple squared-off clock towers of the tidy little downtown.

Although he slept only a few hours last night, he doesn't feel particularly tired. He long ago became inured to sleeplessness; he can get by on three or four hours per night for weeks on end.

The author turns away from the lake, off the gravel path, running now on the hard pavement of the street, far less agreeable to his soles and knees and middle-aged frame.

His apartment is on the next block. He glances at the screen of the phone in his palm, the GPS-driven app that's tracking his run, now at 7.8 kilometers. If he runs past his building, makes another lap around the block, that'll get him past 8.0, a nice even number, a respectable goal.

He doesn't even glance at his front door as he jogs past it, throwing one leg in front of the other, the impact vibrating up his legs. He breathes in sets of two, a couple of short tight bursts of exhalation on consecutive footfalls, then a pair of shallow inhales on the next two strides, a mesmerizing rhythm that lulls him into a spaced-out zone in which he can almost forget who he is, and all the things that keep him awake in the middle of the night. He wishes it was possible to sleep while jogging.

So at first he doesn't register the two men sitting in the car on the corner, facing his direction. A rental car, a pair of clean-cut American-looking heads. No newspaper, no phone, nothing to occupy their attention in the front seat of the shiny white Opel at eight o'clock on a weekday morning, parked on a quiet block in a residential neighborhood.

Fuck.

He continues jogging to the corner, and turns left, picking up the pace unintentionally, adrenaline spiking in his bloodstream, no longer feeling the impact of his strides, nor the soreness in his quadriceps, his muscles growing stronger with the hormonal infusion, his hearing and vision sharper, a strange taste in his mouth.

He turns another corner, onto the block behind his own, and runs fifty more meters, then slows to a walk. He turns out of the street and enters an alley between two tall houses, a tight path with a bicycle rack, a quartet of garbage cans, a red hand-truck.

At the rear of the house he stops. He leans his hand against the coarse cool painted brick, and cranes his neck around the corner. He surveys the backyard of this house, with a low wood fence that separates this yard from his own building's. He looks up at the fire escape, at his bedroom window.

A team could be up there in his apartment, waiting for him, one man hiding on the wall beside the door, another sitting on his sofa, holding a pistol. The two men in the car could be the backup. There could be others, in vans, on motorcycles, at the airport, the train station. He could be surrounded.

He waits one minute, two. He can see his downstairs neighbor knotting his necktie; in the next building a young Dutch mother—in his brain, she's called Dutch MILF—is trying to get her blonde children out the door.

He has anticipated this moment, the discovery that he has been blown, that the people who are looking for him—Charlie Wolfe and his handler at the CIA, or more likely some team of private contractors hired by one or the other of the motivated parties—has found him. He has planned for it. In his coat closet he keeps a go-bag, a nylon backpack with a change of clothes, and a disposable cell phone and its charger, and an empty thumb drive ready to copy his manuscript, and another new passport and credit cards plus a hundred thousand dollars worth of mixed currency—American dollars and euros and Swiss francs and English pounds—and a spare car key, and a dog-eared old wallet-sized photo of a child.

He waits another minute. His breathing has slowed to nearly normal, and he can feel sweat cooling on his back, his chest, his lightweight T-shirt moist and heavy. He's almost ready to move, to hop the low fence that separates the yards, to climb the fire escape, to fold himself through his bedroom window . . .

He walks across the yard, head swiveling left and right, back behind him. He climbs the ladder, hand over hand, up the exterior of the painted brick building to the fourth floor, high above these little green lawns in northern Switzerland.

His peers through his bedroom window. He can see an empty slice of living room, an angled view on the front door. Nothing looks out of the ordinary. But then again, there's not much he can see.

As a rule he leaves this window unlocked, willing to sacrifice one bit of security for another, in this exact situation, right now. He's not terribly afraid of getting burgled in Zurich; what he's afraid of is getting apprehended by the CIA.

He applies pressure with the heels of both palms, pushing up on the old wood, the frame beginning to slide.

That's when he notices the front door opening.

It was after midnight, and nearly all the other tables were empty, the kitchen closed, the restaurant winding down another busy night. The woman leaned back in her dining chair, and the author leaned toward her, anxious to hear what she had to say, desperate to not miss it.

A pair of waiters shared a joke at the service station, while on the other side of the room two busboys stood wearily, dead on their feet. The bartender was sliding a fresh drink across the bar, with a sly smile, to a woman who'd already slid off her stool at least once. The maître d' was reading the *Post* from the back page forward. The music was louder than expected from a place this expensive, and it was Led Zeppelin, of all goddamned things.

And this woman was staring at Charlie. "Yes," she said, "I know who you are."

And Charlie was staring back at her, steely jawed, his whole body tensed, coiled.

And the author's heart was beating so fast he thought he'd croak, right then and there, pitching forward onto the starched white tablecloth. He was holding his breath, running out of oxygen.

And then she said, "You're on television, aren't you?"

She'd had no idea whatsoever what was on the line, that night. She didn't know that their first meeting in the bar had been staged; didn't know that Charlie's arrival to the restaurant had been orchestrated; didn't know that the two men were on the edge of their seats, two unintentional murderers who were toying with the idea of the premeditated crime, against her. She didn't know any of this, back then. Though now she most certainly did.

As it turned out, it wasn't from Ithaca fifteen years earlier that she recognized Charlie. She knew his face from his on-air appearances. The domestic news station was just about to launch, and Charlie was already well known in media circles. Now he was on the verge of being famous to the world at large, and it was apparently this woman's job to be familiar with this ever shifting population. "People on the precipice of fame," she said, "are my business."

So she was not a witness. There was no witness.

The author's relief was immense, an ecstatic relief, incomparable to any mere orgasm. He immediately invited the woman to a second date, the following week.

He scampers down the fire-escape stairs, grateful for the foamy rubber soles of his shoes, nearly soundless on the sturdy framework. He lands on the brick path, retraces his steps through the yards, the alley, running again down the middle of the leafy street, his pace quicker than before, faster than he'll be able to maintain, fighting the urge to turn around, to look for pursuers. Innocent joggers don't check to see who's behind them. He needs to look like an innocent jogger.

He rejoins the stream of exercisers in the thin park along the lake, the sweat-drenched joggers, the middle-agers with their hiking poles, the beefy cyclists with spiky hair in full regalia of garish Lycra straining against sausages both consumed and concealed, interspersed with the business-attired on touring bikes and on foot, heading downtown.

He turns round the busy bend of Bellevueplatz to cross the river mouth at Quaibrücke, running out of steam, slowing down, panting. When he enters the Bürkliterrasse garden he stops, as if this is his purposeful destination, the end point of a planned route. He puts his right foot up on the edge of a park bench, leans forward for a calf stretch, looking back in the direction from whence he came, scanning the crowds. He switches legs, looks in the other direction, while reviewing a mental checklist of his backup plan. His alternative backup plan.

He starts walking through Belvoir on the west side of the lake, the mirror image of his neighborhood, the two areas facing each other across the water. He turns a corner and passes through a modern matte metal gate and continues around the side of the contemporary glass-and-steel building, on a paved path lined with high healthy shrubs. He kneels at the base of the third bush, reaches in to find the knobby trunk, strains his hand around the trunk.

He extracts his arm from the foliage, looks at his palm, holding the small metal hide-a-key box. He slides it open and removes two keys. One of them unlocks the rough-hewn slab of the building's front door, and he walks through the airy lobby, up one flight of stairs to Apartment 4, a sans-serif brushed-steel numeral floating above the ebonized wood.

He leans against the door, straining his hearing, to try to pick up any sounds within the apartment.

Nothing.

He's standing in front of Vanessa's apartment, the sexy management consultant he'd met in the park and then picked up in the Widder for that threesome, who's game for the occasional date, a casual dinner and a satisfying fuck, a quick congenial breakfast before work.

After one of these nights he'd managed to steal her keys, copy them, and return them a few hours later, standing in the lobby of her office building, with apologies; he'd picked up the wrong set on his way out the door. They shook hands when they parted.

Vanessa tends to leave home by 7:45 a.m., at her desk by 8:15 latest. It's now 8:22. He slides that duplicate key into the lock, turns, clicks. The door swings open, heavy and smooth and silent on its well-oiled hinges. His eyes dart around the kitchen, dining alcove, living room, large plate-glass window to a leafy yard, coffee table, wineglasses. Plural.

And a pair of men's shoes.

CHAPTER 45

rad tries for the second time in ten minutes, but again his call is immediately connected to voice mail, *Hi this is Jeff—*

He puts down the phone without leaving a message, and unpauses the music, halfway through what he still thinks of as the second side of *The Rise and Fall of Ziggy Stardust and the Spiders from Mars*, even though he replaced his vinyl version with this CD . . . When was it? Twenty-five years ago?

He stares out the window of his home office tucked into what was built as a maid's room, back in the days when everyone here on Park Avenue had a live-in maid. It's a small room, big enough for only a loveseat and a few bookshelves and a desk with a banker's lamp and a comfortable chair, a casement window that faces the courtyard, and the windows of dozens of other maid's rooms and kitchens and bathrooms and the landings of the stairwells where the teenagers and some of the more desperate stay-at-home moms sneak cigarettes.

Brad had thought he'd been around long enough to see every circumstance in the book-publishing business present itself. He has seen surprise bestsellers come out of nowhere while supposedly guaranteed hits bombed, abysmally. He has encountered ecstatic authors and belligerent authors and authors who, for reasons foreseen and unforeseen, summarily broke contracts or initiated lawsuits or committed suicide or simply flipped out. He has seen books with signatures bound upside down, books distributed with the author's name misspelled on the dust jacket, books missing their final crucial pages or cataloging-in-publication data, books with factual inaccuracies and libelous misstatements and egregious errors of judgment and taste.

But he's never seen this before. He looks down at the manuscript, at his salvation or his ruin, so often intertwined. Glances at his scratch pad, the calculations of the revenue that could be generated by publishing *The Accident*.

He pushes the window all the way open. He peers down, around, looking to see if anyone noticed his window open. He opens his middle desk drawer and removes a small leather jewelry box, bought in a flea market twenty years ago. He digs the box's tiny key out from the bottom of a silver bowl that holds loose change. He opens the box, and peers inside.

Brad pays himself an annual salary of a nice round $500,000, the same amount that the firm has budgeted for the publisher position for a decade now. He's the highest-paid employee, although a couple of other positions at McNally & Sons come close. But as anyone knows who's ever tried to put two kids through college—after a combined thirty years worth of private school tuition—while still keeping Manhattan bedrooms available to them, a half-million per year doesn't make you rich. It barely suffices.

Now it appears that he will never earn more, and quite possibly less, and perhaps even nothing. Luckily when the kids had both moved up to middle school Lucy returned to work, seamlessly sliding back into her job as a schoolteacher. This year her seventy-some-odd-thousand-dollar-per-year salary, after taxes, does not quite cover the maintenance costs of the apartment. But Brad is beginning to suspect that next year her income—and especially her iron-clad health insurance, union-procured and -guaranteed—will come in handy, when McNally & Sons—one of the last remaining independent publishers of any size—will have been sold, and he, the chief executive who presided over its demise, will have been put out to pasture. It's not just Jeffrey Fielder who's staring down the barrel of involuntary retirement.

Brad extracts two baggies from the green leather box. He removes a pipe from one, a pinch of marijuana from the other.

Will anyone ever hire him, ever again? A fifty-something ex-publisher? Or is this the last year of his life that he'll have a regular full-time job? Is this his last *month* coming to work?

Wow, he thinks: the finish line certainly snuck up on me.

He leans on his windowsill, ignites the pipe, and inhales deeply. He holds the smoke in his lungs for a five count, then exhales, into the shared space of the courtyard.

Ahhhh.

"Jesus fucking Christ, Brad." His wife is standing in the doorway, hand on hip. He didn't even hear the door open, what with the David Bowie. "With the *kids* in the house?"

He opens his mouth to respond, but nothing comes out.

Lucy shakes her head in disgust. "Milo still needs a walk," she says, and closes the door behind her.

He returns to his desk, his dilemma, his decision. He has been agonizing about this all day, and all night.

On the one hand, Brad is convinced that whatever damaging revelations are in this manuscript will be absolutely true, and that the thing should be published, and that this greedy unethical bastard should be exposed, while at the same time rescuing McNally & Sons from bankruptcy or takeover, plus saving his own career and livelihood. There's a lot of upside.

On the other hand, it's possible that the federal agent—if that's indeed what that Joseph Lyons guy really is—was telling the truth. That the manuscript is a hoax, perpetrated for the purpose of stock manipulation, hostile takeover, with millions—billions?—of dollars at stake. Lord knows people have done far worse, for far less.

But if the manuscript is true, and Wolfe is in cahoots with black ops of the CIA, then Brad himself could be facing arrest on trumped-up charges, shipped out to Guantánamo. Or simply shot.

He refires his pipe, inhales deeply, exhales slowly.

He picks up his cell phone, and places yet another call that goes through to voice mail. But this time he leaves a message: "Hi Freeley, McNally here. I've given this a lot of thought, and I've decided to go through with it. To try to publish this thing, as instantly as possible." Even the phrase *instant book* makes him tingle. "Please call back to discuss how I should proceed. Thanks."

He places the phone on the mahogany blotter of his boyhood desk, and listens to the lounge-singery *Rock and Roll Suicide*, the end of the album. Then, with the music over, he can hear that Milo the poodle is scampering around the apartment, having heard his name a few minutes earlier, ready for his nighttime perambulation.

Brad hefts his body out of his creaky chair, and puts on his ratty old canvas jacket, its pockets filled with plastic bags and loose change, with ticket stubs and dry-cleaning slips and grocery receipts, a permanent collection of crap that he totes around the neighborhood in this garment that he has owned for thirty-four years.

The agreeable poodle trots in front of Brad down the short hall, and waits at the elevator with his snout pressed up against the seam between the two doors, resolute to be the first to get through any passage, anywhere, anytime.

In the lobby they run into Mr. Benning from 7B, a prissy little sweater-wearing man dragging a prissy little sweater-wearing dog, some type of miniature terrier, excessively groomed, who snarls at Milo, who has the good sense to ignore it.

"That's a good boy," Brad mutters, as the dog immediately pulls the leash and Brad to the curb, and pees against a discarded Twix wrapper. Anything will do. "A good boy *and* a handsome boy. *And* good-looking. That's right." Nonsense. The dog stares at him, expressive eyebrows asking, Can we go? I smell something good over there. Can we go now? Over there?

Brad continues walking Milo along the quiet street, the dog sniffing and turning, intently assessing the aromas of his world.

This will be exciting, Brad thinks. The most exciting, most meaning-ful thing he's ever done—will ever do—in his career. In his life. But it can't be exciting unless there's at least a little danger.

He hears two car doors close in near-perfect unison, from somewhere behind him, a quick *thump-thump*. He notices that the dog stops sniffing at the fire hydrant, spins around on his leash, looking up. Brad chuckles at his dog, the ten thousandth nervous laugh of his life, a half-century's worth of filling uneasy silences with the sound, with the idea, of cheer.

Brad follows the dog's attention, still smiling as he turns, still smiling as he hears the *pop-pop*, still smiling as he feels the sudden bewildering heat spreading through his chest.

CHAPTER 46

"The name is Naomi Berger . . . Yes, I'm sure there's surveillance on her line . . . Why? Because she owns a radical bookshop in New York City . . . Of course, take all the time you need."

Hayden returns his attention to the manuscript in his lap, sitting in the little boat that's bobbing in the moonlit water, gentle waves lapping at the hull. He reads a couple of pages, then the tech comes back on the line.

"Good . . ." Hayden pokes the bud farther into his ear. "Okay, go ahead." He listens to the recorded phone conversation, uploaded from a federal database, between Isabel Reed and her friend Naomi Berger. Then he ends that call.

He nods at Tyler, who's at the helm. "Let's go."

Tyler opens the throttle again, and the boat rips through the water, as Hayden returns to the manuscript, comparing this book's version of events with his own recollections.

"Why are we outside?" Charlie asked. "Have you noticed that it's, um, raining?"

Hayden took a few steps before answering. "*Rain*? This isn't *rain*. You're simply not accustomed to London weather."

He used the tip of his full-length black umbrella to punctuate every other step. He'd been living in England for the better part of a year, and had grown accustomed to always carrying an umbrella. As well as to the continual state of mourning for Princess Diana.

"This is *mist*, Charlie. Rain is something quite different."

"Be that as it may."

"We're outside, Charlie, because it's impossible to *bug* outside, in the wide-open. It's impossible for there to be a little transmitter tucked under the table, or a camera in the wall. It's impossible for someone to be sneaking around in the room behind us."

"Uh-huh."

"And in order to achieve this level of security from undesirable surveillance, we sometimes must tolerate a certain amount of *mist*."

They continued for a half-minute in silence on the lakeside path in St. James's Park, toward the hulking behemoth of Buckingham Palace.

"So have you considered my proposal?"

The park was exploding with spring bulbs, bright bursts of color popping out of all that green, beneath all the dark damp gray.

"I have, Charlie. I have."

"And?"

"Well, I'll tell you." Hayden stopped walking, turned toward to his anxious young companion. "There's a presidential candidate in Italy for whom we don't care."

Charlie tilted his head to the side.

"He has in the past strayed outside of his marriage. We don't know for certain if he's currently, um, *wandering*. But even if not, we doubt it would be difficult to arrange."

Charlie tilted his head to the other side. Hayden wondered if one side was for listening, the other for thinking. Hayden wasn't immensely impressed with young Mr. Wolfe's intellect, but the guy had somehow managed to accomplish things that seemed to be rather difficult to accomplish.

"Are you telling me to entrap this guy, then expose him?"

"I'm not *telling* you to do anything, Charlie. I'm never going to tell you to do anything. You don't work for me."

"Uh-huh."

"What I'm doing is mentioning that the United States of America would be better off if this particular candidate did not prevail." Hayden handed over a small slip of folded paper. "It's a complicated name. I've written it down, to help you remember."

Charlie glanced down.

"Just as we'd prefer it if Saddam Hussein were ousted. If Hugo Chavez had not won that election in Venezuela. If we could do something about the mess down in Kosovo. The challenge in Italy is, by comparison, a much smaller one. But it would also make *far* juicier news coverage. Titillating."

At that moment a dozen ducks emerged from the lake, most of them brightly plumed drakes, and set off across the paved path to a stand of shrubbery, in fresh bud. There must be nests in there, ducks sitting on eggs with infinite patience. There didn't seem to be any ducklings about, not yet.

Charlie turned to watch the waterfowl waddle, as if they might be purposefully interloping in this conversation, perhaps eavesdropping.

"I'm just speculating, Charlie, about international events. And giving you a friendly alert to a news story that could develop. A story that your nascent Italian website might be in a unique position to break, which would certainly help launch that site with a bang. As it were."

"Nice pun."

"Thanks."

Charlie looked off to the left, then the right, slowly. It was almost laughable.

"Listen, Charlie, if you're going to be in this line of work, you're going to need to be less *obvious*. Please don't glance around like that. You draw attention to yourself, and you look like an idiot, and more importantly you make *me* look like someone stupid enough to deal with amateurs. So please."

Charlie nodded. "And if I do this for you—"

Hayden held up his hand. "No, Charlie: if you do this for *you,* for your *own* benefit. Then I can assure you that you will not be investigated or pursued by us. And we will appreciate the outcome. So we will alert you to other similar opportunities, should they arise, in the future."

"And by *we*, you mean . . . ?"

"I mean me."

Charlie's eyes darted away again, increasingly nervous, but to his credit this time he didn't swivel his neck.

"What did you think this was going to be, Charlie? That I'd tip you off to breaking international news because, why? Because I know your *father*? Because out of the goodness of my heart, I want to help you get rich?"

Charlie watched the ducks disappear into the underbrush, instantly hidden in there.

"You came to me, Charlie." Hayden clapped him on the shoulder. "Think about it."

Hayden set off, his leather heels loud on the hard damp walkway, the tip of his umbrella clicking, the sleeves of his new rubberized Mackintosh whooshing against his torso, a raincoat that he'd bought on the same Mayfair shopping expedition as the long expensive umbrella, when he acknowledged that this dismal weather was going to be a part of his life for a long, long time. He should make the best of it. Of everything.

He felt around in the cold but dry right pocket of the Mack until his thumb depressed the stop button, and the record button popped up, and the tape stopped turning.

Hayden glances over the side of the boat, white foam spraying from the black water, speeding toward the horizon's thin string of lights, among which Isabel Reed and Jeffrey Fielder are shacked up somewhere, hiding from him, about to be discovered.

At first, Hayden was expecting this entire mission to be much shorter, more finite, infinitely simpler: find the author, and kill him, and destroy his manuscript. Each year it becomes easier and easier to locate people, anywhere, with cell phones that can be triangulated, with IP addresses that can be pinpointed, with bank cards whose transactions can be monitored, with security cameras at airports and train stations, at banks and gas stations. It's extremely difficult to hide, unless you're very smart, and very careful, and very well-funded.

Unfortunately, the author was all of those things, and hence probably unfindable within a reasonable time frame, using a controllable level of staff. So Hayden turned his focus to the demand side of the eventual transaction. He used Langley's resources to set up round-the-clock electronic surveillance of Isabel Reed—all her computers, all her phones—fed to the desk of a freelance tech named Gunter who occupied a sixth-floor-walk-up garret near the university in Munich.

Because of the post-9/11 warrantless wiretapping program, the systems were already in place to monitor any American, at any time; it wasn't hard for someone in Hayden's position to gain access. And because Isabel was only one person, who could really use only one device at a time, and who slept and ate and commuted and exercised and watched television, it was fairly undemanding to listen to absolutely every word she said on the phone, to read every e-mail she sent or received. Not exactly fun, but not particularly challenging.

Unfortunately, the months of eavesdropping on Reed's New York book-publishing world had yielded nothing relevant. Not one message, not one call. Gunter wanted to shoot himself in the head. Hayden had needed to double the guy's pay, twice.

Hayden packed the chic little nylon suitcase that he'd picked up on a whim in Milan, flew Lufthansa business class to JFK, then unpacked in a modest-size room at an immodestly priced hotel on the Upper East

Side. He combated jet lag by pushing through the long afternoon walking around the Islamic Art galleries of the Metropolitan, grabbed dinner at the bar of an Italian restaurant, and forced himself to stay out until nine, when he allowed himself to collapse. He woke up eight hours later, sufficiently rested and adequately adjusted to GMT −5.

Every morning for a week he set out wearing one of his lightweight travel suits and French cuffs and a subdued silk tie, taking a taxi to a different neighborhood, trudging from publishing house to publishing house, through the winter slush and the surging crowds and the deafening traffic and the soaring skyscrapers, the relentless onslaught of New York City, tall and dense and severely gridded, right angles at every intersection, completely unlike the haphazard layout of European cities with their dead-ends and diagonals and roundabouts, their predictable low-profile architecture and manageably narrow streets. The scale of Manhattan made Hayden's pulse pound.

He walked deliberately, doubling-back on his own path, pausing at storefronts, ducking into delis, scanning and memorizing faces, suddenly hailing taxis. The endlessly exhausting slough of counter-surveillance, a study in the infinite patience required for unreasonable overkill.

Which is why he was taking all these meetings in the first place: overkill. Hayden was fairly certain that the author would entrust his manuscript to Isabel Reed, and he was equally sure that she'd submit it to Jeffrey Fielder. But the difference between fairly certain and completely certain could be the difference between life and death.

So Hayden found himself eluding nonexistent surveillance around Manhattan, pushing through revolving doors into soaring contemporary lobbies or streamlined Art Deco ones, into the Flatiron Building and Rockefeller Center, into squat grungy old buildings and soulless soaring skyscrapers. He'd approach the bunkered lobby desks, and smile at guards wearing navy blazers adorned with the names of security firms. He'd be issued a pass on a lanyard, or a little paper glue-backed badge to stick onto his lapel. He'd sit in the receptionist's anteroom, legs crossed, leafing through a seasonal catalog of forthcoming books, waiting for a secretary to lead him down a book-lined hallway to the corner office.

Hayden would take a seat across from someone a few years younger than him, somber business suits and fashionable eyeglasses, soft fleshy middle-aged executives, impatient with this intrusion but also intimidated, and often bristling with something like contempt.

He would present a badge that identified him as an agent for the National Security Agency. He had business cards to that effect as well, naming him Joseph Lyons. The NSA wasn't the ideal cover for this situation, but Hayden's experience was that absolutely everyone was not only intimidated by the NSA, but also confused by it, unsure of what exactly the agency did, for which branch of government.

He'd set his face into an approximation of moral indignation as he explained about the manuscript, about the hoax that was being perpetrated. When this manuscript did emerge, Hayden said, it would be *absolutely imperative* that he be alerted, instantaneously. If these people were going to be caught, if the hoax was going to be contained and then quashed, time was of the essence, *absolutely critical*.

Hayden shook hands firmly and left behind his phony business card with a real phone number. He'd made a whole box of these cards, 250 of them, a couple of years earlier. They were almost gone.

One evening, he slipped one of these cards to a very likely confederate, and offered him a bribe.

Another evening he met up with a woman he'd known back when he was in Cambridge, a lifetime ago. They'd stayed in faltering touch. Bitsy had been divorced now for fifteen years. After dinner they walked around the block to her apartment, antique Persian rugs and Hudson River School landscapes in ornate gilt frames, a four-poster mahogany bed with obscenely soft sheets, a slow comfortable screw and a warming Armagnac nightcap wearing silk robes in front of the window facing the park, the galaxy of twinkling lights of the skyline, fuzzy from the fog that settled over the dark park like a cold wet blanket.

He snuck out at 3:00 a.m., struck out through the deserted uptown streets, the rows of green awnings of fortress-like apartment buildings, the ornate Beaux Arts facades of limestone mansions, the flapping flags of museums and private schools, the vast expanses of pristine glass that fronted art galleries and clothing boutiques, the big black bags of rubbish on the curbs in front of restaurants, awaiting pickup from the army of garbage trucks that roamed the late-night city like a gang looking for an easy mark, grumbling and proprietary, unchallenged.

Hayden fell back into his hotel bed, wondering what would've been, could've been, if it'd been himself instead of Roger who'd married Bitsy, moved to New York, gone to law school or Wall Street, made this his town, this his life, the whole family together on Christmas ski vacations. He had spent last Christmas alone, in his apartment in Munich, listening to Wagner and reading about Egypt. He spent nearly every Christmas alone.

He left New York the next evening, confident that he'd been appropriately intimidating to the upper echelons of the book-publishing business. Confident that when the manuscript hit the marketplace, he would be alerted, by a variety of people.

On the other hand, it was also possible—it was likely—that the manuscript would never hit the marketplace, that this whole population of informants would never glimpse the thing. Hayden had planned for that contingency as well.

He had even planned for another contingency, one that he'd never admitted to himself. And it was clear to him now, while reading the manuscript in this stolen boat, that he was effectuating a plan he hadn't even realized he'd formed.

Yes, he thinks, I know how this is going to end.

CHAPTER 47

The phone rings, and rings, and rings, then voice mail picks up. Stan ends the call, and instead sends Jessica a text: *Call me. Urgent.*

Something catches his eye out the window, down the hill. It looks like headlights, coming up his long driveway.

There could be plenty of reasons for someone to come driving up to his house at this time of night. Could be the garrulous winemaker from the estate next door, who has a tendency to show up uninvited, not entirely sober. Could be some boyfriend—or girlfriend—of the cook Irene. Could be the ranch hand Logan, returning from wherever Logan goes at night. Could be cops. Could be killers.

It's definitely a vehicle coming up the driveway. Stan wonders what the fuck happened to the security system at the front gate, which he had been assured was absolutely top-flight.

From the house, roads extend in three directions to different destinations on the property. But none offers any egress to the main road. None leads to escape, only to hiding.

As with employing a hot assistant, sometimes owning a thousand-acre ranch, with his nearest neighbors two miles away, has downsides.

Jessica wraps the throw blanket around her shoulders. She thinks she hears her doorbell ring. Could that really be her doorbell? She turns down the music, listens. Yes, it rings again.

"Hello?" She looks through the video-intercom's screen: clean-cut guy, fit, late-thirties or early forties, respectably but not fashionably dressed. A good-looking guy who asks, "Jessica Mendelsohn?"

"Yes?"

"This is Detective Dryden, with the Beverly Hills P.D.? We were on the phone a few minutes ago?"

The man steps back, away from the camera a couple of feet. In one hand, he's holding a briefcase. With the other hand, he reaches into his jacket pocket, pulls out a wallet, flips it open, and holds it up to the camera. Sure enough, that's a badge.

"Oh yes. Hi, Detective. How can I help you?"

"Can you let me in, please?"

She's not too sure about this, not at all. But what's she going to do?

"Sure!" she says, in the forced cheer that she uses to say *thanks!* to hundreds of people every day, in person and on the phone, as part of her performing-parrot act.

She waits by the door, then notices that she's in her bathrobe, and turns to her bedroom to get dressed, but then realizes that she doesn't have the time, and it's better to be securely in a bathrobe than falling out of her clothing. She pulls the robe closed tightly against her chest, her thighs.

Knock. Knock.

She opens the door.

"Thank you. Sorry to bother you. Did Mr. Balzer tell you why we called?"

She shakes her head.

"It's about Camilla Browning. Glyndon-Browning, I guess is her full name. You've met her?"

Jessica nods.

"Well, I'm sorry to tell you, but Ms., ah, Browning is dead. She was in a car accident tonight," the detective continues. "I'm so sorry."

"Oh my God!"

"Yes, it's terrible. And because Ms. Glyndon-Browning—that's what you say, right? Both names?—is not, ah, from the area . . ."

Jessica stares at him blankly.

"And with Mr. Balzer out of town . . ."

"Yes?" She feels like she should know what he wants, but she doesn't. She has spent so much of her life immersed in the plots of movies, but she doesn't realize when her life has slid into one.

"We've been unable to positively identify the body."

Jessica nods, still not getting it.

"And we need to."

"Uh-huh."

"So," he says, growing frustrated, "would you mind coming down to the station? It'll only take a minute."

Oh my God, she thinks: they want me to ID the dead British chick. "Really?" How gross. She wonders if there's any way she can get out of this. "Sure," she says, forcing the cheer. "Give me a minute to get dressed?"

"Of course."

"I'll meet you on the street? I'll pull my car out, to yours?" She places her hand on the doorknob, ready to push it closed.

But the cop keeps his body in the doorway. "It would be better if I waited here while you get ready."

"Um . . ."

He smiles broadly. He really is very good-looking, for a cop. She opens the door and lets him in. "Two secs," she says.

It's when she's in her underwear in her bedroom with the door shut that she hears her phone ringing, out there in the living room, sitting on the coffee table next to her mug of herbal tea and her stack of awesome manuscript. She hurries into a sweater, but there's no way she's going to

313

CHRIS PAVONE

make it out before voice mail picks up. Fuck it, she thinks. Even if it is Stan, he can wait five minutes.

Jessica emerges from her bedroom, pulling her hair out of the sweater, but doesn't see the detective, and falls into a split-second of panic before she realizes that it's entirely justified, because a wire has been pulled around her neck.

The ATV bumps along the rutted path alongside the vineyard, row after row of pinot noir, with clusters of pink roses trained to the stakes at the end of each, which Stan remembers are not purely for aesthetics, but serve some agricultural reason that may or may not involve fungus, or mold, or something disgusting that he didn't expect to be associated with a vineyard, which in the end is perhaps the most surprising pain in the ass in his life, as well as a financial nightmare of epic proportions. Fucking vineyard.

Stan hasn't turned on the headlights—lights would give away his location—and despite the strong moonlight he's having trouble navigating this vehicle in the dark.

At the far end of the vineyard he turns onto the even cruder path that leads up the mountain, into wilderness. There are coyotes up there; he hears them every night. Bears too, sometimes. Wildlife is part of the appeal of this property, this area. Wildlife scares the shit out of Stan.

The engine strains against the ascent, a high-pitched whine. Stan can't remember buying this vehicle, or okaying its purchase. He has no idea how much it may have cost. He doesn't know whether it's a high-end performance machine of some sort, or a barely functioning insipid toy.

The left side of the vehicle rises along a ridge in the path and then thuds into a boulder and then he can fill it tipping over, to the right, it's on just two wheels for a half-second before the balance shifts and it's going over, and Stan is falling out, hitting the hard-pack violently on his thigh and arm, and the ATV comes crashing down on his other side, and he's

314

pinned there, on a dark mountainside, with what feels like a broken leg and a broken elbow and a dislocated shoulder and a gash in his temple, while the big fat rubber wheels continue to spin and whir, a mockery of movement.

He almost can't believe how bad this is, and then of course it gets worse.

CHAPTER 48

The author freezes, standing in the entrance to Vanessa's apartment, the door still wide open to the dim, quiet corridor. This building feels like a business hotel, wall-to-wall charcoal carpets and nickel-finish sconces and uninspired nonrepresentational prints in black metal frames. And he feels like a burglar. Which, come to think of it, he is.

He glances from the pair of men's shoes to the closed bathroom door. He thinks he can hear the shower running from within.

He turns around, looks behind him into the hall. Maybe he should just leave, wait for this man, this alternate recipient of Vanessa's ministrations, to leave. The guy is showering, will probably be gone in ten minutes.

But maybe he can't spare ten minutes. Armed enemies could be flooding the *Bahnhof* with personnel right this minute, not just guns-for-hire but also local *Polizei*, or perhaps Interpol agents, or for all he knows goddamned Green Berets, swarming the airport, erecting roadblocks . . .

His eyes dart around the apartment, flitting over surfaces, shelves, rugs, until his attention lands in the living room. He crosses the space quickly, his feet gliding across the parquet, to the credenza dominated by the flat-screen television next to the dancing green lights of a little black router. He picks up a tall glass candlestick, and yanks out the white taper, and lays the candle silently on the glossy veneer. He hefts the heavy stick in his palm. It'll do.

The blinds are still drawn in the dark bedroom, the linens strewn around, clothing discarded at the foot of the bed. He picks up the suit jacket, a nice soft pinstriped wool, and glances at the label, size 52.

The shower still seems to be running. He hastily pulls on this other man's pants, wrinkled white shirt, jacket; he leaves the necktie on the floor. The pants are a bit short, but within an acceptable margin of error.

He and Vanessa had never had any conversation about an exclusive relationship; it wasn't something he felt entitled to request, considering the essential dishonesty of everything about him. But he never realized just how non-exclusive it was.

He pushes down on the brushed-metal lever, releases the catch, opens the bathroom door. The shower is running in the tub behind the opaque curtain, one of those handheld models, the spray hitting the fabric briefly, billowing out, before being aimed somewhere else, more carefully.

He puts down the toilet seat and hops up on it. He reaches to the top of the medicine cabinet, fully extending the arm that's not holding the candlestick, feeling under the lip of the front of the steel structure, until he finds it, the small screwdriver. He turns to face the wall, still standing on the toilet, and reaches the screwdriver up to the grate that covers the ventilation fan, the air duct. He removes one screw, spinning the tool quickly in his palm, pulling out the little steel cylinder, which slips out of his fingertips, and falls to the floor with a tiny little clank.

Shit. He freezes, staring over his shoulder at the shower curtain, the water still running, no change.

He returns his attention to the second screw, has trouble finding the groove, his nerves catching up with him as the head of the screwdriver slips out once, and again, and a shiver runs down his spine, and he spins around.

"*Merde.*"

The spigot is still running, a full stream aimed at the tiled wall, splattering. The naked man has pulled aside the curtain, standing there dripping, glaring, trying to figure out what action he should take, how serious this situation is. Sometimes people know when they're about to die; sometimes they don't.

"This was a *kid*," Dave said. "Practically a baby."

Charlie nodded sympathetically. "And I couldn't agree more that it was very, *very* unfortunate. I'm heartbroken too."

"No. Not like me you're not."

"Maybe. But that's understandable, isn't it?"

Dave didn't respond.

"Nevertheless," Charlie continued, "it's not like we *made* that happen."

"*We*? There's no *we* in this situation. And you *did* make it happen, Charlie."

For a few seconds neither man said anything.

"What do you have in mind, Dave? What is it you think we ought to do? What do you *want* from me?"

"How long has this been going on?"

"What?"

"This . . . this setting people up."

Charlie rolled his eyes, like a petulant teenager. "How do you think we've managed to get all those scoops, Dave? The exclusives? With a staff that's a bunch of amateur stringers? But somehow—*some*how—we've been beating the wire agencies and cable-news networks, the biggest newspapers, for fifteen years? How do you think that has happened? Luck? Skill? Are you out of your *fucking* mind?"

Charlie held out his hands, inviting answers to his rhetorical questions. "You pretend you don't know anything about the ugly business, Dave. But you do. I know you do. You just choose to ignore it. And you always have. But pretending to not know is not the same as doing something about it. And it's not the same as not knowing. So get off your high horse, you sanctimonious bastard."

"I quit."

"Quit?" Charlie laughed. "You can't *quit*. You think you're a fucking cashier at a 7-11? You're the goddamned COO of a publicly traded company. You signed an ironclad contract."

"So?"

"Not to mention a shitload of nondisclosure agreements. Plus you've been depositing an *awful* lot of money into your bank accounts. For a long, *long* time."

The previous year had been the final year that Preston Wolfe had cut Dave a forty-thousand dollar check, as agreed in the Ithaca hotel room twenty-five years earlier, in the middle of a long desperate night. It had once seemed like a lot of money. It had once seemed worth it, a million dollars, to stay silent. Almost worth it.

"I *own* you, Dave. I've owned you for your whole life, and I will own you forever. And you better fucking remember it."

Neither of them had taken a seat, staring at each other across the clean, uncluttered desk of a man who as a rule didn't handle paper.

"And let's remember, Dave, that *you* were the one who came after *me*."

"What the hell are you talking about?"

"Freshman year? You glommed onto me in the dorm. You rushed the same frat as me. You asked me to room with you." He chuckled, a brief ugly noise bereft of joy. Charlie had been subjugating his haughty temper for decades, but sometimes it proved too potent, and bubbled up from below, setting fire to everything in its path. "You were even the one who suggested the dance club, that night. Am I right?"

Dave steeled his jaw.

"And I get that, Dave, I do. Poor Jewish kid from Brooklyn. A guy like me, I must've looked pretty damn appealing. To a guy like you."

Dave struggled to not rise to this bait, staying silent, steaming.

Charlie took a deep breath. "At this moment, Dave, I need you—Wolfe Media needs you—to handle this Asia deal. For us." The tirade seemed to be over. He would now, as ever, back off. But not all the way. "After that, if you still want to, we can figure out a way for you to, ah, extricate yourself." Trying to defuse the bomb that he himself had constructed, then lit the fuse.

Dave had always been smarter than Charlie; they both knew this, had always known it. Plus Dave was the one who understood the logistics and finances in a way that Charlie had never bothered to learn. Charlie needed Dave, more than he'd ever admit.

"Next spring, Dave. Summer, at the latest."

This was not a winnable argument. Neither man could persuade the other he was more right. Only more strong.

So Dave didn't say anything. There was no betrayal quite like finding out that a lifelong friendship hadn't been genuine.

He flexes both arms, the candlestick and the screwdriver, menacing, glowering, trying to look tough, trying to avoid violence. The naked Frenchman seems to consider lunging, but looks dissuaded by the fact that he's penned into a tall bathtub, plus he's naked, and weaponless.

"Qu'est-ce que vous voulez?"

What do I want? That's a good question. The author shakes his head. *"Rien."* He gestures vaguely with the candlestick, encouraging this guy to stay put. *"Restez la."*

But for how long can he expect this naked Frenchman to do nothing? The guy will call the police as soon as the author walks out the door. Sirens wailing, tires screeching . . .

"Parlez-vous anglais?"

"A leetle."

"I don't want anything from you. *Comprenez?*"

"Oui."

"But I need to tie you up."

The man doesn't understand this.

"Il faut que . . ." He trails off; he doesn't know how to say this in French. He pantomimes, putting his hands in front of him, wrists together as if bound.

320

Recognition crosses the Frenchman's face, then something else, a decision, a resolve.

The author is already running through the apartment again in his mind, the spots where he has left fingerprints this morning, last week, whenever.

"*Alons-y,*" he says, gesturing for the naked man to remove himself from the tub. The author will bind the guy up with the necktie, sitting there on the messy floor of the dark bedroom, surrounded by the evidence of last night's sex. Or this morning's. Vanessa is partial to wake-me-ups.

The water is still running, and the Frenchman takes one tall step out of the tub, then another.

"*À la chambre,*" the author says.

"*Oui.*"

Wet footsteps slapping on the tile, then silent on the carpet of the hall, turning into the bedroom, the author following with the candlestick in one hand and the screwdriver in the other.

Then the naked man spins around, his right fist flying, coming into flush contact with the author's left cheek, an explosion of searing pain, seeing stars, nearly blinded, reacting instinctively by swinging the candlestick with maximum velocity, the heavy glass slapping wet naked skin on the upper arm, rearing back to swing again but the Frenchman has dropped to the floor, is scissoring a leg and knocks out the author's footing, falling on his ass but, somehow managing to hold on to both the candlestick and the small screwdriver, which he uses, as the man lunges, to stab him in the stomach, a deep puncture that freezes the man in place, his mouth a perfect O of surprise and pain, and he staggers backward one slow unsteady step, and another, clutching his gut with both hands.

The author stares up in horror. And the worst of the horror is knowing that this isn't the worst of it, not yet, not by a long shot.

The author leaps to his feet, still holding both improvised weapons, one of which is now bloody. He has never in his life had a fistfight, never took judo or karate or boxing classes, never since childhood hit another person in anger. Never discharged a firearm of any sort, never wielded a nonculinary knife, never until this moment burnished any weapon at any living creature, other than insects.

He once set a mousetrap, which the very first night successfully caught and killed a mouse, tiny and gray, Stuart Little–like. He used kitchen tongs to move the trap, dead mouse and all, into the bag in his garbage can, which he immediately removed and double-bagged and toted down to a basement bin, shutting the lid tightly and retreating to the elevator quickly, a shiver running down his spine.

The next time there was a mouse in the apartment, he decided that the two of them, man and mouse, could coexist peacefully together, co-habitate. It's not as if the mouse was doing him any harm.

Blood is oozing through the fingers of the naked Frenchman, pouring down his abdomen, getting caught in the dense tuft of his pubic hair.

The author swings the candlestick with all his might. At the last moment before impact he closes his eyes, but he can still feel the reverberation in his hand, and he can hear the appalling crack.

He opens his eyes, and sees that he'll need to swing again, at least once more. And this time he'll have to keep his goddamned eyes open.

CHAPTER 49

ayden scans the shoreline of the harbor, the boats bobbing, the pier and docks, the little structure with a flagpole, awnings, outdoor furniture.

He had gotten about halfway through reading the manuscript, then realized he was out of time. So he skipped to the end, read the last few pages, and that'll have to be that. Half the story. Which is a lot more than none of it.

"Empty that bin, will you?"

"Yes sir," Tyler says, and upends the big galvanized bucket, ice packs and beer cans and a bag of pretzels.

Hayden struggles to stand up, his legs tired and sore, his pants wrinkled and a little bit wet. He has been wearing the same clothes for an extraordinarily long time, lightweight charcoal slacks, a pale-blue spread-collar dress shirt, dark-chocolate English brogues with crepe rubber soles. His sport jacket is folded in his bag, and he digs it out, rummages through the pockets, finds a Zippo. Hayden has never smoked, but he has always carried a lighter.

He crumples up a few pages of the assistant's copy of the manuscript, and drops them into the steel bin, and sets the manuscript afire.

———

They tie up the boat alongside a sign that reads 30 MINUTE DOCKING, and walk away from another stolen mode of transportation. Hayden looks around the marina, at all these choices of other watercraft for later. He spots a beautiful Beneteau—fifty-four feet? more?—which looks a lot like the boat his family sailed every summer from the Cape to Maine, delivering and collecting the smaller children from sleep-away camp, making an adventure out of a chore. He also sees a nice big monohull, very similar to the boat he rented a few summers ago in Mallorca. The perfect craft for a long single-handed sail. Yes, he thinks, that's the one.

He and Tyler walk up the dock as if they don't have a care in the world, a couple of fishing buddies, albeit without the tackle. Halfway to land, the wooden dock becomes a concrete jetty, the surface gritty with sand, pebbles, shells dropped by seagulls. Then they're on a leafy street, dense with houses, flowering shrubs, porch swings, imported station wagons.

Hayden is lost in thought, outlining the steps of his new plan, enumerating the challenges, countering with solutions.

They pass a shuttered ice-cream parlor and a post office and a general store, all quiet, and then a woman walking a little brown dog, slowly. An old dog, like Hayden himself, looking up with rheumy eyes.

"Hi," the woman says.

"Good evening."

Hayden realizes they should be making small talk, he and Tyler. Two men on a sidewalk at night should be chatting; silence is suspicious. But he can't think of a damn thing to say.

It was almost a year ago when they sat in a corner banquette in a room filled with white tablecloths and burgundy upholstery, marble columns supporting the soaring, ornately plastered ceiling, waiters wearing black vests with white aprons.

"So. Things went very badly in Finland," Hayden said. "I don't disagree."

Charlie Wolfe was staring down at his untouched Wiener Schnitzel, wedges of lemon, a big white plate. "I can't do this anymore," he said.

Hayden took a bite of sweet spiny lobster. He had access to plenty of good Schnitzel in Munich, but he liked the Bouillabaisse here at his favorite Berlin restaurant on Französische Strasse, a pleasant walk from his office at the embassy.

"It's too dangerous for me, Hayden. To be involved in things like this."

Hayden put down his fork and knife. Wiped his mouth with the big napkin. "You mean you don't *need* me anymore. Now that you're a billionaire."

"I'm not a billionaire."

Now Hayden understood why Charlie wanted to meet in a restaurant. In fifteen years they'd had only one other meal together, a quick lunch in Davos. Otherwise it had had been isolated benches in quiet parks to arrange the mutually beneficial scandals.

"But I've become too visible. And I want to become *more* visible. I can't . . . you know."

This was apparently the end of their long symbiotic relationship, a cordial parting smoothed with a nice bottle of Meursault, very much in public.

Hayden nodded. He picked up his fork and knife again, and took another bite of seafood. Swallowed. "I feel like there's something else. Is there?"

Charlie didn't answer immediately, mustering courage. "Dave found out about it."

Hayden squinted. "To what does *it* refer?"

"The guy in Finland."

Hayden took a deep breath.

"His *kid* was in the house, Hayden. When the police burst in, and he started shooting, and the police returned fire . . . It was a three-year-old boy who got shot. He bled out. While hugging his goddamned *teddy bear*."

"I know what happened, Charlie."

"Well, Dave flipped out. And then some."

"Is it under control?"

"Yes. No. I don't know."

"How'd you handle it?"

"Not as well as I should have."

"Meaning?"

"He was sanctimonious with me, belligerent. And I tried to be accommodating—it's not like I feel *good* about the Finnish guy, and his kid—but I lost my temper. I ended up saying some things I shouldn't have. He was *pissed*."

"Is this reparable?"

"I think so, yes. I hope so. But honestly?"

"No, Charlie, please *lie* to me."

"Honestly Hayden, I just don't know."

Hayden took a sip of the Burgundy, trying to remain calm. This was very bad news. He couldn't help chasing the worst-case scenarios through the corridors of his imagination, and a number of them led through his safe-deposit box in Basel.

Over the years Hayden had used more than a dozen miniature tape recorders, growing smaller and more discreet with each generation, and eventually giving way to the infinitely inconspicuous digital models. Then he procrastinated for a few years before undertaking the considerable and tedious task of transferring all the old analog tapes to digital storage, on CDs. And then more recently from CDs to flash drives. Ever smaller, more easily duplicated, effortlessly transmitted, with increasingly complex and tiresome security.

Or maybe the security isn't really more complex, but Hayden has simply reached that fulcrum of age when all technological advances are the opposite of welcome.

Safe deposit boxes in Swiss banks have, thankfully, been relatively unchanged for the past forty years. Now all his life-insurance recordings sit on a single flash drive, so he no longer needs as big a metal drawer. Then again, he keeps a lot more cash in there than he used to.

CHAPTER 50

hat was nice, she said. A dagger thrust into his stomach, then twisted: *nice*. That's what you say after twenty years of marriage, not after your first time.

"Are you still thinking that we just wait?" Jeff pulls his boxer shorts over his ankles, facing away from Isabel now. He glances down at his penis, sticky and limp and faintly preposterous.

"I don't know," she says. "I'm beginning to wonder if we have to go public, somehow. Have a press conference, maybe. *Try* to have a press conference. Or just present ourselves to NBC or CNN or something, walk into an office and tell our story . . ."

Yes. That this is what people like them would to, in this type of situation. "That sort of makes sense. Doesn't it?" He settles back into the bed beside her, but they're not touching.

"I'm worried that going public only keeps us alive *tomorrow*. Then what, Jeffrey? Do we enter the witness protection program? Are we even *witnesses* to anything? Can we trust the people who are supposed to *protect* us?"

Jeff doesn't answer.

"This is one of the most powerful men in America," she continues. "And he's intertwined with the CIA, operating illegally. They'll *kill* us.

No"—shaking her head—"the only way television works is if the *author* is on it, or someone else with firsthand knowledge. And obviously if the author wanted to do this on TV, he wouldn't have gone to all the trouble of writing the manuscript. He wouldn't still be hiding. He'd just go on TV."

The idea of the author hangs in the air between them, uncomfortably.

Jeff fidgets with his hands. He knows he needs to try harder to conceal the deep simmering resentment that accompanies his long-unrequited love, the festering heart sore caused by rejection, indifference, tepid affection. Because now, as ever, he's sure that Isabel doesn't love him. She had a need and he was at hand, so they're in bed. He's like a fast-food hamburger, not a four-star meal: in a pinch, he suffices. He's a *nice* hamburger.

"Why do you think he doesn't do that? Just go on television?"

Isabel lets out a dismissive snort. "He knows the limitations of TV. Knows there's no way to tell a complex story like this on cable news, which would just reduce everything to a one-ring circus about the single most lurid detail. He wants the audience to understand more. Plus I'm sure he wants the permanence of a book, the validation, the legitimacy conferred by having it out there in the physical world, in stores and libraries, on people's shelves and in their laps and coffee tables. There are still some stories that warrant a book. This is one of them."

"You awake?"

"*Mmmmmmm.*" The halfway hum between awake and asleep.

"Can't sleep," he whispers. "There's too much buzzing around his brain, in bed with this woman after so many years, hiding in this house with this manuscript downstairs, with men with guns out there, maybe looking for him. "Going downstairs."

"*Mmm.*"

Jeff walks down the long hall, the stairs. He closes the door to the stairs, a quiet buffer from Isabel. He doesn't want to wake her.

He switches on the first light he can find by touch, on an end table, a bulbous ceramic thing with a pull chain, a twenty-five-watt bulb, ambered by a parchment shade. Deep shadows creep from every corner, behind every object.

He looks around in the soft light. He thought he'd left his bag here, on this couch. But it's not there. He panics, eyes darting frantically. The panic lasts for only a second because there it is, on the floor, leaning up against the wall. Safe and sound.

Jeff opens the bag, removes the stack of paper, too thick for one hand, nearly a full ream of paper. He deposits the manuscript on the glass-topped coffee table facing the floral-upholstered armchair with the small ottoman, in front of the fireplace. A nice place to read.

He takes two steps across the oval hooked rug, concentric elongated circles in blues and greens and dingy whites. He picks up the bulky fire screen, almost too heavy to lift with one hand, and moves it to the side. He crumples a few sheets of newspaper into the fireplace, atop the thin film of dust and ash, some shards of partially incinerated wood. He settles a fire-starter brick onto the newspaper, and a couple of small split logs on top. He slides open the long, slender box of wooden matches, and removes one, rough-hewn and splintering, its flammable phosphorous splashed onto its tip unevenly, wantonly. He strikes this messy match, and he stoops down, and he tucks the stick under the newsprint. The fire ignites.

Jeff wonders if this is how selling out always happens for everyone, a clear-cut trade-off of integrity for success. He'd always assumed that the sellout was something that happens slowly, gradually, a long-term erosion of willpower, a chiseling-away at idealism, until you get to a point where the decision doesn't even seem like a decision anymore, it's just the thing that you do, and you don't even realize that it's selling out.

But no, here it is, upon him, different from what he imagined, as so many important things seem to end up being. Here it's one fell swoop at a moment of weakness. His company is about to go under, and he knows he will not be one of the first of the newly unemployed to find a job. He's saving his skin. It's so trite.

It's now clear to him that the most heinous part of selling out is that you betray someone's trust. The trust of a friend, a family member, a colleague. Or even just your own trust of yourself, your self-respect. You do something, embrace something, believe something you know you should not. You do something you know isn't right, isn't what you intended to do. Isn't who you wanted to be.

What do you get in return? It's always the same, he imagines: you get success. It may come dressed in different costumes, but it's probably always a similar calculation, for everyone, weighing the desire for some success against the cost of betraying someone's trust.

Maybe everyone thinks the same thing: If it's not me who makes this bargain, who betrays this trust, it'll just be someone else who makes the sellout, someone else who benefits. There is always someone willing to take the bribe, the bait, the opportunity to run the division, the corporation, the world. There is always someone.

Should that person be me? That's the question.

Jeff turns around, looks at the incendiary manuscript. He picks up the top inch. He turns back to the fireplace, and scatters the paper on the small smoldering fire. He blows softly at the gathering flames, and waits for them to catch, engulfing the pages from the bottom. By the light of its own flame, he rereads the top page before it curls and shrivels, then disappears.

He kneels there, feeding small stacks of paper into the growing conflagration, watching the manuscript burn, until every last page is up in smoke.

In the dim light by the front door, he kneels and opens her bag. At first glance he doesn't see it. So he looks more carefully, and removes the large items, and still doesn't see any thick stack of letter-sized paper. It isn't there.

Jeff rises, stands in the foyer, stares into the living room at the licking flickering flames, thinking back through the past hours, driving, shopping at the farmstand, arriving to the house, reading while Isabel prepared dinner in the kitchen, eating on the veranda. Then kissing, and walking upstairs, bed, sex, talking, that phone call.

Then he came back down here, and he burned his copy of the manuscript.

But he can't remember the last time he saw her copy. Did she leave it in the car? Ditch it at the gas station? Did she hide it somewhere in this house? Where would she have had the opportunity . . . ?

He turns on the kitchen light. He starts opening cupboards, and then drawers, one by one, as quietly as possible. There are a lot of places to hide something, in a kitchen. He looks on top of the glass-fronted hutch, and in the cabinet beneath the sink. In the oven. In the dishwasher. In the walk-in butler's pantry and the tiny whitewashed washroom.

And when he eventually finds it, he grins.

The moon is casting dim shadows from the trees on the lawn that sweeps down to the rocky beach, and the moonlight's reflection is shimmering in the Sound, and he can barely see the lights of Connecticut twinkling in a low line across the water. Off to the east, away from the moonlight, the sky is filled with stars.

The slipcovered chair is deep and soft and enveloping, and Jeff sinks low, lower, his feet resting on the ticking-stripe cushion of the ottoman. He hears the creaking of the old wide-planked floorboards upstairs. The squeal of pipes and the distant vibration of running water, the burst of a toilet flushing, the click and hum of the pump in the cellar turning on, running, then a special type of quiet when it stops. Two-foot waves thrum the beach softly, regularly, an acoustic guitar strumming rhythm. He can smell a whiff of salt, carried on a gust of cool early-summer breeze.

He's falling asleep, aware of the dreaminess of his thoughts, the surreal images marching through his brain, like troops trudging through an occupied city. He recognizes these thoughts as dreams; he knows that he's dreaming. But he's also not asleep, not totally; he's still aware of the real world, of real sounds, real sensations. Or at least he thinks he is.

And then he knows he is, because it's a real sound that pulls him into full consciousness, out of the half-asleep dream state: it's a creak from the front of the house, from downstairs not up-, made by something or someone who's not Isabel. It's the creak of the front door halfway through its arc.

Jeff's eyes flash open, but otherwise he doesn't move. This is real; there's someone in the house.

He stays frozen, slouched low in the deep chair, his eyes darting. He's not sure if he can be seen from behind; he may be sunk low enough in the chair to be invisible. Then again, he may not be low enough.

Jeff hears a creak on the floorboards behind him. Another.

He's been holding his breath too long, so he exhales slowly, silently, then inhales just as slowly, straining to be still, to be quiet, to be invisible.

And then a small tinny clang, a little piece of metal landing on the wooden floor. His bathroom sink's washer, falling out of his pocket.

Damn.

It's only a second later that he feels a thing touch his temple. For an instant he's not completely positive, but then all doubt is erased that the thing is a gun when a man says, "Don't move a muscle."

This doesn't make any sense, Jeff thinks. This isn't part of the plan. There aren't supposed to be any guns aimed in his direction. An idea scampers through his brain that he should try to explain to this man, but worries that his explanation may not do anything other than get him shot.

While the man holds a gun to Jeff's head, a second man appears in front of him. A familiar man. Someone Jeff saw once before, months earlier.

He has always frequented a bar around the corner. In the nineties it was Max Fish across from his apartment on the Lower East Side, as well as the Irish pub O'Flaherty's around the block from his office in Times Square. When he briefly lived uptown, the challenge was to find a place on Amsterdam that wasn't perpetually mobbed with drunk ex-frat boys and sorority girls. And when he started spending a lot of his life on Union Square, he struggled to choose a bar that didn't explode with happy-hour revelry every evening.

Because what he's always looking for is elusive: a comfortable place that's neither prohibitively crowded nor depressingly empty. A clientele older than college kids and twenty-something binge drinkers, but younger than the hardcore geezers who hunch over their Manhattans and *Racing Form*s in old-man bars. He wants a ballgame playing on one television in the corner, but not twenty big screens broadcasting the entire league's play. A decent selection of whiskey, without paying eighteen dollars per glass. A kitchen that can produce an acceptable burger, but not a fussy unaffordable patty made with braised short rib or stuffed with foie gras.

What Jeff wants is a place to work after work hours, to bridge the lonely distance between office and bed. In the twenty-plus years that he has lived in New York City, he has cohabitated with another human being for a total of only five; there was a one-year roommate at the get-go, and then a long-term girlfriend in his late twenties, and later a short-term wife. But for the other years he's been solitary, like so many New Yorkers, eating dinner at bars, ordering in Chinese to consume on the couch, turning on the bedside reading lamp at two a.m. without worrying about waking anyone.

This he thinks is the secret to New York City's vast productivity: everyone works all the time to avoid facing their loneliness.

It was a normal lonely evening when Jeff headed to the old bar up on Eighteenth Street, leaving the office in the dark wet cold of early-winter seven p.m., red taillights faced off against white headlights on Park Avenue South, selfish suit-wearing jackasses whose golf umbrellas dominate the entire width of sidewalks, women in short skirts and tall heels trying to hail cabs on every corner, the welcoming glow from shops and restaurants and bars and lounges, customers rushing in and staggering out.

As he turned off the avenue a gust of crosstown wind ballooned his little five-dollar umbrella, snapping a few aluminum ribs. Although the wind was strong, the rain was light, which made his cheap umbrella more trouble than it was worth; he tossed it in the wire-mesh can on the corner, and hustled down the block protected by only his waxy raincoat.

Jeff hung the heavy damp jacket on a peg by the door of the pub. He loves this Barbour coat—it's comfortable and warm, it's waterproof and dries quickly, it has good pockets in the right places, it fits over a sport jacket—but at the same time he hates its ubiquity, its association with a uniform for a team he's not on.

He took a seat on a wooden stool at the far end of the bar, with an empty spot between himself and a pair of unappealing thirty-something women. One gave him a quick once-over, batting over-mascara'd eyelashes over a pink drink in a V-shaped glass, which was not the thing to order in this bar. This was a beer place.

He turned away, unpacked a short stack of proposals from his satchel, his Sheaffer fountain pen from his flannel jacket. He ordered a first pint of ale; he'd order a second with food. He read the covering letters of a few proposals, pitches from agents about why this, that, and the other project should exist in the world, how respected So-and-So is, what a hot topic such-and-such is. Guaranteed publicity. Can't-miss special-sales opportunities. Superlatives and exaggerations and misrepresentations and at least one outright falsification.

A man took the stool next to Jeff, ordered a Belgian ale. Jeff looked up at the sound of the man's voice, urbane and upper-class, out of place in this downtown pub. A voice that belonged in Bemelmans Bar, or maybe the Union Club, visiting from Boston, or from the 1920s.

The two sat in companionable silence for a few minutes while the Knicks quickly went down 12-3, and the bartender busied himself mixing new drinks for the women, then filling a tray of beer glasses for a large group at a table, before heading to the far end of the bar to chat with a better-looking, younger pair of women.

That's when the man said, "You're Jeffrey Fielder, aren't you?"

Jeff turned to face this stranger. Somewhere between mid-fifties and late-sixties; tall and fit, schoolboy spectacles and neatly combed gray hair, well-dressed, maybe too, with a peacocky pocket square poking out of his tailored sport jacket. The type of man you see in expensive uptown restaurants, or boardrooms. Not that Jeff had ever been in a boardroom. Or even really knew what a boardroom was. But the guy didn't look like the type of person who hung around a place like this.

"Do we know each other?" Jeff tried to muster a smile, pushing through the vague discomfort of a mid-forties man with a mediocre memory and a long history of inebriation, confronted with this type of situation. He'd met plenty of people who he later couldn't remember. Especially men. He forgot dozens, maybe hundreds, of men per year. Forgetting men was practically his hobby.

"No." The man shook his head. "You don't know me."

Jeff raised his eyebrows, asking for an explanation.

"I'm a sort of, I guess you'd call it an *enthusiast* about book publishing."

Was this guy a stalker? A frustrated failed novelist, looking for a way to get published? "Uh-huh." Or a rejected writer, looking for revenge?

"I've been studying the book business recently, learning about the process. Agents, editors, writers. Contracts, royalties, legal issues. Libel and such."

Jeff was now fully turned in his barstool, facing this guy. He certainly didn't look threatening, nor was he behaving in a scary fashion; he looked like an art dealer, is what he looked like. But this was definitely a creepy conversation.

Jeff had been stalked once, by the writer of a book proposal who had come to the office with her ineffective agent for a meet-and-greet. Then Jeff had declined to make an offer on the project, as had apparently every other editor during multiple rounds of submissions, and the writer eventually resorted to alternative methods of trying to sell her project. Which included stalking and then propositioning Jeff—boldly and explicitly and not exactly quietly—and after he refused she called his home and nevertheless told his wife that he had not refused, unleashing a whole shitstorm from which his marriage never recovered.

Lesson being that you never know when crazy is going to show up, and there's no real way to protect yourself. So it wasn't really an actionable lesson, so much as simply the revelation of an unpleasant fact of life for anyone who's in the business of making other people's dreams come true, or dashing them.

"How can I help you, Mister . . . I didn't catch your name?"

"You can call me Joseph Lyons. Joe."

"What does that mean? Is that your name?"

"No, not really." The guy smiled. "Mr. Fielder, someday soon—in the next few weeks, maybe, or within a few months—a manuscript will find its way to you. It may even arrive as an exclusive. This manuscript will be about Charlie Wolfe. It will—that is, the manuscript will—"

Jeff appreciated the clarification of the pronoun's antecedent. But this whole thing was making him tingle with fear.

"—purport to be a revelatory, er, *bomb*shell. It may be a full biography of the man's life, or it may have a more limited scope. That aspect of the project isn't comp*lete*ly clear to us, at the moment."

"Who's *us*?"

The man ignored the question. "What *is* clear is that this manuscript will claim that Mr. Wolfe did something, or some things, horrible. Unseemly. Perhaps illegal." He shrugged. "Who knows."

The bartender stopped by, and this man ordered another beer, a pause in his story, looking around appreciatively. "This is a good place," he said.

"Yes," Jeffrey agreed. "There's a lot of liquor."

"Ha! Quoting Hemingway!" The bartender deposited the fresh glass, and this man picked it up, raised it toward Jeff. "*Nicely* done, Mr. Fielder. Nicely done." He took a sip. The bartender retreated.

"But what this manuscript will be, in fact, is a hoax. It's being fabricated right now by a Danish freelancer, for the purposes of scandalizing Mr. Wolfe, collapsing the stock price of Wolfe Worldwide Media, leading to a hostile takeover of the company, and hundreds of millions—or even billions—in profit."

"How do you know this?"

"Because I do."

Jeff snorted.

The man nodded his appreciation of Jeff's dubiousness. "You Jeffrey Fielder, Brown Class of '91, have a checking account at the JP Morgan Chase bank with slightly more than four hundred dollars in it, and revolving debt totaling slightly less than twelve thousand dollars. You live in an apartment 4A in Chinatown with an area of six hundred square feet. The last time you left the United States was two years ago, on a somewhat trumped-up business trip to London. Your favored Internet pornography website is the oldie but goodie, youporn.com."

Jeff cowered at this bit of humiliating invasiveness. "What do you want from me?"

"I have a proposition for you, Mr. Fielder."

"A proposition?"

"Here it is: do everything in your power to convince the literary agent, to convince your publisher, to convince *every*body, that you want to acquire this, publish it."

That sounded like what he'd want to do anyway.

"You want the agent to *not* submit it to other publishers. You want it to be exclusively with you, permanently with you. So that you can *destroy* it."

"Excuse me?"

"You will physically destroy any hard copies. *Shred* them, *burn* them, whatever."

"You're joking."

"If the manuscript is emailed to you, you'll delete the file. If it somehow ends up on other people's computers—which you should do everything you can to prevent—use this." The man reached into his jacket pocket, removed a thumb drive and a business card. "Plug the stick into any USB port, leave it there for five seconds, then remove it. *All* the files will be corrupted, the system will crash, the computer will be electronic scrap."

The man placed the small device and the card on the bar. "If you run into difficulties, if something goes wrong, or if anything happens whatsoever, you call me."

"Anything like what?"

"*Any thing* anything. The agent gets an offer. Or the author contacts you. Or strange men—that is, as strange as me, or stranger—come knocking on your door." The man tapped the card. "That's my phone number. Keep it safe."

Jeff looked down. "And?"

"And what?"

"And why should I do this? Just because you know I'm broke? Everyone knows I'm broke. I haven't committed any crime; you have nothing on me. And frankly it sort of sounds like you're full of shit."

The man nodded. "That's fair. So you want to know what's in it for you. Besides the heartfelt but silent thanks of an ignorantly grateful nation."

"I do."

"Okay, here's what I promise you, Jeffrey Fielder: Once this manuscript has been successfully eradicated from the face of the earth, Charlie

Wolfe will call you, out of the blue. He'll tell you that he admires your track record, your principles. He'll ask if you're interested in publishing his own memoir."

Jeff raised his eyebrows.

"Editors who acquire and edit these types of books, by people like Mr. Wolfe, they're well treated in your business, aren't they? They ought to be. These books generate tremendous amounts of revenue. I'd think that the people who pull in that revenue are rewarded. That's capitalism, right?"

The man leaned toward Jeff. "This is the book that will make you a *star*, Mr. Fielder. An *invaluable* asset. A well-compensated one, with job security. A rarity in today's precarious economic environment. You're how old?"

Jeff couldn't help but notice another solo man walk into the bar, out of the rain. Jeff wondered if this new arrival were connected; he kept his eye on the new guy as he settled at the other end of the room.

"You know how old I am."

"That's true. I do."

"So you're *bribing* me?"

"*Bribe* is not an attractive word, is it? And I don't think it's the operative concept here."

Book editors receive a lot of bizarre propositions. But this had been, by far, the bizarrest.

"And what if I say no?"

"We both know that *no* isn't a viable option for you." The man took another sip of his beer.

"The hoax will never be successfully perpetrated, Mr. Fielder. With or without you. It will be stopped, with arrests and jail if necessary. Perhaps worse."

"Worse?"

"There is no upside to attempting to publish it. There's only upside in preventing the publication. You might as well take advantage of the upside."

The man beckoned the bartender. "I'll settle up, please. And I'll take care of my friend too." The man peeled off two twenties.

Jeff stared into the top of his pint glass, the foam dissipated, now just a flat nut-brown surface.

"This is not *so* bad, is it, Mr. Fielder?"

Jeff didn't answer. In the overall scheme of sellouts, this certainly wasn't as bad as he could've imagined. But it was also not exactly what he had planned as a career-advancement maneuver. Though in fact he had no specific plans in that regard.

"Oh, I almost forgot," the man said, rising from his stool. "There's another reason why you'll want to accept my proposition. The most compelling reason." The man leaned in toward Jeff, the smell of a sandalwood cologne and caramely ale mixing on his breath. "Because if you fail to comply"—he leaned in closer—"I will *kill* you."

"I thought we had an agreement." That same man is now backlit by the glow of the low fire. Jeff's copy of the manuscript is completely incinerated atop the smoldering logs, flames licking from beneath. "Did I misunderstand?"

Jeff can't quite find his voice.

"You were meant to *call* me. If you did something like, say, *flee* from town. Weren't you, Mr. Fielder?"

Jeff swallows, then says, "She threw my phone into the East River."

The man chuckles.

"What was I supposed to do?"

"I guess *not let her* wasn't an option?"

"No, it wasn't. And by the way"—gathering indignation—"can you get that fucking gun off my head?"

The man in front of him nods; the one behind lowers the weapon. Jeff takes a nearly comical breath of relief.

"What are you doing here?" Jeff asks.

"We're finding you. And her. Is she upstairs? Asleep?"

"What do you want from her?"

The man reaches into the waistband of his pants, and pulls out his own gun.

"Come on, Mr. Fielder, don't be disingenuous. You know what I want."

CHAPTER 51

The author climbs back onto the toilet lid, and finishes opening the air duct. He reaches into the dark cavity, where he has stowed a backup set of his most crucial go-supplies, for the unfortunate contingency that just came to pass: his cover is blown, and he can't get into his apartment.

He pulls out another doctored passport, with which he'll be able to cross borders, and a rolled-up rubber-banded wad of cash, with which he'll be able to accomplish many other things. To buy a new identity, to live somewhere else, as someone else.

But he won't have a copy of his manuscript, trapped on the hard drive of his computer, which is already in the hands of his pursuers, whoever they might be, perhaps at this very minute trying to hack the laptop's security system, his encrypted files. Fortunately they will fail. After ten seconds of trying to start the system without the proper authentication, the hard drive will self-destruct, completely wiped out, unrecoverable.

And he won't be able to continue with his treatments, his visits to the plastic surgeon. But that's okay; there's not really anything left to accomplish there. Just the peace of mind that comes from visiting the man who reconfigured your fingerprints, and the other man who reconstructed

parts of your face, so he can tell you that you look all right; good, even. That reassurance has been nice. But it's something the author can live without.

He catches a glimpse of himself in Vanessa's mirror, this new version of himself. The swelling and discoloration are entirely gone; it'd be impossible to notice the incision marks unless you knew exactly where to look, and what to look for. No one would ever glance at this face and say that it has been surgically altered. And in fact it's not terribly dissimilar to his old face—a different point to the chin, a new dimple, a slight slant to the eyes. Definitely enough to confound facial-recognition software. But not so much that he'd need to spend six months wrapped in bandages.

Now after nearly a year of living with one medical challenge or another, he's finally free. His first challenge, when he'd made his decision after that horrible conversation with Charlie, was to become someone who looked like he might be dying. So he started taking CNS stimulants, suppressing his appetite, losing a pound per week for the entire season, enough to loosen up the collars of his shirts, the waists of his pants. At the end there, he even bought a few shirts that were one neck size too big, an extra half inch that really made him look like he was swimming in the broadcloth cotton. Combined with three months of avoiding the sunshine, of poor sleep and weight loss and daily doses of speed, he succeeded in looking like crap. Like a dying man.

And then once he arrived to Zurich, there was the plastic surgery on his face, and the procedures to alter his fingerprints, and the ensuing recoveries, with antibiotics and painkillers, with a variety of muscular and skin treatments.

Will his pursuers ever find that old *Schloss*, tucked away in the mountain forest? They will assume the author is here in Switzerland for alternative cancer treatments, so they'll travel from facility to facility accompanied by Swiss police, brandishing government IDs, demanding confidential patient records. They wouldn't expect that he'd be here for plastic surgery, not a guy who's dying of cancer. So they will not find anything.

But if they come across Vanessa? That will be a problem. They will create a sketch. Then they will find footage from some camera somewhere, an image of a visage that matches. "Yes, that's him," the South African will say in her beautiful Boer accent. But this face will not match the face of David Miller. Will they know definitively that it was him in this apartment, killing this other man?

If they do find Vanessa they will also find that the face she describes matches the face that lives in the top-floor apartment on the other side of the lake, with the self-destructing computer and the paucity of personal belongings. Then they will indeed know what he now looks like, or close enough. And they will have a set of his new fingerprints. All this surgery, for naught.

He'll have to disappear again, farther away, into a less traceable environment. He'll use his squirreled-away millions to make his way to a beach in East Africa, or maybe the South Pacific; he has specific plans for both, and will try the former until it doesn't seem safe, at which point he'll move on to the latter. He'll drink fresh coconut milk and eat grilled fish and pay for the companionship of exotic erotic young women, while he waits for his manuscript to be published, for his venality to be revealed to the world, and for his ex-friend to be vilified, perhaps arrested, convicted.

It's a good thing he finished the manuscript when he did. He now has to hope that Isabel is taking it dead-seriously, and attending to it urgently. She'll no doubt submit it to her on-again-off-again paramour Jeffrey Fielder, who has probably blabbed about it to half of New York, to reporters and scouts and producers, the heft of the truth of the thing creating its own momentum, its inevitability, as it travels through media circles on its way to publication, not just in the print sense of the word, but in the public sense. *Public*ation.

The author arranged for the security detail to protect Isabel for six months. Round-the-clock surveillance, teams of ex-Marines, following her in-person, and using cell-phone-tower triangulation of her mobile's location as backup. Following her through the streets of Manhattan, on subways and taxis, in offices and restaurants, keeping track of Isabel Reed, and keeping her alive.

Maybe the author will call her, from a pay phone in a thatched hut somewhere on the other side of the world. He hasn't spoken to Isabel in a while.

It's remotely possible, the author thinks, that the local authorities won't connect this murder with that fugitive man. One is a local violent crime, the other an international hoax. So it's worth him going to the trouble to obfuscate the line between the two, to try to keep the Americans out of the investigation, to try to keep his identity concealed.

He finds a rag under the sink and sprays it with ammonium chloride solution. He wipes down the apartment, wearing yellow rubber gloves that are too small, cleaning every surface he can remember touching, not just this morning but last Thursday, the week prior, whenever before. Refrigerator and trashcan and coffee press, doorknobs and light switches and drawer pulls, the dangling plastic end to the cord for the thin aluminum blinds.

He steps over the dead naked Frenchman again and again as he crosses the apartment to clean, trying not to look down at the man's open unstaring eyes. He doesn't have the heart to touch those eyes, to close them.

He washes the candlestick and the screwdriver, and places both in a shopping bag, along with his running clothes and shoes. He'll dispose of the weapons as soon as he can, but far enough away from this apartment to make them unlikely to find, difficult to connect to this crime.

In a kitchen drawer he finds the key to her car, a BMW apparently. He hopes this car is parked in an intuitive place; they've never discussed parking, or a car. But sure enough there's one in the corner of a dark low-ceilinged garage that chirps a cheerful response to the remote key, one of a half-dozen BMWs amid twenty cars.

The streets in this residential neighborhood are just as quiet as those in his own, and he has a hard time preventing himself from speeding through the leafy traffic-free lanes, around the soft curves, up the incline, out of town.

It is 9:49 in the morning. Vanessa will not be home any earlier than 6:00, so he has eight hours before she comes home to discover her dead lover, her stolen car. The author will drive south, up and over the mountains; anyone would assume he would take the quicker escapes north to Germany or east to France. He will use local roads, avoiding any potential roadblocks and speed cameras on the highway. Then at Lucerne, when he doesn't have a choice, he'll get on the 2; there aren't multiple options for driving over the Alps.

He should be in Milan by 3:00. He'll abandon the car in a public garage a mile from the train station, then walk to the *stazione centrale* and board the high-speed train to Salerno. By the time Vanessa reports her car stolen—if she even notices, tonight, that her car is gone—he will be on the overnight ferry to Palermo, the most third-worldly city in Western Europe, stray dogs and Gypsy panhandlers and downtown lots filled with rubble. Tomorrow morning he'll cross the Wild West Sicilian countryside, ragged and sere and sparsely populated, to Catania, the incoming port for most of the illicit drugs in Europe, a porous point of departure for someone like him, a discreet American with bundles of cash who's looking for nothing more than a quiet crossing to Tunisia, carrying no contraband whatsoever.

Lost in these plans, he doesn't notice the car accelerating behind him until it's right up on his tail, hugging a long wide curve in the narrow road, and his attention is drawn to his rearview, to—*fuck*—the flashing swirling lights of the police cruiser that's a couple of car lengths behind.

"**C**ome on," he'd said, a quarter-century ago. "Stop. The fucking. Car."

The old Jaguar convertible was still nosing forward in first gear, and Charlie was gripping the wheel tightly with both hands. Dave was shuffling backward, the bumper bumping into his knees. "Charlie, *stop the car!*"

Charlie grinned, laughed maniacally, and threw his head back. But then he didn't bring his head forward again. His face was turned to the dark sky, and the car was still moving, but Charlie was not. He'd passed out.

Dave hopped back a few steps to get distance between himself and the slow-moving vehicle, then ran around the side. He opened the door and walked alongside the car, and hit Charlie on the shoulder to try to wake him up, but it didn't work. So Dave shoved him, slumped him against the gear shift; he shoved again and the guy fell over, halfway into the passenger seat, halfway to the floor, dead to the world.

When the driver's seat was clear, Dave jumped in. Got behind the wheel, and buckled the seatbelt; this was no time to not be wearing a seatbelt. He was terrified that the cops were going to show up, and the girl would still be out there somewhere in the road, running away, and it would be an awful mess. He shifted into second gear.

He couldn't see the girl but thought she must be up around this bend, maybe as much as a quarter-mile away; she'd really been sprinting. By this point she could've come to another intersection, turned onto another street, disappeared. He might be driving around looking for this girl forever.

Dave was furious at Charlie for putting him in this predicament. He considered stopping the car, turning around, driving away from this girl and this problem, going home. Letting Charlie handle himself tomorrow, in whatever fashion that disaster would strike. His own god-damned fault.

But no, Dave couldn't do that.

He began to take the curve, and then Charlie seized awake, and turned to face Dave, arms flailing out, pushing angrily at Dave's arm on the gearshift. Dave glanced quickly between Charlie and the road, still going around the long curve, then turned back to fight off his drunken, irrational friend.

The car came around the curve in the light rain and the deep dark, and there was a sudden flash of movement from the side of the road, not quite on the shoulder, and then a dull thud and a terrified yelp and a sickening crack, and the screech of tires and squeal of brakes.

Then Dave brought the old convertible to a shuddering stop.

He'd spent the better part of Thanksgiving weekend trudging heavily through the bracing late-fall cold, the trees bare and the sidewalks wet and slicked with fallen leaves. He shuffled through the park, amid the dogs prancing in the moist mess, and the smiling bundled-up couples strolling arm and arm, and the joggers in form-fitting bodysuits and synthetic-fiber gloves, and the decrepit old women under woolen blankets in wheelchairs being pushed by indifferent Afro-Caribbean nurses wearing baggy pink scrubs.

He stood across the street from his ex-wife's apartment building, leaning against the rough stone wall of the park, in a light drizzle, a mist forming on his face, his ears raw and red, his hands shoved deep into the pockets of his corduroy jeans. He pulled out his phone, and called.

"Hello?"

"Hi it's me."

"Oh, hi."

"Listen, I'm downstairs. Can I see you?"

She paused, surprised. But then said, "Of course. Come on up."

The elevator was slow and rumbling, an old New York elevator in a big old New York apartment building, the type of structure that doesn't exist in Washington. He never waits in long slow elevator rides in DC.

She was framed in her doorway, wearing a loose wool sweater, barefoot. They hugged.

"How was your Thanksgiving?" he asked, walking into the foyer, scanning the pictures on the walls, faintly hoping he'd come across one of himself.

"Oh, you know."

They walked into the sunken living room, and he saw that the Abstract Expressionist lithograph was still hanging prominently above the mantle, and he felt a small surge of pride. At least he'd gotten that right.

"Your dad was drunk?" he asked.

She chuckled. "Mom too. And Simon. And really everyone except the little kids, and me. They insisted we play football after supper, but it was raining, and muddy, so we all got filthy, and freezing. Then we came back inside and changed into sweats and pajamas while Mom did laundry, everyone sitting around like it was a slumber party, drinking hot cider." She laughed. He still loved the sound of her laugh. "Now that I describe it, I guess it doesn't sound so terrible."

He knew that this was going to be their last amicable interaction, after years of amicable divorce. His ex-wife's opinion of him was soon going to change, for the worse, forever. "No," he said. "It doesn't."

"And you?"

"My mother is just as crazy as ever, so, y'know . . ."

He trailed off. He wanted to just look at her, and hear her voice, for a minute or two. He didn't want to tell her what he was here to tell her, another big fat lie. Didn't want to do that to her, again.

But she didn't say anything, waiting for him to continue, looking at him with the question: why are you here?

"Listen, I'm sick."

She sucked in a deep breath and straightened her posture and started straight ahead, gathering physical strength, to help her gather emotional strength. This is what she did when she heard something that worried her. "What do you mean, sick?"

"I have cancer." His throat caught. "I . . ."

She closed the space between them, opening her arms. As soon as he felt her embrace, he started to cry, tears spilling down his cold chapped cheeks.

"I'm dying, Isabel."

The deal with David Miller wasn't the only one that Preston Wolfe struck that night.

"Dave, give us a minute, will you?"

Mr. Wolfe held out his hand, ushering Dave into the hotel hallway, where he leaned against the wall, then slumped to the ground, and waited.

It was only a couple of minutes.

"No more drugs," Preston told his son. "No more drunkenness. No more lying, lazing around. No more."

He poked Charlie in the chest, a quick hard jab of his forefinger.

"I will fix this. No one will ever know about it. Unless you defy me, Charlie." Another poke, even harder. "And then I will have no mercy. None whatsoever."

Preston Wolfe stepped back and looked at his son, a tall young man who was nevertheless not quite as tall as his father.

"Do we understand each other?"

CHAPTER 52

Isabel turns over in bed, twisting herself up in an increasingly anarchic jumble of linens. She considers going downstairs, finding Jeffrey, also insomniac tonight. Folding herself into his lap, nuzzling into his neck. But perhaps he wants some privacy. Maybe she does too.

She can hear the wind rustling the trees and the surf tickling the shore, but these noises are not soothing. When her demons arrive in the middle of the night, nothing is soothing.

It was more than possible—it was inevitable—to blame herself, to blame her ambition. She'd never thought of herself as especially ambitious, but everyone has important moments, at any level of ambition. In whatever job, there are crucial days.

For Isabel, one of those was dominated by an auction she was running for a hotly anticipated second novel, whose author needed a lot of hand-holding, and whose bidders kept increasing their offers every half-hour, from mid–five figures to high-sixes in the course of the day. This tense, lucrative nine-to-six was followed by a seven-o'clock black-tie that included an honor for—and an interminable speech by—a different author of hers. So this long frantic day, it featured a wardrobe change.

The nighttime portion was equally important work to the daytime; just because there was liquor and food and fancy dress didn't mean it wasn't work. Networking her way through the cocktail hour, the ball-room, the ladies' lounge, the courtyard where the smokers congregated, having one tête-à-tête after another with the who's-who of the business, glad-handing and cheek-kissing and date-making.

The nanny called a couple of times during Isabel's sixteen-hour day, worrying that Tommy's cold or flu or whatever was getting worse. But Isabel's husband was away on a business trip, and Isabel didn't want Lupe to be the one to go to the doctor with Tommy. The nanny's English would be described—generously—as weak, and sometimes that mattered. So Isabel made a pediatrician's appointment for first thing the next morn-ing. She'd catch shit for missing the weekly staff meeting, but sometimes as a working parent that was unavoidable.

Anyone would've done the same thing. In the following months, peo-ple said this to her all the time—anyone would've done exactly the same thing. Except, of course, they didn't.

Isabel returned home after midnight, exhausted. She thanked Lupe and sent her home in a taxi with an extra fifty, and let her cocktail dress fall to the floor, and collapsed into bed.

She was awakened at dawn by the screaming. Tommy was burning up, 106. She rushed downstairs with the boy in her arms, and ran around the block, panting and desperate, until she found a taxi.

"Don't worry, Sweetie," she said. "We'll be at the doctor's in a minute." The hospital was a mile away.

The taxi peeled away from the curb, the eerie blue light washing over the dingy white garbage trucks, the minimum-wagers swabbing down the sidewalks in front of all-night delis, the street-cart vendors position-ing their pastries in front of office buildings, the joggers with reflective stripes down their shorts, the normal business of a city's day starting, coming to life.

"Are we there yet?" Tommy asked, as he had so many times recently. From the backseat of the shiny SUV that was cleaned every week by the guys in the garage, on the drive out to their weekend house. He had asked it on the way to visit her mother-in-law's in Brooklyn, or her parents' house in the Hudson Valley. While heading to Vermont, for a ski weekend; to Cape Cod, to visit friends; to the Bronx Zoo and the Brooklyn Aquarium, Yankee Stadium and Coney Island. It was something the little boy asked, all the time.

"Soon," she said. In the back of the moldy-smelling taxi she pushed the fever-damp hair off her son's hot forehead. On the slippery silver vinyl seat of the taxi, bumping along the potholed street, Tommy shut his eyes, and right then and there he slipped silently into a coma.

An hour later, Isabel's baby was dead. A heart infection, said the young doctor, who had been up all night, up for who knows how long, working. He was tired and frustrated, and perhaps not as tactful as he could've been.

There was, the doctor added, almost nothing she could've done. Almost.

Isabel is agitated, and thirsty, and needs to pee. She rises from bed, and walks to the bathroom, and reaches for the light switch, but then realizes there's enough light from the moon. She doesn't need the electricity, doesn't want to wake herself any more than necessary. She should really be asleep.

She flushes the toilet. Picks up the small glass from its ceramic holder attached to the beadboard wall, and notices a chip in the rim, a small shadow made by the moonlight streaming through the window, a dark little arc in the otherwise pristine glinting circle. She turns on the cold tap, lets the water run, flushing out the rust, the sediment, whatever metals and soils and bits of crud settle in the old pipes of a house like this. She drinks the full glass in one long pull, then refills.

Across the bedroom, the French doors that lead to the small balcony shudder in a gust of wind off the Sound. The room feels stuffy; the doors beckon. She should let in some fresh air; she should step outside, breathe in the salty breeze. She should settle her mind, so she can sleep, so she can survive. Humans needs sleep more urgently than food. And she will no doubt face bigger challenges tomorrow. Perhaps before tomorrow.

Good God, she thinks, what have I gotten into the middle of? How will this end? Isabel knows that she's being chased, trailed. She suspects she'll be found, right here, in this house, soon. These are not people from whom someone like her can hide for very long. In fact, she's surprised she's managed to get this far. She wonders if she's been *allowed* to get here, chased at half-speed to give the appearance of pursuit, to see where she leads, and what she does, and with whom.

Perhaps she's being manipulated, not pursued. Perhaps her plan is not going to work after all. Perhaps she will need help. Perhaps she can get it from an unlikely source.

Even though she's absolutely furious at what's revealed in the manuscript, she has to admit that it took a huge degree of bravery to reveal those truths. Also to orchestrate the vast contrivances, the complex logistics, the resources, the foresight. It was an incredible effort. And the point of all that effort, she knows, is to atone. To seek forgiveness.

An old computer sits on a desk in the corner of the bedroom, a dinosaur of a thing that just a few years ago looked cutting-edge. She powers it up, fans whirring and lights blinking.

Isabel opens the web browser and logs onto her secondary e-mail account, one she hasn't used in years. Her ATM account would be frozen by now, no longer her purview or property; plus it would be easy to monitor, to trace to this IP address. On the other hand, practically no one in the world knows about this older e-mail address. Certainly no one who made her digital acquaintance in the past half-decade. No one who started trailing her recently.

She types rapidly, fingers flying over the keyboard, so much easier than on a handheld device. She re-reads her message once, then hits Send.

———

Isabel takes hold of the door's lever, presses down, releases the catch. She pushes, but the door is stuck. All the doors in this house, she remembers, are always sticking. She shoves, and it budges marginally, but doesn't open.

Isabel turns to go back to bed, but the tips of her fingers linger on the lever. She hates to be defeated by small things. She turns back to the door, determined to lean into it harder. She looks up and down the jamb, trying to identify the tight spot, the sticking spot, the spot where she should apply pressure.

She gives another firm shove, and the door pops open, the glass panes shuddering. She takes one step carefully over the saddle, brings one foot down the few inches to the painted planks of the shallow balcony, just a couple of feet wide. Not wide enough for any furniture, just enough to stand here and watch the sunset, watch the moonrise, watch the sea and the stars.

A gust of wind hits her in the face, a strong slap of salty air.

She looks out over the lawn, the bushes, the trees, everything glinting emerald-black in the moonlight. Another strong gust of wind, this one attacking the opening of the well-worn linen pajama top she found in the hall closet, pushing bare the hollow of her neck, the rise of her breast. Her hand instinctively shoots up to grasp the cloth, to close it, to shield herself.

The door slams shut behind her, blown by the same gust that opened her collar, and Isabel spins at the noise, startled. But it's just the door, slamming in the wind and then bouncing open, a few inches ajar.

She turns back to the sky, to the view. But something inside catches her eye, and she swivels her head to see that the bedroom door is opening slowly. Maybe it's the wind that's causing some type of vacuum that sucks doors open. Maybe not.

She sidesteps toward the edge of the balcony, toward invisibility, and watches. The door opens wider, but still she can't see anything on the other side, where it's only the darkness of a windowless hall, no lights, no nightlights, no moonlight. Just blackness.

The door opens wider, and wider, until it's fully open. But still nothing.

And then she watches a cloth-clad knee come into the moonlight, then a foot. Not Jeffrey's bare foot, but a leather-shod foot. Then another knee and a torso, then shoulders and a head, then a face, and none of it is Jeffrey, but someone she's never seen before, a stranger entering her bedroom in the middle of the night. An intruder. Holding a gun.

She slithers to the side, completely out of view from within, her body flat against the rough weathered shingles.

Isabel glances down. It must be twenty feet to the lawn, a long way. But it's grass down there. It's soft. It may not hurt. She could be fine.

Then again, she could break both her legs, get shot, and die, all in the next couple of seconds. This could be the end of her life, right now.

Another gust of wind, and Isabel's hand again instinctively shoots up to her neckline, just as the door slams again and bounces open, and she realizes that this noise has been noticed by the intruder, that she has practically no time before this man with the gun finds her—

She jumps.

The fall lasts longer than expected, and Isabel has time to think about the impact, to bend her knees, to prepare to squat and roll, the grass wet and cool, dew on her bare knees, dampening the thin linen that covers her back, moistening her cheek as she completes her somersault and comes to a panting, panicked sitting position.

Isabel leaps to her feet, and sprints toward the line of hydrangeas that separate the horizontal plane of the lush lawn from the sheer vertical face of the bluff above the boulder-strewn, pebble-lined beach. She can just make out the break between two shrubs, the cedar gate and its wrought-iron latch, clearer as she gets nearer, a quick flick to release the catch, pulling the door open, wobbly on loose hinges, and then she's taking the rickety stairs two at a time, holding the banister to spin herself around landings, driving a deep splinter into her sole, the searing pain of a small wooden stake driven into her flesh.

She almost cries out, but stifles it.

She continues to bound down the stairs, limping now on her injured foot, an uneven unsteady rhythm, slipping as she spins around another landing, crashing down onto the rough-hewn surface of the weathered wood, weeds invading through the gaps between the planks. Her knee is bleeding.

Isabel looks up to the top of the bluff and sees a figure emerging from the gate, looking down, locating her. She rises again, battered by her own mistakes, and continues gingerly to the bottom of the stairs, to the beach covered with stones of every conceivable size, painful on the bottoms of her bare feet, jumping over driftwood logs, circumnavigating car-size boulders, splashing ankle-deep in the shocking chill of the early-summer water.

She glances back behind her, sees the man leap down the last few steps to the beach.

She rushes past an upended rowboat, then sees a different set of stairs fifty yards ahead, which could carry her back up the bluff, to a neighbor's house and a 911 call, to a driveway, a road, safety, freedom—

Then she hears the crack of a gun, and wonders whether she's been shot.

CHAPTER 53

When Jeff hears the gunshot his whole body seizes, an electric jolt. "What was that?" And a few seconds later, three more gunshots.

The man gives him a what-are-you-kidding look. It was only a few minutes ago that the guy came bursting down the stairs, gesturing into the yard, yelling at his companion, "Go after her!" And then he descended the last few stairs, and turned his attention to Jeff. Waved his pistol in Jeff's general direction. "You stay *absolutely* put." Which is exactly what Jeff has done.

"Those were gunshots?"

"Status?" the man asks.

"Huh?" Jeff says, then realizes that the guy is speaking into some microphone, somewhere. Pinned to his jacket? Implanted in his jaw? Who knows. Who cares.

"Status?" the man repeats, but doesn't get an answer. "Ms. Reed doesn't have a *firearm* here, does she, Mr. Fielder?"

"I don't think so," Jeff says. "But what the hell do I know? Nobody seems to tell me a fucking thing."

"Is that right?"

A few seconds pass in silence.

"Is the manuscript true?" Jeff asks.

"Don't know."

Jeff stares at this guy, this unlikely-looking armed intruder, in the middle of the night in a beach-house living room, protecting the secrets of powerful people.

"Who *are* you?"

"Who do you *think* I am?"

"FBI?"

"Close enough. What's the difference to you anyway?"

Jeff doesn't know. He guesses the guy is right; it doesn't make any difference what organization he works for. "Is your job to prevent this manuscript from getting published?"

"Yes."

"By any means necessary?"

The guy smiles. "That's correct, Mr. Fielder." He brandishes the pistol. "*Any* means. Have you destroyed your copy?"

Jeff inclines his head at the smoldering fire, burned down to low hot flames, the small logs fully engulfed in dancing tendrils of blue.

"Does anyone else in your office have a copy?"

"I gave some pages to my boss, Brad McNally. Not much. Not enough to be a problem."

The man nods.

"It would have been irrational—suspicious—if I didn't give him something," Jeff continues, defending himself unnecessarily. "But that part of the manuscript doesn't contain anything particularly . . ." He doesn't know how to characterize what those opening pages don't contain, in contrast to the rest of the book. "Damaging, I guess."

"Anyone else?"

"No one."

"How did Ms. Glyndon-Browning get a copy?"

"I don't know. I certainly didn't give it to her."

"And Ms. Reed's copy?"

"It's . . ." This is it, the moment when he can complete the sellout, or not. When he can betray Isabel, or not. "I burned it too."

The two men stare at each other.

"There are no other copies here in this house?"

Jeff shakes his head. "So is our deal still, um . . . ?"

"Well," he says, "that depends."

Jeff doesn't know what this means, and is about to ask for clarification when the veranda door opens.

In an instant the man has taken the three steps that separate them, and has raised his pistol to Jeff's temple. A hostage.

Then both men turn their eyes to the door, and they see Isabel limping through, disheveled and bleeding and scared out of her wits, holding a handgun in front of her.

CHAPTER 54

The author takes his foot off the accelerator, but doesn't move it to the brake, unsure of his predicament. Yes this car is stolen, but the police can't know that, not yet. Yes there are murder weapons in the bag in the passenger seat, but the police can't know that yet either. Yes he's a fugitive, a fraud, living under a false name. Can the Swiss police possibly know that?

He looks in the rearview again, his foot still floating between the two pedals, the car incrementally slowing.

Then he decides to floor it. Because there's very little chance that any type of police interaction here on this winding road in the Alpine foothills will not end with him in custody. And custody would lead, almost immediately, to his assassination, a bullet to the brain while he was wearing handcuffs, shaking his head no, a beseeching "Please" his last word.

He feels the accelerator under his sole, and engages the ankle and calf muscles to press the foot down on the grooved rubber panel, tentatively at first, gaining just a few kilometers per hour—

Then his attention is drawn by wild movement in the rearview, the cruiser moving into the left lane, accelerating violently, a bullet shooting past . . . ahead of him . . . and past him, not cutting him off but picking up speed on the straightaway and quickly disappearing from sight, gone, onto business that's not him.

Standing there by the side of the dark Ithaca road in the light rain, Dave realized what was going on, but he couldn't quite believe it. He turned to Charlie, mouth hanging open, unable to say anything, just staring at his friend sitting there, head hanging, devastated.

"I killed her," Charlie concluded, stunned, eyes flat and dead.

Holy shit, Dave thought: Charlie believes that he was the one driving.

What was the right thing to do here? For himself, for his friend, for this dead girl, for the world? The car was Charlie's car, the girl was Charlie's girl, and the drunken bad behavior that caused her death was Charlie's, all of it. If someone was going to have to pay a penalty of any sort for this accident, it should be Charlie. That would be justice. Wouldn't it?

Dave, on the other hand, hadn't done anything wrong, not really. He was the responsibly sober one. He was the one who put a stop to the molestation. He was the one who got the dangerous guy from behind the wheel. He was the one with good intentions here. He was *not* the one who should be punished. No.

Dave looked at the rear of the car, beneath it, the mangled body, blood everywhere.

If Charlie believed he killed this girl, what would happen to him? Would he go to jail? Probably not, this political scion. Would this tragedy force him to change his ways, sober up? Possibly.

On the other hand, what if Dave took the blame for this? What would happen to him? Him, David Miller, he'd go to jail. For a crime he didn't commit, not in intent. And Charlie Wolfe, on the other hand, believed he'd been behind the wheel; believed he'd killed the girl.

It was only for a few seconds that Dave struggled with the decision of whether to tell Charlie the truth. To admit that it was Dave's hands on the wheel, Dave's foot on the gas pedal, when the old Jaguar ran over the girl.

"Yes," Dave said, completely unsure of this course of action, "it looks like you did." And then Charlie took it upon himself to make the unanimous, unequivocal decision to hide the body. To keep the secret. To cover up the crime he thought he committed. Charlie Wolfe, it was clear in that moment, was a heartless bastard, and Dave felt completely vindicated by his decision to let this heartless bastard believe he was a killer.

Over the years Charlie made a great many similar decisions, and Dave had sat idly by, and let him. Dave had unwittingly hitched his wagon to Charlie's star, without ever explicitly intending to. It happened one obvious-seeming choice at a time, one practical consideration after another over the course of a quarter-century, sliding down the slippery slope of convenient amorality, becoming a person he couldn't have ever imagined becoming, until he just couldn't stomach it anymore. That's when he started typing.

Dave had given it a lot of thought over the years, that choice he'd faced on the quiet rural roadside. What was the worse crime: the split-second of unintentional inattention while driving a car? Or the purposeful decision to cover up a vehicular manslaughter while intoxicated, to run away to a luxurious summer vacation in France, letting the dead girl's body rot in a ravine?

Who was the villain in this story?

It had been almost unbearably painful to write the passage in *The Accident* about the accident itself, to revisit the minute details, the sounds and sights, the feeling of the light night rain. Dave was overwhelmed by guilt, and again furious at the unfairness that it was himself behind the wheel, instead of the person who'd been the rapist, the drunk driver, the conspirator to flee from the scene of the crime, to bury the evidence.

So last week he'd sat there at his sleek little computer, facing out onto the glittering Swiss lake, and tried something else: he revised the pages so they conformed to Charlie's understanding of what had happened on that road, formalizing the lie that they'd been living with for the entirety of their adult lives. The lie would live on, in print, in perpetuity.

It was just a couple of pages of text, representing a couple of minutes of life, and death, and a couple of minutes' time it would take to read the passage. Just a dozen alterations, changing the name of the driver from Dave to Charlie.

Dave re-read the passage over and over, debating whether to revert to the actual truth, or whether to disseminate this improved truth, this more true truth, in which it was the bad person who'd done the bad thing.

He hit Save, and closed the document.

He forces himself to concentrate, to try to calm down, to slow the little roadster to 80 kph, humming steadily on the smooth pavement, through the flickering sunlight under the dense tree canopy in the hills above Zurich.

He's still shaking when his phone vibrates, a heart-stopping startle after the adrenaline rush of the police car. The phone is upside down in the passenger seat, and he can't see the screen. He reaches over to turn the device, but his jittery right hand knocks the thing to the floor. He reaches over, taking his eyes away from the windshield for a split-second. He can't quite reach—

No, he thinks. Too dangerous.

It must be Isabel. Does she have news? An offer from a publisher?

He glances over, sees the device lying there on the clean gray carpet. No one has ever sat in the passenger seat, the floor mats have never been sullied with the soles of shoes.

He reaches down again, loses sight of the road again, feels his fingers wrap around the device. As he starts to straighten, his shoulder bumps into the leather-clad steering wheel, and his head too, and he's briefly trapped, panicked—

He frees himself, pops up, straightens his back quickly. He brings his eyes above the level of the dashboard, and sees, too late, his car crash through the low metal rail, out over the side of this mountain . . .

It doesn't surprise him that it's an image of his ex-wife's face that he now sees. Not the age-lined, saddened, tragic face he saw last winter, standing in her uptown hallway, listening to him claim that he had cancer, was dying. But her face from that night years ago, sitting across from him at that Italian restaurant off Washington Square with the grappa and port glasses and plates of cookies and chocolates cluttering the table, leaning away with a playful dimpled smirk on her face, her cheeks flush with all the wine and all the attention, the closing hour of a long first date, before either of them realized this was the beginning of a romance, a proposal, a wedding, a beautiful baby boy . . .

And for a few days back then, he thought he might have to kill Isabel Reed. But he ended up marrying her instead.

It would be ironic if he's really about to kill himself, too, in a car accident.

CHAPTER 55

For a few seconds nobody says anything, or moves, staring at one another in the dim light from the smoldering fire and a single low-watt bulb behind a parchment lampshade.

"What do you think you're doing?" Hayden asks.

"Put down your gun," she says.

He can see that Isabel's knee has been torn open, a flap of gory flesh at the patella, blood streaming down her shin, around her ankle, the top of her foot.

"I don't think so." Hayden can't ignore that her hand is shaking; she may very well shoot him by mistake. That would be an awful shame. He'd considered many possible closing moments to this complicated charade, but getting killed by mistake wasn't one of them.

He feels much calmer than he thinks is appropriate, for the gravity of this situation. He wonders if this is his version of suicide-by-cop. Suicide-by-victim.

"Have you thought this through?" he asks. "Do you imagine I'm going to just walk out of here, and leave you alone?"

She doesn't respond, doesn't even open her mouth.

"You understand that in all likelihood you will *miss*? It's not as easy as you may think to shoot someone from forty feet away."

Hayden presses the barrel of his pistol tighter against Fielder's head, and tightens his grip. Projecting his willingness to shoot the editor in the head, even though he's not at all willing to do this.

"On the other hand, it's really impossible for *me* to miss."

Isabel is still silent, motionless. Making no attempt to advance her position, or change the situation in any way. Which doesn't make much sense. And she's not a senseless person.

"The only question is where, exactly, Mr. Fielder's brains will end up. Spattered on that wall? Or spread across the coffee table? Or just sort of *oozing* out onto the floor?"

Hayden is pretty sure that this woman is trying to trick him again, now. But how? What could she be doing, just standing there . . . ?

She must be killing time. Which means she's waiting for something to happen. Which means she's waiting for some*one*. She's keeping Hayden's focus aimed at this end of the house, because someone else will be coming from somewhere else. From behind.

"Get up." He yanks Fielder by the hair.

"Ouch!"

Hayden drags Fielder backward, to the side of the living room, a wide wall that's hung with a giant jumble of framed photographs, some of which come crashing down at his feet when he leans his back against the wall, with Fielder in front of him as a shield, and beyond the tinkling of broken glass Hayden hears another sound, a creak, and he turns his eyes and his weapon away from Isabel to the far side of the house, the dark hall and the wood-paneled foyer and the front door, which is opening, and he squeezes the trigger and gets off four rounds of splintering wood and shattering glass, a man's yelp and a thud as the guy's body hits the floor, and Hayden repositions his aim and squeezes three more rounds into what's now clearly a dead person, and he rapidly returns the weapon to Fielder's temple as Isabel screams, quick and piercing. And then everything is silent.

"Are there more?"

She doesn't answer, quaking. She's not even aiming her weapon at anything other than the floor.

"*Are there more of them*?" Hayden yells.

She nods. "Another one, shot. I think dead. On the beach."

"Who are they?"

"Bodyguards."

"You have *body*guards? You hired bodyguards?"

"I didn't even know about them. Till a couple of minutes ago."

He understands: the author hired these guys, to watch the agent. To protect her. Not shocking, after all.

Hayden didn't want this to turn into a goddamned bloodbath, but look at this. Blood is pouring out of the holes in that guy in the doorway, dripping off Isabel's gashed knee, no doubt drained out of Tyler somewhere down on the beach, along with this dead guy's partner. And now Hayden notices that blood is also trickling around his own left wrist, his thumb and palm, falling drop by drop to the floor from the tip of his pointer finger. His shirtsleeve feels moist. His left arm has begun to burn.

Hayden has apparently been hit in the arm. *Fuck.*

He has always expected to be get shot, and is surprised that it hasn't happened until now. He's *almost* been shot plenty of times. Hell, he was almost shot earlier today—or was that yesterday?—in Copenhagen. But *almost shot* and *shot* are very different things.

He needs to get the hell out of here.

"Where is it?" he asks firmly.

"What?" Barely audible, shaking her head. "I don't know—"

"*Where's the goddamned manuscript?*" At the top of his lungs.

She cries out, again. Then she whimpers, "Not here. Somewhere safe. In New York."

Hayden turns to Fielder, frozen like a worthless lump of nothing. Hayden can see the plea in the guy's eyes, *Please don't tell her. PLEASE.* Hayden swings the weapon and hits Fielder in the jaw with it.

The guy crumples, crying out in pain.

"You lying bastard." He kicks Fielder in the abdomen. But not as hard as he could've. He turns back to Isabel. "And you're lying too."

His left arm has begun to throb. He's running out of time, and patience. "*WHERE IS IT?*"

Hayden drops his right arm and squeezes the trigger and there's an explosion and a crack of the wood floor and Fielder screams, a hole in his foot. Hayden returns his aim to Fielder's face, now contorted in pain, and absolute terror.

"I *will* kill him," Hayden says, with as much conviction as he can muster. He's not killing anyone else tonight. Hopefully never again.

"No," she says, fighting through tears, "you won't. Look"—she's pointing—"the bookcase. Fourth shelf from the floor, next to that book with the thick red spine."

Hayden's gaze finds the spot on the shelf, a dark glossy circle.

"And there—" She points at a wicker bowl on a console table. "There are others. Motion-activated. Video cameras."

Hayden takes a step toward the bookshelf, as if to yank the thing off and stomp on it. "Don't bother," she says. "They're networked to a laptop that's streaming the video to a server that's, well, *somewhere else.*"

Hayden turns to face the woman, considers coming clean, telling her that she's wrong. Telling her that he'd already disabled this complicated video system, disconnected the cameras from the laptop, wiped the laptop clean. Which he did because he knows why she's here in this house, because he'd listened to her phone conversation with Naomi, because he knew she'd be coming here, even though she'd pretended to go somewhere else, and he pretended to be fooled by that. Because even though she is very clever, he is more clever.

But the person he needs to fool is not her.

He starts walking toward Isabel.

"You would be filmed committing cold-blooded murder," she says.

Hayden is standing just a few steps from her. He admires this woman, her bravery, her deviousness, her diligence. He pities her too, the bad luck she has faced in her life, the death that has surrounded her for two decades now. He wants to explain it to her, wants to tell her that it will be all right. That she will win.

But he can't do that. He needs to maintain his character, his fraud.

"You know what?" he says. "I'm fine with that." He raises his weapon yet again, toward her face, and she gasps.

"*No!*" Fielder screams from behind him. "It's in the kitchen."

Hayden can see in the woman's face that this is true.

"In the freezer."

Hayden strides calmly through the dining room, turns on the kitchen light, opens the door to the densely packed compartment, quarts of frozen clam chowder and pints of ice cream and bottles of vodka and Limoncello and condensed-juice containers and a cryovac'd bag of lobster tails and a box of a dozen ravioli and a big plastic bag, zippered shut, containing a thick stack of paper.

From the bathroom he grabs gauze and surgical tape and tweezers and scissors and iodine and painkillers and a half-filled jar of prescription antibiotics, and dumps these supplies into a canvas beach bag, along with the Ziploc with the manuscript, plus the handgun from the now-dead rent-a-cop, as well as a baseball cap and a big poncho from the coat rack in the foyer, and a box of granola bars and a bottle of water from the pantry.

Collecting these supplies takes him two minutes.

He hustles back through the dining room, into the living room, expecting to see Isabel hunched over Fielder's shot-up foot. But he freezes when he sees her standing in the middle of the room, aiming the pistol at him.

"Don't be ridiculous," he says, but doesn't move. Maybe she's not being ridiculous. "Put that thing away before you hurt yourself. Or is it even loaded?"

She pivots her arm to the side and fires at the wall, then trains the gun again at Hayden. He has two weapons on him, but at this moment neither is in either of his hands.

Perhaps this is the end of it; perhaps this is what he deserves. To be shot here, by an amateur. That would be poetic justice, of a sort. After a lifetime spent among professional agents and assets and criminals and diplomats, in Europe, to get shot by a literary agent at someone's Long Island weekend house. If only there were a pool, he could be found face-down, like Gatsby.

Hayden stares at Isabel, blanched and bloodied yet filled with resolve.

And the thing of it is that she's right, and he's wrong. She should be doing what she's doing, and he shouldn't.

To hell with it, he thinks. If she's going to shoot me, she's going to shoot me.

He starts walking through the living room, staring straight ahead. He can feel her aim follow him across the room, and he's braced for the sound of the discharge, the burning, the pain. He can see himself face-planting onto the bare wood floor, bleeding, dying. There wouldn't be any funeral.

But by the time he reaches the door, he hasn't been shot again. "Good luck," he hears himself say, under his breath, audible to only himself. At least he can allow her the satisfaction of thinking that she outwitted him.

It was a lifetime ago, during the summer before college, that Hayden sailed from Cape Cod to Iceland, across the North Atlantic all the way to the volcanic-rocky landfall of the Seltjarnarnes peninsula on the 64th parallel, the same latitude as central Alaska, or Siberia, or Greenland.

The summertime water was ice-cold; humpback whales were breaching, and porpoises were swimming alongside the boat. All three sailors wept with joy at the sight of the craggy black shore, after three weeks asea, sick of the food and the pitching and the rolling, sick of the boredom, sick of the musty smell of the thin mattresses, sick of one another.

It was a grand irrational adventure, that trip, Hayden and his cousin accompanying his uncle on a mission to sell a beat-up old boat to a distant relative in Scotland—past Iceland, down to the Faroe Islands, then over to Aberdeen—with the sale an excuse for buying a nicer bigger boat, as well as for taking a month-long sail, his uncle spending the entirety of July out of his office, the three of them passing around paperbacks of Norman Mailer and John Updike, heating up cans of Campbell's. A trip none of them would ever forget.

It will be much harder by himself, but not impossible. He will sail across the Sound to Stonington, Connecticut, or in this wind even make it out to Newport, Rhode Island. He will lay in for a long day of buying food and supplies and spare parts and first-aid replenishments; his gunshot is a minor flesh wound, the bullet passing right through his upper arm. He will doctor the hull numbers, buy replacement sails and parts, triple-check all the rigging. Then if the wind is decent, he will be out past the Cape before the weekend, before this sailboat's owner—a weekender, no doubt—will notice that his boat is no longer floating at its mooring. Or maybe the owner won't notice for another week, or two. Harbors like this are littered with underused watercraft.

He laughs when he realizes that this gunshot, the little flesh wound, may help him. The investigators might think he died. He dropped a good amount of blood around that house.

They'll look for him, of course. But no one will imagine that he'd steal a boat, and sail across the Atlantic, and disappear with twenty-plus-million euros hidden in a Swiss-numbered-account slush fund that no one knows exists.

Sitting in the cold Parisian twilight with Charlie, six months ago, Hayden realized that he'd had enough of his life. Of the ethical compromises and the moral dilemmas, of the everyday subterfuges and the intimate dishonesties. Of a carefully managed existence that he had allowed to elude his control, to fall into the hands of someone he shouldn't have trusted, to fall under the sway of an ambition he'd never really had. But ambition, apparently, was a thing you could have foisted upon you, by a more ambitious person.

Sometimes, life conspires to put you in a bad situation, to force you to do something you know you shouldn't. Then what can you do? You do what you have to. You track down and destroy every copy of a manuscript, kill half the people who've read it, scare the bejesus out of the other half, and hunt down and erase the author.

Or you pretend to do all this, and then you disappear.

He identified the town where he will live, a couple of hours north of Reykjavik on the Snæfellsnes peninsula, in the shadow of the Snæfell-sjökull volcano. He rented a house, under what will become his new name, and filled it with furnishings and clothing, a skeleton supply of food. The sheep farmer next-door agreed to keep an eye on things.

Sunlight is beginning to seep over the eastern horizon, but off to the west it's still pure night, the choppy sea glimmering in the moonlight. Hayden secures the rudder. He picks up the bag, and pulls out what is supposedly the last remaining copy of the manuscript, and stares down at the title page, eerily legible in the moonlight.

He continues reading where he left off. And as he finishes each sheet of double-spaced type, he feeds it into the sea, where it floats briefly, absorbing salt water, until it sinks below the surface.

The secret to throwing a fight, Hayden knows, is for absolutely no one to know, ever, that you took the dive.

CHAPTER 56

sabel can't feel her toes, her feet. Everything below her waist seems to be numb. It takes great concentration to force her legs to move, but she manages it, one small step on each foot.

"Why didn't you shoot him?" Jeffrey asks.

"It's not . . . ," Isabel begins, staring at the thing in her hand. "The bullets aren't real." Naomi's gun was used as a prop in one of her bizarre movies. "They're blanks."

Jeffrey considers his bleeding foot. "Could you, uh . . ." He gestures down.

Isabel walks to the bathroom, grabs a hand towel. She returns to Jeffrey, and wraps his wound tightly. She uses the landline to dial 911, intruders, man shot, hurry, thank you.

"What are you going to do with the video?" Jeffrey asks. He's looking blanched, ill, worried.

"Are you okay?"

"Well not really."

"An ambulance is on the way."

"And the video?"

"I don't know. Probably nothing."

He stares up at her.

CHRIS PAVONE

"What good would it do?" she says. "How could I use it?"

He doesn't answer.

"We can't send it to the cops," she continues. "Or the CIA, or the FBI. Who can we trust? Anyone could be on their side. *Anyone.*" Isabel shakes her head. "And anyway, punishing the guy who just left, that wouldn't be the justice we're looking for. He's not the bad guy."

"He *shot* me."

"Not the justice *I'm* looking for."

Isabel hears something, cocks her head. A siren, far away.

"So do you think he's still alive?"

"Who? Dave?"

She can picture her ex-husband, in some third-world paradise in another hemisphere. Africa, maybe, or the South Pacific. He knew Latin America pretty well, and romanticized the various unknowns on the other side of the world. He'd have let his hair grow long, and would be wearing a scraggly beard. But those blue eyes would be unmistakable. "Yes."

"So does this stop him? Or will he just send another copy, maybe to someone else?"

"No. He'll learn that all these people were killed, and he'll want to protect me."

"Is that why you're still alive? Is that why they didn't kill you?"

"Yes. I'm useful, alive. I'm leverage. So the threat of killing me can still hang over Dave."

The sound of the siren is growing more distinct.

"And you really don't have another copy?"

Isabel stares at Jeffrey, wondering again about his loyalty, his honesty. "No."

"Are there others in your office? With your assistant?"

Alexis. Poor girl. That seems like years ago. "Nope. And you?"

Isabel and Jeffrey stare at each other. She's pretty sure he's hiding something. And he looks as if he suspects her of the same.

He shakes his head.

"Then I guess that's the end of it."

It's hard to say which was the most explosive revelation in the manuscript. For the majority of readers, Isabel thinks, it would be that Charlie Wolfe killed a girl. Or that his unwavering instinct was to cover it up, with the help of his Washington-insider father and his business partner.

Other people might be floored by the later actions. How Charlie Wolfe conspired with the CIA to entrap, frame, or otherwise compromise foreign businessmen and politicians, to further American policy interests and to ensure success for the Wolfe websites. How people were killed in this effort. How despite having no political beliefs whatsoever— Charlie's career was driven by the much simpler convictions that his show should have high ratings, that his network should be profitable, and that he should become immensely influential and prosperous—he intended to run for high political office.

But for Isabel, the earth-shattering news was that Charlie Wolfe and Dave Miller once conspired to commit murder of the potential witness to their role in the car accident back in college. They hunted down that witness, tested her, and found that she couldn't recognize them. And Dave ended up marrying that witness. Me, she thinks. I was that witness.

Isabel had sat in the Ithaca police station, leafing through mug shots, then through the pig books of every current class at every college in the Finger Lake region, tens of thousands of small black-and-white photos. This was well before 9/11, before surveillance cameras everywhere, before everyone could be tracked wherever they went. She'd never met the boys who'd left the dance club with Lauren; she couldn't begin to generate a lead.

After a couple of hours, she'd shrugged. "This is impossible."

The cop had nodded, then handed her another book of photos.

Now she knows that at some point that afternoon she had indeed seen head shots of those frat boys, glanced at their faces, glazed over them, moved onto the next, ignorant. And she was still ignorant years later, when she met one of them in a bar, and agreed to have dinner with him another night, and then another, and eventually married the guy, and had a child with him, and went to their baby's funeral together, and split up, and divorced, and she eventually mourned his illness, his death.

His faked death.

The creaky front door is hanging open three-quarters of the way through its arc, affording a view up the packed-dirt driveway cut through the woodland, whose trees are coming alive with light, the sun just below the horizon out there, about to crest the curvature of the earth, dawn breaking clear and cloudless in golden early-summer light.

Isabel's handbag lies on the floor in the foyer near the door, its invaluable contents now seized, impounded, no doubt destroyed. There's a small tear in the leather where she yanked off the tracking device that had been installed by a man in the employ of her ex-husband, trying to keep her safe. There's the pen and the pad where she and Jeffrey exchanged notes, trying to hide their dialogue from phantom enemies who turned out to be protectors.

There are loose business cards floating around in there, as well as bent and wrinkled and torn receipts printed on flimsy paper, which were meant to be submitted to ATM's accounts-payable for reimbursement. Though now Isabel will have to file them away, as self-employed business expenses on next year's tax returns. She'll need to label new file folders. She'll need to *buy* file folders, and pens and Post-Its and copy paper, and a copy machine maybe, and a desk and a chair to go in the office that she'll need to rent, somewhere. Maybe she'll move her business downtown.

One of the receipts in her bag is for eighty dollars, drinks with a prospective client at an overly swanky hotel bar. Another for fifty-two dollars and change, for new hardcover books. Eighteen for a handful of magazines. There are little slips for taxi fares and movie stubs and an airport sandwich with a bottle of water and a packet of spearmint chewing gum.

And there's yesterday's receipt, paid in cash to the twenty-four-hour copy shop: 8¢ per page times 488 pages, for $39.04.

Times two.

CHAPTER 57

The author extracts himself from the deflated airbags that surround him in the driver's seat, like bubble-wrapping around an expensive ceramic vase, packed carefully in a custom-made crate. But someone didn't notice the THIS SIDE UP stenciling, and the car is upside down, all four wheels spinning in the air, going nowhere.

Dave crawls out onto the forest floor. He's not sure if he should try to stand, not confident that his body is intact, functioning. There's nothing that particularly hurts, but maybe that's because he's in shock. Maybe everything is broken, and he's about to die, but can't feel it.

He looks himself over, pats himself down. Astoundingly, he appears to be fine.

He turns his gaze up the side of the hill, to the roadway a dozen feet above, the twisted shards of the retaining barrier. Then he looks in the other direction, past the small uneven plateau upon which his crumpled car is resting, to the steep drop hundreds of feet down the ravine, a deep crack carved by a snow-fed stream through the Alps.

That was an awfully close call. Another one.

He walks around to the passenger side of the car. He sees his phone in there, reaches in, grabs it. He opens the e-mail that he received just before he drove off the road, reads the message. As he hoped, it's from his ex-wife:

Dear D,

I am glad to know that you are alive. I cannot say I will ever forgive you, but I do understand most of the things you've done. And I do appreciate what you are trying to do now with this book.

But it is impossible to publish now. Wolfe is having people killed and copies of the manuscript destroyed. As you know he has many resources and many friends, and he will stop at nothing.

So I will let him believe that he has succeeded in eliminating every single copy of the manuscript. Until the police investigations have ended, until the FBI and CIA have come and gone, until the funerals and obituaries. Until this part of the story has ended.

Then we will begin again.

Love, I